Zelienople
Road

BRIAN LEE WEAKLAND

Word Association Publishers
www.wordassociation.com

Printed in the United States of America.

ISBN: 978-1-59571-570-8

Library of Congress Control Number: 2010931739

Designed and published by

Word Association Publishers
205 Fifth Avenue
Tarentum, Pennsylvania 15084

www.wordassociation.com
1.800.827.7903

To Louann, for always,
and to God's gifts to us,
Jillian Leigh and Caroline Rose.

It's pronounced
Zē(ə)l′-ē-yən-ō′-pəl.
Five syllables.
We were named after a German girl,
Zelie.

-- Honorable Thomas M. Oliverio
Mayor of Zelienople, Pennsylvania
April 29, 2010

Prologue

Curtis Klepper kept a secret from his eleven friends.

He kept it longer than he expected.

But not longer than necessary.

"I can't make up my mind!" he blurted as beads of sweat flung from his balding head.

Ralph Metzgar, the foreman, had enough. He slammed a blank verdict form on his chair and stormed toward an open window. "I need a smoke."

Other jurors aimed dagger eyes at Klepper, except for the hearing-impaired Mrs. Schandelmeier. She was making excellent progress on her knitting and could not be bothered by such histrionics.

Walt Bienick, a retired Butler High School biology teacher, saddled over to the shaking juror. "What's wrong with you, Klepper? You're wound as tight as an endoplasmic reticulum."

Klepper could not answer.

He had orders from his therapist.

Three months ago, Curtis Klepper completed his employer's intervention program. His lack of focus and indecisiveness stymied co-workers at Starbucks in Cranberry Township. Rather than terminating the pleasant young man, his manager ordered probation and required

Klepper to undergo occupational therapy and a mental health assessment.

He was truthful during the evaluation. He didn't drink. He didn't take drugs. He didn't act out fantasies. Klepper was normal in all ways, except one – he could not make decisions, especially if the decision may hurt someone else.

Klepper's psychological evaluation was followed by ten weeks of intensive therapy sessions. Starbucks had retained a newly licensed mental health therapist, Mr. Thad Jordan. Klepper kept all of his appointments with "Dr. Jordan."

He hated every session, though. Dr. Jordan caused great pain.

"Take a seat, Mr. Klepper" were Jordan's first words. Klepper saw two client chairs in the therapist's office. One was a wooden high-back with ripped caning. The other was a plush leather wingback with an open magazine on the seat. Klepper paused. Jordan jotted notes in his journal. Klepper picked up the magazine. He placed it over the broken webbing and then sat on the caned chair.

"Excellent." Jordan scribbled on his pad. He took a candy dish from his desk and put it before Klepper's nose. "Would you like a butterscotch or mint?"

Each session was 45 minutes long. Most of the time was spent in complete silence as Klepper made increasingly difficult choices – whether he should use facial tissues with aloe, whether he should upgrade to Windows 7.0, whether he should flirt with the 18-year-old barista, whether he should roll-over to a Roth IRA.

His final session was most traumatic. Dr. Jordan asked for his client's advice. In the day's mail, Jordan had received begging letters from the American Lung Association and American Heart Association. Jordan only had one check left and $100 to spend.

"If I give money to the Lung Association, necessary research may not be funded by the Heart Association and more people may die of heart disease, but if I give money to the Heart Association ..."

"... people may die from breathing problems," Klepper said.

"Precisely. So you, Curtis Klepper, must decide who gets the money. Who should live and who should die?" It was Dr. Jordan's final exam question.

After thirty minutes of mental terror, Klepper told his therapist to write a $100 check to the Heart Association. He reasoned that people with lung problems die more slowly, so the Lung Association didn't need money right away.

Jordan slapped his patient on the back, released him from care and sent him back to Starbucks with a glowing report. While en route to Cranberry Township, Klepper stopped at Giant Eagle and wired $100 to the Lung Association.

Less than a week later, Klepper received his Jury Summons by mail. A cover letter from the Jury Commissioner congratulated Klepper on being selected "for this most important duty of a citizen in our Commonwealth." The trembling young man read on:

Our great system of jurisprudence commands ordinary people to perform extraordinary tasks. The greatest of these is <u>rendering a verdict</u> of guilt or innocence. You and your fellow Butler County citizens will <u>sit in judgment</u> of the acts of others. You will listen to the evidence, apply the law of this Commonwealth and <u>reach a conclusion</u> as to whether the defendant has committed a crime or not. <u>You will determine</u> whether the defendant will go free or will face incarceration.

This may be the <u>most revered and significant decision</u> you will make in your lifetime. We are sure you welcome the opportunity to make this important contribution to the law.

Klepper hastily scheduled a session with Dr. Jordan.

"Wonderful, wonderful." Jordan reacted to the news. "This is the perfect opportunity to overcome your fear of decision-making once and for all."

"But Doctor, I don't know if…"

"Nonsense, Curtis. You'll be only one of 12 jurors. It's not your decision alone. You can go with the majority and feel good about it. You know, just piggy-back on everyone else."

"Maybe you're right, Doctor. But if I have any problems…"

"Feel free to call me. We can talk about the trial whenever you want. For me, your cure is much more important than whether some criminal goes to jail. Think of yourself, Curtis."

A month later, Klepper looked down the barrel of a gavel held by Butler County's junior judge, The Honorable Mary Anne Graumlich. Klepper was seated in the jury box when the judge inquired, "Do any of you know any reason why you cannot render a fair verdict in this case?" Klepper fidgeted – unable to decide his answer to the question.

Seconds later he was sworn in as Juror Number 4.

Klepper's jury panel was assigned a capital murder case. There had been much publicity in the Pittsburgh area press, but Juror No. 4 had not followed the coverage. The irascible Judge Graumlich ordered jurors not to read newspapers or to talk about the case with anyone. Klepper heeded the advice, except during his weekly therapy sessions with Dr. Jordan.

"I can't follow the evidence, Doctor. The police couldn't find the murder weapon, there was no forcible entry of the house, and different fingerprints were everywhere. Nobody knows the motive. There's no sense about this. But other jurors act like they understand everything."

Jordan, secretly excited about this window into the jury's thinking, feigned disinterest. "Remember our goal,

Curtis. You don't need to examine every piece of evidence and every word of testimony. All you need to do, at the end of the trial, is to vote with everyone else. And when you do..."

"I know, I know. I'll be cured."

"But, in the meantime, tell me everything the jurors say to you. Then I'll instruct how you can react. Nobody will know that you're just going along for the ride."

Foreman Metzgar sucked all traces of tar from his cigarette and returned to his prey.

"Klepper, man up!" Metzgar stuck his index finger between the juror's eyes. "I don't care for wussy guys. You know what I mean?"

The jury room was quiet for the first time in four hours. Metzgar poised his finger like a stiletto ready to dissect Klepper's skull. Marion Rouzer, a retired Bell Telephone operator, gasped. Tydville Stones, part-time mail carrier, tried to calm herself by picking hair from her sweater. Physical therapist Bob Hunter hunkered down, hoping not to see blood.

"Say the word, GUILTY!" Metzgar shouted into Klepper's ear. "Say it!"

"But the judge said we should reach a unanimous verdict without doing violence to our individual decisions." Klepper tried to reason with the enraged foreman.

"Oh, Mr. Klepper," Metzgar said sweetly. "Nobody here wants any violence. Does anybody here want violence?"

The other jurors nodded innocently, except for Mrs. Schandelmeier who smiled as she knitted two and pearled one.

"No, there won't be any violence," Metzgar continued, "UNLESS YOU VOTE NOT GUILTY!"

A quick smack on Metzgar's head ended the confrontation. He turned to see Juror No. 2, Beatrice Hileman, holding a plastic flyswatter. "Sit down, Ralph. I'll handle it."

Hileman, a registered nurse for 45 years, was as impatient with Klepper as the others. But she favored a softer approach.

"Mr. Klepper, you seem like an intelligent man," she said. "And you seem to be a good-hearted person."

"I am a caring individual." Curtis nervously rubbed his hands.

"That's true," Beatrice continued. "And all of us care, as well. We care about the poor man who was savagely gunned down while he sat in his living room chair. We care about his family, his friends and his neighbors who struggle to recover from this heinous murder."

"Yes, I suppose..."

"Of course, Curtis. We're here to do the right thing for all of these victims." Beatrice grasped his shaking hands and looked into his fright-filled eyes. "We're here to make sure justice is carried out."

Metzgar tapped his last Winston on the jury table. "So what'll it be, Klepper? Eleven of us say he's guilty. We've been here for six hours. We're all tired and we want to go home. What do *you* say?"

"G-g-guilty, I suppose." Klepper seemed almost relieved to make his decision.

Metzgar scribbled his signature on the jury verdict form and buzzed for the bailiff. "Let's go," he muttered to Beatrice, "before the bastard changes his mind."

Calls of "We have a verdict!" echoed through the Butler County Courthouse. Court personnel, dozens of reporters and selected members of the public filed into the ceremonial courtroom, reclaiming seats they established during the week-long trial.

A side door opened. Jurors, heads bowed, entered the box. Metzgar proudly waved the verdict form like a sharecropper holding a deed.

"Have you reached a verdict?" Judge Graumlich asked.

"We have, Your Honor." Metzgar stood and unfolded the form. "We find the defendant…"

"Stop!" The judge covered her ears. "Say no more! It's my job to read the verdict. Just hand it to the bailiff."

Metzgar complied and sat.

Judge Graumlich read the verdict form in silence. She relished the few moments of power while courtroom observers hushed. Then she handed the paper to her bailiff, who pronounced a "guilty" verdict.

"Do you wish the jury to be polled?" the judge asked defense counsel.

"Yes, Your Honor."

"Very well. Juror Number One, is the verdict as read your verdict?"

Metzgar stood and with profound conviction responded, "Definitely, Your Honor."

"Juror Number Two, is the verdict as read your verdict?"

Beatrice Hileman nodded. "It is, Your Honor."

"Juror Number Three, is the verdict as read your verdict?"

Mr. Bienick affirmed.

"Juror Number Four …"

Klepper rose. His eyes scanned the courtroom. From the back row, Dr. Jordan smiled at his patient and winked his approval.

"Is the verdict as read …" Judge Graumlich raised her voice to grab Klepper's undivided attention. "… *your verdict?*"

Klepper's eyes darted from Jordan to the defense attorneys. He could see their mounting anxiety with every juror response. He looked at the district attorney, whose warm smile seemed to convey reassurance for a guilty verdict. Finally, he saw raw fear in the eyes of the defendant, whose life and death hinged on Klepper's answer. How could he be certain that the defendant pulled the trigger? There were no eyewitnesses. Much of the Commonwealth's evidence surrounded motive and opportunity, but no finger on the trigger.

Other jurors seemed so confident in finding the defendant guilty. But how could Klepper live with himself if he made the wrong decision? If he only had more time to think.

"Ah, just a moment, Judge."

Afraid that her jury was unraveling, Graumlich took control. "It's a very simple question, Mr. ..."

"Klepper."

"Mr. Klepper. What did you decide? Guilty or not guilty?"

Klepper looked toward Dr. Jordan again. The therapist was mouthing the word, *guilty*.

"You told foreman Metzgar that the defendant was guilty. Right, Mr. Klepper?" The judge tried to hasten the young man's response.

"Objection," a defense attorney shouted.

"Overruled." Graumlich slammed her gavel. She turned to the indecisive juror and tried another approach.

"Well, Mr. Klepper, did you decide that the defendant is *not guilty*?"

"No, Your Honor, I did not decide that."

The judge exhaled. "Very well, Mr. Klepper. You may be seated.

"Juror No. 5, is the verdict as read your verdict?"

Chapter One
The Spree

Throughout the trial, it was called "that awful night."

Three vicious crimes in two hours. Four seriously hurt. One dead.

By midnight on Friday, August 14, the sleepy town of Zelienople was wide awake. A killer was in its midst. Gates were closed. Doors were bolted. And those late night trips to the convenience store were postponed to mid-day.

That awful summer night changed everything.

The spree began at Yer-In Yer-Out convenience store on South Main, across from the Catholic cemetery. About 9 p.m., a part-time clerk named Harold McCoy was unraveling jammed receipt tape in his register when he heard a click. He turned to find a handgun shaking wildly only inches from his face.

Harold stumbled backward. His eyes rolled up. Oxygen drained from his head, and his body fell sharply against a cigarette rack. The wire display stand cut a gash in his scalp.

Zelienople police responded at 9:30 p.m. after a gas customer found Harold cowering under cartons of Winstons. The cash register door was open and empty. The assailant had stripped clean the rolls of Pennsylvania Lottery tickets as well.

Before paramedics loaded poor Harold onto their stretcher, he mumbled to police. "I think it's a concussion," he said, rubbing his temples.

"Who did this to you, Harold?" one cop asked.

"Everything seems blurry to me," Harold replied. "All I remember was that gun. It was cocked and in my face. What an awful night!"

He then lost consciousness for a few days.

While Harold was being whisked to the trauma center, police fielded another emergency call. According to a dispatcher, three people were injured by a gun-wielding man about ten blocks away on Arthur Street.

When police arrived at the address, they found 30-year-old Nata Prybelewski compressing a wound to her abdomen and tearfully wiping her father's face and neck.

Stanley Prybelewski and his wife, Minka, both in their 70s, had been enjoying the night air on their front porch when they were attacked. A young man in a black hoodie pushed Stanley off his swing, and pointed his pistol at Minka.

"Give me that ring!" he shouted, viciously grabbing her hand. Minka resisted, cursing him loudly in Polish. They tussled onto the porch floor. His gun fired accidentally into the night air.

Nata heard commotion and ran from kitchen to porch. She saw a wild young man wriggle the diamond ring from Minka's twisted hand. Minka hollered for help as she flailed her fists at the assailant.

A streetlight five houses away cast enough light for Nata to locate her mother's ceramic watering can. She hurled it at the intruder, plunking him squarely between his shoulders.

"Stop thief!" she screamed while backing away from the awful scene.

He stood and turned. Nata tried to study his face, but the streetlight behind him cast shadows. She couldn't make out his features. She observed only three things: his wide, pulsating eyes, his rapid breathing, and what was either stubble or dirt on his chin.

Then he shot her.

Porch lights in the neighborhood clicked on. That second gunshot sent weekend hunters to their gun cases. Within minutes, an impromptu Arthur Street posse formed in the street near Prybelewski's house.

The Neighborhood Watch captain phoned 9-1-1. Several neighbors, with dogs on leashes, quickly searched on foot, but to no avail.

The perpetrator had slipped away.

"Friday Night" purred and moaned. She hugged her lover tightly under the wrinkled sheet. Then she did that one annoying thing: she licked his neck.

Zelienople's young police chief, Andy Faxon, rolled to his side, wiping his neck with a pillowcase. Twice he had asked "Friday Night" to refrain from such cervical salivation. Apparently, it simply was a bad habit – one that his daiquiri-plied date undoubtedly practiced on other lovers. Andy tolerated her drooling tongue for a simple reason – why allow one momentary bad habit to spoil an hour of good habits?

Andy knew her name was Sherry. And, like a true gentleman, he sweetly uttered her name at appropriate intervals during tender moments. A little encouragement goes a long way, he learned from the Pittsburgh singles scene. Sometimes all the way. But he thought of her as his Friday night appointment, nothing more. Appointments properly scheduled can avoid unpleasant conflicts, especially when you have a "Saturday Night" as well.

The bedside clock read 10:30 p.m. "Friday Night" was on her back. Her mouth was open, her breaths were heavy, and her mission, accomplished. Andy stroked her soft face. Her olive skin was supple to his touch. Her makeup was light and accented the perfect symmetry of her cheekbones and full lips. She was beautiful, he thought. With an athlete's agility, Andy tenderly lowered himself onto the sleeping girl and slid his arms behind her shoulders.

But any thoughts of an encore performance were immediately erased by a ringing telephone. Andy looked at the caller I.D. and rolled his eyes.

"I've got to answer it," he told the woman, whose fingernails were gouging his lower back.

"They'll leave a message. Hold me, Andy."

"Police business, Friday, er, Sherry. Let me grab the phone."

He reached for the nightstand, his abdomen sliding over her mascara. He pulled the telephone to his ear. "Yes? What is it?"

"Chief, you need to get to Arthur Street," his detective said. "We've had two armed robberies in two hours. Four people are in the hospital."

Faxon cradled the phone into his shoulder, pinching "Friday Night's" fingers.

The detective heard a female moan.

"Man, what time is it?" Faxon wiped his forehead with the bed sheet. "I must have been working out for three hours."

"Andy, put the weights down or whatever else you have there. We need you as soon as possible." The detective grew weary months ago of his chief's interest in physical pleasure rather than police work. "Your daddy was always the first cop on the scene. That should have rubbed off on you."

Another comparison with the great Chief Walter Faxon. Andy could never live up to his father's reputation. Vietnam War hero. Relentless fighter of organized crime. Long-time president of the Pennsylvania Association of Police Chiefs.

"Walter Faxon" was a name that calmed fears, that brought peace and security, that kept trouble away from this western Pennsylvania town.

Sure, Andy resented the comparison. But he brought in on himself.

After the beloved Chief passed away at his desk last year, Andy deposited his inheritance into a campaign fund. He printed thousands of highway signs using his dad's campaign slogan: "Fix it with Faxon."

At only 28 years old, with a thin law enforcement résumé, Andy Faxon swept past a field of qualified unknowns to become Zelienople's youngest police chief. He retained all of his father's majors and captains, hoping that the department would run itself. Almost immediately, however, the force was hammered by civil rights lawsuits, an employment discrimination class action and a budget crisis.

At management meetings, he found himself constantly asking, "What would Walter do?" One officer boldly answered: "He would lead us."

Now, with a vicious criminal at large in Zelienople, Faxon faced his first test as a law enforcement chief. This was not the time to be naked in a bedroom.

"Friday Night," sensing that her appointment was completed, gathered her clothes. "Don't worry about me, Andy. You go ahead with your little police business."

"I'm sorry, Sherry. Let's do this again, real soon ... How about next Friday?"

Andy zipped his warm-up jacket and closed the garage door behind him. Arthur Street was only four blocks from his home on Ziegler. He jogged casually toward the whirring blue lights, exchanging waves with curious bystanders.

"What's going on, Chief?" one called out. "Have you caught the guy?"

Andy kept jogging, secretly hoping that the armed criminal wasn't hiding in nearby shrubbery or trees. If his muscles weren't so sore, Andy could rip the criminal limb from limb. That is, if the goof didn't have a gun. Andy was scared of guns.

Two plainclothes detectives had cordoned off the crime scene with yellow tape. They took measurements on the porch while a uniformed police officer drew a sketch. Andy approached and stepped over the tape.

"Your report, detective?"

"My report will be done in a week. You can read it then." The detective sneered at the chief and returned to his measuring.

"I want your respect and your report, detective!" It was Andy's first push back.

"Well, sir…" The detective paused to summon some patience. "Two attacks within a mile of each other. Both robberies. Both involving a handgun. Cash, lottery tickets and jewelry taken. Two victims physically assaulted and an unarmed female here was shot.

"Paramedics responded and determined that the girl's injury was the most life-threatening, so they pulled her from her parents and took her to the trauma center. The parents gave a few details to officers before they were transported."

"Description?"

"Not much to go on, Chief. Young male, thin, slight build. Nobody had a clear look at him. Could be white, black, Hispanic …"

"Clothing?"

"Black hooded sweatshirt, blue jeans. That's about it."

"Same description in both incidents?"

"The convenience store clerk fainted when he saw the gun, so not much help there. We're hoping to find a surveillance camera at the store. The woman who was shot here, name is Nata, probably had the best opportunity to see his face."

"Have her help with a police sketch." Andy made his first leadership decision.

The crowd swelled to about 50 people as a television news van edged down Arthur Street. Within minutes, searing lights on metal poles illuminated the scene. Reporters pressed to the front, pointing their microphones like swords to part the crowd. Two uniformed officers blocked them from the porch steps.

Andy turned to his detective. "Handle this, will you? I don't have the time or patience to deal with the media right now."

Rapid-fire questions from reporters occupied the detective long enough for Andy to ponder, "What would Walter do?" His daddy probably would be trolling the neighborhood on foot, flashlight in one hand, service revolver in the other. By now, the old chief would have tracked down this punk, pounded him into submission and then dragged his sorry ass before these klieg lights for the angry public to spit on him. Then, Andy thought, we all could sleep, knowing that Chief Faxon and his Zelienople justice system were in full control.

But Andy was not Walter, a fact known to all his cops and suspected by the growing crowd on Arthur Street.

"Chief, chief!" One reporter pushed aside the lead detective and thrust a microphone toward Andy. "Why aren't you chasing this criminal?"

"Yeah, yeah. Let's go git him!" a neighbor yelled.

"Calm down." Andy raised his arms to make peace. "Please allow your police officers to complete their investigation here."

Andy whispered to his detective, "Did anybody see which way he went? Toward New Castle Street or Main?"

"Nobody saw a thing, Chief. He just vanished."

Andy leaned on the porch railing. He cleared his throat and addressed the nervous neighbors. "Based on eyewitness accounts, the suspect is a black male, about 20 years old with stubble on his chin. He is wearing a dark, hooded sweatshirt and jeans. We have reason to believe that he is headed west on Rt. 288 and is likely in Beaver County by now."

"Let's chase the son of a gun!" a woman shouted. "If you don't want to go to Beaver County, we sure will!"

Andy tried to calm her. "Ma'am, I don't think that's a good idea, we will…"

The chief's advice was unheeded. Most of the neighbors had already hopped into their trucks and SUVs. Andy heard a loud rumble fade as the convoy headed west on New Castle Street.

"Does anybody know whether our robber was driving or walking?" the new chief asked his officers.

"Based on the timing of these two crimes, I think he likely walked," a detective replied.

Andy looked out at the now-deserted neighborhood. Except for hoarse barking by the McCloskeys' geriatric mongrel, Arthur Street was disturbingly still. For the first time, Andy regretted his decision to run for police chief. This was supposed to be an easy job – low crime rate, elderly population. Nothing ever happens here, his daddy used to complain.

But everything changed that awful night.

And it was about to get more awful.

Tom Zachary returned to bed after a bathroom visit. His wife, Marcy, was curled under a single sheet. Their bedroom had finally cooled after a steamy evening. But it wasn't the temperature, humidity or soft mattress that kept Zachary awake; it was the unpredictability of his young newspaper reporter. Being the Kane News-Leader owner was reason enough to be sleepless, but being young Matty Moore's editor could downright lead to insomnia.

Matty began his summer internship at the News-Leader innocently enough. He learned to edit handwritten news releases from the Mount Jewett Garden Club. He gathered police reports, sized photos and fielded calls from subscribers whose newspapers fell into puddles, thorn bushes or elk droppings. Only lately did Matty develop a nose for news, and he hadn't been the same sweet teenager since.

The Kane News-Leader, rural McKean County's only weekly newspaper, had suffered its worse revenue loss in twenty years before Matty's summer stint. Locals said the newspaper was becoming irrelevant, what with all the information they could find on the Internet and cable television. Tom Zachary tried to compete by starting a News-Leader website but abandoned the costly project because no one had enough technology experience to update it. So he decided to focus on what local newspapers do best: run stories about local people and print names, names, names.

Matty never disagreed openly with Zachary's philosophy. Instead, he volunteered his spare time to do some old fashioned journalistic digging. Over the summer, his stories about unsolved murders and skullduggery brought readers back to the News-Leader. His byline sold newspapers, and Zachary's bottom line was no longer so bottom.

Now, at midnight and after two hours of tossing in bed, Zachary was wide awake and thinking. Was his intern too excited about his news reporter job? Did Matty know the line between gathering news and making it? Was he simply "too close" to his latest project: confirming that Billy Herman was indeed the killer of former Pennsylvania state police commissioner Frank "Josh" Gibson?

Zachary watched his sleeping wife. Marcy had rolled to the center of the bed, like always, and her elbow pointed at his ribs, like always. It was no use, trying to carve a sleeping spot on this mattress; might as well get dressed, he thought.

Marcy mumbled into her pillow and withdrew her dagger elbow. Zachary turned to face her.

"I can't sleep," he whispered.

"That's three nights in a row," she said. "I'm going to ask Dr. Fisher for a Flomax prescription."

"No, no. It's not that," he said. "I'm just thinking about things. My mind won't rest."

Marcy sighed. "Vytorin or Lyrica or whatever that pill is that comes with butterflies at night. Fisher will have something to stop your thinking."

Zachary flicked on a lamp beside the bed. "Instead of medicating me, Marcy, you should ask me what I'm thinking about. And maybe if we work through these issues, I'll get some sleep."

"Let me guess," she said. "It's Matty, the dead police commissioner and the exposé that never seems to be written. Is that it?"

"Oh, Marcy. What can I do? The kid is fixated on this story, but I'm afraid he's going off the deep end. Do you know what he told me yesterday?"

"Zzzz."

" Marcy, wake up and listen! Matty said he went to the cemetery to dig up Gibson's grave to get a DNA sample. Can you believe that? I mean, thank God that Gibson's widow had some of Josh's hair in an old brush."

Marcy's elbow sprang from her side and poked Zachary's rib. "Why can't we talk about this in the daytime?"

"Just listen to me, Marcy. I'm starting to feel drowsy the more I talk. So Matty takes Gibson's hair sample to the state police barracks in Kane and some Swedish pathologist matches the hair with dried blood on a shovel…"

"Huh?"

"Yeah, Marcy. She seemed Swedish. Her blonde hair was tied up in those little braids and she had beautiful white teeth…"

"Was she wearing a low-cut lace apron and ski boots?"

"Not that I recall. Anyway, Matty said the shovel was Gibson's murder weapon. He said there was other blood on it, probably blood from the murderer."

"So the state police will solve it, Tom. Go back to sleep."

"You don't understand, Marcy. Matty has the crime all figured out. He didn't tell the police his solution. He said the cops would have to 'buy the newspaper' if they wanted the story."

Marcy sat up. "So what you're telling me, Tom, is that Matty is doing his own investigation and that he…"

"Will likely confront the murderer," Zachary interjected.

"Well, that's stupid," Marcy said. "You can't be responsible if your reporters do something so stupid."

Zachary excused himself for another bathroom visit. Marcy, now wide awake, was doing the thinking.

"Tom," she called through the closed bathroom door. "You didn't tell Matty it was OK for him to track down the killer, did you?"

Silence.

"Tom? You wanted to talk."

Flush.

"Tom, tell me you told Matty to let the state police handle it."

She could hear water running in the sink and a pump, pump of the soap dispenser.

"Tom, you wouldn't place your reporter in danger, just to get a news story? You wouldn't do that, would you, Tom?"

Zachary emerged with a sheepish grin. He flicked off the lamp and dove under the sheet. "Good night, Marcy. I think I can sleep now."

Marcy lay on her back, her eyes glued to a lazy, humming ceiling fan.

"Tom? Answer me."

"Lunesta. That's it," Zachary said into his pillow. "Lunesta has the little butterflies. Remember that commercial, Marcy? These yellow butterflies float through your open bedroom window at night and, with their little feet, gently close your eyelids."

Zachary turned onto his side to avoid her elbow.

"Don't worry, Marcy. We'll get a prescription for you in the morning."

Connoquenessing Creek travels north then east then south, seemingly cutting through everybody's back yard or close to it. You could wade across it without water touching your waist most of the year. And at its widest point, you could skip a stone three times before it would plug into the far bank.

But the creek might as well be a mile long and 100 feet deep. Nobody wanted to touch the water. Nobody wanted to boat or fish or skip a rock. Upstream from Zelienople, a steel-making plant had poured tons of waste nitrates into the Connoquenessing. For as long as the steel plant made money, the creek was toxic, nothing more than a dumping ground for chemicals. Once their creek was polluted, trespassers dumped old appliances and mattresses.

Years ago, western Pennsylvanians canoed and kayaked on the creek. They started near the Butler Reservoir and casually paddled past Harmony and Zelienople. Creek currents guided kayakers through forests and farmland on its meandering, southwest course. Thirty miles and a couple hours later, the creek poured them into Beaver River near Ellwood City. More adventurous kayakers would continue south for another hour, until Beaver River emptied into the Ohio River, twenty miles downstream from Pittsburgh.

Those days on the creek were long gone. Industrial waste, litter and stench ended all recreational uses there.

So, late on that awful August night, no one expected to see a kayak on the murky Connoquenessing. Nobody watched for anyone paddling upstream through the sludge and muck. None of the neighbors stopped to investigate beneath the bridge at New Castle Street.

Why would they look? Who would want to get near the stinking water, they would later ask. To them, the polluted creek no longer was a route of travel. They would echo police investigators: any criminal who would use the Connoquenessing as an escape route was ingenuous – contaminated with toxins, but ingenuous.

A few hundred yards upstream from the New Castle Street bridge, creek waters tousled over a rocky shelf. Sputtering sounds of the rapids easily obscured splashes of footsteps. On that awful night, nobody heard the low rumble of a kayak being dragged up a sandstone bank.

Nobody, including Billy Herman.

Herman's house was tucked behind clusters of maples only a few dozen yards from Connoquenessing Creek. The old wooden farmhouse was set back hundreds of yards from its access highway, Zelienople Road. Views of the house were by invitation only. And Herman invited no one.

Locals said the property probably held historic significance, although none of its owners bothered to research and no effort was made to uncover its secrets. Built in 1894, the structure was oddly angled, probably to take advantage of afternoon sun. Land records showed an original simple cabin, which was "improved" between the great wars. Wings, gables and dormers were added over the years, whenever property owners found money to spend. New rooms protruded from every angle, each with windows and most with splendid views of the creek.

A succession of owners kept the house in good repair since its original construction. The present owner, however, largely neglected it.

Access to the house was blocked by an iron gate. Less imposing chain link fencing secured the property's frontage with Zelienople Road. Past the gate, a macadam path extended about 500 yards and then branched into a circular driveway to the front door. More difficult access also was available by foot through the woods or by portage up Connoquenessing's rocky bank.

Billy Herman was a big believer in security. The former Pittsburgh police officer investigated enough murders to understand the value of a dead-bolt lock and, when properly concealed, an electrified fence. The Zelienople property was perfect. Close enough to Forest Golf Club and remote enough to the rest of the world. When Herman retreated to his castle at night, he slept soundly.

On August 14, scotch in hand, Herman sat quietly in his study. A double window provided a view across the creek toward New Castle Road and Grandview. About 11 p.m., his slight intoxication notwithstanding, Herman noticed a stream of headlights exiting town. A police cruiser, lights flashing, roared past minutes later. He monitored his police radio and learned of the armed robberies. In his stupor, however, Herman double-checked his front-door lock by accidentally opening it.

Within a half-hour, Herman slumped more deeply into his recliner. Radio reports of unproductive police efforts bored him. The criminal obviously escaped. Police had no leads. The description seemed too general. And, in any event, the wrongdoer likely was far away from Herman's castle on the creek.

So the former cop emptied his glass, belched and struggled to his feet. Alcohol dimmed his motor functions. Herman shuffled down a hallway, bouncing from wall to wall. He fell into his bed. To the outdoor sounds of crickets and water tumbling over the sandstone rapids, Herman dri1 at midnight.

He would soon be awakened by the crashing glass.

Chapter Two
The Frisk

Gloria Negley always slept on her left side. She heard things better with her right ear – things like rain popping through an open window, a baby whimpering and the call of a distant whippoorwill.

These subtle sounds were strange and much less comforting than the noisy jet engines and Amtrak whistles that dominated her Philadelphia neighborhood. But she was miles from home and, she thought, a world away from civilization.

Friday was her second night at Leigh-Rose Mansion, the governor's home in Kane, Pennsylvania. She was invited by her daughter Ann, the First Lady of Pennsylvania. Gloria, mother of four and grandmother of nine, knew the routine – Grandma must help out when a grandchild is born.

But getting to Kane exhausted the poor woman. Six hours of airplane connections and a bumpy bus ride from Bradford wore her down. By the time she dragged her suitcase from the underbelly of a Greyhound, Gloria felt like a great-great-grandmother.

On this warm August night, she kicked off a sheet. The guest room clock read 2:52 a.m. A soft wind ruffled the curtains. Wind chimes rattled from the front porch below. She heard crickets and leaves rustling. Then, most disturbingly, she heard footsteps on the staircase.

Gloria lifted her head from the pillow. Her
Ann, was sleeping in the master bedroom a
away. Her granddaughter, Hannah Maria, fidge
crib next door.

The governor's staff had left the mansion hours earlier.
No security was posted in the house. State police troopers
had guarded the front gate, but perhaps an intruder slipped
past them, she thought.

Footsteps continued down the hall away from the guest
room and past Hannah's nursery. Gloria quietly stood, moved
to the door and opened it an inch. She looked into the dark
hallway in time to see a man enter Ann's room and close the
door behind him.

Gloria tried to scream, but no sound came out. She slipped
into Hannah's room and hurriedly locked the door. The baby
stirred but didn't cry.

"Jimmie, Jimmie is that you?" Ann's muffled voice eked
through the walls.

"Yeah, dear," the governor replied. "I tried not to wake
you. Sorry."

When Gloria heard Governor Bailey's voice, she
exhaled and slumped into a rocker next to Hannah's crib.
The governor was supposed to be in Harrisburg, she thought.
Why was he home so early in the morning? She strained to
hear conversation in the next room.

"You don't have to turn on the light. Jeez…"

"Are you all right, Jimmie? You look exhausted."

"Six hours on the road. I guess that can tire you out."

Jimmie Bailey, young heir to the Bailey political machine,
was indeed an unconventional governor. He seemed to
follow his own schedule, and it changed from day to day.
Ann understood his impulsiveness and generally tolerated
his peculiarities. But this unexpected return to Leigh-Rose
in the wee hours could not go unchallenged.

"Don't you know what time it is?" She challenged him. "It's dangerous to be driving alone at this hour. You could fall asleep and run into a tree. You're too valuable to me and to Hannah to be acting so recklessly. You're not a teenager anymore, Jimmie."

"I know what I'm doing, Ann." Jimmie stepped into the dark bathroom. "You're my wife, not my mother. Stop treating me like a child."

"Come out here where I can see you." Ann raised herself up on one elbow. "What are you wearing? Blue jeans and a T-shirt? It looks like there are dirt and grass stains on your pants. Where were you tonight, Jimmie?"

He didn't answer, preferring to gargle and spit instead.

Ann stood and belted her robe. She walked around the bed and moved to the bathroom door. His silence bothered her. Perhaps he was keeping a secret. Given his grimy appearance at the moment, she didn't suspect that he had been unfaithful, unless he was mud-wrestling with another woman. Something was amiss, though; nobody gets this dirty driving from Harrisburg.

Jimmie tossed his T-shirt into the bathroom trash can. He removed his sneakers and soggy socks. Ann watched him as he unzipped, pushing down his jeans and rolling them into a ball. He couldn't get undressed fast enough, as though his clothes were somehow incriminating.

She pressed him further. "Did the car break down?"

"No. The car didn't break down."

"Well, did you get lost?"

"No, I didn't get lost either."

"Did you fall into a ditch or something?"

"No, Ann. I'd rather not talk about it." Jimmie splashed cold water on his face and arms. Ann noticed minor scratches on his ankles.

"It looks like you were hiking through the woods and got cut. You need to clean these scratches. I'll get some disinfectant spray."

Jimmie dabbed a soapy washcloth on his wounds as Ann reached into the medicine cabinet. She saw him wince as he rubbed his right calf and brown blood stained the washcloth.

"Here, spray a little of this." Ann looked into his eyes and saw a momentary fear. He regained his composure quickly.

"OK, Ann, I probably should tell you. You'll find out eventually."

"I always do."

Gloria tried to stop listening. This was none of her business. Little Hannah stretched beside her and gurgled. Gloria flung a cloth diaper over her shoulder and raised the baby from her crib. Hannah's skin bore the soft perfume of baby powder. It was a familiar smell to the woman – the scent of rebirth, the scent of innocence.

She kissed Hannah's forehead and combed the baby's wispy hair with her fingers. Whatever uneasiness the infant sensed from her parents' tone of voice was ebbing. Sounds from the master bedroom had softened. Hannah snuggled in her grandmother's arms, finding warmth and love.

"There, there, sweet girl." Gloria wrapped a receiving blanket tightly around the baby. "Everything is all right. Go to sleep."

After only a few days at Leigh-Rose Mansion, Gloria had forged a close bond with her newest grandchild. But she couldn't stay for more than a week; she had other children and other grandchildren to visit as well. She understood the pressures for new parents and helped whenever she was asked. Ann wanted her mother close by, at least until she gained enough confidence to be a mother herself. Jimmie relented to the visit, although he walked on eggshells whenever another Negley was nearby.

"A fight!" Ann's angry voice broke the morning quiet. "You were in a fight? With whom?"

Gloria strained to hear Jimmie's response, but it was a whisper. She placed Hannah on her side and raised the crib railing. Why would a governor be in a fistfight, she wondered. What kind of a place is Kane, Pennsylvania?

Maybe it was time for Gloria to return to her civilized Philadelphia.

Matty Moore, Kane News-Leader intern extraordinaire, needed just one strand of hair.

And he was so close to it.

Dr. Greta, the Swedish forensic pathologist, was standing by at Kane's state police barracks. Matty had promised to deliver a DNA sample to her. He had said it would match a blood stain on the Josh Gibson murder weapon. Matty had told her it would reveal the killer.

The DNA that Dr. Greta could pull from that hair would be astounding, he thought. With a little of this nucleotide and a little of that nucleotide and some laboratory hocus pocus, Dr. Greta would conclude, within a reasonable degree of medical certainty, a perfect DNA match and an airtight case against the killer – Billy Herman. At least that's what Matty expected.

First, though, he had to find Herman's house at the head of Zelienople Road.

Matty eased his Mustang over a rise on Perry Highway about 1 a.m. He saw road flares and circling blue lights about a half-mile ahead. More than a dozen vehicles and cars were stopped before him in a line facing south. Another line of cars traveling north had been stopped as well. He pulled beside a tractor-trailer and noticed the driver's meaty arm resting through an open window.

"Hey, buddy," Matty called to the truck driver. "Are you on the radio? What's going on here?"

The driver's head poked through the window. In the flickering blue light, Matty noticed the trucker's long hair, earrings and lipstick.

"Yea, sweetie, I have," the woman replied.

Matty could hear the occasional barking of a police dispatcher through the woman's radio. He stepped closer to hear the transmission.

"Are they checking for drunk drivers?" Matty asked.

"No, it's the borough police. They don't do much with drunk drivers. From what I hear, seems like there's a criminal on the loose. So they're checking all the cars and trucks on Perry Highway."

"Crap!" Matty said. "How long have you been sitting here?"

"About 15 minutes, and we haven't moved. The police are taking their good old time."

When the line moved forward a few feet, Matty returned to his car. He pushed the shift stick to park and reclined in his seat. A few minutes later, the lady trucker walked back to his driver's window and tapped on it.

"Here's some warm coffee from the 7-Eleven," she handed him a cup. "I didn't drink it yet."

"Thanks." Matty felt the warm Styrofoam. He peeled back the plastic lid and took a sip. The woman started to walk back to her truck when he asked her to wait a minute. Maybe there was a news story here, he thought.

"What are the police saying about this criminal? Pretty dangerous, huh?"

"Tell you what, dear," she answered, "let's go sit in my cab and talk because I can't see if the traffic is moving from here."

Matty obliged. He followed the woman alongside her rig and climbed to the passenger door. Grasping a few well-placed handles, he maneuvered himself into her passenger seat. Through the bug-stained windshield, he saw that traffic had not budged an inch.

The woman popped into her driver's seat as nimbly as an acrobat. Matty watched her push some fast food trash from the center console onto a single mattress behind her seat.

"This is your home?" he asked.

"Yeah, pretty much."

"What are you hauling?"

"Computers, big screen TVs, junk like that. I never really look at the stuff. They just pack it in, hand me this paper and I drive it to Point B."

From his higher vantage point, Matty watched police officers down the highway searching every compartment of a travel trailer. Each car was searched in about ten minutes. Traffic inched forward. Matty looked at his watch: 2:30 a.m.

"I thought they were looking for a criminal," Matty said. "But it looks more like a search for drugs."

"You seem pretty nervous, young fellah," the woman said. "You have some bad things in that Mustang? Maybe you ought to dump it out now."

"No, no. I don't do drugs. I just don't want cops rummaging through my car."

After a few minutes of awkward silence, the woman thrust a wrapper in Matty's face. "Beef stick? Will cure your hunger."

"Ah, no thanks." Matty was repulsed.

Traffic moved up one car length. The police radio blurted an update: no capture of any suspect in the "Zelienople shooting."

A shooting? Maybe Matty had blundered into a breaking news story. He considered calling his editor for advice, but the hour was late and Tom Zachary would be more cantankerous than ever. Matty's only interview prospect at the moment was the grisly-looking truck driver to his left.

"You didn't tell me there was a shooting, ma'am," he said. "Was somebody killed?"

"All they said on the radio was that four people were hurt, one of 'em was a girl who was in pretty bad shape. I was waiting to hear if she died. Try some of this Jumpin' Java Juice; it will keep you awake through Thursday!"

"No, thank you," Matty replied. "I'm real curious about this criminal on the loose. Have police given any description?"

"Sho-o-o-o-t," she said in four syllables. "The borough police give a description? Hell, no. If they gave a description over the police radio, these hills would be crawling with more hunters than the first day of buck season. But I did hear something on the CB radio."

"What was that?" Matty asked.

"This is third-hand. You know, truckers hear everything and pass it on. Sometimes the facts get a little mixed up. Anyway, one of them said he overheard Andy, the police chief. Andy told his deputy that the shooter was a black man wearing a hooded sweatshirt, or maybe the sweatshirt was black. Andy said the criminal has real spooky eyes."

Well, that's a problem, Matty thought. He partially fit the description – the part about being black. But Matty wasn't wearing a hoodie and, as far as he could tell, his eyes weren't spooky. He hoped the police would not delay him too long.

"Fried pork skins?" The woman rattled a bag in his face. "Good for a meal on the go."

Matty shook his head no. "The cars are moving up, so I'd better go," he told her. "Listen, it was a pleasure meeting you, and I hope you make it through the search OK."

She extended her hand to him. "Likewise, Mr. …"

"Moore. Matthew Moore."

"Sarah. Sarah Shoup. My pleasure." She shook his hand. "Now you go back to your car and throw away all that dope you got stashed. Cause the cops will find it."

Matty smiled as he eased his feet to the roadway. He slammed the passenger door, and Sarah inched her rig forward. Matty returned to his Mustang and reached for the driver's door handle.

Suddenly, he felt a hand grasping his shoulder.

"Make no sudden moves," a voice behind him ordered. "Slowly put up your hands."

Matty did as instructed. A flashlight trained on his face.

"What's your name, son?" A uniformed officer emerged from the shadows and stood before him.

"Matthew Moore."

"Where are you going, son?" a voice behind him asked.

"I'm a newspaper reporter," he answered. "I'm here working on a story."

"We don't recognize you. What newspaper are you with?"

"Kane News-Leader, Pride of the Alleghenies."

Matty's hands were sharply pulled behind his back, and he felt handcuffs clicking on his wrists. The officer bent Matty over the hood of his car and frisked him.

"Don't get cute with me, son. Let's start this conversation again. What newspaper are you working for?"

The officer behind pulled Matty's hands upward, causing the cuffs to tighten.

"Kane News-Leader."

"Never heard of it. How about you, Charlie? Ever read the Kane News-Leader?"

"Nope, and I ain't never heard of Kane either. Where is that?"

Matty heard the officers laugh, but he tried to stay composed.

"McKean County, almost in New York. I'm a reporter for the local newspaper. My press credentials are in the glove compartment. If you just let me…"

"Hold still, young man. We'll be searching the car. We just have a few questions first. Like, where were you about 9 o'clock?"

"I was with my girlfriend. We were in my apartment in Kane."

"Her name?"

"Megan Broward. She's a student at Edinboro University."

"Do you own a gun, Mr. Moore?"

"No, never have. In fact, I've never had a gun in my hand. I'm a newspaper reporter. Why can't you believe that?"

A third officer who was searching the car poked his head from the passenger door. "He may check out, Sarge. There's a press tag here with his photo. It says, 'Matthew Moore, reporter.' But, just to be sure, I think we should check with the newspaper."

"I agree," the sergeant said. "Who's your boss?"

"Mr. Tom Zachary, my editor," Matty replied. "He'll confirm everything. There's his phone number on the press tag."

Zachary answered on the third ring. "Y-y-y-ess?"

"Sorry to bother you sir. This is Sergeant Weber of the Zelienople Borough Police. We're doing a criminal investigation and we've stopped a young man who claims to be a reporter for your newspaper…"

Zachary sat up. "Matty? Is he in some trouble?"

"No, sir. He's in no trouble. Can you describe him?"

"Ah, he's 19 years old. He's African-American. He drives a yellow Mustang and…"

"Thank you, Mr. Zachary. You've been helpful."

"… he's an excellent writer, really digs for his stories. Seems to go the extra mile…"

"Thank you, Mr. Zachary."

"And another thing, he has a nose for news…"

"He seems to be following a news story here in Butler County tonight," the sergeant said.

"Well, Matty probably needs some direction from me. Could you put him on the phone for a minute?"

"Sure, Mr. Zachary. Just for a minute. Here he is."

Sergeant Weber removed Matty's handcuffs and handed him the phone. Matty braced for a tongue-lashing from his editor.

"Hi, Mr. Z."

"Matty, what the hell are you doing? We don't care about news in Butler County…"

"Got it, Mr. Z," Matty said as the officers listened. "I'll find out if police have any leads on the Zelienople robber. You want me to hang out at the police station?"

"Get your butt out of there, Matty." Zachary whispered through gritted teeth.

"Sure thing, boss. I'll get some information on the victims and I'll find some witnesses. Save some front page space for me."

"Maaattyyy. Don't play games…"

"See you in a few hours, Mr. Z." Matty closed the phone and handed it to the officer. "He wants me to stay here until something breaks. Is there any way I can get past your roadblock?"

The sergeant directed Matty to return to his car. He radioed ahead to allow Matty's Mustang through the checkpoint.

"One more thing, officer. Could you direct me to Zelienople Road?"

About 3:30 a.m., Matty found Billy Herman's front gate. Iron bars blocked the entrance. Matty did not want to park in such an open area, so he drove a few hundred yards north and pulled into the woods. He could see Herman's house in the distance. He climbed over the chain link fence and stepped carefully through the brush.

Herman was probably home, Matty thought. House lights were on. A black Tahoe was parked at the front door. If Matty's experiences with Herman were any guide, Herman was probably drunk. And hopefully he had passed out.

Shortly before Matty reached the clearing, he tripped and fell. He stifled a moan. A single barbed wire strung a few inches from the ground had scored his ankle. He paused and listened for any alarm he may have triggered. Hearing nothing, Matty moved forward to the black Tahoe. He opened the driver side door.

A police siren wailed in the distance. The Zelienople neighbors' trucks were returning south to Butler County. When the citizen convoy rumbled past Herman's front gate, Matty hunched down in the Tahoe. The diversion was brief.

Matty raised his head. He looked back at Herman's house. No lights had turned off or on. Everything was deathly still.

He aimed his pen light on the driver's upholstered headrest. He studied the seams for a tiny piece of evidence. He concentrated on his task, the late hour troubling his eyes. He pushed the fabric with his thumb, and there it was. Matty pulled it from the headrest with tweezers and placed it in a zip lock bag.

A little strand of gray hair. A little something for Dr. Greta to study.

And with that, Matty retraced his steps, hopped the fence and sped home.

Chapter Three

The Discrepancy

"Governor Bailey please. Tell him that Padgett is on the phone."

Dennis Padgett, the governor's personal financial planner and money watcher, nervously tapped his head with a pencil. Four years into the job and he still couldn't figure out where the money was going. Sure, his boss had millions, but Padgett sweated the details – the thousands and hundreds.

His was an impossible job. Padgett was supposed to control finances, but what could he do or say? Governor Bailey insisted upon online banking; he moved funds willy-nilly from one account to another with the click of his mouse. No investment was safe from the governor's ad hoc spending habits. Padgett needed to take control. Now.

"Yeah, Dennis," a groggy Jimmie Bailey answered the phone. "Why are you calling on Saturday morning?"

"I'm reconciling your accounts, Governor. I noticed a pretty big wire transfer overnight. Just making sure it's OK."

"The thirty-thousand? Yeah, I did that. Don't worry about it."

"Where did the money go? I've got to account for it somehow."

"I said not to worry about it, Dennis. I'll get it back."

Exasperation was setting in. The young accountant couldn't push his boss much further, and he knew it. He had no other job prospects.

Padgett had ended a promising career as a trust officer at Mid-State Bank's Smethport office. He had been under the wing of Mid-State's branch manager, who found the lad to be "smart, sensible and deceptively ruthless in making money." Three years as a bank teller and loan officer gave Padgett a track record of success. His promotion to trust officer at age 26 was unheard of at the powerful bank.

Before long, whispers at the Smethport office reached the ears of upper level management: Padgett was gunning for the branch manager position. How ungrateful! How Machiavellian! A backstabber!

Rather than retreating to his office cocoon, Padgett decided to expand his power base beyond the bank. He reached out to his powerful trust customers by joining their social clubs and frequenting their charitable events. He contributed generously to local politicians and judicial candidates. He sponsored a Little League team. He began dating a former Kane High School homecoming queen. It seemed like all the right moves for a rising superstar.

With his new powerful friends, everyone thought Padgett was untouchable at the bank.

Everyone but his paranoid branch manager.

Little criticisms began popping up. First, a sticky note on his computer monitor mentioned something about his cluttered workspace. Then, he overheard the branch manager complaining that Padgett should not be eating at his desk. A few days later, he received a critical email from corporate headquarters about "not being a team player."

Padgett soon noticed other little changes. His favorite cinnamon swirl doughnuts no longer were part of the Friday morning dozen. His parking place was reassigned beside the dumpster. And, worst of all, he was scheduled to work Saturday mornings.

After a few months of increasing abuse, the branch manager and corporate human resources director paid

Padgett a visit. They closed the door behind them. "Uh-oh," Padgett uttered. He knew what was coming.

Before they handed him a pink slip, a secretary interrupted. Judge Horace Van Lear, the respected and feared chief judge of McKean County, was on the phone. The branch manager and H.R. director slumped in their chairs. They heard the judge's sonorous voice boom through the receiver.

"Dennis, my boy!" Judge Van Lear exclaimed. "I enjoyed our chat at the Bench-Bar Charity Ball last week."

"Always happy to donate my time and talents to your worthy causes, Judge." Padgett smiled at his office visitors.

"How are things going at Mid-State, son?"

"My customers are happy, Judge. But I don't think management here appreciates me. Can you believe they trimmed my lunch hour to 15 minutes?"

"Well, son, I'll be golfing with your CEO tomorrow and I'll fix that."

The branch manager and H.R. woman skunked out of Padgett's office. Judge Van Lear then appointed Padgett as special administrator for the largest estate in McKean County history – the $50 million estate of Governor Brock Bailey. It was apparent to Judge Van Lear that the executor, Jimmie Bailey, was squandering assets before the estate was closed. Van Lear needed a competent money man to safeguard the estate.

Over the next few months, Padgett had two jobs. He tolerated his now-secure bank job while working diligently to locate and protect the Brock Bailey fortune.

Brock Bailey was the sole heir to Keystone Oil Company. His father, William, had amassed a fortune in cash assets as Keystone grew throughout the early 1900s. The company was sold before Brock graduated from college. Brock never worked in the oil business. Rather, he studied law and became a state senator.

A highly publicized kidnapping of his wife catapulted Brock into the state spotlight. He ran for governor and won in a landslide. Shortly after he announced his re-election campaign, Brock's limousine was sideswiped by a tractor-trailer on Pittsburgh's Fort Pitt Bridge. The limousine plunged into the Monongahela River. The governor's body was missing for months before being recovered downstream in the Ohio River.

Jimmie Bailey campaigned for governor to succeed his father. Meanwhile, Brock's estate case was winding through Judge Van Lear's court. Word reached the old judge that Brock's money was being wasted by Jimmie. Van Lear devised a plan to stop that.

The plan's key point was the honest and competent young banker.

Padgett threw himself into the task with wild abandon. With Van Lear's help, he muscled onto Jimmie Bailey's homestead with police troopers and demanded to secure all estate assets. Jimmie, having enjoyed the security that only millions in cash assets can provide, resisted the intrusion. Only after Jimmie's friend and attorney, Bill Pennoyer, intervened was Padgett given access to the loot.

And there was beaucoup loot.

Tens of millions of dollars. Cash. Jimmie pulled dozens of fire-safe boxes from under the floorboards of an outbuilding. He displayed his wealth to Padgett. Never had the young banker seen so much currency in one location. He was both awestruck at the fortune and dumbfounded by Jimmie's stupidity of hoarding such cash.

So Padgett set to work. The cash was counted and deposited in safe accounts. He compiled a detailed report for Judge Van Lear. He concluded that Jimmie squandered about $4 million, leaving a balance of nearly $46 million for distribution to heirs.

Attorney Pennoyer argued that Jimmie was the sole heir, so it didn't matter what he squandered. Unfortunately for the new governor, Van Lear found another heir – an illegitimate son of Brock Bailey and his housekeeper. The estate was split in two. The other heir was a black teenager from East Liberty. His name was Matthew Moore, the aspiring journalist.

Padgett complied with Judge Van Lear and set up trust accounts for Matty Moore. The minor would not receive a distribution until his 18th birthday. When that day arrived last year, Matty took control of a third and promptly purchased a new Mustang. Matty had his own trust officers; Padgett was more concerned with Jimmie's share of the Brock Bailey estate.

The new governor became impressed with Padgett's financial acumen. The young man seemed to have a golden touch with Jimmie's money. Before long, he asked Padgett to quit the bank and work full-time as his financial advisor. Terms of the deal were too good to pass up. Jimmie would set up Padgett in a newly renovated Victorian house in Kane. All of his office and household expenses would be paid. His mother, father and brother could live there in luxury, expense-free. Best of all, Padgett would receive 10 percent of whatever income he generated from the Bailey estate funds.

Never before had a money manager enjoyed such a thrill. Imagine nearly $50 million in cash to place in the portfolio of your choosing! Some government bonds here, mutual funds, money market cash and, for some wild action, venture capital and commodities. Padgett scrutinized the balances of his funds every hour. He steered Jimmie's fortunes successfully through lean times and fat times. After four years, Padgett nearly doubled Jimmie's wealth.

But occasionally, maybe a few times a year, there would be a blip. An unexpected withdrawal or transfer of funds by

Jimmie. No preauthorization by Padgett. No post-transfer explanation by Jimmie. The money, sometimes tens of thousands, would simply be gone.

Last night, Jimmie withdrew $30,000. Again, without explanation.

Now Jimmie was on the telephone and Padgett was asking him for a reason. And the best Jimmie could do was a promise to pay the money back.

"All right, Governor. You'll pay it back. I'll enter it on the books as a draw against funds to be reimbursed." Padgett made a notation on his calendar. "Is there a payback date?"

The governor paused.

"Well, I don't need a firm date," Padgett said. "We'll say the money will return before year's end. Is that acceptable?"

"Yeah, OK."

"And you can't tell me what the money was spent on?" Padgett asked.

"Not right now. Listen, I'm a little tired from my trip last night, so if you don't mind…"

Padgett relented and ended the call. Maybe $30,000 is too insignificant a sum in the land of $100 million, he thought. And $30,000 is certainly too insignificant even for a Type A financial planner, whose job and family home are at stake.

Good Shepherd Catholic Church stood as a beacon of hope for the hopeless of Pittsburgh's Hill District. Hope for a warm cup of soup. Hope for shelter from the city's extreme heat or cold. Hope for eternal salvation, especially for those few souls who attended early morning Mass. Tanya Harper was one of those souls.

Tanya converted to Catholicism after a conversion of her own. She was former housekeeper to Governor Brock Bailey and mother of his illegitimate son. Brock paid her $2 million to keep quiet about their affair. Extreme guilt about her secret life and estrangement from her son, Matty Moore, led to an impulsive act – dumping the entire $2 million cash into the Good Shepherd Church poor box. But after that donation, Tanya found her son, met her future husband and gained a new purpose in life.

Father Frank McWilliams, Good Shepherd's founding pastor, trusted Tanya with the church key. Every morning at 6:30, Tanya unlocked the burglar-resistant front door, set the thermostat a few degrees below comfortable and flicked on the appropriate lights. Because Saturday's Mass was poorly attended, lighting needs were slight -- just two spotlights on the altar and two lanterns above the center aisle. As Mass progressed, the rising sun would provide sufficient light for those literate enough to read Missals.

Tanya scanned the pews for any street people who hid after Friday prayers. The place seemed to be deserted. She continued down the center aisle, blessed herself before a side altar and entered the sacristy. Father McWilliams would not arrive for another ten minutes, so she uncorked the sacramental wire and poured some into a glass chalice.

As she unfolded freshly laundered altar linens, she heard the side door unlock. The door knob twisted back and forth. Tanya waited for the characteristic thump of Father McWilliams's left shoulder to pop the door. She stood back. Nothing. The door knob twisted again. Tanya heard a sigh that didn't sound at all like her pastor's voice.

"Wait a second," she called.

Tanya pulled the knob with all her strength, and the door swung open. Standing outside was a magnificent sight. She fell to her knees and bowed her head.

"Please rise, young lady. You embarrass me."

"Oh, Your Most Excellency … was that correct? You're more excellent than Father McWilliams."

"Nonsense. That is not possible."

Archbishop Herbert Ostrow, long-time head of the Pittsburgh Diocese, puffed his chest and motioned for Tanya to step back. He swept past the woman, his blazing red garments cutting a sharp trail in the morning twilight. He carried a shepherd's crosier and held a mitered cap. His burgundy roped belt wildly swung inches from her face. Tanya reached for his hand. "Your ring."

Bishop Ostrow allowed her to kiss his ring and then helped her stand. She was only a momentary distraction, though. The renowned cleric's eyes immediately darted about the small room. "The vestments? Where are Father's vestments?"

"Here they are, Your Most Excellency. Father keeps his best vestments in these wardrobe bags." Tanya opened a small compartment above the radiator. Bishop Ostrow gasped when he saw a lifeless sparrow with a glassy stare inside the bag.

"Good gracious, Lord! How long has that been there?"

Tanya picked out the bird by its heavenward legs. "Couldn't be more than a week. Father wore this little number last Sunday."

Disgust was over the bishop's face. "What other varmints do you have in this church?"

"Whatever's in the neighborhood," she replied. "Cats, rats, bats…"

The bishop carefully pulled a green cassock from the bag before dusting himself of invisible contamination. He directed her to re-zipper it. She watched him pray silently over the chalice and communion wafers. He mouthed Latin words as he touched Father Frank's steel crucifix.

"Mass is 7 a.m., right?" he asked her.

"Yes, but Father usually starts ten minutes late. Gives our ladies time to finish morning Rosary and the men time to clear derelicts from the vestibule."

Bishop Ostrow peered from the sacristy door. In the dull light, he studied some few sad faces. He watched the Good Shepherd hopeless shuffling toward their pews.

"Is Father Frank all right?" Tanya asked, startling him.

"Don't be alarmed," he replied. "I'm visiting all parishes in the diocese. It's part of our study, called 'The Doors to Christ.'"

"What does that mean, Your Excellency?"

"Our numbers are falling, young lady. Especially young people. Not so many priests anymore. You know that, right? So when someone opens the doors to a Catholic Church, we want them to be welcomed in, to feel at home."

Bishop Ostrow returned his eyes to the spotty congregation at Good Shepherd. He sighed and continued.

"The Lord's House should be a place of life, a place of joy. When you open the Doors to Christ …, well," he waved his hand over the congregation, "it shouldn't be like this."

Despite his admonition, Tanya was becoming alarmed. Good Shepherd was her second home, her place of life, her place of joy. But what could she say to the big man in the cardinal-colored clothes? Nothing. Nothing, really.

"How long have you been a member at Good Shepherd, young lady?"

"About five years."

"Why?"

Nine o'clock had always been their Saturday tee time. Art Diddle, Dave Morganthal, Dr. Frischetti and Billy Herman. Their names were not penciled on the starter's list. The 9 o'clock slot was simply labeled, "The Boys." Everyone at the club understood. It was tradition.

So it happened on the third Saturday in August that tradition was broken. As usual, Art was teed up precisely at 8:59. As usual, Dave wore his Alcoa sun–visor and poor attitude. As usual, Doc had iced his portable beer cooler. But, as unusual, Billy Herman was not puffing on a Cuban and propped up by his 3-iron.

"Should we wait?" Diddle asked. "I've taken my three practice swings."

"I don't know," Morganthal replied. "Check the parking lot."

"Anybody got his cellphone number?" Frischetti asked.

"Nope, never called him," Diddle said. "Never had to. He was always on you like a bad rash. Let's hit and maybe he'll show."

"I don't like this," Morganthal snapped. "You can't hit yet. Not until Billy is here. It's Forest Club tradition."

"Screw tradition," Diddle barked. "I feel a good drive coming on, a 300-yarder. I'm gonna smack it."

"Stop, Art!" Frischetti threw his arms over the anxious golfer's shoulders. "Don't you think we owe it to Billy to wait a minute or two? What if he fell at the bag drop and broke his leg?"

"Or maybe he got drunk and overslept," Diddle pushed his buddy back. "Let me go. I'm gonna bring this course to its knees."

Morganthal slammed his driver into his golf bag. "It's no use, fellas. I can't play golf without my best buddy. You go ahead. I'm gonna look for Billy."

At precisely 9:06 a.m., the threesome jumped into Frischetti's pickup, heading for Zelienople. Twenty-five minutes later, the truck pulled to the locked front gate of Billy Herman's property.

"I don't see his car," Diddle said. "Just that black Tahoe. Are you sure this is his house?"

Morganthal consulted his navigation system. "Three twenty-two Zelienople Road. Yeah, this is it."

"Oo-wee," Diddle said. "Nice digs for a retired cop. Where did he get the money for this?"

"Not golf bets, that's for sure," Frischetti chuckled.

"Look, here's an intercom," Morganthal said. "Let's give him a ring and wake him up."

Diddle exited the truck and picked up the receiver. He heard a ringing tone. There was no answer. He pulled on the iron gate. It gave a few inches.

"You're skinny enough to squeeze through there, Art," Frischetti hollered.

Diddle twisted his torso and inhaled. The iron bars jabbed into his Polo shirt, streaking it with rust stains. He inhaled more deeply and squeezed his hips through the opening. Soon he was standing on Billy Herman's driveway.

"Go on up to the house," Morganthal ordered. "If you hustle, we can tee off before noon."

Diddle began his 100-yard march to the distant house. In the filtered morning sunlight, he noticed the treed front yard covered with poison ivy and, curiously, lines of barbed wire stretched low to the ground.

All was quiet.

He stepped onto Herman's furniture-less front porch. The main door was closed, but a screened side window was open. Diddle rang the doorbell and waited. After a minute, he rang the bell a second time. Still no answer.

Diddle knocked. He turned to his friends beyond the gate and shrugged his shoulders. He could see Morganthal directing him to knock on the window.

Diddle nodded. He stepped from the porch and moved to the window.

He raised his fist to knock.

That's when he saw the body inside the living room.

That's when he screamed.

Chapter Four
The Escape

Zelienople police rammed a public works department backhoe through Billy Herman's front gates. The iron bars mangled and parted. Chief Faxon's police cruiser was the first to enter.

Andy Faxon had received a call only minutes before. A murder report. The first murder in Zelienople in five years. This one followed two vicious armed robberies. Residents were terrified. The robber on the loose was now a murderer at large. All eyes focused on Chief Faxon – attention he didn't welcome.

His cruiser stopped several hundred feet from Herman's front door. Faxon and his major walked past the parked Tahoe. They met the first responding officer and Herman's golfing buddy, Art Diddle.

"Anybody go in yet, officer?" Faxon asked.

"No, sir. Take a look through the window. No doubt he's dead."

"Good Lord!" Faxon peeked through the window and shuddered.

"Let's go in, Chief," the major said.

"No," Faxon blurted. "I don't want anyone to touch anything. Get this man, Mr. …"

"Diddle," Diddle said.

"Mr. Diddle should be out of this area. Take him to the station for questioning. And keep other officers posted at the front gate."

"But, Chief," the major interrupted. "I've got thirty years of experience in major crimes. You should send me in, at least to search the house. The killer may still be in there."

"Good point." Andy paused to scratch his head. "Position our people in a circle around the house. Let's secure the property first. Then…"

"Then I go in, Chief? We'll take Rodriguez and Burns. They're good investigative officers. We won't spoil any evidence."

Faxon held up his hand. "Stop it, Major. You're not going to run this investigation. The people elected me, so I make the decisions. And I have a better idea. Get me Elliot Chen on the phone."

"Chen, are you nuts?" the major shouted. "That publicity hound? He's not a cop, Chief. He's a damn television personality. This is police work!"

Faxon's neck stiffened and his face changed from amber to violet. "Are you disobeying my order, major? I said to get me Chen on the phone. Is that clear?"

"Yes, sir," the chastened officer replied.

Elliot Chen was not easily reached. His only listed telephone number poured callers into a 1970s answering machine in a Sewickley warehouse. The machine identified the business, "Chen Forensics;" its president and owner, "Elliot Lin Chen, M.D.," and its valuable role in the universe: "If you wish to retain Dr. Chen to analyze and solve with absolute certainty any and all medical, criminal or histological anomalies worthy of his examination, please leave your name and number at the tone."

Chen was globally known as an expert medical examiner. His knowledge of the human body and, particularly, how it shuts down was without peer. His analyses of crime scenes, often based on easily overlooked scraps of evidence, were brilliant and his conclusions, uncontroverted. When Elliot Chen said it was so, it was so.

He spoke with authority and precision. Prosecutors feared his testimony in major murder trials. He based every conclusion of guilt or innocence by drawing patterns with bits of physical evidence – how the victim's eyes rolled back, how far the blood splattered, whether the wounds indicated a left-handed assailant. Every shred of evidence supported his certain conclusion because, as he constantly testified, "Every dead body tells a story. We must listen."

Success after success in the courtroom thrust Chen into the national spotlight. Cable news shows added Chen to their expert panels every time a celebrity knocked off a spouse. The nation was riveted to his controversial opinions. He urged viewers not to accept the easy solution to a crime. "Why would the accused movie star have no blood stains if he violently stabbed his cheating wife?" he would ask.

His unpopular but smartly supported viewpoints unsettled his neighbors' thirst for immediate justice. So Chen became a prophet without honor in his own community. He was vilified by the legal establishment and, eventually, the medical establishment. His business in western Pennsylvania was under siege.

Chief Faxon, however, remained a fan. Chen was a towering intellect, someone with a curious mind and a fresh perspective. Faxon recalled his first meeting with Dr. Chen in a Butler County courtroom. Faxon, a summer intern with the county district attorney, watched the famous doctor testify in a manslaughter case. Despite nasty cross-examination by a prosecutor, Chen remained cool and methodical. His testimony was simple and unassailable: Fact A leads to Fact B, which leads to the conclusion of Fact C. Each fact was based on indisputable laws of nature. If you denied Dr. Chen's conclusion, you had to deny gravity or the laws of nature. Even Faxon became convinced that Chen was correct and his boss was wrong. The jury voted to acquit.

Faxon also remembered Chen's devastating criticism of the Butler police. When the manslaughter victim was discovered in a restaurant kitchen, police did not seal the building. Short order cooks were permitted to visit the kitchen to take their belongings, and outside vendors were allowed to stock kitchen supplies. Rookie officers turned over the dead body to find a wallet. Chen testified that the crime scene was too contaminated to yield any fruitful evidence – an opinion repeated in front-page headlines in Pittsburgh newspapers.

Chief Faxon wanted none of that. His first murder investigation would be done according to Chen. The dead man sprawled in that living room deserved the finest investigation possible, Faxon thought. A Chen investigation.

"OK, Chief, we've secured the perimeter," the major radioed his boss. "No one will get in or out."

"Good. Anything else?"

"Yeah. That Black Tahoe parked at the door, that's a stolen vehicle with a stolen license plate."

"When was it stolen?" Faxon asked.

"The Tahoe was stolen a few days ago from a convenience store up north in McKean County. The license plate was stolen from a passenger car in Warren, Pennsylvania," the major replied.

"Who's the thief, the killer or victim?" Faxon asked.

"No description of the thief. Maybe the killer stole it and left it here during the murder."

This is getting more complex, Faxon thought. His crime scene was expanding by the minute.

"Well, major, secure the vehicle. We'll dust it for fingerprints after we talk to Chen."

Governor Jimmie Bailey had only one appointment on Saturday afternoon. His chief of staff, Bill Pennoyer, had scheduled it weeks ago – before their alleged "fight."

His two visitors waited in the governor's study. Bailey hurriedly buttoned a starched shirt and cinched his necktie. Ann watched him in silence, still dumbfounded by his late night antics. She would pursue a more complete explanation after his 2 p.m. appointment.

Bailey stood outside the closed study door and cleared his throat. He made his usual grand entrance.

"Ellis," Jimmie roared as he greeted his guests. "And this must be Mary Anne Graumlich. I'm delighted to meet you."

The slight woman with big red hair stood and shook his hand. "The pleasure is mine."

"Governor, our firm is so honored that you may appoint Mary to the bench," said Ellis Casale, a prominent Butler County trial attorney and major contributor to the Bailey for Governor campaign. "She is anxious to serve the people of our great Commonwealth."

The governor sized up the woman. She seemed extremely young. He pulled her résumé from a file. University of Dayton graduate. Ohio Northern Law School. Recent partner at Casale, Dodge and Schumann. Thirty-three years old.

"Well, Ms. Graumlich, any attorney with a recommendation from Mr. Casale is highly considered in my administration," Bailey said. "Please be seated."

Bailey certainly owed his campaign supporter some favors, but appointing such an apparent lightweight to the Butler County Court of Common Pleas was a bit unusual. Perhaps a short interview would assuage his fears, he thought.

"So Ms. Graumlich, tell me about your work at the Casale firm."

"Oh, dear," she said with a giggle. "I work in commercial transactions, nothing real sexy, Governor. We put together real estate deals and incorporate small businesses."

"That's important work, I suppose," Bailey observed. "Surely, Ellis lets you do courtroom work, too. How many trials have you handled?"

"Let me interrupt, Jimmie," Ellis snapped. "You can't measure her abilities just by counting the number of trials. She has many fine attributes. She's honest, loyal and disciplined. Mary has a wonderful sense of humor and, surely you can tell that she has unlimited potential."

Bailey stood and gestured to Casale. "If you will excuse us, Ms. Graumlich, I'd like to speak with Ellis privately."

The governor took his friend across the hall to a reception room.

"Ellis, what the hell is going on? She would be a disaster as judge. Why are you pushing her?"

"Jimmie, our firm contributed about $35,000 to you for re-election. We have campaigned and supported your party candidates throughout Pennsylvania. Until today, we have not asked you for any favors."

"No, but I don't see …"

"Listen to me, Governor. You have two choices. You can appoint Mary as a Butler County judge and hope that she grows into the job, or you can throw us out of your house. But if you do the latter, don't expect Casale, Dodge and Schulmann to give you one more dime."

"But why this woman? Certainly there are more qualified attorneys in your firm," Jimmie pleaded.

"Oh, there are. And those attorneys are making us a lot of money."

"And Mary Anne Graumlich is not?"

"She did, until we made her a partner. Now she's just a thorn in our side. Complaining about this and that. Demanding a full partner share, but not bringing in any business."

"So you want to get rid of her?" the governor asked. "Just want to kick her up and out of the way?"

"Precisely."

"That's not my idea of good government, Ellis."

"Screw that idea, Jimmie. Ninety percent of the judges appointed in this Commonwealth are just like Mary – unable to survive in private practice."

"That's pretty harsh, Ellis. Especially from you. These judges have helped you and your firm win millions in verdicts. How can you say they're deficient?"

Casale winked and flashed a mischievous smile. "No one will fault you for this appointment, Jimmie. Mary's a female. She's a Butler native. We haven't had a woman on the Butler bench for years. They'll send her for judicial training. And, when she puts on that robe, she'll be as arrogant and merciless as the rest of them."

Jimmie recognized some truth in his argument. Perhaps Mary Anne Graumlich was not a qualified or deserving choice. But she seemed like a safe one.

"OK, Ellis," he replied. "I'll appoint her."

"Great. Our partners will be so pleased."

"But the appointment only lasts for a year. She'll have to run for election. If she screws up, the voters will reject her. Don't be surprised if she's back on the Casale, Dodge doorstep looking for a job."

Casale laughed. "Voters? Throw out a judge? That will never happen. After all, we've never had a major trial in Butler County. If she screws up, the voters will never know."

Bailey pulled his necktie and opened his collar button. "You go tell Mary the good news. I can't face her."

With that, the governor returned to his bedroom for a needed nap.

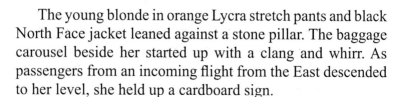

The young blonde in orange Lycra stretch pants and black North Face jacket leaned against a stone pillar. The baggage carousel beside her started up with a clang and whirr. As passengers from an incoming flight from the East descended to her level, she held up a cardboard sign.

It read: "Pennoyer."

Beyond the terminal doors waited an unmarked airport limousine. Its engine revved. Inside were a nutritionist, a life coach and a registered nurse. All waited for arrival of their new patient from Pennsylvania.

Bill Pennoyer, a hastily packed tote bag over his shoulder, nodded to the girl and they walked briskly to the waiting mini-bus. Pennoyer flung his tote on a shelf behind the driver. He said nothing. Across the aisle were grim-looking faces and eyes seared with unnecessary compassion. He absorbed the stares, too tired and depressed to make conversation.

The limousine emerged from its subterranean parking space and into the sharp Colorado sunshine. Within minutes, Denver's airport was miles behind Pennoyer. He closed his eyes and tried to forget the past 24 hours.

"Mr. Pennoyer?" One of the women tapped his shoulder. Pennoyer had nodded off and slumped toward her.

He straightened and, without opening his eyes, told her, "I don't want to be here. Do you know that?"

"Nobody wants to be here, Mr. Pennoyer," the nurse across the aisle remarked. "For you, though, it's an important first step in your recovery."

Pennoyer bit his lip and repressed an urge to commandeer the bus. How could his friend Jimmie be so insidious to force Pennoyer into rehab? Not that he had any addiction. Jimmie's idea was just to get Pennoyer away from Pennsylvania for a few months. Rehab – that would be his cover. No one ever asks any more questions when you're in rehab, he thought. God bless you, people think. Finally, you're taking care of that awful personal problem.

"I'm Catherine, your life coach." A forty-something woman, an obvious plastic surgery survivor, handed Pennoyer a clipboard with some paperwork. "I'll help you through the admissions process."

Pennoyer took her pen and studied the forms. The heading of each page was the same: "Castle Rock Center for Lifestyle Wellness – A Biochemical and Holistic Approach for the Treatment of Drug and Alcohol Addiction." He was directed to check each and every box that described his chemical of choice. As Jimmie instructed, Pennoyer only checked "Alcohol."

The second page was a consent form for treatment. Questions on the third page only sought financial information. Catherine stopped him there.

"Mr. Pennoyer, simply sign the third page. Your treatment has been paid for."

"You've received the wire transfer?"

"Yes, sir," Catherine answered. "The $30,000 sum will cover the initial 45 days. Each successive thirty-day period will require an additional $10,000. Do you understand?"

"Forty-five days should be sufficient," he replied.

"Fine," she said. "We'll design your treatment plan for 45 days. This will require a great deal of dedication and focus on your part. It may be very difficult to erase years of demons in only 45 days."

"You don't know me very well, Catherine."

The limousine pulled off an interstate exit and turned onto a two-lane road. Pennoyer could see white-capped mountains forming a wall to the west. Outside his window were countless acres of prairie grasses matted down by constant winds. Air inside the vehicle was hot and stagnant. Fatigue set in.

"How much farther?" he asked.

"Another hour," the nurse answered. "We'll be there in time for dinner."

Pennoyer didn't feel like eating. All he wanted was a hot shower and a change of clothes. He was still dressed in last night's clothing – a green T-shirt covered with a dark flannel jacket. His muddy jeans, which dried on his flight, were torn at the ankles. He had no time to dress for Colorado. He looked like a drunk. He apparently needed help. He was sure these drug addiction counselors were accustomed to such sloppily dressed patients.

"There are some things you need to know about the Castle Rock Center," Catherine said. "For example, we take privacy very seriously. You may recognize some of our patients. We have treated the addictions of famous people – show business stars, politicians, business leaders. It is important that you respect their privacy."

"I understand," Pennoyer said.

"In return, our patients will respect your privacy. We know that you are Governor Jimmie Bailey's chief of staff. Mere mention that you are treating with us could cause embarrassment to the Governor…"

"That would be a shame," Pennoyer said sarcastically.

Catherine waited until he returned her eye contact. "Listen, Mr. Pennoyer, Governor Bailey's act of referring you to our center was an expression of friendship. You must understand that. Don't be resentful. You will understand this wonderful gift when your addiction is cured."

Pennoyer didn't understand how he ended up in this situation. He was a successful attorney, then a well-respected sports agent. He worked closely with his friend, Jimmie Bailey, and ran two winning gubernatorial campaigns. Pennoyer was highly regarded as an effective chief of staff, having excellent rapport with the State Legislature, the judiciary and political bigwigs in Pennsylvania.

Now, he was running away from it all – pushed into a rehab center in remote Colorado with only the clothes on his back and whatever provisions he stuffed into his canvas tote.

"Where am I sleeping tonight?" he asked the women on his bus. "On a cot in some concrete cell with a bunch of drunks?"

"Oh, no, Mr. Pennoyer," Catherine answered. "You'll have a private room with a bath. Here is our brochure. You see, each room has a 40-inch plasma TV and a balcony that overlooks our heated Olympic-size pool."

Pennoyer studied the Castle Rock brochure. Each photo was stunning, especially those of the 18-hole championship golf course.

"Breakfast is served from 8 to 10 every morning in our garden room. You'll have a full range of menu items, including pancakes, scrambled eggs and fresh fruit. Our nutritionist makes sure that your diet conforms to your individual biochemical needs."

"Certainly." Pennoyer gulped. "I would expect that."

"Then, before lunch, you'll participate in our individual life lessons where we determine your psychological and physiological needs. In the afternoons, we concentrate on stress therapy, which may involve social interaction in our Jacuzzi and deep-tissue massage by our specially trained therapists."

"I could do that."

"So you see, Mr. Pennoyer, treatment of this terrible addiction will require sacrifices on your part. Are you up to the challenge?"

"Yes, Catherine." He extended his hand. "And please call me Bill."

Chapter Five
The Sermon

Jessie Krone arrived at the Kane News Leader office within ten minutes of her editor's frantic call. Tom Zachary used the word, "emergency," at least a dozen times in his voice mail. He knew that only an emergency would rouse his office manager on a Saturday.

It did.

"This better be serious, Tom." Jessie flung her purse on the business counter. "What's your problem now?"

Zachary peered over the partition of his cubicle. His face was flushed. His hands combed through his hair. It could be a look of desperation, Jessie thought. Or, more likely, another acting job.

"My computer, it's gone!" Zachary exclaimed. "Someone put this little box here in its place. Do you know anything about this?"

Jessie sighed and walked to his desk. She flipped open the box, revealing a monitor and keyboard.

"This is your new netbook, Tom. Don't you remember? You approved these little laptops for the editorial staff. Matty said they're faster and more convenient, and you can take them on the run to a story and …"

"I approved this??? Matty recommended this??? How much did they cost?"

"Gates Hardware had a special. Matty paid for six of them. He wouldn't take any money, said it was on him."

"But my computer, Jessie, my 286, it's gone! My best writing was stored in that computer." Zachary put his head in his hands. "My great ideas are lost, forever!"

"Relax, Hemingway. Matty saved your great ideas on this flash drive." Jessie handed Zachary the tiny device.

"Very funny, Jessie. My ideas would fill this room. How could they be all on this little stick?"

"Trust me," the office manager replied. "There's enough storage on this little baby to handle every original idea that ever hatched in this office."

Zachary logged onto his Associated Press site and scrolled through the day's headlines. "I-79 Roadwork to Continue Another 10 Years." "Governor Considers Female Attorney for Butler County Judge." "Pirates Extend Losing Streak." "Zelienople Crime Spree Ends with Murder."

"Gosh, Jessie, look at this." He opened the Zelienople story. "Matty called me last night. Some police officers stopped him at a roadblock. I guess they were looking for this murderer."

Zachary read a summary.

"One person is dead and four others injured in a series of assaults and home invasions in Butler County overnight. Zelienople police are investigating. No arrests have been made."

Jessie looked over his shoulder. "That's beyond our coverage area, Tom. Why would Matty be down there?"

Zachary knew. Matty was hoping to retrieve DNA evidence from Mr. Billy Herman – evidence that may link Herman to a murder five years ago. Just one hair was all Matty needed to prove that Herman's blood stained the same shovel that killed police commissioner Josh Gibson.

Should he tell Jessie?

"Tom, answer me. Why was Matty in Butler County last night?" Jessie persisted.

"Kids these days. You just can't control them."

"Tom ..."

"OK, Jessie. He was trying to find a hair."

"Huh?"

"Try to follow me, Jessie. Matty thinks he's solved the Josh Gibson mystery. State troopers found a shovel at the foot of Kinzua Bridge only a few yards from where Gibson's body was found. The shovel had two different types of blood on it. DNA tests showed that one blood type came from Gibson. Apparently, he was attacked with the shovel."

"And Matty thinks the killer's blood is also on the shovel?"

"Yes. So he sneaked out last night to visit the killer's house..."

"So he could get something with the killer's DNA?"

"Right," Zachary confirmed. "A hair. That's all."

Jessie's next breath required more oxygen, so she sat. "And how was Matty supposed to get this hair? Just pluck it from the killer's head?"

"I dunno," Zachary replied. "Kids these days, you just can't..."

"Tom, you knew about this? You just stepped back and let an 18-year-old summer intern go sleuthing around a killer's house – all for a news story? Are you serious?"

First Marcy yelled at him, now Jessie. Why can't these women understand the importance of good investigative reporting, Zachary asked himself. After all, the last he heard, Matty was safe and talking to police.

"Relax, Jessie. Matty knows what he's doing. He's a responsible kid."

"Responsible, my derriere." Jessie hyperventilated again. "You were right, Tom. This is an emergency!"

Archbishop Ostrow ended Saturday's Mass readings and closed his oversized Missal book. He stood behind a lectern and faced his congregation. A rosette stained glass window above the balcony filtered the angled morning sun and cast an eerie glow throughout Good Shepherd Church. The color mesmerized him momentarily, like a toddler's eyes fixed on a candle. He cleared his throat. His choice of words was most important. And he delivered them softly but resolutely.

"My brothers and sisters, thank you for allowing me to celebrate Holy Mass in your house of faith. Good Shepherd Church was established here in the Hill District of Pittsburgh by your pastor, Father Frank, only about 15 years ago. Many of you remember how we converted an old warehouse, knocking out walls, building a steeple, designing the altar. Many people donated their time and skills for this place of worship.

"I am honored to declare Father Frank's mission an overwhelming achievement. He has brought joy where there was despair. He has created a community of faith where there was hopelessness. He has brought God's word to the barren wasteland. And, like the Good Shepherd, he has tended to his flock with great and lasting success.

"But the success is not this building, not the bricks and mortar, not the wooden pews. The success that God measures is the strength of your love, your spirit, your devotion. I feel that strength today, and no matter what happens you must keep that strength and trust in the Lord.

"Let me tell you a true story. In 1789, after our young nation gained its independence, a small expedition was exploring the Ohio River, not more than a few dozen miles from where I stand today. The expedition was led by Samuel Holden Parsons, a former brigadier general in the Continental Army. The purpose of the expedition was to find a route from the Ohio River northward to the Great Lakes. Their goal was to locate the source of the Cuyahoga River, which flows into Lake Erie at what is now the city of Cleveland. So the men traveled by canoe, north from the Ohio and upstream on the Beaver River. The month was November.

"General Parsons had sent word upstream to a block house below Beaver Falls that he would be there for dinner that night. However, a steady snow had fallen. The assistant, who handled their horses, took the land route was slowed by poor weather. During his difficult journey, the assistant found the general's canoe pulled onto a Beaver River shore. The canoe was empty. The assistant discovered tracks in the snow. He assumed that General Parsons had stopped to warm his feet by walking about, so the assistant traveled on to the block house.

"Night came, and General Parsons and his party had not arrived. The following day, about noon, an empty canoe floated past the block house. It was broken into pieces. Some of the general's personal belongings were pulled from the wreckage.

"It was not until the following May that General Parsons' body was discovered on the banks of the Beaver River. The body was temporarily buried there, but the grave's precise location remains a mystery today.

"As do I, Samuel Parsons had a task. He explored western Pennsylvania to find a cost-effective trade route. My task is to explore Pittsburgh Diocesan churches to find ways to save money and to keep our mission of faith. Samuel Parsons communicated ahead so that his host could be prepared. Likewise, I am here today to communicate with you.

"However, I do not want our diocese to suffer the same fate as General Parsons' canoe. We are traveling upstream and the waters are treacherous. With limited funding and dwindling church contributions, we must steer our canoe to safe shores. That is why I have begun a new program called, 'Doors to Christ.' We will identify which church facilities are necessary to serve our faith communities. For example, is it necessary to operate St. Agnes, St. Cecelia and

St. Ignatius, which are within one square mile? Would it be more economical for the diocese to provide transportation to a more distant church than to suffer the costs of continued operation of small parishes? Could our diocese be better served by merging congregations and eliminating some of our underperforming ministries?

"These are difficult questions, my brothers and sisters. But, you understand, these are difficult economic times for all of us. Therefore, during the next few months, I will be visiting dozens of our parishes and speaking with clergy and laity. I fervently hope that the good people of Good Shepherd will join in this effort.

"Now, please stand and we'll continue with the prayers of the faithful."

Tanya Harper rose from her pew and walked solemnly to the altar. She bowed slightly to Archbishop Ostrow. She stood before the microphone, brushed aside a tear and opened her prayer book.

"For the people of Good Shepherd, may they take comfort in God's word and in His mercy, let us pray to the Lord," she said, raising her arms for the congregation's response.

"Lord, hear our prayer."

The archbishop stood to the side, obviously relieved that his dire sermon didn't prompt an exodus by Good Shepherd's faithful.

"For the men and women of our military, may God keep them safe, let us pray to the Lord," Tanya continued.

"Lord, hear our prayer."

"For what else shall we pray?" Tanya asked the congregation. She noticed a white cane raised in the air. Mr. Robinson, the church's blind head usher, stood. He had never before spoken during daily Mass.

"For the bishop's canoe," he said solemnly, "may God not smash it too bad, let us pray to the Lord…"

Fame had not spoiled Dr. Chen's passion for his work. When he received word that Zelienople police wanted him to examine an unspoiled death scene, he grabbed his medical satchel and raced to Butler County. In the world of forensic pathology, every second counts.

Chen was hustled through police barricades shortly before 10 a.m. He jogged up the long driveway to where Chief Faxon waited with a police photographer. Enthusiasm spilled from Chen's every pore. He grabbed Faxon's hand and shook it heartily. He gushed with praise for the chief's decision to preserve the scene from contamination. After all, how often is a fresh dead body first touched by a medical professional rather than a rookie cop?

They entered the foyer without a sound. Before them, about twelve feet inside the living room, was a grisly sight. The body of a middle-aged man, dressed in a lime green golf shirt and Sansabelt slacks, was sprawled face-down on the hardwood floor. The victim's left arm was under the body. The right arm was extended. About two inches from the fingers was a small caliber pistol.

Chen directed the police photographer to take as many photos as possible from a distance of five feet from the body. Nothing was to be touched.

"I knew your daddy, Chief." Chen stepped past Andy and bent down to open his bag. "Walter was a first-rate policeman. He would be proud that you are handling this investigation with such care."

"Thank you, I respect your ..."

"Rule number one," Chen interrupted Faxon's attempt to praise him. "Rule number one ... do you know what that is?"

"Get photographs?" Faxon responded.

"No. Rule number one at a death scene is this: don't move the body." Chen rummaged in his bag and pulled out two latex gloves. "Important evidence can be gleaned from the position of the body and things that are close to the body. Did this man fall on this spot, or was he dragged here?"

"How can you tell that?" Faxon asked.

Chen stepped closer to the dead man. "If he were dragged here, there likely would be a trail of blood. I don't see that. Secondly, his clothing would be bunched or pulled into a certain direction. His clothing is not bunched. So initially I would say that his body was not moved."

"Could be a suicide, Dr. Chen?" Faxon speculated. "The body wasn't moved and there's a weapon right there."

"I'll leave those conclusions for your medical examiner, but…"

"But what?" Faxon knew that Elliot Chen never shied away from a medical finding or a legal conclusion.

The pathologist crouched to the floor and sniffed. "This gun has not been fired. Does that answer your question about suicide?"

"Not totally. Suicide is always a possibility," Faxon said.

"I suppose so. Except for this." Chen pointed to a bunch of frayed threads on the victim's back. "Exit wound here."

Faxon stepped a bit closer. Chen knew his stuff. Suicide victims rarely shoot themselves in the chest. Murder was more likely.

"When did you get the first report of this shooting, Chief?"

"About 45 minutes ago. A golfing buddy found him here and called us."

"Has he been identified?" Chen asked.

"Not positively. No next of kin has been involved. We escorted the golfing buddy to the station for a report. Not sure if he actually saw the face because he did not enter the house."

Chen reached down and checked the man's neck for a pulse. "Well, his identity is not important now. We'll get that later. Let me continue my examination."

Faxon watched Chen remove surgical instruments, tubes and a syringe from his bag. Chen laid a towel on the floor and arranged his tools. "I don't have my recorder, Chief. Could you take some notes for me?"

"Sure."

"Just write down what I say, and I'll transcribe your notes later."

"OK."

"August 15, about 10 hundred hours. Victim is a white male, approximately 50 years old, no pulse, no respiration. Body position available by photograph, but largely resting on left side from waist down, knees bent. Upper body is in a prone position, head slightly bent toward victim's right shoulder. Right arm fully extended with index finger pointed away from body. Photographs will indicate presence of unfired handgun within inches of index finger. Am I talking too fast for you, Chief?"

"Yeah, a bit."

"Well, write faster then."

Chen gripped the dead man's jaw and then tried to turn the wrist. Chen tried to manipulate the man's elbow and knee joints to no avail.

"Should I write down that rigor mortis has set in?" Faxon asked.

"My dear boy," Chen replied. "Rigor mortis does not 'set in.' Rigor mortis is 'fixed.' Write that down."

Chen tried to move the larger joints, but the corpse was completely stiff.

"So what is the time of death?" the chief blurted.

Chen sighed in mock exasperation. The excitable young chief anxiously awaited a proclamation from Chen – the hour, minute and second of the victim's demise.

"I'm good, but I'm not that good." Chen hated to disappoint the young chief, who was obviously in awe of the pathologist's massive talent. "The best we can do is a range of time, usually in hours. Especially when time passes before we find the body."

"But Dr. Chen, I saw this show on TV where crime scene investigators narrowed the time of death to a certain hour and ..."

"Excuse me, Chief, and I don't mean to be impertinent, but we're talking hard science here, not Hollywood. My career didn't get this far by making wild-ass guesses. When I reach a conclusion, it's based on facts, facts, facts. For example, rigor mortis begins within a half-hour to two hours after death. It is fully fixed within six to 12 hours. Mr. X, here, is as stiff as steel, so he's been dead at least six hours. Probably closer to 12."

Faxon was disappointed.

"But there are other tests," Chen continued. "If a dead body remains in one position for several hours, gravity takes over. When the heart stops pumping, the hydrostatic pressure of blood causes it to settle. The blood begins to collect in those parts of the body closest to the ground. We should be able to see reddish or purple markings in those spots."

Chen carefully lifted and turned the dead man's legs. "Let's pull up these pant legs and take a look."

Faxon watched Chen reveal purplish marks on the man's calves and knees, just as the doctor predicted.

"So he's been dead for a few hours," Faxon said. "That's nothing we didn't already know."

"Ah, but here's the trick, Chief. If you take this body back to the morgue and all of these purplish splotches from his prone position stay in place, then livor mortis is present. If that happens, the heart stopped at least six to eight hours ago."

Chen directed the police photographer to snap pictures as Faxon helped him turn over the body. The dead man's face was strikingly maroon. Both men were careful not to touch anything near the chest wound.

"Hmmm," Chen pressed the man's soaked shirt. "Not much bleeding here. That's a bit strange."

"Why would that be, doctor?"

"I really don't know."

Chen measured the bullet wound to the abdomen. He asked Faxon to make a quick sketch of the entry and exit wounds in his notes.

"One explanation for the small amount of bleeding could be that Mr. X was dead before he was shot. If cardiac activity was already stopped, then bleeding would be reduced."

Chen lifted the man's eyelids and examined the blood vessels underneath. "No sign of trauma to the body, no sign of asphyxiation. Of course, something internal could have killed this man, but that will have to wait for an autopsy."

"An autopsy," Faxon said. "Yes, we will do an autopsy. Who does that, Doctor?"

"Usually, your county coroner will select a medical examiner. But I would like to be present, if you agree."

"Certainly. I want you to be there."

Chen nodded. He took an empty syringe and directed the needle inside the dead man's eye socket. He withdrew a small amount of fluid before returning the dead body to its prone position.

"One more test, Chief, and this is a bit indelicate."

"Should I watch?"

"Be my guest."

Chen unhooked the Sansabelt waistband and slowly lowered the pants. He inserted a rectal thermometer as deeply as he could.

"What are you doing?" Faxon asked.

"Trying to answer your question."

"You mean, the time of death?"

"Yes, Chief." Chen read the thermometer and smiled. "Take another rectal reading in precisely five hours, then let me know. Here, you can use this."

Chen placed the thermometer into Faxon's hands.

"The body cools about one degree Celsius per hour until it reaches ambient temperature. Your job is to find out the ambient temperature later today."

Chen repacked his bag and stood over the stunned police chief.

"But, Doctor, I can't…"

"Don't worry, Chief. It won't hurt him."

Chapter Six
The Thermometer

Matty Moore, exhausted from his overnight adventures, slept on his apartment sofa. Beside him, inside a zipped sandwich bag, was "the hair." Standing over him and holding a plate of pancakes was Matty's friend, Megan Broward.

"Ahem," she started with a whisper. "It's 11 o'clock. It's late for you, even for a Saturday."

Matty opened one eye. The Fraley Street apartment's windows were open. He heard traffic noises. Then he heard the clanging of dishes from the Golden Wheel Restaurant below.

"What time did you say?" He lifted onto one elbow.

Megan kissed his forehead and swirled the plate before his nose. "I'd say breakfast time, but I ate three hours ago."

"Gosh, Megan, you should have waked me up before this!" Matty swung his feet to the floor and rubbed his eyes.

"You were sleeping so soundly, I hated to wake you. What time did you get home last night?"

Matty didn't remember looking at his watch. He recalled little after finding one gray hair inside Billy Herman's Chevy. Zelienople seemed far away now. After all, two hours of driving alone in the blackness of Allegheny Forest can dull a man's memory.

"Late, Megan. Real late. I guess I just crashed on the couch."

"Did you find what you were after?"

"Yeah. Right here." He showed her the sandwich bag. "You have to look really close. There's one strand of Billy Herman's hair."

Megan held up the bag toward a sunny window. She squinted while twisting the bag in all directions. "Well, if you say so."

"Come on." Matty took her arm. "Let's get this sample to Dr. Greta before noon. She can work on the DNA testing over the weekend. My story deadline is Tuesday. Mr. Zachary is going to flip out. News-Leader Page One, here we come."

"I'll drive if you eat on the way," Megan said, grabbing her keys and a bottle of syrup.

Matty folded his sandwich bag twice and stuffed it in his jeans pocket. The teenagers rambled down two flights to the ground floor restaurant. They acknowledged a naughty wink from Toolie, the waitress, before taking the rear exit. Megan's Volkswagen was parked in back.

Kane's state police barracks were a dozen miles away. Megan hopped behind the wheel. After Matty and his hair were situated, she aimed the Volkswagen west on Route 6. The winding road cut through a forest thick with pines. Warm midday sun encouraged Matty to nod off. Megan glanced at her sleeping friend. She noticed scratches on his left arm. His sneakers were streaked with orange-colored dirt. He looked like he had been crawling on his belly through a boot camp obstacle course.

As she had all night, she worried about Matty's safety. His courage in tracking the nefarious Billy Herman to his home in Zelienople seemed abnormal. If Herman was a killer, why did Matty risk his life last night? Somehow, a front-page story in the Kane News-Leader didn't seem to be a good enough reason to Megan. There had to be something more.

The Volkswagen slowed for a curve. Matty clutched the sandwich bag as his head bobbed forward. He awoke with a smile. Megan patted his knee, and he turned to face her.

"Matty, you should let the police do their work," she said. "You're only 18. Not even in college yet. And here you are doing the work that trained criminologists should be doing. Promise me that this is it. No more sneaking around at night, snooping in people's houses."

"I wasn't snooping in people's houses," Matty answered. "I just went into a parked car."

"But that wasn't your car, Matty. That's like breaking into someone's house."

"No it's not, Megan. The car wasn't locked. It was out in the open."

"Where was it?"

"Near Billy Herman's front door."

"So you walked right onto his property?" Megan asked.

"No, not really. I had to climb the chain link fence first because his front gate was locked. You see …"

"Matty! You trespassed!"

"Keep your voice down, Megan. This is the state police entrance here."

She pulled her car into the barracks lot. She turned off the ignition and rested her head on the steering wheel.

"Did anyone see you?" she asked softly.

"I don't think so. It had to be close to 4 a.m."

"Listen to me, Matty. This is serious. You're about to hand over to the state police a piece of evidence you collected while you were trespassing…"

"I'm not going to tell them that," Matty said.

"If that turns out to be the killer's hair, don't you think the troopers are going to ask you a lot of questions? And the first will be: where did you get that hair? You know that."

"They don't have to ask, Megan. They can read it in the newspaper. I'm going."

Matty reached to open his side door. Megan quickly pushed the childproof lock button. Matty's door handle was frozen stuck. He was imprisoned.

"Let me out, Megan. I've come this far. I can finally nail Billy Herman."

Megan took a deep breath before letting him have it. "You're obsessed with him, aren't you, Matty? Ever since you tried to interview him about Josh Gibson's murder and he knocked you down, you've tried to get even."

"That's not true, Megan. I'm just after a news story."

"Like hell, Matty! You could have called the police and had him arrested when he hit you in front of the courthouse, but you wanted to get even."

"No, Megan. That's wrong."

"Matty, I've tried to figure out why you're acting this way. It's so bizarre. You knew that Billy Herman stole your car, but you didn't file a police report. Instead, you tried to track him down."

"I got my car back, so it wasn't important …"

"Let me talk, Matty. And I'm only saying these things to help you, not to hurt you."

"Well, calling me 'obsessed' doesn't help …"

Megan turned on the ignition and sped back to the highway. Matty rebuckled and, through his side mirror, saw Dr. Greta frantically waving at them. Matty made no effort to stop the car.

"Matty, you've got to rethink this whole situation," Megan said sternly.

Perhaps his girlfriend was right, Matty conceded in his mind. The same hair that could land Herman in Pennsylvania's electric chair also could send Matty to jail.

As the Volkswagen raced back to Kane, Matty pushed the plastic bag deep into his pocket. Maybe he'd hold onto that hair just a little longer, he thought. He wasn't quite ready to surrender his Page One story.

Not yet.

Sweet aromas of roast beef and garlic potatoes filled the Padgett house. Julia Padgett, matriarch and chief cook, directed husband Paul to set the dining room table. She slowly stirred a pot of gravy as her son, Michael, whipped potatoes. Saturday night dinner was an hour away.

Their Victorian mansion at the elbow of Clay Street was truly a home. For nearly two years, the Padgett family enjoyed their house and their two-acre lot rent-free. Their generous landlord was the governor. Julia's older son, Dennis, was Governor Bailey's financial advisor.

Dennis Padgett's office occupied a converted sun room on the second floor. It overlooked Glenwood Park. To the south was Kane Manor, a popular bed and breakfast. At times, Dennis was distracted by guests of the Manor, coming and going at all hours of the day and night. And he was annoyed by Manor guests who wandered off its nature trail to pick fruit from his black cherry trees or to cross-country ski over his backyard. But the Padgetts were in no position to complain. They had to be good neighbors because the governor said so.

For the first time that day, Dennis smiled. He smelled roast beef, heard pleasant sounds from the kitchen and sensed the joys of family.

Otherwise, his morning was mundane. He had crunched numbers. First, he totaled Jimmie Bailey's household expenses. Then, he reconciled the governor's checkbook. Finally, he reviewed the balances in Bailey's seven accounts. But one transaction stuck in his craw – the governor's overnight fund transfer. Without explanation, $30,000 had gone "poof." Although Bailey was unconcerned, this "loss" from the boss's money market account disturbed the young accountant.

"Dennis!" Julia called. "Time for dinner!"

"Be right there, Mom."

Dennis closed all the file applications on his computer but one. He stared at the money market account online. The governor had accessed the account overnight. Sometime after midnight and before 6 a.m., funds were transferred. Where did the money go?

"Dennis, let's eat before the potatoes get cold." Paul yelled upstairs.

"Be right there, Dad."

Dennis closed his laptop computer and stood. Through the side window, he could see a stream of limousines circling the Kane Manor driveway. A small, smartly dressed crowd gathered at the front entrance. He watched a bride and groom exit the first car and greet the crowd. Together, they filed into the Manor. The innkeeper, an ex-Marine sergeant, ordered the drivers to park at the side entrance. Then he directed some musicians to set up inside the front porch. Dennis noticed the innkeeper take the arm of an older woman, probably the bride's mother, and escort her into the Manor.

When Dennis walked into his downstairs dining room, Julia, Paul and brother Michael already were seated. He took his usual seat at the far end. Then Paul lowered his head to say grace.

"Dear Lord, thank you for this food we eat and for the many gifts you have provided to our family. Thank you for this house and for the generosity of Governor Bailey. We pray for your continued blessings. Amen."

The roast beef platter circled the table in record time. Forks and knives stabbed and slashed in choreography of consumption. After the first few bites, however, Dennis picked at his plate – a fact noticed by his mother.

"Is something wrong?" she asked. "You don't like my cooking?"

"No, no, everything's delicious. I guess I'm just not hungry."

"This is not like you, Dennis," his father said. "Is everything OK with the governor? You've been working on his books all morning. Aren't the figures adding up?"

Dennis hesitated to share his frustration. Why worry his parents?

"You know, I really can't talk about the governor's finances," he said. "That's confidential."

Julia spooned more gravy over his beans and patted his cheek. "There, there. Just eat and you'll feel better."

Michael looked up from his empty plate. "Food was great, Mom. Can I be excused?"

"No," his father said. "Something is eating at Dennis. Let's help him."

Dennis pushed back from the table. His anxiety was obvious. He felt responsible for his family's fragile living situation. As long as he stayed in the good graces of Jimmie Bailey, they could live in this beautiful house, and the governor would continue his stipend for their living expenses. But, keenly aware of Jimmie's impulsive behavior, Dennis knew that all of this could be taken away tomorrow.

"Talk to me, son." Paul leaned toward him.

"OK. I guess I need to talk to someone. But this is all a family secret. Promise?"

They all nodded.

"Something began a couple years ago," Dennis said. "Money started disappearing from the governor's accounts. At first, it was ten thousand, and then a few months later, another ten thousand. I would ask Jimmie what was going on, but he would tell me nothing, saying either that it was none of my business or that he was just taking care of some matters.

"So, I made up entries to justify these withdrawals – general things like 'debt payment,' or 'account transfer' or 'general expenses.' I didn't feel comfortable about these entries, but I figured he was the governor and he owned the money."

Julia shook her head. "That's right. It's his money. Don't worry about it."

"Last year, the amounts got larger," Dennis continued. "Eventually these withdrawals exceeded one hundred thousand. When I asked him about it, he got combative. So I dropped the subject."

Paul interrupted. "Why does this concern you, son? If he's got something else on the side, it's his business, not yours."

"What do you mean, Dad? Something else on the side?"

Paul looked across the table. "OK, Michael, you can be excused now."

"But Dad…" Michael protested.

"You're excused. Now go!"

The younger son took his plate to the kitchen sink, turned to see his father's stern glare, and exited to the rear yard. When Paul saw Michael on his bicycle riding up Clay Street, he returned to Dennis's question.

"If it's one thing I know about politicians, son, especially married ones – they always have a girl waiting in the wings."

"Oh, Paul, for goodness sake," Julia responded.

"No, seriously. It's women that make men spend all their money. I'll bet you that Jimmie Bailey is keeping a girlfriend on the side. He's paying her rent, giving her gifts, maybe even paying her hush money."

Dennis had considered that possibility. But Jimmie and Ann seemed like such a perfect couple. He never heard them argue. And now, with a baby girl, the governor could never stoop so low, he thought.

"It's gotta be something else," Dennis said. "Maybe he has a gambling problem. Maybe he's in debt to some bookies or some mobsters."

Julia, ever the believer in human kindness, would hear none of this. "Have you considered that maybe the governor is a secret philanthropist?"

"Huh?" the two men said simultaneously.

"He's a multi-millionaire. He has so much money that he feels guilty. Look, he's given us a place to stay. That came from his heart. Maybe he's donating money to worthy charities."

"But, Mom, if he's giving money away to charities, he would tell me. He could take tax deductions. Jimmie's no philanthropist. No, this money is going elsewhere."

Paul agreed. "Dennis is right. The governor is doing something rotten. Why, one look at the sneer on his face would ..."

"Dad, let's just cool it. Right now, the governor is our best friend. I just don't want to be involved in anything criminal."

"Criminal?" Julia exclaimed. "Why would you be involved? You're just handling his books."

Dennis knew his mother would be correct in a perfect world. But often accountants were dragged into criminal court as co-conspirators. He had to find out what Jimmie was doing, and find out fast. On Monday morning, he would trace the $30,000 wire transfer.

His boss would never find out. Dennis knew how to cover his tracks.

"Drugs!" Michael burst through the back door. "I bet it's crystal meth."

"Shhh, Michael," Julia scolded. "Watch your tongue."

Dinner was over. Michael was ordered to wash the dishes – a punishment for verbalizing what everyone was thinking but none could truly imagine.

"Mr. X" lay stiff on a table at the Butler County morgue. It was time for his final temperature reading. Chief Andy Faxon unrolled a paper towel, revealing the once-used rectal thermometer.

Faxon waited for the medical examiner to arrive. Faxon grew more impatient with every passing minute. Dr. Chen had stressed that a second temperature reading should be taken at the morgue that afternoon, and he had handed the thermometer to Faxon. Two o'clock came and went. So did three o'clock. Still no medical examiner.

The reading had to be taken, but Faxon was repulsed by the idea. To accomplish the task, somebody had to turn over the dead body or twist Mr. X into a contorted position. Hopefully, that somebody would not be Faxon. How badly did he really want to know the time of death? He looked at the thermometer needle and cursed it.

Suddenly, the door sprung open. Elliot Chen, his white lab coat neatly pressed and buttoned, swept into the room. A young female assistant carried his bag of medical supplies.

"Thank God." Faxon wanted to kiss his hand, but he remembered where it was a few hours earlier.

"I'll take that," Chen said, retrieving the thermometer. "Help me turn him over."

Chief Faxon pulled on a pair of surgical gloves and together they turned the corpse. Chen wasted no time and performed his test. He reported the results to his assistant and took a second reading. Same result, he told her. Then they flipped Mr. X onto his back and covered him with a sheet. Chen violently shook the thermometer and placed it beside the corpse.

"Well, I guess that concludes my work here, Chief." Chen closed his bag with a definitive snap. "Thank you for contacting me in this case."

Faxon looked puzzled. "What was your reading, Doctor? I mean, can you tell me the time of death?"

"I have a pretty good idea, Chief. But, you know, I have not been retained by the police department. Not yet, at least." Chen stepped to the door.

"Wait! We contacted you, so doesn't that mean we retained you?" Faxon begged.

Chen only smiled. "Sir, there's only one way to retain me. Surely, you understand. I have a business to run. That takes money. I don't work for free."

Faxon was speechless.

Chen stopped in the doorway. "Your father, Walter, would have this case solved by now. Be careful you take all the rights steps. Again, it was a pleasure meeting you."

"But you can't just walk out," Faxon said. "You have evidence. You know when he died, and you're not telling me."

Chen relished the situation. "Chief, I don't have any evidence. I only have opinions. You have all the evidence right there, lying on the table. Here's my card. If you want to retain me, call this number and work out the business arrangements. Until then, good day."

Faxon watched helplessly as the famous pathologist made a grand exit. The chief was alone in a cold room. He picked up the thermometer. It read 65 degrees, the same temperature as the room's thermostat setting. Chen had erased the reading and dared Faxon to repeat the test. It was a dare Faxon was doomed to lose.

"Don't worry," he said to the corpse. "You're safe with me. I don't do thermometers."

Chapter Seven

The Identity

Only four hours earlier, on the first tee of his beloved Forest Club, Art Diddle was waggling his driver and preparing to hit the shot of his life. Sunlight had sparkled through the trees. Sparrows were chirping. Before him, an expansive fairway streaked with morning dew waited to welcome his little white ball. His world was at peace.

Funny how things change.

Diddle was now screaming: "That's all I know. I swear it!"

"Sit down, Diddle!" the Zelienople police detective shouted back. "I'm not through with you. Give me complete answers and tell me the truth!"

Diddle was the unfortunate fellow who discovered a dead body.

The interrogation at police headquarters had entered its second hour. Most of the questions seemed irrelevant to Diddle. Police asked about his family history, his personal relationship with the victim and whether he used drugs or alcohol. At first, Diddle was annoyed. Now he was downright angry. He paced the floor until his golf spikes ripped the carpeting.

"Can I go now, detective?" he asked. "There's nothing more I can tell you."

"Just a few more questions, Diddle. That is, unless you think you need a lawyer," the detective countered.

"I don't need any stinking lawyer. I have nothing to hide."

"Then tell me this: how were you able to get past the iron gate and reach the front door?"

"I'm skinny. It seemed like an emergency. Billy never missed a golf date. I pushed on the gate hard enough to squeeze through. I had to get to my friend."

"Your friend?"

"Yeah, Billy Herman is my friend," Diddle said, realizing that he never uttered such a sentence before.

"Tell me what happened next."

"I walked down his driveway until I came to a parked SUV."

"Herman's car?" the detective asked.

"Nope. That wasn't his car. He drove a British import, low to the ground and with a smelly exhaust. I never saw the Tahoe before today."

The story checked out. The Tahoe had been reported stolen days earlier. Zelienople police theorized that the vehicle was a key piece of evidence.

"So you looked through a window and you saw a dead body." The detective read his notes. "Are you positive that it was Billy Herman?"

"I couldn't see his face, but just from his body type, I assumed…"

"Don't assume, Diddle. Nobody has positively identified the victim. We can't locate any family members in the area. We're trying to find his dental records, but it's the weekend and we're having trouble. Someone who knows him must identify him."

Diddle didn't like where this conversation was heading.

"How long have you known Billy Herman?" the detective asked.

"Close to 10 years. We golf together every Saturday. But we're not close. He didn't talk about his business on the golf course. We knew that he retired from the Pittsburgh police and moved to Butler County. Other than that, he was a mystery. None of us socialized with him. He stayed pretty much to himself."

"A classic loner?"

"Yeah," Diddle replied. "Billy was a classic."

The detective closed his file folder and opened the interrogation room door.

"Are we done?" Diddle asked.

"No, not yet. We're going for a short ride."

Diddle's heart jumped. "Am I under arrest? Are you taking me to jail?"

"Worse than that," the detective said. "I'm taking you to the morgue. We need someone to identify the body. You're the only one who admitted to being Billy Herman's friend."

He escorted Diddle to an unmarked police car. They spoke little on their 18-mile trip to Butler County's government center. Diddle followed the detective through a long hallway, up a fire exit stairway and into an older building. The morgue was identified by hand-painted lettering on a frosted glass window. The detective knocked twice. Chief Faxon opened the door.

Inside were two walls of long filing cabinets dating from the 1940s. An oak table with a slate counter occupied an alcove to the right. Faxon directed Diddle to the table. A white sheet covered the body. Diddle noticed a pungent odor.

Faxon stationed Diddle at the head of the table and slowly pulled back the sheet.

Diddle nodded. "That's Billy Herman, the son of a bitch."

"Why do you say that, Mr. Diddle?" Faxon asked.

"He owed me 25 bucks."

The three women in Jimmie Bailey's world were, in decreasing order by age, puzzled, frustrated and hungry. His mother-in-law, Gloria Negley, couldn't understand why a governor would involve himself in a fistfight late at night. His wife, Ann, was annoyed by Jimmie's refusal to reveal details of his overnight adventures. And his daughter, Hannah, as always, yearned for a feeding.

They sat quietly in their discomfort as afternoon sunshine streamed through the porch windows. Gloria had calmed the baby for most of the day, but Hannah's intensifying squirms and whines began to wear on her. She handed her new granddaughter to Ann. The baby looked back with a self-satisfied smile. The squirms and whines worked.

Jimmie was upstairs, asleep in bed. His Saturday appointment had concluded, and he had told Ann that he wasn't feeling well. No opportunity for her to ask questions. No chance to find out what happened. She had kissed his forehead, turned on the window fan and left.

Gloria sat next to her daughter on the porch swing. Her eyes surveyed the sprawling front yard of Leigh-Rose. Everything outside was so beautiful and perfect, she thought. Everything inside? Not so perfect.

"You look sad, Ann. Is everything all right?" she asked.

"I don't know. Maybe I'm reading too many pregnancy and child birth books. They say my hormones are probably too low, and that affects my mood."

Gloria put her arm around her daughter. "The first few weeks are the most difficult, Ann. It takes some time to adjust."

Ann stroked Hannah's cheeks. The baby's eyes closed. "I still can't believe I'm a mother. Seems like everything happened so fast. One day, you're building your career and the next, you have this new life in your hands."

"You'll be a terrific mother, Ann. Your children will become the most important people in your life. No matter what else happens, you must protect your children."

Ann wasn't sure what her mother was saying. What may happen? She continued to rock the swing and let the comment pass.

"There will be dark times, my dear. I've had a few when I raised my children," Gloria said. "The important thing is for you to be strong and steady. Your children must understand that, if everything else falls, their mother will still be standing."

Ann's hormones were too low to let another comment pass.

"Mom, what are you saying? I won't be standing alone. Jimmie is here with me. He'll be the best father ..."

"Oh, yes, Jimmie," Gloria interrupted. "I'm sure he'll try his hardest."

"Mother! Are you insinuating that Jimmie will be an absent father? He loves Hannah. He's been with me every step of the way. I can't do this without him."

Gloria removed her arm from behind Ann's shoulders. Truth is, she never truly liked her son-in-law and believed Ann deserved better than a wealthy, good-looking politician. She never shared her perceptions with Ann. How could she? Her daughter was smitten so quickly with Jimmie Bailey that any objective evaluation of the boy would devastate her.

Hannah awoke. Her cry pierced the thickening air.

"There, there, little girl," Ann said, raising her baby over her shoulder. "It's OK. Daddy will be up soon."

Gloria suddenly felt unwelcome. Perhaps her advice was unwelcome, too. Ann was becoming a good mother, and it was clear that she already was a protective wife.

"I didn't say anything critical of Jimmie," Gloria said.

"It's what you didn't say, Mom."

"Your father and I love you, Ann. We always will. And we want you to know that, whatever happens, you're still in our hearts and we support you."

"Mother! Stop it!" Ann exclaimed. "My life is here. Our lives are here."

"Surely, dear. You're right. I have no business saying anything."

Ann handed Hannah back to Gloria. "I'm sorry. I'm just a little depressed. I'm sure it's a hormonal thing. In a few days, I'll be better, you'll see."

"If you want, I'll stay until you feel better," Gloria offered.

Ann appreciated the offer. Since Hannah was born, she felt alone in Leigh-Rose Mansion. She didn't feel comfortable talking with the staff about her feelings. She missed talking with her friends in town. And, most significantly, Jimmie seemed distant and disengaged since the birth.

"When do you suppose Jimmie will be down for supper?" Gloria asked.

Ann glanced at the clock. "It's getting late. Maybe I should check on him."

"I don't mean to pry," Gloria said, meaning to pry. "But I overheard you and Jimmie arguing early this morning. Is everything all right?"

Ann sighed. "To be honest, no. He came home about 3 this morning. He was a mess, covered with dirt and scratches. He said he was in a fight."

"Good gracious." Gloria feigned ignorance. "Who?"

"He told me he got into an argument with his chief of staff, Bill Pennoyer."

"That nice young man? He seems so easy-going," Gloria said.

"Bill is a sweetheart, not a violent bone in his body," Ann said. "None of this makes sense to me."

"But why would they fight?" Gloria asked.

"I asked Jimmie that question," Ann said. "He shrugged me off. This is all so strange. He and Bill have been best friends for years. They never had any disagreements before."

Gloria tried to put a good face on the situation. "Ann, this is politics. Things can get heated – even between friends. Maybe, they both reached their boiling points. Hopefully, all those bad feelings are behind them. You want my advice?"

"I suppose," Ann replied cautiously.

"Don't push Jimmie too hard on this. When he's ready to tell you what happened, he will. ... Now let's get some dinner on the table."

Ann agreed, and the two women toiled in the kitchen as Hannah watched from her bouncer seat. The work eased Ann's tensions, until her mother asked a question.

"Did you say Jimmie had a lot of scratches?"

"Yes," Ann replied.

"Not bruises?"

"None that I could see."

Gloria hesitated, but decided to ask one more question: "And he was in a fight with a man?"

"Saturday Night" was special. She was the only girl Chief Faxon trusted with a key. With a chilled bottle of Pinot Grigio in one hand and a frozen pizza in the other, "Saturday Night" a/k/a Roberta, slammed shut Faxon's front door with one thrust of her talented hips.

As usual, Andy's place was cluttered with unrefrigerated leftovers. Dirty dishes were stacked in his sink. A slimy concoction of powdered wheat germ and shredded carrots had encrusted in his blender. Dumbbells of varying weights were scattered about.

She followed a trail of dirty clothes from the laundry room to Andy's master bedroom. Fortunately for her, the bed had been stripped and a clean set of silk leopard print sheets were on the mattress. Unfortunately for her, Andy was not.

Roberta assumed that Chief Andy was working overtime, so she had expected an empty house. All day long, radio stations warned of a murderer at large in the Zelienople area. Everyone was told to lock their doors and not to answer them for any reason. A desperate criminal was on foot, news reports said. He had a gun, she heard. And he will likely shoot to kill.

So "Saturday Night" kept Andy's drapes closed. She didn't want interruptions by any desperados. Unlike other Saturday nights, she decided not to light mood candles, play soul music or burn lavender incense. Andy would understand, she thought. Tonight they would limit themselves to tactile stimulation.

Roberta undressed and stood before Andy's open closet. Half of his clothes were on hangers and half were balled up on the floor. She searched for her favorite T-shirt, the tattered blue one from Grove City College. It didn't smell fresh. It smelled like Andy. She pulled it over her head and stretched the fabric over her thighs.

Then she slid under the bedcovers. To wait.

To wait for the front door to open.

And soon it did.

Castle Rock Center for Lifestyle Wellness welcomed its newest patient with style. Bill Pennoyer stepped from the airport limousine and onto a waiting courtesy cart. Together with Catherine, his "life coach," he was whisked toward his private villa. Along the dirt path, Pennoyer counted 15 prairie dogs, five predator birds with scary beaks and three coiled snakes.

"Where are the humans?" he asked.

"You will see." Catherine answered without looking up. She was busy making notes on her hand-held computer.

Five minutes passed. They passed a sign, reading, "D Sector." Underneath the letters were painted daffodils.

"Is this my sector?" Pennoyer asked.

"Yes. You will have a complete orientation when we arrive." Catherine gave him a cursory smile and returned to her data entry work.

Undaunted, Pennoyer tried to keep the conversation going. "This is pretty remote out here. I guess nobody has made a successful escape."

"Mr. Pennoyer, our task is to help you escape from your addiction," Catherine countered. "If you don't take this seriously, we will fail. Do you understand?"

Pennoyer had no choice. His boss, Jimmie Bailey, ordered him into rehab. It was, Bailey said, "the perfect cover."

The motorized cart rolled into a covered space. A doorman, dressed in jeans and a suede shirt, took Catherine's hand and helped her from the cart. He then motioned Pennoyer to follow his "life coach" up a stone stairway. At the top, they were greeted by a uniformed guard who scanned the bar code on Catherine's name tag. Pennoyer followed her into a revolving door that led to an opulent lobby.

A ruggedly handsome man wearing sunglasses passed them in the revolving door. Pennoyer took a glimpse, then did a double-take when the doors stopped. "Hey, isn't that …?"

"Please be discreet, Mr. Pennoyer," Catherine scolded. "Our guests are entitled to their privacy, remember?"

"Ah, yeah, but I'm sure that was the guy in the tabloids. You know, the one who got high and wrecked his car and …"

Catherine covered his mouth with her hand. "You may see people who look familiar. Some of them are celebrities. But everyone can fall prey to temptations, to the evils of alcohol and drugs. They deserve a chance to get better, without the glare of television cameras and without the drooling public. Don't you agree?"

"Geez, he's in rehab." Pennoyer couldn't let it go. "I never thought he was in such bad shape. Maybe if he just had someone to talk to, someone to level with. A friend. Then he wouldn't turn to drugs. I can talk to him if you like."

"Absolutely not, Mr. Pennoyer. We have licensed professionals here. We call them addictions counselors. Two of them will be assigned to you tomorrow, in fact. Our clients are not permitted to talk to each other about their addictions unless we're in a group setting."

"I don't know why I can't, you know, give them some support..."

"Again, Mr. Pennoyer. Absolutely not. You do not understand what factors in their lives led them into addiction. Each client has personal triggers. And if you don't recognize these triggers, you may accidentally lead them into a relapse."

Pennoyer understood, but that didn't stop him from scrutinizing every face in the lobby. Beautiful, rich, mostly young. They gathered at a lavish lounge beside the registration desk. Shamelessly, the pretty people slurped their acai berry smoothies and snacked on vegetable chips. Could things get more miserable?

"Stephen will assist you with your bag," Catherine said, forgetting that Pennoyer traveled very light – one tote bag. "A specially designed dinner is waiting in your villa. Report to the front desk for orientation tomorrow at 8 a.m."

Catherine shook his hand and directed him to follow the doorman through a glass-enclosed corridor. At the far end was a security door. Stephen swiped his badge over a pad and a locked clicked. He opened the door and told Pennoyer to take his private elevator to the third floor. Pennoyer grabbed his tote and handed the man two dollars.

"No, sir," Stephen said. "No money is exchanged here."

"How long have you worked here, Stephen?"

"About five years."

"Good pay?"

"Decent."

"Meet a lot of famous people?"

"Don't ask."

Stephen stepped back as the elevator doors closed between them. When they reopened three floors up, Pennoyer was astonished. His villa looked like a pricey Aspen ski lodge. Two open stories with a bedroom loft. A complete kitchen of stainless steel and marble. Floor to ceiling windows with stunning views of the Rockies.

As Catherine had promised, dinner was served. But he recognized nothing on the table. Twigs, sprouts, compressed vegetables masquerading as meat and a bowl of fresh fruit. He searched for a salt shaker, but found none. Perhaps, he thought, excess salt was a triggering mechanism for beer lovers. That's why he found no pretzels or peanuts or popcorn. Catherine didn't want to trigger his urge for a beer, he surmised.

He never wanted a beer so much in his life.

Pennoyer gobbled the twigs and sprouts. He chased the vegetable patty with a bottle of green tea. Still hungry and still tired, he collapsed on the sofa. The last 24 hours had taken its toll. His body was dirty and aching. His nerves were unsettled.

His mind could not shake the horror he had witnessed

Pennoyer indeed had demons, but they were not due to alcohol. His demons could not really be blamed on anybody or anything. He was simply in the wrong place at the wrong time.

What he did, anybody in his shoes would have done.

Pennoyer opened his tote bag. Inside were a change of underwear, his shaving kit, his bank cards and a few shirts he had grabbed before racing to the Pittsburgh airport.

And one more thing. A micro-audiocassette tape that could prove his innocence.

Chapter Eight

The Ballet

Some men enjoy a Saturday night date with their wives. Some men prefer patronizing the arts rather than watching television at home. Some men are incurably romantic.

Tom Zachary was not one of those men.

"Tell me again why we're here," Zachary whined as his wife pulled him into the Kane High School lobby.

"The Spencers invited us, that's why," Marcy said through a forced smile. "Their little girl, Brittany, is dancing the lead. Can't you behave?"

"No. I don't know the Spencers or Brittany. I don't like dancing. Music gives me a headache. It's too hot in here."

The more he spoke, the less she paid attention. Too many people were watching them, she thought. The crowd included many of her friends and co-workers. Marcy was the school's assistant principal. She didn't want her petulant husband to cause any embarrassment.

"Gary Spencer owns Gates Hardware, remember Tom? He's the News-Leader's major advertiser. The least you can do is to watch his daughter perform with her dance group."

Marcy was right again. Sometimes Zachary was so absorbed with writing news stories for the weekly paper that he forgot to schmooze with local business people. After all, without advertising revenue from Gates Hardware, the News-Leader would be reduced to an on-line blog. Hardly a week passed without Gates buying at least one page of advertising.

"I suppose I can suffer through this, Marcy. Don't let the Spencers catch me sleeping, though."

Kane High's auditorium seated about 600. The community's performance of "Romeo and Juliet" included a dance troupe of 30, an orchestra of 24 and a children's chorus of nearly 50. With all of their parents, siblings, grandparents, aunts and uncles shuffling down the aisles like huddling penguins, Zachary was feeling claustrophobic. He hated to give up his aisle seat until the show's director told everyone to move to the center.

"There's Susie Spencer over there," Marcy told her husband. "Yoo-hoo, Susie!"

Zachary turned around. Patrons were moving into the aisle. An older couple who looked somewhat familiar smiled to him and sat directly behind him. Zachary tried to recall their names. Maybe he wrote a story about them years ago. Maybe they operated a store on Fraley Street. Maybe he saw them at the Golden Wheel Restaurant.

"Isn't this exciting, Tom?" Marcy jittered in her seat like a teenager at a rock concert. "We need to get out more often, don't you think?"

Zachary nodded perfunctorily. His mind was trying to sort out the couple behind him. After a few minutes, he whispered to Marcy: "Look behind us. Who are those people?"

Marcy turned. They were absolute strangers to her.

"I don't know, Tom. But the Brosgalls are seated a few rows back. Her hair is orange tonight. Can you believe it?"

"Shh, Marcy. They're talking." Zachary leaned back, trying to catch a word or two.

"The Brosgalls went to Italy this summer," Marcy continued. "Rained the whole time, so they just ate their faces off…"

"Marcy," he whispered. "Not now. I'm listening. They just said something about Jimmie Bailey."

"Tom, that's rude to eavesdrop," Marcy said.

Zachary ignored her. Any gossip about Governor Bailey was infinitely more interesting than the overfed Brosgalls. He squirmed in his seat so that his good ear would catch more of the mystery couple's conversation.

Man's voice: "Dennis was very disturbed. I never saw him like that before."

Woman's voice: "Just because the money was missing?"

Man's voice: "Thirty thousand. Just gone overnight."

Woman's voice: "Nobody's money but the governor's. I say let him be."

Man's voice: "Aren't you curious, Julia?"

Woman's voice: "Maybe a little. What I don't understand is where Jimmie Bailey is sending all of this money. What did Dennis say, hundreds of thousands over the year?"

The auditorium lights flickered and dimmed. The couple stopped talking. Zachary leaned to his wife.

"Did you hear that? Jimmie Bailey is paying someone under the table."

"Oh, Tom," Marcy whispered. "For once, stop being a newspaper reporter and enjoy a night out with me."

"I have to find out who these people are." Zachary started to turn around. Marcy stopped him with a tight grip on his shoulder.

The community orchestra began its overture. The curtains parted, and the leotarded dancers sprung to their toes. Marcy sat in wonder. Zachary sat in suspense.

A horde of dancers parted, leaving Brittany Spencer alone under a spotlight. She performed an arabesque and twirled about the stage. After her short solo, a young man in white tights leaped into the light and gently raised Brittany in his arms. The voices behind Zachary started again.

Man's voice: "Look at Michael. Way to go, son."

Woman's voice: "Oh, Paul. He's our beautiful boy."

Zachary grabbed Marcy's program. In the dim light, he squinted to read the performer names. But middle age and small print don't go together.

"Marcy," he whispered. "Look at this. Who is dancing the role of Romeo?"

"It says, 'Michael Padgett.' Someone you know?"

Zachary's mind clicked like tumblers of a combination lock. "Padgett" was the fellow's name from Mid-State Bank. Zachary vaguely remembered the young banker in Judge Van Lear's courtroom. The old judge appointed Padgett to handle Brock Bailey's estate after son Jimmie frittered away millions of dollars. What was Jimmie up to now?

Marcia elbowed Zachary. "Get your mind on the ballet."

Zachary curled the program in his fist. The couple behind him, Padgett's parents, had stopped talking. Son Michael had pranced off stage, replaced by 20 maidens with pancake makeup and matching up do's. The ensemble danced for what seemed like hours to Zachary. Finally, after a crescendo featuring a loud clarinet squeak and dropped cymbal, the curtain fell and house lights returned.

Before Marcy could talk, Zachary turned around. Paul and Julia Padgett began to stand for intermission. Zachary recognized them as the couple who rented the house at the bottom of Clay Street. Zachary loved to snitch black cherries from their backyard tree.

"That was certainly entertaining," he said, stopping Paul from his exit. "These young people are so talented, especially the male lead."

"Thank you," Julia said, beaming. "That was our son, Michael. I don't believe we've had the pleasure…"

"Tom Zachary's my name. This is my wife, Marcy. And you are?"

"Paul and Julia Padgett." Paul extended his hand and they shook.

"Padgett, Padgett," Zachary stammered. "Are you any relation to Dennis Padgett?"

"Yes, sir, he's our older son," Paul answered.

"A wonderful young man," Zachary said. "I interviewed him for the News-Leader a few years back. We printed some stories about the Brock Bailey estate. You remember?"

Julia smiled. She was proud of her sons and eager to share their successes – even with a snooping newspaper editor. "Dennis works for Governor Bailey now. Does all of his personal financial work."

"Is that right, Julia?" Zachary said. "That's wonderful. I'm sure Jimmie is a terrific boss. Do you read our newspaper?"

"Well," Julia laughed, "I just clip out the coupons. Paul does the reading."

Zachary turned to Mr. Padgett. "Have you seen our monthly column, 'Where Are They Now?' We should do a story on Dennis, don't you think?"

Paul became uneasy. "You'll have to ask Dennis. He probably won't tell you much. It's private what he does with the governor's money."

Zachary put his arm around the man's shoulder. "We're not going to pry about the governor's finances. We're not interested in that."

"Good." Paul squirmed.

Zachary paused to let the man explain his response. No explanation followed.

"Should we be interested in that, Paul?"

They agreed to meet at "the stoplight" at 10 p.m. Fraley Street at Greeves.

Matty was alone. His friend Megan had fallen asleep an hour ago. It was her typical response to Saturday night meat loaf at the Golden Wheel. Comfort food always works. In contrast, Matty had the uncomfortable baked chicken and corn fritter special. He would be awake until midnight.

The young man waited with a zip lock bag in hand. No traffic passed. The stoplight changed to a yellow blinking light. He watched headlights coming from the west. Dr. Greta said she would be driving a small pickup truck.

Megan had warned him not to share "the hair" with the state police. She worried that Matty would be forced to say whose hair it was and how he obtained it. Megan trusted that her friend understood that he could be prosecuted for trespassing.

But Matty was too curious. He had to know. Was Billy Herman's blood on the shovel that killed the police commissioner five years ago? Matty was so close to proving his theory that Herman was the cop's murderer. He couldn't stop now. Surely, Megan would understand, he thought.

The small truck turned into the restaurant parking lot. Matty waited nervously as Dr. Greta walked toward him. She was smiling; he was not.

"I'm glad you called, Matty," Dr. Greta said. "But I don't know why all of this is such a secret. If you know the murderer's name, you'll have to tell police sooner or later."

"We're not working for the police, doctor. We're just testing a theory. That's what I told you over the telephone. This is all confidential – between us."

He handed her the bag. She lifted it up to the streetlight.

"One hair? That's all? We like to have more of a sample, Matty."

"You told me one hair was enough. I didn't have time to get anything more."

Dr. Greta placed the sample into an evidence bag. "Are you paying for this test?"

"I hadn't thought that I ..."

"Matty, either you pay for it or the Commonwealth of Pennsylvania will pay for it and, if the Commonwealth pays for it, they get the report."

"The report goes to me, Dr. Greta, and not to anyone else – especially the police. How much do I owe you?"

She looked him over. Tall, handsome, young, bright and eager. If only she was 20 years younger, she thought, he would receive an entirely different answer.

"Nothing," she said. "Nothing yet. But if there's a match, you have to tell me who the sample is from."

Matty didn't like the deal. But, at the moment, he had no other offers.

"OK. You'll find out."

She shook his hand in a very professional manner.

"And one more thing, Dr. Greta, no matter what happens, no matter who asks you, we didn't meet here tonight. Got it?"

"Promise."

Matty watched her step carefully over the gravel parking lot and return to her truck. Soon its taillights vanished over the horizon. When Matty returned to his apartment, Megan was still asleep. He lay beside her and wondered if he did the right thing.

"Saturday Night" waited and waited for Chief Andy to come home. In fact, she waited so long it became Sunday morning.

About 1 a.m., "Saturday night" a/k/a Roberta realized how cheap she was. She met Andy only a few weeks ago, and now she was half naked and alone in his bed. What kind of self-respecting girl would throw herself at a stranger just to share intimate moments every seven days? Certainly not Roberta.

The smell of Andy's T-shirt around her neck began to annoy her. Roberta was scrupulously clean at home. How could she live with a slob like Andy? Dirty dishes, dirty laundry, dirty floors, dirty windows. If it wasn't for his dazzling smile and tender touch, she would have run from his house, screaming all the way home.

Roberta felt itchy. Maybe it was the sheets. Someone had washed and folded them before she fixed the bed. Maybe the bedclothes weren't totally dry. Maybe mold had set in. She smelled his pillowcase and then sneezed.

Her questions kept coming. Why would a police chief own silk, leopard print sheets? Were they a gift from another girlfriend? From his sister, maybe? From his mother? Eeech! What kind of a pervert is this guy?

Roberta slid from the bed. Using only the moonlight that shone through Andy's bedroom window, she located her underwear and outerwear. She stepped into her pumps. It was time to go. He could call her later if he wanted, she thought. He had some explaining to do, especially about the sheets.

As she buttoned her blouse, Roberta heard a click at the front door. Then she heard soft steps. That rascal, she thought. He's trying to sneak in. Roberta was swept with excitement. Should she jump back into bed? Or should she surprise him behind the door? Startling a cop during a murder investigation was probably not a good idea, she thought. So she curled up on Andy's easy chair in the corner and pretended to sleep.

Roberta listened as the footsteps moved from living room to dining room. She heard drawers being pulled open and not being shut. She heard the clink of silverware and glasses. She grew uneasy when she heard a chair being knocked over and then the splatter of a drawer's contents being dumped on the floor.

Footsteps moved to the kitchen. Again, drawers were pulled out and overturned. Seconds later, she heard footsteps in the powder room. The mirrored medicine cabinet door was thrown open and glass shattered. One by one, each medicine bottle was inspected and then thrown to the floor.

Roberta was gripped with fear. Either Andy was drunk and violent or … the alternative was unthinkable.

Having no place to hide, Roberta decided to block the bedroom door. Andy's dresser would do the job, but she didn't have the strength to move it. To the side of his closet, though, were 25-pound iron weights. One by one, she slid about a dozen of them to the door and wedged them between the hinges and the wall. Then she moved his chair and nightstand to secure the weights in place.

With trembling fingers, Roberta dialed 9-1-1 on her cellphone. She tried to talk over the noise outside Andy's bedroom door.

"There's a burglary in progress," she told the dispatcher.

"Address, ma'am?"

"I don't know the address. It's on Ziegler."

"Zelienople?"

"Yes, hurry."

"Your name, ma'am?"

"Uh, I'm a neighbor. Please hurry."

"I'm sending someone over now. Please wait in the street."

"Uh, I can't …"

Suddenly, the bedroom door was shoved open several inches. Roberta came face-to-face with the intruder. She screamed. He reached inside and grabbed her hair. With all of her strength she pushed the door with her hip. He yelped in pain as the door jammed into his forearm. He released her.

Sirens sounded from the distance. Within seconds, flashing blue lights illuminated the house. The intruder abandoned his prey and fled on foot. Roberta slid to the floor and cried.

She heard a police cruiser slowly pass the house. A second police car pulled into the driveway. She jumped when she heard the front door open again.

"Roberta, Roberta, are you all right?" Andy called.

"Yes. Help me. I'm in the bedroom."

Andy stepped over the broken glass and burglarized mess. Roberta removed her fortress behind the door. She hugged him hard.

"He was here, wasn't he?" Andy asked.

Roberta could only nod and hug him more tightly.

"Did you see him?"

She nodded again, backed from him and tried to regain composure. "I looked into his eyes. They were big and it seemed like they were throbbing. He was like an animal. He was breathing like a wild animal. Oh, Andy."

"The dispatcher said there was a burglary on Ziegler Street. Did you call that in?"

"I did, Andy, but I didn't give the address or my name."

Thank God, he thought. Zelienople's police department didn't need to know about the extracurricular affairs of its chief.

"Was he white, black, Hispanic, what?" Andy asked.

"He was white, Andy."

"Are you sure?"

"Yes, I saw him, like, this far away," she said, spreading her hands about 12 inches apart.

"What was he wearing, Roberta?"

"Like a zip-up black sweatshirt. I didn't see anything else." She hugged him again and together they walked to the bed. He sat down with her. "I need something to drink, Andy."

He took her hand. They stepped over the wildly scattered debris in the kitchen. Andy retrieved a bottle of water from his refrigerator and handed it to the trembling woman. She clung to him and took a swallow.

"Listen to me carefully, Roberta. I will take this information and make it part of the investigative file. There's no need for you to get involved in this."

"Thank you. I'm very upset. I can't talk to the police right now."

"You've been through a lot tonight, Roberta. Let me take you home."

The doorbell rang. Andy directed Roberta to stand behind the laundry room door. She thought his behavior was strange, but complied. He opened the door and met a uniformed officer. Roberta heard him step outside and pull the door behind him. A few minutes later, he returned to her.

"I didn't want the officer to see my home was vandalized," Andy told her. "Imagine how embarrassing that would be for a police chief."

"Guess so," she said. "None of this will be reported?"

"Surely, you understand, Roberta. You know, the situation here with us, you're alone in my house, you were confronted in my bedroom. That could ruin me. We'll catch this guy and he'll be executed or put away for a long time. Trust me."

"What about my description? I had a good look at him, Andy. I could make a positive identification for you."

Roberta was his best witness; his other witnesses were unconscious, half-blind or dead. But Roberta was a witness who had been undressed in his bedroom. Andy imagined the cross-examination at the killer's trial:

Q. How long had you known Chief Faxon?

A. About three weeks.

Q. Did you sleep with him?

"Objection!" the district attorney would shout. "No relevance."

The defense attorney would argue that Roberta, by canoodling with Faxon, had an undue bias in favor of the police – likely a winning argument.

"Overruled," the judge would order. "Answer the question, ma'am."

A. Yes, I slept with Chief Faxon.

Q. How often?

A. Every Saturday night.

Andy was certain. Nobody needed to know those details.

Chapter Nine

The Sauna

When he heeded the call many years ago, Father Frank McWilliams understood that loneliness would follow. His friends from seminary had dispersed to various parishes. They reunited rarely, usually for a funeral of one of their own. Time had claimed his mother and father. He spent nights alone in the rectory, alternating between prayer and thought.

As pastor of Good Shepherd Catholic Church in Pittsburgh's poorest neighborhood, Father Frank understood that his personal isolation paled by comparison to the sorrows of his congregation. At least, he had a home, he had food, he had a purpose.

But his solitude was profound. Turning 65 without family and without fanfare was difficult. He could complain to no one. His was a life of service to others. Deep inside, though, behind his ever-present smile and disarming charm, he was a lonely man.

Father Frank's path to the priesthood was unusual. The outgoing son of a Brackenridge steel worker, he worked summers on the coal barges. He traveled the Pittsburgh rivers in oppressive heat. He befriended the men who gave an honest day's work. He loathed the men who dodged work. He grew to distrust the steel company, his union bosses and everyone else who came by their money easily. For McWilliams, there was no religion on the barges, save for occasional, unflattering references to the Almighty. His language was the saltiest.

When young Frankie graduated from high school, a full-time position awaited at the Allegheny-Ludlum steel plant. The hours were long, but the pay was good. For an 18-year-old, the job seemed like the logical next step. His father pushed him hard to accept the offer. His mother, however, was quiet. When he asked for her opinion, she handed him an envelope from Duquesne University.

"Don't tell your dad," she said. "Open it up."

McWilliams pulled out a form. He scanned it quickly and returned it to the envelope.

"No," he told his mother. "I'm not going to make anyone's quota."

"Frankie, listen to me. Think about it. Nobody in our family ever went to college. Why spend your life in the dirt and smoke of Brackenridge?"

"Hard work never killed anybody, Mom."

His mother bowed her head and mumbled a prayer. Suddenly, he felt deep soreness from the day's hard work. He didn't enjoy pain.

McWilliams completed the application for a four-year diversity scholarship. A few months later, he received the call from Duquesne. Shortly before graduating cum laude in philosophy and religious studies, McWilliams received "the call" from a higher authority.

After his ordination, Father Frank returned to the Pittsburgh Diocese and was assigned as an assistant pastor at an affluent South Hills church. He handled his priestly duties competently, but something was missing. A year later, he convinced Archbishop Ostrow to assign him to a mission – not a mission to a third-world country, but a mission for Pittsburgh's poor and needy.

Lacking a Catholic presence in the Hill District, the Diocese charged McWilliams with starting a parish called

"Good Shepherd." He found an abandoned warehouse on Centre Avenue and, with financial help from his Duquesne friends, built a church. His most helpful friend was Governor Brock Bailey, heir to the Keystone Oil fortune.

Archbishop Ostrow, liberal in compassion and conservative with a buck, gave McWilliams a short-term commitment: "make Good Shepherd a self-sustaining parish in ten years or it will be consolidated with Saint Agnes Church."

McWilliams took the challenge. He built his parish with people. Ten people attended his first Sunday Mass. The church grew to more than 300 families. Good Shepherd became a community center and a source of hope for those in despair.

But McWilliams didn't build the parish with money. His Sunday collections were the lowest in the Diocese. His heating bills for the converted warehouse were enormous. Vandalism and vagrancy were constant problems. Good Shepherd was saving souls, but not saving cash.

As collection money dwindled in the Diocese and budgets tightened, Bishop Ostrow began the painful process of church consolidation. He had rescued Good Shepherd from the ax in past years, only because he kept his ten-year commitment to Father McWilliams. Increasingly, though, he endured complaints from his administrators. Good Shepherd was a drag on the Diocese, they said. Few priests wanted to celebrate Mass in such squalor, let alone reside in a rectory located in Pittsburgh's high crime neighborhood. St. Agnes, a more prosperous parish, was only two miles away, they pointed out. Consolidation seemed to be necessary.

Bishop Ostrow prayed mightily for public relations advice. In a dream, he witnessed the heavy wooden doors of Good Shepherd swing open. Marching from the church were regiments of expressionless people. Some were crying. Some were leaning on crutches. Some carried prayer books and chanted in Latin. His dream ended with the doors falling from their hinges and the entire Good Shepherd warehouse imploding into dust. His prayer for public relations advice was not fruitful.

He relayed the dream to his secretary. She gave him two pieces of advice: first, to stop eating pizza before bedtime and, second, to think about the doors in his dream. They opened and they fell upon the power of some unforeseen force, "like the doors to Christ," she told him.

Bishop Ostrow returned to his study and developed the "Doors to Christ" program, for which he took complete credit. Ostensibly, "Doors to Christ" would evaluate the fiscal performance of all parishes in Pittsburgh. In reality, though, the only "doors" to be closed were Good Shepherd's.

Father McWilliams knew what was coming. He was notified by letter from the diocesan administrator. "All Catholic facilities are included in our study," the letter said. "Any facility that fails to meet our minimum requirements for fiscal stability may be subsidized through this office, may be supported by private funding sources or, at last resort, may be terminated."

McWilliams knew that his ten years was up. This was his pink slip.

His congregation knew as well. Bishop Ostrow's sermon at yesterday's Mass left little doubt: Good Shepherd's doors would soon fall from their hinges. Everyone understood that McWilliams, the priest who fanned their faith, had little power to keep their church alive.

Unless he could find money.

Quickly.

Zelienople police knew the victim's name: Billy Herman. They knew he died from a single gunshot to the chest. They knew the gun by his hand had not been fired. They knew his murder followed a spree of armed robberies in the town. They had completed 90 percent of their investigation of the murder scene.

But they had no suspects.

Sunday was not a day of rest for Chief Faxon's detectives. Nor could it be. The community was gripped with fear. The robberies seemed so violent; the murder, so indiscriminate. Rumors swept through Butler County that a woman had been murdered. A caller to the 9-1-1 operator reported a burglary in process on Ziegler Street, but when police arrived there was no woman on the street. Had she been abducted? And killed? Detectives struggled to check out dozens of leads, all of which were dead ends.

Reporters pressed for updates, but police were mum. Details of Billy Herman's death were withheld from public consumption. Fears of copycat murders prompted police to clam up. Nobody had to know the manner of death, how the body was discovered, how entry was gained into the house and, most significantly, the bizarre evidence that a large rock had been thrown through Mr. Herman's bedroom window.

Throughout the day, Billy Herman's creek-side home was scrutinized for evidence. Detectives spent hours theorizing what happened to Herman's bedroom window. The rock, which was discovered amidst broken glass, was carefully dusted for fingerprints. Investigators measured the glass-splatter pattern to determine the force used to throw the rock. And they concluded that entry was not attempted through the bedroom window. The rock incident likely was meant to scare Mr. Herman, they concluded. Police found no fingerprints on the rock.

The handgun that was found only inches from Herman's hand was fully loaded and, obviously, unfired. If the killer had intended to fake a suicide scene by placing the gun near

Herman's hand, it was a vain attempt. The handgun's serial number was tracked. Herman apparently purchased it years earlier at a Virginia gun show. It was never traced to a crime. The only fingerprints on the gun were his.

In the living room, police found a brass bullet, which was lodged in a wall behind Herman's liquor cabinet. Police determined that the bullet was fired from a .38-caliber revolver. Ballistics tests would be performed later. The slug's location was consistent with the trajectory of the entrance and exit wounds of the victim.

Based upon their review of the crime scene, police concluded that entry was likely through the front door. Whether the intruder had a key or the front door was unlocked, police could not determine. Because entry apparently was not forced, detectives surmised that Herman opened the door for his killer after the killer threatened him by throwing a rock through his bedroom window.

No doorknob, light switch or wall column escaped dusting by crime scene investigators. Fingerprints were lifted from every room.

Zelienople's lead detective was intrigued by the 5,500-pound chunk of evidence parked outside. How did this stolen vehicle end up in Herman's driveway? Did the killer drive it? How did it get past the locked front gates? The detective ordered a full fingerprint dusting.

Police also were scrambling for a physical description of the attacker. They knew only one person who had a reasonable look at the man – Nata Prybelewski, the 30-year-old woman who was attacked on her parents' front porch. Nata's condition had been upgraded to "stable" overnight. She was able to see visitors in her hospital room.

Detectives Adams and Keating were assigned to conduct the interview. Accompanying them was Higgins, the department's sketch artist.

Nata was sitting up in her private hospital room. Her mother, Minka, who lost her diamond ring in a struggle with the robber, was conversing in Polish. A nurse escorted the detectives to Nata's bedside.

After the usual pleasantries, detective Adams got down to business.

"Here's the description we have so far, Ms. Prybelewski. A young man, maybe in his early twenties. About six feet tall, more or less. Olive or darker complexion. He wore a black hooded sweatshirt. Can you give us a better description?"

Nata was still shaken. She bit her bottom lip and nodded to the detectives.

"This is not easy for me," she said. "I saw him fighting with Mama. He had her on the floor of our porch. He seemed shorter than six foot."

"Tell me about his face," Adams said.

"I didn't really see him up close. He was about ten feet away. The light was not good. Our porch light was out, and the streetlight cast shadows."

"Any details would help us, Nata."

The woman tried to remember, but her recollection was spotty.

"The black sweatshirt, I remember that. It was zippered in the front. He wore the hood…"

"His face, Nata. Tell us about his face."

She paused. "His face was dark. His features were dark. If I had to make a guess, I'd say he was black."

"Not Asian or Hispanic?" Adams asked.

"No, definitely not."

"And not white, right Nata?"

She paused again. "Again, I'd have to guess he was black."

"His hair, Nata. Was it closely cropped like a black man's hair or was it long?"

"It wasn't long. I'm sure of that."

Adams waited for detective Keating to finish taking notes. Higgins grabbed a sketch pad from his briefcase and pulled a chair beside the bed.

"Before we ask you to assist Officer Higgins in his sketch, is there any other detail about the robber we should know?" Adams asked.

"There was stubble on his face, like he hadn't shaved that day. And his eyes…"

"What about them, Nata?"

"His eyes were set apart and it seemed like they were beating like a heart. I'll never forget those eyes, the last things I saw before he fired his gun."

Minka cradled her daughter and asked detectives for a moment without questions.

Adams looked at Keating's notes. "Black male, six feet two inches, unshaven, 20 years old, eyes wide and throbbing."

Nata had composed herself. So Adams continued.

"If you saw him again, would you be able to identify him?"

"I think so," she answered feebly.

Minka pleaded with her eyes. The detectives knew what she was thinking.

Find him soon.

Group therapy sessions at the Castle Rock rehab center were held at 8 a.m. in the Peony Pavilion, a short walk past Contemplation Gardens. All new patients, euphemistically called "patrons," were to gather for orientation at Peony. Strict orders were given to all. No talking. No cellphones. And no revealing clothing.

Bill Pennoyer, avowed alcoholic, had ironed his only shirt and brushed his thinning hair. He looked presentable in the bathroom mirror. Just a trace of derelict, he thought. These addiction counselors can be fooled, but he wasn't sure whether the real alcoholics would call him out. Thank goodness he learned his acting skills in Pennsylvania politics.

Today's new patrons numbered about 20. Each took a seat in the pavilion's circular conference room. Above them were celestory windows, specially designed to cast sunlight upon one chair at a time. Pennoyer eyeballed the group. He didn't recognize anyone and, thankfully, no one appeared to recognize him.

"Welcome to your new life!" a man's voice thundered over the sound system as television screens lowered from the ceiling. "This is Castle Rock, where you will take your first steps toward clean living. All is possible, if you try."

Images of the rehab center property, interspersed with happy, youthful faces, flashed on the monitors. Pennoyer endured about ten minutes of the self-promoting video; the faces around him became more interesting.

The middle-age woman beside him was tall, slender and restless. Uppers, he thought. The freckled purple-haired boy beside her was motionless. Drugs from his mother's medicine cabinet, Pennoyer surmised. All the red-nosed guys were probably drinkers. The fat man with the perpetual grin? Oxycontin was the best guess.

While the video droned, the sunlight beam moved toward a woman directly across the room. Who was she? Golden hair, soft blue eyes, a sultry angular face with pouty lips. A lady in the fullness of life, Pennoyer thought. Couldn't be more than 25 years old. Not a wrinkle. Not a frown line.

Clearly, she was uncomfortable under the sun's glare. She pushed back her chair and leaned away from the sunshine. Pennoyer admired her silky skin, the way it flowed perfectly from her chin, past her collarbone and southward to a hint of cleavage.

He was mesmerized. While other patrons stared blankly at the monitors, Pennoyer studied every inch of the woman.

She was surely an actress or model, he thought. Perfectly proportioned and perfectly alluring. He caught a fleeting glance from her and returned one. She smiled coyly. So did he. She kicked off her shoes and wiggled her toes. He unbuttoned his sleeves and stretched his pudgy arms behind his head.

He thought he heard her giggle.

During the next hour, professional addiction counselors made their speeches as they paced between Pennoyer and his new blonde friend. Every word they said was gibberish to Pennoyer's ears. He struggled to look around them, to see across the room to the intriguing woman.

Pennoyer's counselor, Catherine, took the microphone. She had noticed her new patron's attention disorder. Her comments were sharply directed to him.

"Although we travel our road together, we remain as individuals here at Castle Rock," she said. "Each of you will have a separate treatment plan. Each of you will make unique sacrifices and lifestyle changes. You must respect your neighbor's privacy. Therefore, please do not disclose to others the nature of your addiction."

Catherine explained that patrons with similar additions were not segregated by housing. "Whether you are staying at the Tulip Cottages, the Lilac Cabins or the Azalea Villas, your neighbor's demon may not be your own."

Pennoyer waited for his friend to make eye contact. When she did, he drew a question mark in the air. She cupped her palms with her fingers straight up. Tulip! That's where she's staying. Another glance to her. She was holding up seven fingers. Room No. 7!

When orientation ended, Pennoyer felt like a teenager at a Fort Lauderdale hotel. He had connected with a beautiful girl. What more could he ask for? He watched the young lady talking to a counselor. She smiled at him over her shoulder and walked away with the older woman. Pennoyer noticed a paper she had left on her chair. He slipped it into his pocket a second before Catherine took his arm.

"Mr. Pennoyer, please follow me to your evaluation session."

He followed Catherine up an escalator to a small conference room. Seated inside were his nutritionist, a physical conditioning coach and a little man who was identified as his hypnotherapist. They questioned him about his alcohol history.

For the next two hours, a piece of paper was burning a hole in Pennoyer's pocket. He asked for a bathroom break because the suspense was killing him. When the door shut behind him, he read the note: "Sauna at the Tulip exercise facility, 9 pm."

Pennoyer gulped. He could feel blood rushing to every capillary.

When the appointed hour arrived, Pennoyer was wrapped in a pool towel and stoking the heated coals in an empty sauna. The exercise room hours had ended at 8 p.m., and not a soul was in sight. Perhaps this was her joke, he thought. Why would a beautiful starlet hook up with a blubbery thirty-something in a sauna after hours?

At 9:15, while a bead of sweat tenaciously hung from his nose, the sauna door opened. His dream girl, wearing a pool robe that was one belt tug away from exposing her worldly charm, sauntered in and sat beside him.

"You looked like you needed a friend this morning," she said with the sweetest smile.

"I did," he said, "and still do. What's your name?"

"Roxanne Randle, but my friends call me 'Roxy.' How about you?"

"Bill Penn ... Pencil. Bill Pencil."

"That's an interesting name," she cooed. "You should be in show business."

"Are you?" he asked. "Your face looks so familiar."

"As a matter of fact, I am. I hold suitcase number 17…"

"On 'Take It or Leave It?' I love that show. So you are a model."

"Yea, but not model behavior. That's why I'm here at Castle Rock." She ran her fingers through her hair. Her robe was opening wider. "How about you, Bill? What do you do?"

"I'm in politics…"

"Politics, like Congress? I think those senators are so cute."

"Well, I'm a senator myself," he fibbed. "From Rhode Island."

She saddled up closer. "I used to date a guy from Rhode Island. He was from Hartford. But he wasn't a cute senator. Just a guy."

It doesn't get much better than this, Pennoyer thought.

"What's your addiction, Bill? I know we're not supposed to talk about it, but I get real curious."

"Sometimes I drink too much. But it's not real serious." Pennoyer felt a tingling on his right foot. Was that her toe? The heat was building. Sweat leaked into his eyes. He squirmed.

"You shouldn't be in this heat too long, Bill. It's not good for your heart."

"I'm OK. I guess my eyes are stinging a bit."

Roxy stood and faced him. "Don't worry, I'll wipe that sweat." She grasped the lapels of her robe and sensuously rubbed his forehead. He wanted to stop time.

"So what are you in here for, Roxy? What's your addiction?"

"Oh that. I don't really like to talk about it," she replied.

"No, seriously, we're friends. You can tell me. What is it?"

"Well, I suppose I can tell you, Bill. It's sex."

Chapter Ten
The Suspect

Dennis Padgett tried, but his access was denied.

Being the governor's financial advisor was not enough to crack the privacy firewall of Mid-State Bank. Padgett shut down his computer. His quest to find out where Jimmie Bailey mysteriously wired $30,000 required a personal visit to Mid-State's Smethport office.

Padgett hadn't set foot in the bank since he quit his job as trust officer five years ago. He had burned every bridge in the process. Except for a bridge with Shawna, senior loan officer.

On Monday morning, before the bank opened, Padgett tapped his key on Shawna's office window. She opened the bank's rear door, and Padgett hopped inside.

"Can't stay away, Dennis?" she joked. "How long has it been?"

"Not long enough," he replied. "Is Murphy still running the show?"

"Yeah, we can't get rid of him," she answered. "Don't worry, Dennis. You're safe here for an hour or so. Murphy won't arrive until ten."

"Great, Shawna. That will give me enough time to track a wire transfer."

"The governor's account?"

He nodded and handed her the account number. She fired up her computer as he pulled a chair beside her.

"You know, I'm not allowed to do this. We've got privacy rules." Shawna's warning fell upon deaf ears. Whenever Jimmie Bailey was involved, nobody followed privacy rules.

They stared at the screen while numbers downloaded from the bank's server. Bailey's money market account had only 25 transactions in the past year – most were modest deposits and withdrawals. Two entries, though, piqued Padgett's attention: Friday's $30,000 transfer and a series of ten $9,000 transfers three months earlier.

"Looks like someone was trying to avoid the $10,000 cash reporting requirement," Shawna said. "These $9,000 transfers should have set off your alarm, Dennis."

"I didn't do that, Shawna." Padgett maintained his innocence. "I had no idea..."

"Let me trace the bank routing number," she said, making a search for number 0769323. "Central Bank & Trust, Butler, Pennsylvania. That's where the $90,000 went."

"Whose account?" Padgett shot back.

"I can't really..."

"Shawna, I'm a signatory to this account. My name's on it. I need to know where the money went!"

She turned the computer screen away from him. After a few keystrokes, she studied the screen. Then she jotted a name on her legal pad.

"Would you like some coffee, Dennis?" She stood up.

"Not right now. Just tell me the name."

"I'll be right back, just make yourself at home." Shawna left the office, but turned around in time to see Dennis reading the name on her notepad. When he returned to his seat, she re-entered with two cups of machine coffee.

"Let's see, where was I?" she said, tapping her keyboard cursor and highlighting the Friday wire transfer. "This is bank routing number 7073452. First Bank of Littleton,

Colorado. Payment of $30,000. Transfer successful at 7:35 a.m. Mountain Daylight Time."

"The payee?" Dennis asked.

"We have rules, Mr. Padgett," Shawna playfully scolded. "I am not permitted to release that information to you."

She scrolled to the next page. Her eyes lit up briefly. She bit her lower lip and wrote a long name on her legal pad.

"More coffee, Mr. Padgett?"

"Yes, more coffee," he replied. "Take your time."

She smiled, took his half-filled cup and walked to the hall. Padgett leaned over her desk. He read her writing upside-down; "Castle Rock Center for Lifestyle Wellness." In the margin, Shawna had written: "If I were you, I'd take my name off this account."

Padgett understood the loan officer's concerns, but decided it was too premature to drop his name. Jimmie would be tipped off and may fire him, he thought. Better to investigate the Castle Rock Center. It could be a donation. Maybe Jimmie was a philanthropist, as his mother suggested. Or maybe Jimmie was a drug addict, as his brother suggested. Or maybe Jimmie was a crook, as his father suggested.

"Here's your coffee, Dennis." Shawna startled him when she returned. She handed him a warm ceramic mug, which he held in his hands like an adult security blanket. She pushed some papers across her desk and rolled back in her chair.

"You may want to read these federal guidelines for reporting cash transactions of $10,000 or more," Shawna said. "I'm sure someone with your financial background understands that these big cash transactions must be reported – if not by you, then by the bank. Otherwise, it looks like money laundering by a criminal enterprise."

Padgett knew she was right. Either he would report the transfers to the feds or, now that Shawna was aware of the transfers, Mid-State would report them.

"The $30,000 cash transaction looks legitimate, but the ten $9,000 transactions will raise red flags," Shawna said. "I don't want you to get into any trouble."

"I'm sure they're all legitimate," Padgett replied, not being sure of anything.

Shawna led Padgett to the back parking lot. They shook hands and she pressed a business card in his palm.

"Let me know what you want to do," Shawna said. "In the meantime, here's the name of a criminal defense attorney who's done work in this area. You may need her advice."

Fifteen minutes ago, Padgett came looking for answers. He drove away with a hundred questions. Four questions bothered him greatly.

What is Castle Rock Center?

Did the governor have a substance abuse problem?

Why did Jimmie Bailey pay $90,000 to a man named "William Herman?"

Would Dennis Padgett land in jail?

Mary Anne Graumlich strode into Casale, Dodge & Shumann on Monday morning with a Friday afternoon attitude.

"Let's pack up and get the hell out of here!" she yelled to her support staff. "Don't keep the new judge waiting!"

The Casale firm's most underproductive attorney was heading to the Butler County bench. But not before she ridiculed her secretaries and extracted her pound of flesh from the law firm partnership.

"Ms. Graumlich," one secretary said timidly, "none of these cases has been reassigned to another attorney. What should I do with these files?"

"How the hell should I know? You know these attorneys as well as I do. Ask them yourself. ... And one other thing..."

"Yes, Ms. Graumlich?"

"From now on, it's 'Your Honor.' Got it?"

"Yes, Your Honor."

Ellis Casale, the firm's managing partner, endured the 33-year-old's tantrum for the last time. He called her into a side conference room and shut the door.

"You're not a judge yet, so this is probably my last chance to speak to you attorney-to-attorney," he began.

"Make this quick because I'm taking my kids to Kennywood Park this afternoon," she said.

"Mary, on behalf of the firm, I wish you well in your new career as Butler County judge. Your service here at Casale, Dodge and Schumann has been rocky at times, but we want you to know that your talents will be missed."

"Thank you for damning me with such faint praise," Graumlich said. "What about my final partnership distribution?"

Casale placed a yellow portfolio folder on the table. When she reached for it, he leaned on it with his fist.

"Our independent auditor has reviewed the firm's financial situation," Casale said. "He has taken many factors into consideration, including your buy-in share, the value of our holdings and earnings based upon your caseload and clients. I think you will find the number very generous."

Graumlich paged through the folder and read its conclusion. She glared at Casale with fire in her eyes.

"This is outrageous!" she shrieked. "There are eight partners in this firm, and my share is exactly one-eighth!"

Casale shook his head in disbelief. "How is that unfair?"

"How can you be so stupid, Ellis? Or should I say so dishonest? I have brought great honor to this firm. Governor Bailey has selected me to be a judge. In the history of this firm, no one has ever served as a judge. I should be compensated for rising to this level."

"Mary, surely you don't think …"

"Think I should be paid a fair compensation for the status that I have attained and the prestige that I have bestowed upon your little group of thieves, here? Absolutely!"

With that, she threw the portfolio across the room, scattering loose pages along the flight path. Attorneys who had gathered outside the door ran to their offices. Secretaries hid in the file room. The Casale receptionist placed calls into voice mail.

"What do you want us to do, Mary?" Casale braced for an impossible demand.

"I want a 25 percent bonus above that number," she demanded. "That's the least you can do for Butler County's newest judge."

"I-I-I can't do that," Casale answered. "That would look like we're buying a special favor from you."

Graumlich pointed a well-manicured index finger at him. "Ellis Casale, are you accusing me of an ethical violation? Because if you are, I will not hesitate to report you to the Supreme Court disciplinary board. You cannot threaten a judge."

She picked up the file folder and flung it toward her senior partner. He ducked the missile. The flying folder ripped through an oil portrait of the late Mr. Schumann.

Through gritted teeth, Casale had the final word: "Here is my threat, Graumlich. If you don't get your arrogant ass out of this office in fifteen minutes, I'm calling the police."

"You'll regret you said those words, Casale." Graumlich sneered.

"Maybe," he replied. "But I sure felt good saying them."

Jimmie Bailey canceled all of his appointments. He was not to be disturbed. No calls and no mail were to cross the threshold of his home office.

Everyone obeyed those orders, except for Ann.

She entered his office quietly. Jimmie was admiring a trophy, one of the many mementoes of his professional baseball career. Things were more fun then. Being a husband, father, political target and, lately, a law-abiding citizen were much more challenging.

Jimmie was not surprised by her visit. He knew why she was there. His late hours and his phony explanation for them didn't fool his wife. She wanted answers. She deserved answers. Only this time, it was better that she didn't know the truth.

"Did your cuts heal, Jimmie?" Ann began with an innocuous question, designed to lead to more damaging answers.

"Yeah," he said. "And I still don't want to talk about it."

"And Bill, is he all right?"

"I don't know about Pennoyer. He's not at work today."

She saddled closer to him, trying to make some progress.

"What was the argument about, Jimmie? Why did you fight? You were best friends."

"I don't want to talk about it." Jimmie set down the trophy and stared at the wall.

"Guys only fight over two things, girls or money. Which was it, Jimmie?"

"It wasn't over a girl, Ann," Jimmie said sternly. "Just let me alone. This is none of your business."

"This is my business, Jimmie," Ann pleaded. "Tell me. You can confide in me."

"I don't want to talk about it. Why can't you understand that? Just get out!"

Ann felt a horrible pain in her stomach. She bent forward and regained her balance by grabbing his trophy shelf. Jimmie did not come to her aid, but rather stepped away toward the window. Ann turned and reached for the door.

"Something awful has happened, Jimmie. I feel it. Something that can destroy us and destroy our family. You know what it is. You can't fix it by yourself."

He continued to look through the window. The high August sun was scorching Leigh-Rose Mansion's front lawn. Shining beyond the perimeter hedges were chain link fences installed to secure the governor's property. Jimmie was jailed in his own house, while being incessantly interrogated by Ann. Their awkward silence lasted only a minute longer.

"Open this door for me, open this door for your wife," Ann ordered.

"If you want to fix this, whatever this is," he whispered, "don't ask any more questions."

She pushed open the door and turned back to him.

"When you're ready to talk, I'll be upstairs with Hannah."

"Just go," he said. "There's nothing you can do."

Ann fought back tears as she ascended the stairs. Her mother, Gloria, met her in the baby's room. Ann welcomed her hug and strong shoulder. Hannah was sleeping soundly.

"Did he talk?" Gloria asked.

"No, Mom. He's hiding bad news from me. He's very withdrawn. Jimmie has only acted like this once before, after his father died in the tornado on Kinzua Bridge."

Gloria stroked her back. "But he eventually told you what happened, right?"

"Mom, it's the most difficult thing for Jimmie to open up. I want him to share the bad things with me as well as the good. He doesn't see me as his partner; he sees me as someone he must protect."

"Jimmie loves you, Ann. Be strong. He will open up to you when he's ready."

Ann wanted to be patient, but her instincts said otherwise. If one person in the fight didn't want to talk, maybe the other one would.

She vowed to track down the missing Bill Pennoyer. And she knew the man who could do it for her – an unscrupulous private investigator from Harrisburg, Sylvester Sylvaney.

Pressure was building on Chief Andy Faxon. The Billy Herman investigation was growing colder by the minute. His terrorized constituents in Zelienople Borough, the ones who loved and respected his dear father, Walter, were turning on him abruptly.

Talk show callers were demanding instantaneous results. Surely, there were suspects, they cried. Surely, Chief Faxon can slap handcuffs on somebody and make them talk, they complained. Maybe those rumors about the chief were true, one caller said. "He's too mamby-pamby to arrest anyone. He's waiting for someone else to get murdered first." To which another caller remarked: "Yeah, and then the slime ball will be sentenced to probation by some criminal-coddling judge!"

Even less constructive was the County crime-stopper telephone hotline. About 300 calls were screened. None of the tips produced suspects that remotely resembled witness Nata's description. No caller made any reference to a rock thrown through Herman's bedroom window, nor gave any corroborating evidence about the .38 handgun, the stolen Tahoe or a possible motive.

Faxon's widespread distribution of the police sketch yielded no telephone calls. The sketch was a shadowy face with uncertain features. Faxon's deputy chief said the sketch eliminated about 60 percent of the Butler County population, including only 10 percent of the police department.

Ballistics tests on the bullet fragment plucked from Billy Herman's living room wall confirmed only the caliber of the murder weapon. Police were unable to trace the bullet to any stolen handgun or to any weapon earlier used in a crime. An autopsy of Herman concluded only that he died of a single gunshot wound. The medical examiner speculated that death occurred between six to 12 hours before the body was first examined by Dr. Chen at 10 a.m.

So when the hotline telephone rang on Monday at noon, expectations were low. The caller, a truck driver named Sarah Shoup, had some information that "may be of help," she said.

That awful night, when her rig was stopped for a police checkpoint, she met a young driver who seemed to fit the description.

His name was Matthew Moore, she said. His Mustang was stopped behind her truck, and they chatted for about an hour. According to Ms. Shoup, the young man was "very interested" when she told him about a shooting in Zelienople. She described him as "excitable," as though he "was hiding drugs in his car."

Mr. Moore was "wearing something black," but she didn't remember if it was a hooded sweatshirt. He was "tall, pleasant looking and had a day's growth of beard," she told police. She denied that his eyes "were pulsating," but said he probably wasn't on drugs at the time. "If he was toking up," she said, "he would have eaten my fried pork skins."

Ms. Shoup then reported that Zelinople police were conducting a roadblock on Perry Highway. "A few of the officers stopped Matthew Moore and asked him questions," she said. "They probably have his name and address in their records."

Detectives rummaged through the Perry Highway roadblock records. They found a report written by Sergeant Weber describing his encounter with Matthew Moore last

Saturday at 3:30 a.m. He had told Weber that he had been with his girlfriend, Megan Broward, at an apartment in McKean County earlier in the night. He knew nothing about the robberies in Zelienople, he said. Detectives pulled his driver's license photograph. The 18-year-old marginally resembled the police sketch – enough to prompt detectives to page Sergeant Weber.

By the time Weber arrived at headquarters, the detectives had assembled a comprehensive file on their newest suspect. No criminal background. Honors graduate of Stender High School in Pittsburgh. Summer employment at the Kane News-Leader. His parents, Stephen and Tanya Harper, had clean records as well.

"Remember this guy?" Detectives showed Weber the driver's license photograph.

"Sure do," he replied. "He was driving a beefed-up Mustang south on Perry Highway. We questioned him at the traffic stop because he fit the description."

"Did you search the car?"

"Yes, but we didn't find anything," Weber said. "He said he was a reporter working for the Kane newspaper. Said he was on a story."

"Did you check that out?"

"Yes, sir. We telephoned his editor just to confirm."

The detectives conferred among themselves. Matthew Moore seemed like another dead end. He was clean, he had a reason to be on the road at that hour and, most significantly, he was heading southbound – the wrong direction for a fleeing felon.

"Thank you for your time, Sergeant Weber," the lead detective said. "We've got the wrong guy."

Weber took his cue and started to leave. Then he remembered something.

"I don't know if this is important or not," he told detectives. "Right before we waved his Mustang through the checkpoint, he asked for directions."

"To where?"

"Zelienople Road."

Chapter Eleven

The Fingerprints

Tuesday at noon was the "ABSOLUTELY FINAL DEADLINE" for Wednesday's News-Leader. Tom Zachary bent that rule only once – in July 2003, when a tornado destroyed Kinzua Bridge. As the editor often reminded his staff, "only an act of God can move my deadline." Given this inflexibility, most of the newspaper's work occurred on Mondays.

So Zachary opened the News-Leader office at 6 a.m. Monday. He flicked on overhead lights and, as he often has done since purchasing the struggling newspaper years ago, proofread pages of display advertising copy. He corrected a supermarket ad promoting sales of "Fried Children." Just last week, he caught a typographical error on the Beasley Auto Sales insert, which proudly touted its "40 years of continuous horrible service." He corrected it to "honorable." What errors he didn't catch were found by readers.

As the sun peeked over Fraley Street and morning traffic broke the outside stillness, Zachary sipped his coffee and sighed. How he dreaded another slow news week.

Zachary's upcoming edition was disappointing. After a string of sell-outs, largely due to exclusive photographs of the governor's baby girl, the News-Leader was mired in August doldrums. Local news was confined to garden club meetings, family reunions and livestock auctions. News about high school sports would not begin for another two weeks. And hot weather had drained the enterprise from his reporters.

The editor scanned a morning news summary from Associated Press. As usual, no stories pertained to the News-Leader circulation area. The state news concerned only Pittsburgh and Philadelphia. Things looked bleak for the "Pride of the Alleghenies."

One good news story could save the edition, he thought.

Zachary discovered one by accident.

Someone had left three copies in the office printer. On the top sheet was written: "Hold for DNA test results." Zachary read the second and third sheets with great interest.

COLD CASE SOLVED:
COMMISSIONER GIBSON MURDERED
IN KINZUA VALLEY
By Matthew Moore
News-Leader Staff Writer

Frank "Josh" Gibson, one-time Pennsylvania State Police Commissioner, was not a despondent suicide victim after all. His death five years ago at the Kinzua Bridge was a murder.

State police told this reporter last week that a murder investigation has begun in earnest following the discovery of Gibson's blood on a shovel found near the death scene.

Police investigator Cal Heinrich said the initial suicide determination was based upon Gibson's battered body being found under the 300-foot-tall railroad bridge. Suicide was assumed, he said, until the murder weapon was found in bushes close to the spot.

"*This discovery confirms what many of us always believed,*" *Heinrich said. "Josh Gibson wasn't the kind of man to take his own life. Someone did him in.*"

Dolores Gibson, the commissioner's widow, was not surprised by the newly-announced murder investigation. Reached by telephone at her Wexford home, Mrs. Gibson remembered her husband's joyful attitude and positive outlook.

"*Josh enjoyed his police work and enjoyed life,*" *she said. "He's not the kind to jump off a bridge, I'll tell you. But who would kill him? That's what I don't understand.*"

State police have retained forensics experts to extract evidence from the shovel. Police have confirmed that blood stains on the shovel are of two different blood types. One type, near the blade, matched with Gibson's. Other blood stains near the handle are likely from the killer, police said.

Gibson's death was the topic for an investigative series in the News-Leader this summer. We reported that Gibson was lead investigator in the disappearance of Pennsylvania Governor Brock Bailey. Assisting Gibson was Pittsburgh police detective William "Billy" Herman, who abruptly retired after Gibson's death.

Police reports from the Bailey investigation revealed that Gibson and Herman often disagreed with tactics and procedures. The reports also placed Gibson and Herman together in Kinzua Valley shortly before the commissioner's death.

Herman, now residing in Zelienople, recently was arrested in McKean County for reckless driving. He was released on bond and awaits trial.

This reporter spoke to Herman immediately after his pre-trial release. When asked what he knew about Gibson's death, Herman said he was not strong enough "to push that fat man off the bridge." Without giving any other details, Herman added that Gibson "was dead before he hit the ground."

[Hold this next paragraph until Dr. Greta confirms DNA results!]

Preliminary DNA testing on a hair sample taken from Herman positively matched the blood sample from the murder weapon, according to a Harrisburg scientist.

Zachary drew a big red "X" over each page. None of this could by published without a thorough emasculation by the newspaper's attorney. Every journalist should know, even a young enthusiastic one, that you can't publish a story accusing someone of murder. That's libel. Newspapers get sued. Zachary had no insurance for that.

Wait a second! William Herman? Hadn't he seen that name on the morning news wire?

Zachary returned to his computer and pulled up the Associated Press summaries for Pennsylvania. He read the fourth story, dateline Zelienople:

Police identified the murder victim as William G. Herman, 54, former Pittsburgh police officer. Herman's body was discovered at his Butler County residence early Saturday. Details surrounding the death were not reported. Herman had been a key investigator in the 2003 disappearance of Governor Brock Bailey.

Zachary was stunned. His summer intern had traveled to Zelienople overnight Friday to find DNA evidence linking Herman with the Gibson death. Now Herman was dead.

The News-Leader clock read 7:30 a.m. Some of the shop workers and staff members were arriving. Matty Moore was not among them. Where could he be?

Minutes before 8 o'clock, office manager Jessie Krone stepped to her desk with a blueberry scone and a scowl. She hated Mondays, and she dreaded the next eight hours with her neurotic boss.

"Jessie!" Zachary called a millisecond before her teeth clamped into her breakfast. "Look at this!"

She read the summary and studied a photograph of the murder victim.

"Billy Herman, yeah, that's him," Jessie said. "That's the guy Matty was following for his big story. So somebody put a bullet in him."

"Jessie, don't you realize?" Zachary said. "Matty was going to Herman's house to collect evidence this weekend. Maybe he got mixed up in this."

"I told you, Tom. I told you, I told you, I told you ..."

"Don't blame me, Jessie. This was all Matty's idea."

"You should have stopped him, Tom. But no-o-o-o-o, you wanted him to get this story, so you could sell more newspapers! Look at what's happened. I told you ..."

"Ok, you told me," Zachary shouted. "Now find him!!!"

Sylvester Sylvaney hopped onto the first plane out of Harrisburg. The peripatetic private eye landed an hour later in Bradford. After a twisting mountain ride through the Alleghenies, Sylvaney arrived at Kane Manor.

Travel was simply a part of the job. How could he track down cheating husbands, malingering employees or assorted scoundrels without chasing after leads? People paid him big money to snoop for them. He found that most of their cases were mildly entertaining. This jaunt, however, was especially intriguing: he was summoned by the First Lady of Pennsylvania.

Sylvaney was familiar with Kane Manor. He often entertained local politicians and business leaders there. When you run the most expensive investigative agency in the Commonwealth, you rely on wealthy clients. Sylvaney signed up quite a few in northwest Pennsylvania, usually after dinner and a drink at Kane Manor.

Reservations were made for 7 p.m. He had requested a table for two in a private room near the veranda. He called ahead for a chilled bottle of white zinfandel. Experience had taught that every woman loves rosé wine, that wine glasses are more subtly refilled with rosé and that white zinfandel produces lively conversation.

Sylvaney was met by the Manor's owner, Gregory Harkins. The ex-Marine, a loose apron flung over his shoulder, led his guest through a dark corridor to a secluded waiting area.

"Sorry to leave you here," Harkins said. "Orders from the lady."

"I understand. We must be discreet."

Harkins nodded and disappeared down the hall. Sylvaney paced the floor for several minutes. He overheard Harkins attending to other diners and placing orders with the cook in the kitchen. Sylvaney looked down the corridor and watched hotel guests carry their luggage up the grand staircase. A teenage busboy hurried past him with a tray of dishes. Dusk was settling in.

Harkins returned with a note. Sylvaney unfolded the paper.

"Please come alone to veranda. Hurry. I must return home soon."

Sylvaney took his briefcase and walked briskly past the dining room. He unlatched a pair of French doors, leading to a side patio. In the fading light of an August evening, he saw the radiant First Lady alone and teary-eyed.

"Mr. Sylvaney, I don't know if you remember me…" Ann spoke softly, as though the conversation were being taped.

"A few years ago we met," Sylvaney answered. "Yes, I remember. At that visit, you asked me to investigate Jimmie Bailey. I never expected you would marry him."

A tentative smile crossed her lips. "I never expected that as well."

Sylvaney prided himself on judging people, but he couldn't read Ann Bailey. She was obviously in pain, probably caused by her husband. But they just had a baby girl, the governor was re-elected and there was no hint of infidelity – Sylvaney usually picked up on such rumors.

"You were very mysterious on the telephone, Mrs. Bailey. So I assume this is not just a personal visit."

"Please call me 'Ann' and I'll call you 'Sy.' I'd like to keep everything informal."

"Certainly. Does Governor Bailey know that I'm here?"

"No," she said emphatically. "Nobody knows, except for Gregory. He's a trusted friend."

"And you don't want anyone to find out, right?"

Ann nodded yes.

"All right, I'm sworn to secrecy," Sylvaney said with mounting curiosity. "What service can I provide for you this time?"

"I want you to locate my husband's chief of staff. His name is Bill Pennoyer. He has been missing for several days. Jimmie won't tell me where he is. I am very concerned."

Sylvaney flipped open a memo pad. "When did you last see him?"

"He came to work at Leigh-Rose Mansion on Friday. He left with Jimmie at the end of the day. They were to drive to Harrisburg. But Jimmie returned early Saturday morning. He was dirty and bleeding, and he told me he had a fight with Pennoyer."

"Anything else?"

"I don't want the police involved. I don't want any missing person's report. For my sake and Jimmie's sake, I want you to handle this alone and report only to me."

Sylvaney shook his head in agreement. "But this isn't much to go on. I don't know ..."

Ann slid an envelope stuffed with cash across the coffee table. "You said you were the best."

"I won't disappoint you, Ann."

"And one more thing, Sy. Thank you for ordering wine, but white zinfandel is much too sweet for me. Next time, order a pinot."

He would not underestimate Ann ever again.

Matty wasn't late for work. He was "gathering news" during breakfast at the Golden Wheel Restaurant. His favorite news source, waitress Toolie, interrupted his black cherry pancakes with incessant gossip. She refused to write his check until he promised to investigate rumors about the Ladies Guild rigging its Bingo wheel. Guild secretary, Marla Ronan, "a horrible player," Toolie said, "won the past five Bingo jackpots. Something smells."

Matty appreciated the tip, but his mind was elsewhere. Despite his girlfriend's warning, Matty had trespassed on Billy Herman's property, lifted a human hair sample from a parked vehicle and handed the evidence to Dr. Greta for analysis. Megan criticized him for getting too close to his story and said police should obtain evidence against Herman.

Dr. Greta hadn't called with the results, so Matty's theory that Herman's DNA matched a sample from the blood-stained shovel was still untested. Deadlines were fast approaching for Wednesday's edition of the News-Leader. His blockbuster story was being held up by a slow-moving Swedish pathologist. He could wait no longer.

"Toolie," he interrupted the talkative waitress, "I'm expecting an important call on my cellphone. Could you put in another order of hotcakes?"

When she was out of earshot, Matty flipped open his phone. He dialed the Kane state police barracks and had Dr. Greta paged. Toolie stood over him and filled his coffee cup. Matty's mean stare chased her away.

Dr. Greta took the call in her lab. Matty detected disappointment in her voice.

"I'm sorry, Matty," she said. "I've run the test three times and each time there were insufficient characteristics."

"No match?"

"No, Matty. Your hair sample and the blood on the shovel do not match. I was putting together a written report for you…"

"Oh, no, don't bother, doctor. Your word is enough for me." Matty's voice communicated his dejection. Maybe Herman wasn't the killer after all, he thought.

"Where was this hair taken?" Dr. Greta asked. "Directly from the person's scalp?"

What the hell, Matty thought. If there were no match, the police won't ask him any questions. So he might as well tell Dr.Greta.

"I took it from the headrest of a vehicle, not from the man's head. So maybe it was someone else's hair," Matty told her.

"Do other people drive the car?" Dr. Greta asked.

"Yes," Matty replied, remembering that Billy Herman had stolen the Tahoe. The hair was probably from the true owner, he realized.

Meanwhile, seven blocks east on Fraley Street, two plainclothes detectives paid a visit to the News-Leader offices. After producing their badges and frightening Tom Zachary, the detectives asked about Matthew Moore. They "had a few questions for the young man." Had he worked there last Friday? Whom did he know in Zelienople? And where did he live?

Zachary pressed the detectives for details, but they resisted. He confirmed that his summer intern was at work last week, and he claimed ignorance about Matty's contacts in Zelienople.

"He has an apartment at the General Kane Boarding House up the street, but he may be out on a news story at the moment," Zachary told them.

The detectives smiled, apparently satisfied by the information. When they left, Zachary quickly dialed Matty's cell number. It was busy. Zachary's call was dumped into voice mail.

"Matty, listen to me carefully," Zachary's message began. "Billy Herman was murdered late Friday night in his house. Two detectives are on their way to your apartment to question you. Don't tell them anything without an attorney. Got it? I hope you get this message…"

He did, but not in time.

Matty ended his call with Dr. Greta and sipped his coffee. As he poured maple syrup over his second plate of pancakes, he noticed two men entering the restaurant. One sat at a table yet to be cleaned by Toolie. The other man approached Matty.

"Mr. Moore?" he asked.

"Yes, sir." Matty dabbed his mouth with a napkin.

"My name is Adams and his is Keating. We're detectives with the Zelienople Borough police. We just have a few questions."

Matty felt a buzzing in his pocket. Someone had left a message on his telephone.

"Do you know a man named William Herman?" Adams asked.

A million thoughts raced through Matty's head. Herman probably saw him trespassing and called the cops.

Maybe Dr. Greta and the state police knew he broke into Herman's vehicle and took the hair sample. Maybe he was in big trouble.

His cellphone buzzed again. Matty stood and placed his palms on the wooden dining table. "Wait here," he told them. "I have to take this call."

Matty walked past the daily menu board and leaned against a waitress station. He noticed Adams staring at him. The other detective had pushed Matty's plate and silverware to one side and was sprinkling white powder on the table.

Zachary's message hit him like a bolt of lightning. Herman was murdered about the time Matty was trespassing! And now two Zelienople detectives were dusting the table for fingerprints.

Matty tried not to shake. He pretended to be talking on his phone. He was stalling for time. He prayed that God would send someone to help him. His prayers were answered.

"Do you mind telling me what you're doing, for the sake of Peter?" Toolie cackled at the detectives like a bantam rooster. "I'm the lady who cleans these tables, and you're just dumping dirt on them."

Keating slid the impressions into his briefcase. "Sorry, ma'am. I spilled some sugar."

"And you're a lying sack of crap," she shot back. "I've been waiting tables here for 50 years. I know what sugar looks like. AND THIS LOOKS LIKE COCAINE!"

Adams and Keating turned a bright shade of purple. Dozens of diners twisted to witness the commotion. Toolie pummeled the detectives with a drink menu. She grabbed Keating by his hair.

"See that sign, Buster? That says 'Zero Drug Tolerance.' We don't tolerate your ilk, so hit the road!"

The embarrassed detectives stumbled out the front door, barely remembering why they had visited Golden Wheel

Restaurant. After instructing her other diners to "get back to your food," Toolie found Matty hiding behind the bar.

"You in some kind of trouble, Matthew?" Toolie asked, pulling him to his feet.

"I dunno, Toolie. Those were cops."

"Those wimps? They sure don't make cops like they used to."

Matty's phone rang. The caller ID showed Tom Zachary's office number. Toolie directed him to take the call in her break room.

"Did you talk to them, Matty?" Zachary asked.

"No, Toolie chased them away," Matty replied.

"Good," Zachary said. "I was serious about getting an attorney. You need to talk to someone in confidence."

"How did Herman die?"

"He was shot through the chest. They found him in his living room Saturday morning about 9 o'clock."

Matty remembered the scene. The house lights were on. The front door was open. There were no sounds. Matty had been about thirty feet away from a murder. That's why police detectives wanted him to talk.

He needed an attorney.

Chapter Twelve

The Fashion

Bill Pennoyer awoke with a song in his heart.

An hour with Roxanne in the sauna indeed produced sweet music, perhaps the "Melody of Love." Pennoyer hadn't heard such a rhapsody in many years.

Feeling more vim than viral, Pennoyer eagerly anticipated his first day of Castle Rock Center therapy. He downed a breakfast of wheat germ flakes and soy milk. He mustered three pushups without a pause between them. He even noticed new growth on his bald spot. Pennoyer was ready to greet his substance abuse counselors with a renewed sense of self-worth.

At precisely 8 a.m., someone knocked on his villa door. He peered through the peephole. Outside his door was a white-haired gentleman with black aviator-style glasses. His diamond earring sparkled in the hallway light. He held a garment bag over his shoulder.

Pennoyer opened the door and the man dashed inside with a bunny hop. He handed over his garment bag.

"Here," the man said. "A gift from Roxanne."

"What is this?" Pennoyer unzipped the bag. Inside were designer shirts and slacks. The man smiled proudly and handed Pennoyer his card.

"Phillipe Loreaux? You?"

"*Oui. C'est moi.*"

"The famous fashion designer?"

"*Mais oui.*"

"*Mon Dieu!*" Pennoyer exclaimed, pulling clothes from the bag.

"These are from our autumn collection, *monsieur*. You like?"

Pennoyer removed a hanger from the top shirt. It wasn't exactly his style, ruffled sleeves and a V-neck enclosed by shoelaces. The second shirt was brilliant red and buttonless. The third was more traditional in style but emblazoned with hypnotic stripes. Each shirt tapered at the waist. Perhaps a few more weeks of wheat germ, he thought, and maybe his physique would be more European.

"All sizes are *grand*," Phillipe lamented, having underestimated his customer's girth. "We can make *petit* modifications if *nécessaire*."

"No, no," Pennoyer said. "You've inspired me, Monsieur Loreaux. I intend to lose a few kilos with exercise and diet. *Grand* will be my size. You'll see."

Phillipe helped him into the striped shirt. A few snips here and a couple buttons moved there and Pennoyer was reasonably clad. The pants were snapped with a small struggle as well.

"Roxanne tells me that you have a problem with the bottle," Phillipe said. "*Moi aussi.*"

"You are a patron here as well?" Pennoyer asked.

"*Oui.* This is my third visit to Castle Rock. I hope my last."

Pennoyer listened patiently as the famous designer unloaded his psychological torment, his tortuous childhood, his unrequited loves and his unrelenting struggles with liquor. After feigning interest in the elegant man's psychoses, Pennoyer asked the only question that truly interested him:

"What do you know about Roxanne?"

"Oh, she is my little saint," Phillipe replied. "I met Roxanne quite by accident several years ago. I was in the sauna and she…"

"*Pardon*, Phillipe," Pennoyer interrupted, not wishing to hear any more sauna stories. "What is she like? Does she have family and friends?"

"Roxanne is all alone, unfortunately. She has so much love in her heart, but she cannot find others to love her. So she moves aimlessly through life, absorbing any affection she encounters. She confuses sex and love. No one can break through her addiction."

Pennoyer never understood mental afflictions. Now he was plum dab in the universe of crazy people with crazy problems. Somehow, Roxanne didn't seem to fit in.

"So she has bounced from one bed to another, one *garçon* to the next," Phillipe continued. "At day's end, she has no friends, no love, no promise of fulfillment. *Très terrible!*"

Pennoyer looked into the wardrobe mirror. He pulled in his ample gut. If Roxanne was looking for *amour*, he would gladly be her *premier garçon*. But how could he tell her? Apparently, every male patron of Castle Rock Center has partaken of the lady's weaknesses. Why would she trust him over her other paramours?

"Phillipe, do you have affection for Roxanne?" he asked.

"She is my friend, *mon amie*, nothing more."

"But you were in the sauna…"

"Roxanne is not my type," Phillipe said with a wink.

Pennoyer jotted notes on Castle Rock Center stationery. Phillipe turned away, giving him privacy. The message to Roxanne would be simple and easily understood. Pennoyer had emptiness in his heart also. He wanted to be her friend. Last night was special, but he understood that she needed something more. He had a secret to share with her, a secret too serious to share with anyone else. He trusted her, and he needed her.

His letter had a postscript. They would meet at the sauna tonight at 9.

Pennoyer sealed his note inside an envelope. He handed it to Phillipe.

"Please deliver this to Roxanne, and tell her I'm very grateful for her gift," Pennoyer said.

"*Certainment.*" Phillipe walked to the door and turned. "Don't tell my addictions counselor that I was here, *s'il vous plaît.* Two drunks like us are not permitted to rendezvous, *n'est-ce pas?*"

"*Je comprehend,*" Pennoyer replied with his finest French accent. "*Nous desirons un bon vin blanc ou champagne! C'est dommage.*"

Phillipe began to sweat. Tremors followed. "Bourbon," he muttered. "Do you have any? It's been so long…"

Pennoyer held the man's shoulders to steady him. Catherine, his life coach, had warned him to avoid contact with other alcoholics. One casual comment, she said, may "trigger relapses in fellow patrons." He never expected it would be so accidental.

The shaking stopped after a few minutes. Pennoyer handed his guest an iced green tea from his refrigerator. Phillipe seemed to have regained control.

"*Merci beaucoup,*" he thanked Pennoyer as he entered the empty hallway. "I shall deliver your note to the beautiful Roxanne."

Pennoyer retreated to the quiet of his apartment. The day's group therapy session would begin in one hour. His session was limited to alcohol abusers. Roxanne would attend the sex therapy session on another floor. Maybe they would meet at the canteen for lunch. Surely, she would have read his note by then.

All he wanted to see was her smile.

Then he wanted her promise to keep his awful secret.
A secret on the audiotape buried in his tote bag.
A secret his heart longed to release.

Matty Moore had a sick feeling, the kind that dries
the throat and shortens the breath. His was a feeling of
powerlessness, being haunted by the unknown, and being
pursued by forces stronger than he was. Time and destiny
were merging quickly. Panic was his closest neighbor.

Matty had visions of doom as he drove south toward
Pittsburgh. He had ducked from a police interrogation into
the murder of Billy Herman. They had his fingerprints. If
he talked, then he would reveal his entry onto Herman's
property that fateful night. And if he refused to talk, then
he would become the lead suspect. So Matty decided to
flee from Kane and take refuge with his parents in their
Shadyside condominium.

Horrible and disconnected thoughts consumed him like
a bizarre dream. Police investigators would surely discover
that Matty had an altercation with Herman at the McKean
County Jail. Matty had accused Herman of killing Josh
Gibson. Herman struck Matty and fled. Matty, bleeding and
dazed, had stumbled across the street and into a coffee house.
There would be witnesses there, he thought. Police would
develop a motive: that Matty was "getting even."

How many people knew that Matty was trying to pin a
murder on Herman? Zachary knew. Probably Jessie. He told
Megan about it. Megan even knew that Matty had trespassed
on Herman's property and had taken evidence from a Chevy
parked there. Megan would be interrogated by police, and
probably would be called to testify against him, he thought.

Did he have an alibi? Not really. He was alone in his
car, driving from McKean County to Butler County in the
darkness of an August night. He was stopped by police at

a roadblock on Perry Highway at 2 a.m. He remembered telling the sergeant that he was heading to Zelienople Road. That's where Herman lived and died.

Matty arrived in Shadyside before dinner time. He parked behind his parents' condo building and took a rear stairway. He knocked the secret knock. His mother, Tanya Harper, opened the door.

"Mom, I need an attorney." Matty blew inside. His eyes were wide and he was short of breath.

"Matty, what's happened?"

"There was a murder and the police want to question me." He closed the door and motioned for them to move from the window.

Tanya slumped onto a chair. Her husband, Steven, overheard and ran to the room. "What's this all about, son?" he asked.

"My editor, Mr. Zachary, says I shouldn't talk to anyone, except an attorney. He said that anyone I talk to could wind up being a witness against me."

"Good Lord, Matty!" Tanya hugged her son. She felt a softness in him that she hadn't felt since he was born. He needed her, but he couldn't talk to her. She hated that, but she understood.

"You want Buddy Spence?" his father asked. "He got your Uncle Mitch off on that drunk driving charge. And he's cheap."

"Hush, Steve. We're dealing with a murder now. Matty needs the best lawyer money can buy." Tanya thought a second. She had just watched the news. A powerful state legislator was recently acquitted in a high profile racketeering case. His attorney was gloating at a press conference. What was his name?

"Alfonzi. Tony Alfonzi. Italian kid from Penn Hills. They say he never loses a case." Tanya flipped through the Yellow

Pages. "Here's his number. His office is downtown on Fort Pitt Boulevard."

"Take me there," Matty told her.

They traveled quickly through Oakland, west on Centre Avenue and past Good Shepherd Church. Tanya recited a "Hail Mary" as she saw Father McWilliams sweeping the front steps. She had hoped to ask Matty for a sizeable contribution from his trust fund to keep the church alive, but now was not the time. Matty's money was needed for a less divine cause.

The Harpers and Matty entered Alfonzi's steel and glass office building before 5 p.m. Tanya convinced the attorney's battle-worn secretary to schedule an emergency appointment. They waited in Alfonzi's posh lobby, surrounded by framed newspaper clippings of the great trial attorney's courtroom victories. Few of the successes were murder cases.

At 5:30 p.m., an exodus of legal staffers began. Some of the lighting was scaled down. The receptionist applied lipstick and finger-brushed her hair. She was heading for Happy Hour at Mitchell's. The forced air cooling system shut down, and the offices were quiet except for a jarring voice down the hallway. Minutes later, that voice stopped, and the Harpers heard approaching footsteps.

A short, balding man swaggered into the lobby. He wore a rumpled white shirt with a bow-tie half visible under his double-chin. He flashed a smile that exuded supreme confidence. Matty distrusted him immediately, but he wasn't looking for a friend. He was looking for a savior.

"Antonio Alfonzi." He introduced himself with a handshake. "I go by Tony. I have a few minutes. How can I help you?"

"My son, Matthew, is in some trouble with the police," Tanya answered. "He won't give us any details because he doesn't want us to be witnesses in the investigation."

"That's smart," the attorney said. "He can talk to me, though. How old are you, Matthew?"

"Eighteen, sir. I've never been in trouble before," Matty said.

"Step into the conference room." Alfonzi led Matty into a richly appointed room. A wall of windows revealed stunning views of Monongahela River and Mount Washington. He sat at the head of a marble conference table. Alfonzi spoke to Tanya and Steven: "If the two of you will excuse us for a few minutes…"

He looked into the teenager's anxious eyes. Retrieving a yellow legal pad from a credenza, Alfonzi asked the most important question: "Do you have money?"

"I do, enough to pay your fee," Matty answered.

"I don't come cheap."

Matty pulled a blank check from his wallet. "How much do you want?"

"Murder case?"

"Yes, sir. I'm a suspect in the Zelienople murder."

Alfonzi licked his lips. He had read newspaper accounts of the crime. He appreciated the intense pressure on Zelienople police to find the murderer. And he knew the Borough's police chief was young and inexperienced, someone who likely would botch the investigation. Alfonzi thrived on such cases. He wanted a piece of this action, so he had to set a fee high enough to make a lot of money but not too high to scare the client away.

"Initial retainer of $50,000, nonrefundable," he announced.

Matty filled in the check and handed it to him.

Alfonzi scrutinized it. "Matthew Moore Trust Fund, it says. So you can write me a check just like that? How much is in your trust fund?"

"When I turned 18 this year, I was able to access a third of the total. That was about $8 million."

The attorney's eyebrows rose involuntarily. He tried to control his glee. "Your account is about $8 million total?"

"No," Matty answered. "That's the third I received this year. The total trust funds are about $25 million."

Alfonzi gulped before folding the check and stuffing it in his shirt pocket. "So that's $50,000 now and, if you're indicted, I'll receive a second nonrefundable retainer of $100,000."

"That would be fair, I suppose," Matty said. "Someone who never loses a case deserves a larger fee."

Ever the businessman, Alfonzi obeyed Rule No. 1: Get the money first, and then manage the client's expectations. "Well, Matty, I can't guarantee that we'll get you out of this mess, but I promise to do my very best."

"I suppose you'll lose a case sometime," Matty said. "I just hope it's not mine."

After assuring Matty that their interview was in confidence, Alfonzi adeptly extracted his client's personal history. He learned that Matthew Moore was an illegitimate son of the late Governor Brock Bailey and, therefore, a half-brother to Governor Jimmie Bailey. He learned that Matty received his fortune in the private settlement of Brock Bailey's estate. And he learned that Matty was an aspiring newspaper reporter with a summer internship at the Kane News-Leader.

But when Matty began to talk about his exposé about the Josh Gibson murder and his suspicion about Billy Herman's involvement, Alfonzi held up his hand.

"Stop! No more," he said. "From here on, I'll ask specific questions."

"Why?" Matty asked. "It would be easier for me just to tell you these things."

"You don't understand criminal law, Matty. If you tell me that you committed a crime, then I know whether you're guilty or not guilty."

"So what? You're my attorney," Matty said. "I can tell you everything, right?"

"If I know you're guilty, then the rules of ethics prohibit me from putting you on the stand and asking you questions. If I know that you're giving perjured testimony, I could lose my law license."

"I'm not guilty, sir." Matty glared at his hired gun.

"Again, stop it. You paid for my advice, so take it. Just answer my specific questions."

Matty couldn't tell his boss. He couldn't tell his parents or girlfriend. Now he couldn't tell his attorney. The whole legal system was frustrating.

Alfonzi pushed his chair closer to the table. He looked Matty in the eye.

"Don't reveal to me anything that you did," the attorney said. "I only want to know what others did, do you understand?"

"Yes, sir. Let's continue."

"All right. What do the Zelienople police know about you? What evidence do they have to implicate you in this murder?"

Matty recalled a few things. "They stopped me at a roadblock on Perry Highway on the night of Billy Herman's murder. I told them I was heading to Zelienople Road. That's where Herman lived."

"How soon was this before the murder?" Alfonzi asked.

"This was about 2:30 a.m. I don't know the time of the murder. The body was discovered about 10 o'clock Saturday morning."

Alfonzi understood that timing would be critical. He jotted a note to hire an independent forensic pathologist. The kid would be paying another fortune for experts, he decided.

"What else do the police know?"

"They have a description of an armed robber that terrorized the town that night. I may fit that description."

"Yes. I saw that police sketch. That would be weak evidence without a more positive identification. Anything else?"

"Maybe fingerprints."

Alfonzi's defense was strong until that tidbit. "Fingerprints, where?"

Matty could only speculate. He told his attorney a convoluted story about trespassing on Herman's property and entering a parked Chevy Tahoe there. He assumed police took fingerprints from the door handle, steering wheel and dashboard. He told Alfonzi about the aborted police interview at the Golden Wheel Restaurant and about the detective dusting for fingerprints at their dining table.

"So you don't know if they have a match, do you?" the attorney asked.

"No, sir."

Alfonzi scratched his head. Without a fingerprint match, police would not be able to place Matty at the scene. His remark about traveling to Zelienople Road, a 30-mile stretch, would not be sufficient proof to arrest him for murder. His resemblance to a poorly-drawn police sketch would be the weakest evidence against the young man.

"Billy Herman was a retired police officer who lived a hundred miles from you. What possible motive would you have to kill him?" Alfonzi ventured to ask.

"Other than him knocking me unconscious and stealing my Mustang? None."

Alfonzi sighed. There was more to the Matty-Billy relationship. "Explain."

Matty related the incident outside McKean County's Jail. Matty had accused Herman of killing Josh Gibson. Herman responded by punching Matty and fleeing in Matty's car.

Herman then abandoned the Mustang at a convenience store and stole the Chevy Tahoe.

"Herman was shot, Matty. Did you have a gun?"

"No, never had my hands on one."

Alfonzi scribbled a final sentence on his legal pad: "Motive, yes. Opportunity, yes. Means, no."

Chapter Thirteen
The Arrest

Chief Faxon enjoyed momentary relief. Cacophony from irate callers on talk radio had been deafening until Faxon issued his press release: Zelienople Police identified a prime suspect in Friday's criminal spree. That announcement should take some pressure off his department, he thought.

But once radio listeners learned that no arrests had been made, telephone lines lit up again.

"If Andy Faxon knows who did these awful things, he should get that killer off the streets!"

"Faxon should corner him in an alley and gun him down. That would save us all the cost of a trial."

"Put a slug in the bum before he gets an attorney!"

"If only Walter Faxon was chief, we could all sleep at night."

Andy tried to shake off criticism, but soon realized that his deputies had similar attitudes. He overheard two of his top colonels complaining about his lack of decisiveness. Andy's inflexibility with department rules hampered the investigation, they said. If Adams and Keating hadn't encountered the suspect face-to-face, against Chief Faxon's rules, there would be no fingerprint match – the only hard evidence linking Matty Moore to Billy Herman's murder.

Those deputies, however, did not interview "Saturday Night," Andy's weekly bedmate. She had encountered the Zelienople robber outside the chief's bedroom door. She told Andy that the man was white. Matty Moore, the prime suspect, was not.

So Andy developed a plan to eliminate Mr. Moore from suspicion. His plan involved "overselling" Matty Moore to the district attorney. Andy would promote Mr. Moore as the armed robber of the Yer-In Yer-Out convenience store, the assailant of the Prybelewskis and the killer of Billy Herman – all rolled into one. Certainly, the district attorney would laugh Andy out of the courthouse. No one could be arrested for these heinous crimes on such flimsy evidence, he believed.

Faxon's appointment with Gil McFadden, Butler County district attorney, was set for 2 p.m. at McFadden's office. Faxon brought detectives Adams and Keating, as well as the complete investigative file. He expected the crusty prosecutor to adjourn the meeting by 2:30, with a firm admonition to collect more evidence. He was wrong.

McFadden had a different plan. After 20 years as Butler County's top law enforcer, McFadden's star was falling. Rumors abounded that he spent his six-figure salary and most of his workday visiting computer gambling sites. Two of his assistants recently quit amid allegations that McFadden asked them for personal loans. His wife quietly filed for divorce. In a last ditch attempt to revive his reputation, McFadden welcomed the Zelienople challenge. He couldn't wait to convict somebody, anybody for the crimes. And the sooner, the better.

Faxon and his deputies waited outside the prosecutor's office. A large oak door muffled the voices inside. Adams and Keating, clutching the Herman investigative files, fidgeted in their seats. The cops never conducted such a serious investigation. And they never fingered a suspect with such a thin thread of evidence.

"Let's skip this step, Chief," Adams told his boss. "We'll make the arrest first, and then we'll involve the DA."

"Yeah, Chief," Keating agreed. "Once we turn this file over to Mr. McFadden, he'll leak information to the media and his office will take the credit."

Faxon sat quietly. He wanted McFadden to review the case. The seasoned prosecutor, despite his gambling addiction, was astute enough to point out the case's weaknesses. Faxon's deputies would learn to gather more evidence rather than criticize their chief.

The heavy door swung open. Faxon stood as several assistant DA's with huge smiles filed past him. Inside, standing behind an unkempt desk was a grinning McFadden.

At six-foot four and maybe 180 pounds soaking wet, McFadden could double for Abraham Lincoln under the right lighting. His was a face built with unforgettable features – feather-duster eyebrows, sunken cheeks and wrinkles that his recent divorce undoubtedly deepened. He shook his guests' hands and dragged a third chair before his desk. Adams set the bulky files on a side table and stretched his sore arm.

"Gentlemen, you have had some success I hear," McFadden said.

"Yes, sir," Faxon answered. "After three days of intense police work, we have identified a person of interest…"

"Come, come, chief," McFadden interrupted. "We do not use that term here. Is he a suspect or is he not a suspect?"

"He is our prime suspect," Adams said. "In fact, he is our only suspect."

"Very well," McFadden said. "What do you want of me?"

Faxon really wanted the district attorney to deflect some pressure. "With all of the publicity and this being a murder case…"

"A capital murder case, I might add."

"Yes, sir." Faxon noticed delight in the DA's eyes. "A capital case deserves a proper arrest. We'd like your office to obtain an arrest warrant from the magistrate."

McFadden relished a chance to involve himself immediately at the case's genesis. If his daydreams came true, McFadden would soon be standing in front of a bank of microphones and announcing the biggest news event in Butler County history. His office would prosecute, he would tell the assembled throng, and "justice would be meted out expeditiously, with the same compassion this horrible criminal showed upon Zelienople!" How could McFadden lose in his upcoming re-election bid after this show?

"Have you prepared an affidavit to present to the magistrate?" he asked Faxon.

"An affidavit? Well, no, we thought you would handle that."

"Young man! Your father, God rest his soul, never asked me for an arrest warrant without a sworn statement. You must lay out sufficient evidence to make a *prima facie* showing that the suspect likely committed the crimes. Can you do that?"

"No," Faxon said. "I'm not sure we can do that, yet."

"Hogwash!" McFadden wasn't about to let this golden opportunity slip him by. "Work with me, Chief. Certainly, you have enough information in those huge files to point a finger at … at…"

"Matthew Moore. He's a black 18-year-old from Pittsburgh," Keating added.

McFadden allowed that name to roll around his head. Matthew Moore, Matthew Moore. He was going to be spending the next few months condemning Matthew Moore to the judge, to the jury and, hopefully, to the executioner.

Adams pulled a manila folder from the investigative file. "Fingerprints, we have fingerprints, and they match."

"Match what?" McFadden asked.

"Fingerprints we found in the dead man's car. A perfect match."

"So what?" McFadden challenged. "The kid didn't kill a car. You don't have a match at the crime scene?"

"No," Faxon said.

"You have two other crime scenes, the convenience store and the Polish family's front porch," McFadden recalled. "Any matches there?"

"No, sir," Faxon said.

The district attorney shook his head. He was determined to find more evidence in the file. "What else do you have, chief?"

"Mr. Moore was stopped by one of our sergeants at a road block on Perry Highway around the time of the murder," Faxon answered. "He said he was a newspaper reporter working on a story. We checked with his editor, who gave him cover. But his excuse was weak because he worked at a newspaper in McKean County. He had no reason to be in Butler County."

"Now we're getting somewhere, men," McFadden said. "Lying to police in an investigation. That's obstruction of justice in my book."

"One problem, sir," Faxon said. "Moore was traveling south toward Zelienople a few hours after the convenience store and the Prybelewskis were attacked."

"A minor detail," McFadden stuttered. "Maybe he was going back to the scene of the crime. Lots of criminals do that."

Faxon was stunned. McFadden was glossing over irregularities in the evidence. The veteran prosecutor was digging his heels into Matty Moore. Faxon tried to restrain McFadden's enthusiasm.

"We have no motive. We have found no relationship between Herman and Moore…"

"A random act of violence," McFadden said. "This is common in drug cases."

"The kid is clean, no drug record," Faxon said.

"A teenager out for a joyride after midnight? Are you kidding me? He was high on something. After we arrest him, we'll do a urinalysis."

"Our investigators have not found the murder weapon," Faxon continued.

"After your detectives interrogate this kid, he'll tell you all you need to know," McFadden responded.

"In addition, we can't fix the time of death," Faxon said. "Maybe police stopped Mr. Moore after Herman was already dead."

"Chief Faxon, there are no absolutes on the time of death. Your daddy knew that."

Andy reached his boiling point with the dishonorable DA. "My daddy didn't make excuses when the evidence didn't add up, sir!"

McFadden suddenly became less Lincolnesque and more grotesque. His face wrinkled by double. "Give me that file, Faxon! I'll write the damn affidavit! You'll get your arrest warrant in three hours. That's how efficient we are in this office."

Andy realized his major miscalculation. He had placed his oh-so-careful investigation into the hands of a sleazy politician whose career hanged by a thread. Hopefully, he thought, an innocent man would not be hanged as well.

Tom Zachary did his best thinking between his second and third Texas Hot Dogs. His hunger was abated just enough to stimulate his sleeping neurons. Today's mental challenge was this: how to interview the governor's financial advisor without scaring him.

"Jessie!" the editor called to his assistant. "Call this number and ask for Dennis Padgett. Tell him that the News-Leader wants to feature him in next week's issue. You know, 'Where Are They Now?' See when he can sit for an interview."

"What's all this about, Tom?" Jessie had worked with Zachary for 10 years. His *modis operandi* was transparent to her. "What's Governor Bailey up to now?"

With a mouth-load of chili dog, Zachary could only grunt an answer.

"So Jimmie's doing funny business with his money?" Jessie interpreted his reaction. "What makes you think Dennis Padgett will tell you any details?"

After a swallow and cola rinse, Zachary revealed his scoop. "Marcy and I overheard Padgett's mother and dad at the community ballet. Jimmie was wiring hundreds of thousands of dollars to unknown people and refused to explain anything to Padgett."

Jessie was not impressed by his scoop. "That's what makes America great, Tom. People can spend their money any way they like. This wasn't tax money, right?"

"No, Jessie. And everything might be on the up-and-up. But Jimmie and I go back a long way. Something smells here."

Could be the onions, Jessie thought. But maybe her boss was onto something. Governor Bailey had been acting strangely. He was holed up at Leigh-Rose Mansion and failed to attend a General Assembly ceremony. His office had canceled all appointments for the week. And his chief of staff, Bill Pennoyer, was suddenly "on vacation," according to his voice mail recording.

Jessie returned to her desk and made the call to Padgett's home office. The accountant stubbornly refused an interview, telling Jessie that he was too busy at the moment. Jessie sensed that Padgett was nervous. His responses were more furtive than forthcoming. So Jessie changed the subject; she asked about his parents, his brother and their cherry trees. He opened up just a crack, and she stepped in.

"If you don't want to be interviewed, I totally understand," she told him. "Many people would rather keep their name out of the newspaper. Tom speaks to people often, just for background information."

"So people talk off-the-record?" Padgett asked.

"Sure," Jessie said. "Tom absolutely respects the confidentiality of his sources. He would never reveal your name if the conversation was off-the-record."

The anxiety in Padgett's voice faded. Jessie decided to close the deal.

"When should I tell Tom that you could meet him?" she asked.

"Thursday afternoon, about 2. We'll talk here at my Clay Street office. Be sure to tell him that every word, absolutely every word I say will be deep background. My name cannot be revealed in the newspaper. I could lose everything."

Jessie agreed to his terms. She flashed a thumbs-up to Zachary.

"Mr. Padgett has some secrets to reveal," she said. "He wants to talk, but he's scared."

"Jimmie intimidates everyone around him," Zachary said. "But he shouldn't intimidate me or the Kane News-Leader."

Jessie chuckled at her editor's bravado. Not once did Zachary reveal in print Jimmie's many transgressions. The governor had a free pass with the News-Leader in her view. The juvenile arrest of Jimmie after he "accidentally" shot his father was never reported. Jimmie's cover-up of his father's death in the Kinzua Bridge tornado was suppressed as well. Could Zachary muster enough backbone to expose the latest Jimmie Bailey scandal?

She watched her boss as he wiped away chili sauce that had dripped on his necktie. She answered her question with an emphatic, "maybe not."

Zelienople police investigators Adams and Keating happily accepted an arrest warrant from the district magistrate. The warrant directed: "Any duly appointed law enforcement officer of the Commonwealth of Pennsylvania to secure at once the person of Matthew Moore." The magistrate found probable cause only for the crime of grand theft auto. Evidence had not supported an arrest for murder nor aggravated assault and robbery.

Adams and Keating were content. They welcomed an opportunity to nab Matty Moore without interference by a 90-year-old waitress. They hoped to interrogate him at police headquarters and force him to confess to every crime. They planned to convince the teenager to be honest and, perhaps, he would avoid a death sentence.

But, first, they had to find him.

With the blessing of Chief Faxon, Adams issued an all points bulletin. Law enforcement agents throughout western Pennsylvania were to watch for a bright yellow, late model Mustang. According to the bulletin, officers should "approach with caution because the driver, Matthew Moore, is wanted in connection with armed robberies and murder."

When the bulletin was issued, Matty and his parents had already returned to their Shadyside condo. Matty had parked his Mustang inside an alley garage. The Harpers and their now-infamous son were trading impressions of Attorney Alfonzi when Matty's cell phone rang.

"It's Megan," he told his parents. "She's probably worried about me."

Matty took his phone to another room and pulled the door behind him. "I'm OK, Megan. I'm with my parents in Pittsburgh."

"No, you're not OK, Matty." Her voice was shaky. "The state police were here looking for you."

"What did they say?" Matty pushed the door fully closed.

"They asked if this was your apartment and whether I knew where you were," Megan said. "I really didn't know where you were or when you were coming back."

Matty slid to the floor. He whispered, "Did they say anything about Billy Herman?"

"No, nothing about that. They asked if they could come into the apartment and I let them in. One of the troopers was looking around the rooms while the other asked me more questions."

"Like what?" Matty asked.

"Like whether you owned a gun. … Matty, what's going on? Are you in trouble?"

"Megan, you're my best friend ever. I want you to remember that. But I really can't say anything to you. That's what my attorney told me."

Matty heard sobbing on the other end of the call. He didn't know what to say to ease her mind. A tear came to his eye, and he said, "Megan, I love you."

After a pause, Megan gathered a breath. "I love you, too, Matty. Don't let anything bad happen."

Three police squad cars eased down Elmer Street, stopping in front of the condo building. Two officers ran to the rear and secured a back entrance. One officer, gun drawn, stationed himself at the front entrance. The least senior cop climbed to the second floor landing. He knocked violently on the Harpers' door and shouted, "Police!"

Matty dropped his call with Megan. He found Alfonzi's business card and quickly dialed his direct line. Before the attorney answered, Tanya and Steven entered the room and told Matty that he was being arrested.

"Are you Matthew Moore?" the officer asked.

"Yes, sir."

The policeman snapped Matty's hands behind his back and cuffed them. He spun the teenager around and radioed for back-up. Matty stood complacently as the officer read his rights. He heard the words, but the whole scene was so surreal he paid no attention.

"Where are you taking my son?" Tanya pleaded.

"Step aside, ma'am." An officer grabbed Matty by his handcuffs and pushed him into the hallway. Matty bowed his head as they passed by other condo owners' open doors. Tanya followed at a distance. Another officer held out his arms to keep her from the squad car.

"Station three, ma'am," he told her. "That's where he'll be processed."

"I don't want my baby in jail!" she hollered. "Matty, we're coming to get you!"

After Matty's personal items were inspected, the arresting officer handed Tanya a cellphone, watch and wallet. Matty's father put his arm around Tanya's shoulders. They watched the two police cars turn left toward Centre Avenue.

The cellphone buzzed. Tanya answered it.

"Matty, this is Tony Alfonzi. Sorry I missed your call."

"Sir, this is Tanya. Matty was just taken away by the police. They handcuffed him."

"Mrs. Harper, try to relax. Don't panic. We knew this day would come," Alfonzi said.

"I feel so helpless, like there's nothing I can do to help. Matty said nothing to us. Tell me what this is all about, Mr. Alfonzi."

"I'm so sorry, Mrs. Harper. Everything I know came from Matty. And everything he tells his attorney is protected by the attorney-client privilege. I can't talk to you about this."

Tanya looked at Steven. "The attorney won't tell me anything either."

"Give me that phone!" Steven yelled. "That's bullshit! We're Matty's parents. He's only 18. Tell us everything, now!"

Alfonzi snorted. "Listen to me, Harper. Matty is my client, not you, not your wife! Matty paid me to represent him, not to repeat confidences to you. Don't interfere with my work, do you understand?"

"NO!" Steve yelled louder into the phone. "THIS IS BULL…"

Click.

Chapter Fourteen
The Line-up

Sylvester Sylvaney was a digger. Like a squirrel scratching for January acorns, Sylvaney plowed deep to discover his prey. No snippet of fact was too insignificant to ignore. No childhood friendship was too outdated to overlook. No fingerprint or footprint was too slight to escape his notice. When a client was paying Sylvaney to find a missing person, he unearthed enough information to author a biography.

His client, Ann Bailey, was an adequate starting point for his research. She knew a few helpful details about the missing Bill Pennoyer. Ann told her private investigator that Pennoyer was 36 years old, never married and constantly fighting a weight problem. She said that her husband, Governor Jimmie Bailey, was a friend to Pennoyer since college, and that Pennoyer was best man at their wedding.

Ann provided Sylvaney with several recent photographs. One showed Pennoyer at the governor's inaugural ball. Another was his official portrait as the governor's chief of staff. She even gave Sylvaney a photograph of Pennoyer holding Hannah Bailey, her infant daughter.

Sylvaney, a retired Secret Service agent, had contacts in every investigative agency known to the federal government. Consequently, he was without peer in ferreting out personal data. He obtained a copy of Pennoyer's driver's license from his home state of New York. He discovered Pennoyer's date of birth and, through some clever techniques, his Social Security number. From there, he followed a simple path to Pennoyer's bank records and credit card numbers. With only a few hours of computer searching, Sylvaney learned every significant detail of Bill Pennoyer's life.

The profile that emerged was of a competent and dutiful servant to the governor. Like the moon, Pennoyer cast none of his own light, but only reflected light from the governor. Whatever Pennoyer did either was expected by Jimmie, was approved by Jimmie or "fit in" with the governor's philosophy. Pennoyer's true identity was unidentifiable. Sylvaney assumed that the object of his search was instructed by Jimmie Bailey to lay low, to stay out of sight. His assumption was reinforced by Governor Bailey's recent lack of concern for his buddy. Certainly, Sylvaney thought, an on-the-job chief of staff is critical for a governor. Pennoyer had been missing from work for nearly a week.

As discreetly as possible, Sylvaney inquired about the missing man with legislators and agency directors in Harrisburg. Each of them said the same thing: Pennoyer was with the governor at his home office in Kane. Only a few recalled seeing him in the past two weeks. Most notably, a Senate secretary remembered Pennoyer on the Capitol steps last Thursday. "He seemed upset," she told Sylvaney, "as though he had lost his best friend." She did not notice any cuts or bruises. A Capitol guard recorded a log entry for Pennoyer on Thursday at noon. "He told me he dreaded the long drive back to Governor Bailey's home," the guard told Sylvaney.

An asset search reported that Pennoyer owned one vehicle, a late model Jeep Cherokee. Ann had told Sylvaney that the Jeep was not parked at Leigh-Rose Mansion, nor was the vehicle parked in Pennoyer's reserved space near the Capitol.

Sylvaney spread the photos on his desk. He studied the man's features: a round, puffy face, blue eyes, a lock of hair combed over his forehead, tight pursed lips. His complexion was pale. He was easily more than 200 pounds, most of which was packed around his waist. Pennoyer obviously ate well during the past few years. More obvious was his lack of exercise. Sylvaney discarded any thought that Pennoyer took a hike in the Alleghenies or a canoe trip on Pine Creek. Wherever Pennoyer was, Sylvaney concluded, he was sitting, eating and relaxing.

Having learned all he could about the man, Sylvaney asked himself, "If I were Bill Pennoyer, where would I go?" He thought for a moment and then jotted some notes. Someplace remote, somewhere away from people, likely outside Pennsylvania.

Second question: "If I were Bill Pennoyer, how would I get there?" Sylvaney made a list of modes of transportation. Pennoyer could drive into upstate New York and into New England, or he could take a flight. "If I flew," Sylvaney wondered, "what airport would I use?" Not Harrisburg, because Pennoyer was known there. No smaller airports because their flights would not get him far enough away fast enough. Sylvaney narrowed the choices to two, Philadelphia or Pittsburgh. Because Pennoyer was last seen in Harrisburg, he likely drove the shorter distance to Philadelphia, Sylvaney reasoned.

So the private investigator sent an assistant to scour the long-term parking lots of Philadelphia International Airport for Pennoyer's Jeep. Two hours and $12.00 later, he told Sylvaney no luck there. Sylvaney concluded that the Jeep was probably at Pittsburgh International Airport, 300 miles to the west.

The following day, Sylvaney set out on the Pennsylvania Turnpike. He arrived at the Pittsburgh airport's parking garages by mid-day. There, in space 3,034, was Pennoyer's

Jeep. Its wheels were painted with dried mud. Dirt was splattered over its windows. Strapped to the roof was a heavily scratched orange kayak.

Pennoyer had flown. But what airline and what destination?

Sylvaney deftly popped the door lock. He reached above the visor and found Pennoyer's parking stub. The time recorded was Saturday, August 15 at 05:30. Pennoyer had arrived in time to board any flight departing at 6 a.m. or later. Such evidence was not helpful to the investigator; Pittsburgh's airport has dozens of departures at that hour.

Sylvaney noticed that mud had been tracked into the car as well. Tossed in the back was a pair of muddy hiking boots. Fast food discards littered the passenger seat. Papers in the glove box confirmed the vehicle was Pennoyer's.

Despite Sylvaney's consummate experience in extracting information, he hit a dead end. He realized that tracing Pennoyer to a specified flight would be impossible. Airlines observed strict privacy rules. Passenger names were released only upon an emergency or court order. Any attempt to gain such information by circumventing federal law could land him in jail.

He needed help – someone with information that could be purchased or stolen. The best place to start? Jimmie Bailey's hometown newspaper.

About halfway between Hollyhock Hills Dining Hall and Petunia Place Gift Shop was a bright yellow stucco building, bearing the sign, "Snapdragon Fitness Center." The 12,000-square-foot gymnasium was the pride of Castle Rock Center. Most of the rehab patients were required to participate in some form of exercise. Those with eating disorders or body image problems were teamed with personal fitness trainers.

Other addict patients, like Bill Pennoyer, designed their own workout routines.

Sporting the latest Phillipe Loreaux activewear, Pennoyer signed in at the front desk. He shuffled his flabby Lycra-covered legs upstairs past a horde of sweaty stationary bicyclists. He paused to watch a class of glowing women gyrating on yoga mats. He walked past muscle-bound men, some older than he, in the free weight area. He avoided studying his reflection in full-length mirrors that covered the walls; Pennoyer was well aware of his physical flaws. He never had a good reason to exercise, until today.

Exercise was synonymous with pain. That was Pennoyer's credo whenever a physician admonished him for poor diet, excessive weight and high blood pressure. He rationalized that walking to and from his refrigerator was sufficient exertion, that roasted peppers and sausage canceled each other out on his pizza, and that nobody's death certificate ever credited "high cholesterol." None of his friends had ridiculed his habits or concerned themselves with his health. Pennoyer watched his waistline expand steadily without interest, let alone alarm.

All of that would change today.

Love is a powerful motivator.

He had a 9 p.m. date in the sauna.

"Mr. Pennoyer, I presume." A trim young man with a buzz haircut and snugly fitting polo shirt held out his hand. "My name is Erik, and I have the pleasure of designing your circuit training regime."

He squeezed the corpulent corpuscles out of Pennoyer's hand. While the injured man tried to regroup, Erik flipped open a laptop and accessed Pennoyer's rehab file.

"Your treatment plan does not require cardio, Mr. Pennoyer. This will be a self-designed exercise program, then. Tell me what your fitness goals are."

"Please call me Bill." Pennoyer winced, pressing his hand under his left arm pit. "I don't know how to say this, Erik. I want to look sexier. You know, move some weight from here to there."

"I see," Erik replied. A little vein beside his forehead was popping as though he were laughing on the inside. "Sexy is good. But first, let me ask you some questions. When is the last time you engaged in sustained exercise?"

Pennoyer thought a few seconds. "I guess in law school about 12 years ago. I played racquetball on the weekends."

"No weight training?"

"I never saw the point of it. Too much grunting and too much pain."

"How about aerobic exercise? Jogging, swimming, anything like that?"

Pennoyer shook his head. "I'm sorry, Erik. That was too time-consuming."

"No need to apologize, Bill. We'll start off slow and build you up. After a few weeks, you'll notice positive results, better tone, less body fat..."

Pennoyer didn't have a few weeks, only a couple of hours. Surely, Erik could design some exercise to improve his appearance a little by 9 p.m.

"Suppose you wanted quicker results, Erik. What would you do?"

"Assuming my risk factors were low, the surest way to lose weight and gain muscle is a combination of intense cardio workouts and resistance training. See that gentleman over there on the treadmill? He's here every afternoon. He runs on that machine for an hour, then he does two full circuits on our Universal machines. He's been here about 60 days, and he's lost nearly 30 pounds."

Wow, Pennoyer thought, that guy looks great. What would Roxanne think if Pennoyer lost 30 pounds?

"That's the routine for me," he told Erik. "Let's get started."

The trainer smiled. He often dealt with patients who viewed rehab as a spa. Many of them desired to re-enter society with a cleansed mind and renewed body. Pennoyer's length of treatment was only 45 days. Short of surgery, Erik's treatment plan could not erase 12 years' accumulation of fat in six weeks.

He led Pennoyer to the center of a circular room. Arranged around them were 12 bulky machines. They resembled futuristic torture devices – iron bars, chains, strapped pedals. Each of them warned where not to put your fingers, chin, feet and other appendages. Erik handed him a towel. "You'll need this," he said. Pennoyer dabbed his forehead; the sweat already started.

Erik programmed the machines to their lowest resistance. He taught his student how to maneuver the bars and pulleys. "Work yourself until you feel a burn," he said. "If you have difficulty breathing, stop and rest."

After Pennoyer completed his first circuit, Erik excused himself for another personal training session. He told Pennoyer to complete a second trip through the machines. They would meet tomorrow at 4 p.m., he said.

Pennoyer dutifully completed the bench press machine. He examined his upper arms in the mirror. His mind foolishly perceived some improvement. But it was not enough. He decided to try a treadmill next to the fit gentleman. By the time he hobbled over, the man's pace was dialed down to a slow walk.

"Excuse me, sir," Pennoyer interrupted the man's decompression. "I'm new here. Could you show me how to operate this thing?"

"Sure," the man replied. "Just step up here, attach this kill switch clip to your arm and we'll program it. What's your weight?"

Pennoyer blushed. "I'll enter it." He pushed three numbers.

The man had no reaction. "From one to ten, what level are you?"

"I'll say five."

"OK. We'll say five. We'll do a moderate uphill for 15 minutes with a five-minute cool down. Now, push that start button."

Pennoyer hit the red button and the belt beneath his feet started to slide. He gripped both side bars as the walkway angled upward. The Lycra between his thighs rubbed together and caused uncomfortable warmth. As the belt accelerated, Pennoyer started to jog.

"There you go, buddy." The fit man slapped Pennoyer's back. "You're doing great. Let's up that speed a bit."

Pennoyer grimaced as the man punched the up arrow five times.

Nata Prybelewski was released from the trauma center in early evening. Her discharge instructions included bed rest whenever possible and daily application of topical antibiotics at the site of her bullet wound. Doctors did not restrict her travel. She had no medical excuse when Zelienople police escorted her to their station.

Nearly a week had passed since Nata was accosted on her parents' front porch. In the shadows of an August night, her assailant stood ten feet from her and fired a single shot. Before Nata fell, she glimpsed his face. Since that moment, she had been interrogated by dozens of detectives and officers and left each of them unsatisfied. She simply could not describe the man with detail. It was all so quick and so traumatic.

Nata was whisked into a rear service entrance. She was led into a darkened room. Police told her to stand behind a row of electronic components, wires and light projection equipment.

DetectiveAdams introduced himself again.After inquiring about her health, he asked if she was taking any medication that could affect her memory or powers of observation. She said no. He then pointed to Detective Keating to leave the room.

"Miss Prybelewski, we've invited you to help us this evening in making another identification of the person who shot you. We are conducting a line-up. In a moment, six individuals will be standing against that far wall. You will see them, and they will not see you. It is important that you maintain your composure. If you see the man who shot you, do not scream, don't cry, don't run."

"Have you caught him? Oh, dear God, I hope you caught him." Nata started to shake.

"I hope we have, Nata. You can help us by identifying him. But don't point. You can whisper in my ear."

The terrified woman shook her head. A female cop tried to calm her as a side door opened. Six young men, all wearing black hooded sweatshirts stepped in line along the front wall. Five of them were white; the sixth was Matty Moore.

Nata studied each face carefully. She eliminated two suspects immediately; they were much too short. Her assailant had been at least six feet tall. Person number 3 had a distinctively long nose. She would have remembered that, so number 3 was eliminated. Person number 4 was smiling and his face was covered with freckles. He had no facial hair other than peach fuzz, so number 4 was eliminated.

Person number 5 was tall, had whisker stubble and looked menacing. Nata had seen that face before. But where? Number five certainly fit her physical description, but something about him was disturbing. She would return to number 5.

Matty Moore was number 6. He could be the suspect, Nata thought. Number 6 had a darker complexion, and he looked like the only candidate stressed out by police custody. Number 6 had a 5 o'clock shadow. His eyes were set apart, like she had described to police in their interviews. But she didn't remember the assailant being quite that tall or quite that young.

Nata convinced herself not to be too persnickety. She really didn't have a great view of the criminal. His features were fuzzy in the late night shadows. The police weren't asking for 100 percent certainty. They only wanted her to pick out one of the six men. Surely, the detectives have gathered much evidence that points to either number 5 or number 6. Her identification wasn't all that important. Besides, she thought, Adams and Keating would not have driven her from the trauma center and set up this line-up if they didn't have a good suspect in it.

Nata returned her view to number 5. She had seen that face on her parents' porch that night. She remembered the pain from her wound. She recalled the siren of an approaching ambulance. There was great commotion on the porch. Police officers had responded to the scene while a crowd of neighbors pressed in. Her elderly parents had been struck by a violent stranger. She was filled with rage and despair.

Dozens of voices filled the air. One voice had been very distinctive.

Nata now whispered into the detective's ear. "Can they say something?"

"If that would help, Miss," Adams replied. "What would you like them to say?"

"I want them each to say, 'Compression, Compression.' Just like that."

Adams began with number 1 and ended with Matty. Nata heard exactly what she wanted. Number 5 could now be eliminated. She remembered a Zelienople police officer helping to load her into the ambulance. The officer shouted the words, "compression, compression," to one paramedic while pointing at her bullet wound. Nata now realized that police placed one of their own in the line-up.

By process of elimination, Nata made her choice. She whispered "number 6" into Adams's ear.

"How sure are you?" Adams asked.

"He's the only possibility," Nata answered.

Adams directed Keating to remove the six men. He asked Nata to sign a form to memorialize her selection. Another detective offered to drive her home.

Once the witness and suspect were safely absent, Adams turned on the lights. At the rear of the room stood Chief Faxon. Beside him was a young lady wearing a guest pass.

"Number six," Adams announced. "Positive identification. He's our man."

Faxon turned to his guest, a lady he usually entertained on Saturday nights. "Do you agree with our witness?"

"He's not your man, Andy. He's not the man who ransacked your house. And I'm positive about that!"

Chapter Fifteen
The Prosecutor

Archbishop Ostrow convened the diocesan council. He had seen enough of Good Shepherd Church. He was ready to decide its fate.

The cleric, dressed casually in short sleeves and black slacks, arrived last at the emergency meeting. Attendees, a mix of priests, nuns and lay leaders, surrounded a super-extended walnut table in an ornate conference room. Each of them had paged through an initial draft of "Doors to Christ," the bishop's plan to consolidate parishes in the Pittsburgh Diocese. Now they anticipated Ostrow's explanation. Why was he closing some doors and not others?

"My dear friends," he began as he always began, "this report is preliminary, but it challenges all of us to make difficult choices in these difficult times. The overview summary on page three highlights the overall decrease in parishioner contributions. While our flock is growing, the per capita donation had dropped nearly 25 percent in the past two years. This decrease has been particularly acute in three parishes."

A bar chart on page 4 ranked parishes by loss of contributions. Most of the bars were dipping below the x axis. Council members easily noticed the underperformance of three parishes: St. Anselm dropping by 40 percent; St. Stanislaus, down 43 percent, and Good Shepherd, falling by 61 percent.

Page 5 depicted decreasing membership at 14 parishes. Good Shepherd ranked last again, having lost 16 percent of its members in the past year.

Council members understood the consequences. This study would not have been commissioned by Bishop Ostrow if he didn't have a purpose. At least one church was on the chopping block.

"Our Holy Father has entrusted me with the stewardship of this diocese," Ostrow asserted his authority. "But your input and consent are vital to me in these very difficult decisions."

No translation was necessary. Ostrow was asking his council for cover; he didn't want the faithful to condemn him alone for closing churches. Any decision to shutter a church, no matter how financially sound, ignited loud public rancor. Ostrow wanted council to deflect blame; the group had to vote.

"You will notice that our report makes no recommendations, so I'm asking for a motion by one of you," he said. "Without courageous action, we are heading toward insolvency."

A hand shot up to his right. Ostrow pointed to it. "Father Mark?"

The bishop's financial assistant, as previously rehearsed, spoke with resolve, "I move that the diocese terminate St. Anselm, St. Stanislaus and Good Shepherd." Another young priest, yet to be assigned to a well-to-do parish, seconded the motion.

"Discussion?" the archbishop asked, knowing that discussion would ensue.

Sister Rosalia, a tall, bespectacled nun, whose royal blue habit was always starched and pressed, raised her hand. Ostrow looked about the room for an alternative speaker, but found none.

"This is indeed sad," said Sister Rosalia, self-proclaimed conscience of the council. "Last year, we closed St. Mary Magdalene and St. Michael the Archangel. Three more closings this year? Surely, some of our wealthier parishes can donate their collections to the less fortunate."

Profit-sharing was not a popular concept among the churches. Ostrow knew that borrowing from St. Peter's to pay St. Paul's would cause a greater cry than simply closing St. Paul's. So he allowed Sister Rosalia's comments to atrophy and die.

"Any other discussion?" he asked.

Long-time editor of the Pittsburgh Catholic, Daniel O'Sheen, raised his hand. The bishop pointed to him with greater hope.

"Can we phase in these closings?" O'Sheen suggested. "We'll close Good Shepherd immediately and work with the others to raise funds."

Voices around the table seemed to welcome the suggestion. The motion was withdrawn and another made to close Good Shepherd. Ostrow sensed a victory.

"Point of order!" Sister Rosalia raised her hand, to the bishop's chagrin. "Do we need a unanimous vote or a simple majority?"

Ostrow glared. Nothing short of unanimity would deflect all the blame. If there were dissent, he figured, the public would sense a controversy among council members and, ultimately, conclude that Ostrow railroaded the action.

"My dear Sister Rosalia," he sweetly answered. "Do you object to the motion? I think it is eminently reasonable. Now, I won't be involved in this vote. But, certainly, everyone around this table understands that we act as one, that as members of one body we are divinely inspired to speak with one voice and to act with one heart. And if a house be divided against itself, that house cannot stand…"

"I withdraw the point of order," Sister Rosalia interrupted.

"Call for the vote," O'Sheen said.

"Just a minute." A voice from the corner spoke up. Retired auxiliary bishop John Hogan raised a feeble arm. Courtesy required council's complete attention. "Has the pastor been notified of this situation?"

"Yes," Ostrow answered. "I have spoken to Father Frank McWilliams at length. Plus, I celebrated Mass last Saturday and advised the congregation of our financial study. It is a troubled parish. Costs are high. Vandalism and vagrancy are problems."

"Good Shepherd..." Hogan searched his memory. "We started that parish about ten years ago. I remember now. Father Frank had an excellent idea to bring faith to the poorest neighborhood in Pittsburgh. Are you saying that his mission was a failure?"

"Oh, no, Bishop Hogan." Ostrow began to backpedal. "Father Frank has done all he can. It's this economy. Things are getting worse..."

"Fiddle, Herbert, fiddle the economy. Money is always a problem. We can't just hang the Sword of Damocles over the heads of every pastor in this diocese. The moment their collection baskets are empty, we drop the sword? How can they operate under such pressure?"

Ostrow recoiled as heads were shaking in agreement with the old bishop. He had to change the dynamic.

"Father Frank will be reassigned, Bishop Hogan. His parishioners will only travel a few miles to the nearest parish. We are not abandoning anyone."

"Herrr-berrrrt," Hogan scolded him. "I've sat quietly in these meetings for the past ten years. I have not spoken while you and these good-intentioned people have eviscerated our churches. We sell them like commercial properties. I drove by St. Anthony's the other day; it's now a restaurant. They tell me the old marble altar is used for the Sunday brunch."

"But Bishop Hogan, we can't operate on faith alone," Ostrow pleaded.

The old bishop enjoyed his infrequent burst of power and insolence. "I'm the only person in this room who can disagree with you, Herbert. We **can** operate on faith alone. I have faith that if we commit this diocese to find resources to operate Good Shepherd Church, God will provide. What have we done to provide help to this parish? Has anybody taught Father Frank how to raise money?"

Ostrow was speechless.

No vote was taken.

Jimmie Bailey emerged from his cocoon by week's end. He breezed through his correspondence, finished calls to legislative leaders and signed off on a proposed budget – all before noon. The dark clouds that had been over his head had dissipated. He was smiling again.

For his staffers at Leigh-Rose Mansion, the governor's new attitude was infectious. Although Bill Pennoyer's mysterious and unexpected "vacation" prompted rumors, Governor Bailey's aides were working happily long into the night. Bailey's legislative initiatives were well-received by politicians and the public alike. His proposals for privatizing state liquor stores and extending hunting seasons swelled his public approval rating. Whatever had been bothering the governor was past news, his aides agreed.

Ann Bailey welcomed her husband's new disposition, and her hiring of Sylvester Sylvaney to track down Pennoyer mollified her. She needn't harangue Jimmie for his account of last Friday. Sylvaney was to nab the information from Pennoyer himself. In fact, given Sylvaney's reputation for efficiency, she had expected a full report by now. Ann would learn Jimmie's secret later. She decided to enjoy her husband's company in the meantime.

Gloria Negley, Ann's mother, agreed to watch baby Hannah for the day. Ann cornered Jimmie in their walk-in bedroom closet. She suggested they arrange a private movie screening at the Smethport eight-plex.

"What's showing?" he asked.

"We have two choices, 'Death of a Man Named Vulture,' that's a murder mystery, or a romantic comedy about..."

Jimmie stopped her. "The romantic comedy is perfect. Let's take some wine and we'll reserve the private screening room."

Ann smiled. "We need time together, Jimmie. You don't have to talk or think about anything."

He held her hand and looked in her eye. He was the same boy who proposed to her five years ago, she thought. He was charming then and, if he threw off the mantle of being governor, could be more charming now. But his charm could mask his personal torments, as well – the kidnapping and loss of his mother, the abuse by and violent death of his father. At times, Jimmie seemed to act with impunity, as though his family traumas entitled him to such behavior. It was this Jimmie, the one with dark secrets, who frightened her. He squeezed her hand and patted it. She patiently waited for him to speak.

"Ann, I apologize for the way I've acted this week," Jimmie said. "Something terrible has happened, and I think you should know."

She braced for another confession by Jimmie. But she didn't push him.

"I've known something a long time, and I never knew how to tell you, or whether I should tell you," Jimmie said. "But I believe, if we handle this properly, everything will turn out all right."

"Sure, Jimmie. You know I'm here for you." Ann closed the closet door to hamper any eavesdropping by her mother.

"Bill Pennoyer has a problem, a big problem," Jimmie said. "I've tried to help him, but it got to be bigger than both of us."

"What kind of problem, Jimmie?"

Bailey closed his eyes. At this point, he could have told her either of two things. He chose the lesser.

"Bill has a drinking problem."

"Oh, my," Ann sighed. "I never knew."

"He kept it from everyone, except for me. Last Friday, we were packing up at the governor's mansion and he found a bottle of Jack Daniels. Damn nearly drank the whole thing."

"That doesn't sound like Bill. I knew his appearance was looking poor, but I never thought he was an alcoholic."

"Worst I ever saw, Ann. So I told him to get help. That's when we got into a fight. He realized then that he had to check in."

"What do you mean, Jimmie?"

"Bill is in rehab now, Ann. He's getting treatment. I didn't want to tell anybody, but then I realized that you were so concerned."

Ann was concerned. His story had a bit of a smell. She never saw Bill Pennoyer drinking anything other than an iced tea or, occasionally, a Rolling Rock Beer. How could Bill possibly be working so efficiently under her nose while hiding a drinking problem?

"Where is his rehab center, Jimmie? Maybe I could send a card."

Jimmie was ruffled. He didn't want any more specific questions.

"I-I-I don't know, Ann. Bill called me a few days ago and said he found a rehab center out of Pennsylvania. I just pray that it works, Ann."

Butler County's district attorney Gil McFadden gambled on poker, football games and ponies. After years of practice, he was still terrible at it.

An occasional winning trifecta or miraculous windblown field goal only whetted his appetite for more "action." His next big jackpot was always just around the corner, or so he thought. In the meantime, his salary, retirement accounts and his children's inheritance inexorably flowed into the pockets of virtual bookies on gambling websites.

Last March, his net worth started to dip into negative numbers. He finagled a second mortgage on his ex-wife's house. He signed up for new credit cards to pay the balance on his older ones. He dipped into campaign funds to pay his loudest creditors. Everything would be repaid, he thought, as soon as his gambling luck turned.

McFadden was stacking debt upon debt. His house of cards was teetering, poised to collapse with the next dunning letter or debt collector phone call. His $160,000 salary paled in comparison to his mountain of debt. So McFadden reached out to his friends, including long-time associates in the prosecutor's office. But he didn't ask for their sympathy or support, he asked them directly for money. Fifty dollars here, a hundred there. He promised to pay everyone back "with interest." He never did.

Two of his assistants, under daily pressure to pay McFadden their spare cash, resigned without explanation in June. A month later, McFadden lost his secretary, his best investigator and both summer interns. Others in the office worked behind closed doors, pretended to take telephone calls when McFadden paced the halls or took frequent personal days. They all knew what he was doing behind his closed office door, but no one had enough courage to challenge him or repel his advances. Rule One in Pennsylvania politics was strictly observed: keep your mouth shut.

Lately, as the rats around him were abandoning ship, McFadden shoveled heavier caseloads upon his more faithful assistants. To keep his office afloat, McFadden took on more legal tasks – cutting into his computer time. Immersion into criminal cases eased his temptation to visit gambling websites, but not enough to cure his addiction. What he needed was one major case, like a capital murder case. That would divert him away from goshdarnpoker. com and bookiedelight.com, at least for a few months, he thought.

McFadden ran his fingers through Chief Faxon's murder investigation file. He pulled photographs from the various crime scenes and read numerous reports from Faxon's lead detectives. Although Faxon did a good job with the resources at his disposal, some pieces were missing. Most notably, McFadden thought, Zelienople police had not secured videotape from the Yer In-Yer Out convenience store. One officer had reported presence of a security camera focused on the sales counter, but did not follow up. Secondly, Faxon noted that renowned forensic pathologist, Dr. Elliot Chen, had examined the murder victim. No test results were in the file, however.

Several facts comforted the district attorney. Police had arrested a suspect whose fingerprints were recovered inside the victim's vehicle. The suspect had been stopped by police on Perry Highway, possibly before the murder. And, most significantly, a key witness in an earlier armed robbery positively identified the suspect.

McFadden's task was not daunting. He assembled the bits and snatches of evidence into a criminal complaint, charging

Matthew Moore with armed robbery, aggravated assault, grand theft auto and first degree murder. Sure the murder evidence was thin, he realized, but the witness identification was sufficient to guarantee a conviction. After all, he thought, Butler County's jury pool is drawn from voting rolls and property records – likely resulting in an older, conservative jury. What chance would Matty Moore have in court?

The district attorney, eschewing temptation from his computer, grabbed a yellow legal pad and drafted the complaint:

In the Court of Common Pleas of Butler County, Pennsylvania

Commonwealth of Pennsylvania v. Matthew Moore, a/k/a Matty Moore

Now comes the Commonwealth, through the undersigned duly authorized District Attorney, and files the following criminal charges against defendant Moore, and avers:

1. On August 14 in this year of Our Lord, defendant Moore, with premeditation and willfulness, entered into the dwelling place of William Herman of the Borough of Zelienople, with the intention to do bodily harm, and intentionally killed William Herman, thereby committing the offense of murder in the first degree in violation of Pennsylvania's Criminal Code;

2. As part of the commission of aforesaid murder, defendant Moore engaged in theft of a motor vehicle owned by another, with the intention to permanently deprive rightful owner of the use and enjoyment of said vehicle, in violation of Pennsylvania's Criminal Code;

3. Further, defendant Moore committed an aggravated assault upon Harold McCoy and committed an armed robbery of the Yer In-Yer Out convenience store on South Main Street, Zelienople, in violation of Pennsylvania's Criminal Code;

4. In addition, defendant Moore committed three counts of aggravated assault upon Stanley Prybelewski, Minka Prybelewski and Nata Prybelewski, all of Arthur Street, Zelienople, in violation of Pennsylvania's Criminal Code.

That should scare the kid into a quick guilty plea. Hey, wait a minute! McFadden dropped his pen. That's exactly what the prosecutor feared. No trial. No glory. No chance to rehabilitate his image in the office. A quick plea would free his time and send him back to his gambling websites.

Better to string Mr. Moore along, McFadden decided. Don't reveal all of the evidence, but just enough to keep the kid guessing.

So McFadden shredded his criminal complaint and scheduled his case before the grand jury. In his vast criminal law experience, McFadden knew that he could secure a presentment from any grand jury despite flimsy evidence. Without a presentment, McFadden's weak case could be contested in open court. The judge and defense counsel could find flaws and perhaps fatal deficiencies in the evidence before trial. McFadden, ever the poker player, decided to hide his cards for now.

Twenty-three grand jurors from Butler County, mostly retirees who were very agreeable with anybody from the district attorney's office, heard Matty Moore's case in 30 minutes. McFadden quickly secured his presentment against Moore for murder, armed robbery, aggravated assault and grand theft.

Matty Moore's arraignment was scheduled before a Butler magistrate the next morning. McFadden assumed the 18-year-old was indigent and required a court-appointed attorney. He was shocked to learn that Antonio Alfonzi was holding for him on Line 2.

"I'll be making an appearance for Mr. Moore at tomorrow's hearing, Gil," Alfonzi told his old nemesis. "What are the charges?"

"Robbery, assault, stolen car," McFadden replied. "And, oh yeah, murder."

"Murder?" Alfonzi screamed into the phone. "That's preposterous, and you know it."

"The grand jury says I've got an excellent case, Tony. You might want to treat me with a bit more respect."

Alfonzi ably acted the part of a defense attorney outraged by prosecutorial overreaching. "You can't convict him, Gil. He's innocent."

"That's your opinion, Tony, not mine." McFadden hung up the phone with a smile. Every case is a crapshoot, he thought, especially when a jury makes the decision. Attorneys like Alfonzi were the gamblers. If they took their clients to trial, the jury's verdict would decide life or death.

McFadden's gambling was much less serious. He closed his door, turned off his lights and clicked on his computer.

Chapter Sixteen
The Gift

Dennis Padgett wondered why the Kane News-Leader would be interested in his work as the governor's bookkeeper. His long days were spent fussing with numbers. No reader would be titillated by that, he thought.

Tom Zachary's office had provided few clues. The editor reportedly would write a short column bringing readers up to date with Padgett's career. Padgett envisioned the story's angle: a former trust officer at Mid-State Bank in Smethport, well-known and well-liked, was now toiling in obscurity for the governor. For a brief moment in print, Padgett would emerge from the shadows like Punxsutawney's groundhog before returning to his hole. It all seemed so pointless.

Nonetheless, Padgett prepared for the newspaper interview as scrupulously as business school grads chasing a Wall Street job. He outlined his personal history with Governor Bailey, the governor's commitment to affairs of state and his future plans. He would praise Governor Bailey. Any details about the governor's business affairs and wealth, however, were "off the record." Those were the ground rules.

Zachary arrived at the Clay Street address shortly before 2 p.m. Padgett accompanied him to his second floor office. Bright afternoon sunshine streamed through one wall of windows. Zachary's wingback chair offered a view of the Kane Manor bed and breakfast.

"So you can see everyone who comes and goes at the Manor?" Zachary asked.

"All the celebrities in Kane," Padgett said, chuckling.

"Marcy and I haven't stayed at the Manor for years. Is the Marine still in charge there, what's his name?"

"Gregory Harkins," Padgett replied. "Yes, he's still fixing it up, a never-ending job. You should interview him for your column some day."

"That's an idea. He probably has some stories to tell."

"More than I do." Padgett figuratively threw cold water on his interviewer.

Zachary leaned forward. He shook his head and clicked his pen. "I don't think so, Dennis. You've got stories to tell. There's some money missing, I hear."

Padgett had underestimated Zachary's investigative skills. The editor's nose was on the trail of Jimmie's wayward spending. But how much did he know? And who told him?

"Listen, Tom, everything we talk about can't be printed. That was the deal, right?"

"Right." Zachary would have agreed to any deal at the moment.

"Look around, Tom. All of this – the house, furniture, utilities, my office equipment – all of it comes courtesy of Governor Bailey."

"I understand, Dennis."

Padgett wagged his finger. "If you so much as breathe my name, my entire career will be finished. Or if Jimmie or some judge pins you down on threat of contempt or imprisonment, you cannot reveal me as your source. Got it?"

"Wild horses couldn't drag your name out of me, Dennis. I'll swear to that on a stack of bibles. Now can we talk?"

Padgett reached over and grabbed the steno pad from Zachary's hand. "There will be no notes from this conversation. You can rely only on your memory. If anyone points a finger at me, not only will I deny everything you print, but I will sue you and your newspaper for every dime. Understood?"

"Yes, sir. You can trust me, Dennis. Here, take my pen, too."

Padgett sighed. He was still hinky about this off-the-record interview. But he decided to take it one question at a time. Zachary would have to drag details from him. "OK, Tom, ask me a question."

Feeling naked without pen and paper, Zachary folded his arms on his chest. He leaned backward and cleared his throat. Experience told him that Padgett would terminate their conversation at some point of extreme discomfort. Better to start slow and increase the pressure, he thought.

"Other than Governor Bailey, do you manage assets for clients?"

"No, just the governor's. All of my eggs are in one basket."

"I see. Do you offer the governor investment advice or …"

"Governor Bailey trusts me with all of his assets, Tom. I have discretion to make investments, budget his personal expenses and pay his bills. My job is to free the governor's time so that he can attend to his executive duties."

"So you make all of his expenditures, do you?" Zachary asked. "You write out the checks and handle everything?"

That was the arrangement Padgett wanted, but Jimmie tapped his funds occasionally for unexplained reasons. Recently, his large wire transfers triggered cash reporting rules. Padgett hoped that he would avoid criminal liability under money laundering laws. He viewed this interview with Zachary as an opportunity to distance himself from Jimmie's potential criminal behavior.

"No, I don't handle everything," he told Zachary. "Jimmie has access to several of his accounts."

"The governor made some withdrawals from his accounts recently, right?"

That question seemed innocuous to Padgett. "Yes, he did. Nothing wrong with that."

Zachary stammered. "I'm not accusing anyone of anything. Jimmie Bailey can spend his money however he wants. And he doesn't have to get approval from you, right?"

"Correct, Tom. I'm just the bookkeeping guy."

"Well, don't sell yourself short, Dennis. You do more than bookkeeping. You feel responsible for the governor's financial empire. There are millions there. You've done a great job in earning him more millions over the years…"

"That's right. We've done very well."

Zachary sensed an opening. "So you take great pride in your success?"

"Yes, we've done very well."

"And, every time Jimmie withdraws money, that hurts your pride?"

Padgett was growing skeptical of his leading questions. "What are you driving at, Tom?"

"Tell me about the thirty thousand that vanished last week." Zachary cut to the quick.

"Damn it, Tom! How do you know about that?"

Zachary feigned journalistic integrity. "I've got sources, Dennis. Wild horses couldn't drag their names out of me."

"OK, this is all off-the-record. Last weekend, I was reconciling Jimmie's accounts and I found a wire transfer of $30,000 from his money market. I asked him about it and he refused to explain it. That should have been the end of it…"

"I know. It's the same old song; Jimmie can do whatever he wants with his money. But you went a step further, didn't you?"

Padgett flashed a look of terror. Did Zachary tail him to the bank on Monday morning? Did he know about the loan officer tracing Jimmie's wire transfers? As long as everything was confidential, he thought he should tell the whole truth.

"Yes. I was concerned about Jimmie. There were other transfers that he refused to explain. I am a signatory to his accounts, so I felt I should know."

"You found out where the money went?" Zachary asked.

"The thirty thousand dollar transfer was traced to the Castle Rock Center for Lifestyle Wellness. That's all I know."

Zachary's fingers twitched without a pen. He needed to remember the name, so he repeated it. "Castle Rock Center for Lifestyle Wellness. C-R-C-L-W. Can I write that down?"

"No notes!" Padgett was firm.

Zachary looked out the window. Kane Manor was in view, its tall chimneys and lead glass windows were features of a "castle." A landscape "rock" was "centered" in its circular driveway.

And, if his story panned out, the News-Leader would make money – definitely contributing to Zachary's "lifestyle wellness."

First Lady Ann Bailey was first to hear Jimmie's explanation for Bill Pennoyer's absence. And she was first to doubt it.

According to her husband, everyone should back away and give Pennoyer a chance to recover from his drinking problem. No one should bother the poor man, Jimmie said. Word of Pennoyer's stint in rehab should stay in-house, Jimmie advised her.

He also told her that Pennoyer spoke by telephone after he arrived at the rehabilitation facility. Ann decided to test his honesty. She could retrieve Pennoyer's telephone number and time of the call by flicking a few buttons on Jimmie's cell phone. When she reviewed his calls, nothing stood out. His story about Pennoyer seemed to be another lie.

"Let's go for a ride, Mom," Ann hollered to Gloria. "We'll take Hannah with us."

Ann felt an urge to leave Leigh-Rose Mansion before she confronted Jimmie. She had to respond to him calmly. She needed time. And she needed a secure telephone call with Sylvester Sylvaney.

"It is a lovely day, Ann," Gloria said. "We should shop a bit before sundown."

Ann was silent until they pulled from the Leigh-Rose driveway. "Mom, did you ever meddle into Dad's business?"

Gloria was puzzled. "No," she replied. "Not really. When I was your age, wives raised children and kept the house. I never saw the checkbook or paid any bills. There were certain things a husband was supposed to do. As long as he was working and came home with his paycheck on Friday, I was happy."

"Maybe, you're right."

Ann stared through the windshield as she drove west toward Kane. Hannah had fallen asleep in her car seat. Gloria reached around to straighten the baby's nodding head. She turned to see a tear in Ann's eye.

"You're troubled again, dear," Gloria said. "You can talk to me."

"Jimmie is saying things to me that don't make sense. I don't know if he's protecting me from the truth or if he's in some trouble. Either way, I feel left out. He doesn't trust me anymore."

Gloria wanted to ask what Jimmie had told her. But motherly concern outweighed her curiosity.

"Jimmie is under a lot of stress now, Ann. Pennsylvania politics can be a pressure-cooker. Plus, he's a new father without enough sleep…"

Ann patted her mother's leg, sending her a subtle message to stop making excuses. Both women knew that Jimmie's strange behavior could not be justified by lack of sleep or petty politics. Neither had affected him before this week.

The car turned down Clay Street and into the winding driveway of Kane Manor. Ann asked her mother to watch the sleeping Hannah while she made a quick visit. She knocked and pushed open the heavy porch door. She met innkeeper Gregory Harkins in the foyer.

"Mrs. Bailey, to what do I owe this pleasure?" he greeted her.

"I apologize for making a pest of myself, but may I use your telephone to make a long-distance call?"

He escorted Ann to his office and closed the door when he left. Ann sat at the innkeeper's tidy desk and dialed a very private Harrisburg number.

Sylvaney was happily surprised by the intrusion. "I see by my caller ID that you're waiting for me at our favorite restaurant."

"I'll make our dinner reservation after your work is done, Sy," she responded coolly.

"That will give me incentive, Ann. So far, I've located Mr. Pennoyer's Jeep at the Pittsburgh Airport. He apparently flew out Saturday morning, but his trail is cold."

"Maybe I can warm it up," Ann said. "Jimmie told me today that Pennoyer checked himself into a rehabilitation center for alcohol abuse. That should narrow your search."

"Alcohol abuse?" Sylvaney laughed. "That's a good one. I've done a thorough search on Mr. Pennoyer's history, and there's nothing to suggest such a thing. He hasn't missed a day of work in four years. He keeps up a hectic travel schedule. And his credit card records show no purchases of alcohol. If Pennoyer is an abuser, he keeps it well hidden."

Ann had to agree. But Sylvaney's job was to be absolutely thorough. Such high-level work for the First Lady demanded such scrupulousness. "Assume that Bill Pennoyer's problem has been well hidden, Sy. Check it out for me, OK?"

"OK." Sylvaney sensed a rebuke by his famous client. "Did the governor tell you the name of the rehab center?"

"No, Sy. How many could there be?"

After two circuit trainings, thirty minutes on the treadmill and three power shakes with booster protein, Bill Pennoyer collapsed on a yoga mat. His flabby body could take no more exercise and nutrition. His Lycra fitness gear was drenched in sweat. Every muscle ached, especially those he never knew he had.

Pennoyer felt so rotten that he felt great. Blood was pumping to muscles that had been dormant for years. His scalp was tingling with new blossoms. He could look straight down and see his toes. His new-found limp had a macho air. His arms swung wide to compensate for the new muscle mass, or painful swelling, of his upper back.

Just one session in the gym and Pennoyer was a new man. Fat cells had blown apart and endorphins raged in their place. Others may not have noticed, but Pennoyer saw results – a slimmer waistline, broader shoulders and a new zeal for life.

He returned to his villa for a relaxing shower and two Advils. A short nap recharged his batteries. At 7 p.m., he reheated a serving of tofu lasagna. He chased dinner with a cocktail of cranberry juice and diet ginger ale. By 8 p.m., he covered himself with musk body spray and headed for the

Tulip recreation center. He had a 9 p.m. appointment in the sauna.

Pennoyer was fixated on his new friend, Roxanne, the sex addict. What a terrible malady, he thought. A young, attractive blonde, offering her very self to strangers while desperately seeking acceptance and security. Pennoyer wanted to be her special friend – that one man who could unselfishly bear her physical affection and yet lead her to true love. He yearned to be her personal addiction counselor. They would schedule session after session after session. He would design a step approach to ease her down slowly. Serious addictions cannot be overcome "cold turkey," he thought.

The Tulip gymnasium was filled with noise as Pennoyer approached. He peered through the front doors and saw dozens of his fellow rehab patients crammed into temporary bleachers. Catcalls and cheers echoed through the building. On the floor, ten behemoth basketball players were battling.

Roxanne stood when she saw him. She waved for him to sit beside her on the top row. He noticed her T-shirt, her eyes and her waving hand, in that order.

"Aren't they great?" she hollered to him over the din.

Pennoyer squeezed beside her, not particularly excited by the game. He put his arm around her shoulder and gently kissed her cheek. She didn't notice.

"That's Corky Anders of the Phoenix Suns, and there's Jo Jo Riley of the Celtics. What athletes! They really put on a show." Roxanne bounced with every dribble.

"I didn't know Castle Rock sponsored professional basketball exhibitions," Pennoyer said. "Guess you get your money's worth here."

Roxanne threw back her head and laughed. "You're kidding, right? These players are patients here. They're just as sick as you and I. They come here to get clean."

Pennoyer watched the players run like racehorses, stop on a dime and toss the basketball with a perfect arc. The ball smoothly swished through the net. Then they backpedaled to the opposite end with greater speed than he could flat out run. With every basket made, Roxanne called out the player's name and shook her T-shirt.

"You know everybody!" he hollered over the noise.

"I'm good with names and I never forget a face," she said, before suddenly jumping and shaking. "Way to go, Surfdog! Ruuuh, Ruuuh!"

"Surfdog?"

"Yeah, Bill, Surfdog. Sometimes, I have special nicknames." Roxanne pointed to the player as he toweled off on the sideline. He winked to her.

Pennoyer, realizing why she was so good with men's names, grabbed her hand and stood. "Come on, Roxanne, let's go. It's about 9 o'clock. The sauna will close soon."

"Oh, Bill," she said, sighing. "I don't feel like the sauna tonight."

Her sad words drained the blood from his newfound muscles. She put her head on his shoulders and sniffed. The aroma from his body spray took hold of her.

"Instead, let's walk back to my place," she said. "I have a gift for you."

Pennoyer's blood rushed back like high tide. They stepped through the cheering crowd and into the crisp Colorado night. Soon they were alone on a path to the Tulip cottages. Her cottage was on the far end. Unit 7 was located away from Tulip gymnasium noise and closer to the Front Range Mountains, now bathed in moonlight.

Roxanne keyed open her cottage door. The place was immaculate. Fresh flowers in matching crystal vases decorated tables in her foyer and dining area. Pillows were fluffed and perfectly arranged on her love seat. Unlike Pennoyer's villa, there was no underwear balled up in a corner and no aluminum cans on the kitchen counter. Even the air smelled clean.

"You said you had a gift for me," Pennoyer reminded her.

She touched his nose with her index finger. "You're still a little boy, Bill. So excited, aren't you?"

Getting there, he thought. Her gift would surely help. "What is it?" The suspense was killing him.

She tossed pillows from the love seat and pulled him upon it. "You know, Bill, all day every day we go to these therapy sessions. We're told to be strong. We're told to face our demons. And there comes a time when we have to test ourselves, to see if we're making any progress. Are you making progress with your drinking problem, Bill?"

"I think so, Roxanne. I haven't had any alcohol for about a week now."

"That's wonderful, Bill. Do you think you're cured?"

"I don't really know. Perhaps."

She retrieved a brightly wrapped box from under her coffee table. "Here, Bill, pull the ribbon and open it."

Pennoyer peeled away the wrapping paper. Inside was a bottle of Johnny Walker scotch whiskey. Roxanne watched for his reaction, so he made his fingers tremble.

"Do you want to take a drink, Bill?"

"Yes, yes, I do. I-I-I guess I'm not cured yet."

Roxanne opened the bottle and poured two shot glasses. She downed hers and turned to Pennoyer. "It's all right, Bill. Sometimes you just need a taste if you're not fully cured."

Pennoyer threw back the drink and felt its warmth flow down his throat.

"Thanks for the gift, Roxanne. But I'm so sorry I don't have a gift for you."

"Oh, yes you do," she replied, bending down and expertly removing his belt with her teeth. "I'm not fully cured either."

Chapter Seventeen

The Expert

Elliot Chen, world-renowned forensic pathologist, had lousy people skills – at least with living people.

He could tell you what a corpse ate for dinner last Thursday, but would rarely accept dinner invitations from friends. He preferred bladder examinations to card parties. The only Bloody Mary that captured his attention was more likely a stabbing victim than a cocktail.

Nevertheless, Chen understood that dead bodies never paid his bills. His business relied on money from living stiffs. As much as he hated to do it, sometimes he needed to talk with people who talked back.

So when he read a Pittsburgh newspaper story about Matty Moore's arrest for Billy Herman's murder and saw the accompanying photograph of defense attorney Antonio Alfonzi, Chen sensed a business opportunity.

He had worked with Alfonzi a few years back. The attorney had paid Chen's bill on time, a rare occurrence these days. But the pathologist had a stronger objective than simply Alfonzi's money. Chen had not been paid by Chief Faxon for hours spent in travel and examination of Billy Herman's body. If, instead, Chen shared his knowledge with the criminal attorney, he would punish Faxon and the Zelienople police for not paying his retainer.

"And you are…?" Alfonzi's receptionist struggled to remember the visitor's name.

"Elliot Chen." He handed her his card.

"Dr. Chen! Oh, I am so sorry," she apologized. "I should have remembered. The Cafardi case, right?"

Chen nodded with a prideful grin. He recalled his brilliant performance in court. Despite eyewitness testimony, fingerprints, motive evidence and defendant's violent criminal history, Chen's analysis of the dead body swayed the jury. "The stab wounds were made by a left-handed killer," he told jurors. "Mr. Cafardi is right-handed. *A fortiori,* he is innocent of this crime. These are unassailable truths!" Everyone in the courtroom knew that Cafardi did it, but Chen had injected enough reasonable doubt and personal charm to eke out an acquittal. Chen's reputation as a formidable expert and powerful advocate had been firmly established. His fees rose exponentially.

"I'll tell Mr. Alfonzi that you're waiting," the receptionist said.

"Don't bother," Chen said. "I'll surprise him."

Alfonzi heard the pathologist utter the name, "Tony," as he passed every open door. By the time Chen reached the corner office, Alfonzi had secured his checkbook and closed his working file folders. Chen's reputation included a roving eye and a nose for assets.

"Come in, Elliot. What brings you to my doorstep?"

"Thought you needed me to pull your ass out of the fire again, Tony."

"Still basking in the Cafardi case, Elliot? You were just one piece of the puzzle. Cafardi won because he had a great attorney."

Chen opened an antique humidor on Alfonzi's credenza. He pulled out a cigar and sniffed it. "You smoke this shit, Tony? Business must be tough."

Alfonzi closed the box, nearly snipping the pathologist's highly-trained fingers. "That's Cuban, and, no, business is not tough. Just got a capital murder case and getting a lot of press. The phone has been ringing non-stop since Sunday."

"Yeah, I've read the story, Tony. The kid's in big trouble. He matched the description and he was trolling around the neighborhood after midnight. Black kid, too. How's that going to play with a jury outside of Pittsburgh?"

"Don't worry, Elliot. He's innocent."

"They all are." Chen mocked him. "But some of them walk and others get the electric chair. It's a risky business you're in, Tony. If I were you, I'd never refuse an offer of help."

Alfonzi's review of the records in *Commonwealth v. Moore* revealed a weak case for District Attorney McFadden. No murder weapon, no motive and no witnesses placing Matty Moore at the murder scene. McFadden had a police report that Matty was driving to Zelienople Road at 2 a.m. Saturday, which conflicted with eyewitness identification in a Zelienople home invasion four hours earlier.

Why was Dr. Chen pushing himself into the case? The victim was shot once in the chest and died at the scene, Alfonzi recalled. What more could a forensic pathologist add?

Chen stuffed two cigars into his coat pocket. He turned to the scowling attorney and said, "Downpayment for what I'm about to tell you."

"OK, Elliot, I'll bite. What do you know?"

"Plenty," he replied, landing with a thud on a client chair. "Walter Faxon's boy, Andy, the Zelienople police chief..."

"Yes, I've heard of him," Alfonzi interrupted.

"...didn't want anyone to touch the body until I arrived at the murder scene."

"You, you examined Billy Herman? Gawd, you get your fingers everywhere."

Chen smiled at the thought of his fingers in Alfonzi's wallet. First, he had to close the sale. "We did a full examination at the scene and a second examination later in the Butler County Morgue. It was a beautiful death, Tony. Clean entry and exit wounds, not much blood, no perceptible physical trauma elsewhere. The victim fell in a heap on the floor. Other than his unfired gun that was inches from his hand, nothing else was remarkable."

Alfonzi listened for any shred of information helpful to Matty. Nothing was there.

"So what, Elliot? You haven't told me anything new. Why should I hire you?"

Chen raised his feet and rested them on Alfonzi's desk. He bit off the end of a cigar and pretended to puff smoke into the startled attorney's face. "I'll say two words to you and you'll strike me a check for $100,000."

"I doubt it."

"Timeline."

"That's one word," Alfonzi replied. "And I'm not paying you."

"Impossible timeline."

"Well, you've piqued my interest, but I'll need more than two words to hire you," Alfonzi said. "What makes the police timeline impossible?"

Chen sized up his prey. Obviously, the attorney would not commit to a six-figure expert fee without more to whet his appetite. He decided to state his theory but withhold his examination records until the check cleared.

"When I arrived on the scene about 10 a.m. Saturday, rigor mortis was present," Chen said. "So Herman had been dead for some time, at least six to eight hours. He was face down on the floor, and blood had collected to the lowest areas of his body – his forehead, left hip, left arm and knees. That confirmed my six to eight hours conclusion."

Alfonzi calculated that Herman was dead at least by 2 to 4 a.m. Matty was stopped at the Perry Highway police roadblock at 2 a.m. No timeline problem yet, he thought.

"Chief Faxon kept asking me to determine the time of death," Chen said. "Faxon was very interested in that. So I did some other tests."

"What did you tell him?"

"Nothing. He didn't pay me. Simple as that."

"So when was the time of death, Elliot?"

Chen held out an open palm. "How badly do you want to know?"

"MATTY!" The collective scream from Kane News-Leader staffers echoed through the newsroom. Nobody had expected the popular summer intern to be freed after his murder arrest. And his editor never expected to see his star reporter back at work.

Tom Zachary pushed through the group of well-wishers and embraced Matty like the Prodigal Son. "How in the world…? Did they come to their senses and drop the charges?"

"I wish I could say that, Mr. Z. I'm innocent. All of you know that I couldn't harm a flea, but the Butler County prosecutor won't let me go."

"So why are you here?" Zachary asked.

"We had a bond hearing," Matty replied. "Our magistrate set the bond extremely high, thinking there's no way I could pay it. Boy, was he wrong!"

Zachary well knew of Matty's enormous trust account. Whatever Matty had paid was worth his temporary freedom, he thought.

"I'll bet people in Butler County are outraged that you're walking the streets, Matty. Just like that, free as a bird."

"Not exactly, Mr. Z. My attorney had to make some promises to the magistrate," Matty said.

"Like what?" Zachary was getting a bit leery.

"Because my job is here, I'm confined to McKean County. I'm allowed to go back and forth to my job, but at night ..." Matty paused, not quite ready to tell him the other condition.

"Go on, Matty. Don't be nervous. Whatever the magistrate ordered, we'll make adjustments. What is it? You have to wear a monitoring device? You have to stay in your apartment and have food delivered? Tell me."

"Well, Mr. Z, the magistrate was reluctant to release me unless I was living in a stable, family environment. You know, I have to live in a place with a father figure and a mother figure. So I'll be moving in with you and Mrs. Zachary this afternoon."

"WHAT??!! This isn't happening!"

"Just temporarily until the trial. May I call you 'Dad'?"

Zachary's mind reeled. How could he tell Marcy? How quickly could he convert her sewing room into a spare bedroom? How could the magistrate free Matty but imprison the Zacharys in one fell swoop?

"There's one thing you probably don't know about me, Mr. Z..."

Zachary braced for another bombshell.

"I have a severe allergy to processed meats, like hot dogs."

Mary Anne Graumlich was minutes away from her robing ceremony. A new judge has to look her best, she thought. So $150 for a hair permanent and style, $175 for an original Phillipe Loureaux dress, and $230 for upper lip electrolysis were necessary expenses. Her only unnecessary expense was $1.50, her cost for a used Bible at the Goodwill Store; the county should provide a Bible, she complained.

Butler County's ceremonial courtroom had been scrubbed and polished for the investiture. Extra seating was available along the mahogany-walled aisles. Even the gallery, long-closed for structural deficiencies, was opened for media representatives. Hundreds of prominent western Pennsylvania politicians, attorneys and courthouse observers started filing in to the lavish courtroom an hour earlier. Notably absent was anyone from Casale, Dodge & Schumann. Graumlich's former law firm would celebrate the "loss" of their most incompetent partner later at the 1901 Tavern & Grill.

Graumlich waited impatiently in chambers. In ten minutes, she and Butler County's President Judge Samuel Lovecchio were to emerge through a side door and greet the throng. Judge Lovecchio had anticipated this moment more than anyone had realized. For the past five years, he was the sole judge for Butler County. Mounting caseloads and time-consuming administrative tasks sapped his energy. At 67 years of age, and with his Florida townhouse beckoning, Lovecchio was more than ready to shovel all unpleasant duties upon a junior judge.

"Enjoy this moment, young lady," he said to Graumlich. "They'll love you now, but in a few weeks they'll be talking behind your back."

Graumlich ignored the old man as she closed her compact case. She slipped off her pumps and massaged her pinched toes.

"I remember my investiture," Lovecchio continued, as though he had an audience. "My wife, God rest her soul, never looked as radiant. She held the Bible for me, and my three daughters gathered beside me for the oath. Happened right here. That was thirty years ago. Seems like yesterday."

"That's nice." Graumlich dismissed the senior judge with iciness.

"Is there anything you want to ask me, young lady? Anything about being a judge, your duties, ethics, responsibilities? Anything at all?"

"As a matter of fact, yes," Gramlich replied. "Why do you refer to me as 'young lady?' I'm 33 years old. I've been a practicing attorney for nearly 10 years. I graduated near the top of my class at Ohio Northern Law School. I've formed corporations. I've drafted covenants not to compete. I've sat in on small claims cases and even depositions."

Lovecchio already knew his successor was barely an attorney. He hadn't realized how ill-tempered she would be.

"Don't refer to me as a young lady, Judge Lovecchio. That demeans me in front of everybody." Graumlich pursed her lips, which Lovecchio interpreted as a sign of anger. Tension eased when she applied fresh lipstick.

"Very well," he responded, somewhat chastened. "I shall address you as Judge Graumlich or Your Honor."

"That would be appreciated," Graumlich said, fussing with her hair.

Fifteen minutes before the appointed hour, seating in the courtroom was scarce. District Attorney McFadden was holding ten seats for his staff, but three were not taken. Latecomer Antonio Alfonzi tried to slip into one of them.

"Hey, Alfonzi, those are saved for the DA's office," McFadden called to his rival defense attorney.

"Sue me!" Alfonzi hollered back. He was constantly annoyed by arrogant prosecutors. None of them survived by their wits and business instincts, he reasoned. They drew regular paychecks, ate well and enjoyed absolute job security. If they couldn't move their butts into the courtroom fast enough, Alfonzi thought, they didn't deserve a seat.

McFadden was enraged by the private attorney's insubordination. He stretched across three seats and grabbed Alfonzi's lapel. "I said those seats are saved, buddy."

Alfonzi shrugged from his grip. "You're a horse's ass, Gil. You and your office are a joke. I can smell the incompetence from here!"

"What you'll be smelling is your client frying in the electric chair," McFadden retorted. "You better enter a guilty plea soon for that kid or he's toast!"

"That's very funny, especially coming from a pro-life politician." Alfonzi trotted out a low blow. "Don't use my client to revive your dying political career, Gil. That's one gamble you're sure to lose."

McFadden's blood pressure shot up to stratospheric levels. He rose to his feet so quickly that he pushed over two folding chairs. "I'll knock you on your ass right here, Alfonzi!"

Before the DA could swing his fist, the courtroom bailiff intervened. "Gentlemen, is there a problem here? We could take this matter out into the hall."

Alfonzi looked at his rival with disgust. "No problem here. None at all. I'll sit somewhere else, somewhere with real attorneys."

The bailiff stood between them, and tempers cooled. McFadden eased into his chair and pretended to ignore Alfonzi.

"I have two words to say to you, Gil. 'Impossible timeline.' Just remember those words when we're in trial," Alfonzi said.

"What does that mean?"

"You'll find out soon enough." Alfonzi bluffed. He didn't know what those words meant. Not yet. Not until he paid Elliot Chen an enormous expert fee.

The courthouse bell pealed. Chatter stopped. The bailiff called for order. All stood as Judge Lovecchio and the prospective judge entered. When the crowd was seated, a court clerk read a proclamation from Governor Thomas James Bailey. Mary Anne Graumlich was formally appointed to a vacancy on the Court of Common Pleas of Butler County. The proclamation was adopted by Judge Lovecchio, who issued an Order that Ms. Graumlich be sworn.

After the oath and after sustained applause, Graumlich stood behind a lectern. Her speech would be short but biting.

"Thank you, my friends. We start a new chapter today for Butler County Courts. As your first female judge, I will sweep away the misconception that only men can do this job."

Lovecchio squirmed as the audience stared at him for a reaction.

"For too long, courts in Pennsylvania have been dominated by the old guard, by men who slavishly hold to outdated judicial thinking and outmoded courtroom technology," Graumlich continued. "We stand at the dawn of a new era, a time for fresh thinking, for new ideas."

For the first time since Oktoberfest, froth appeared on Lovecchio's lips.

"Change is coming to your Common Pleas Court," Graumlich pronounced. "Your judges will work longer hours. We will work on weekends. We will toil unceasingly until our docket is up to date. In fact, as a sign of our devotion to this mission, Judge Lovecchio and I will provide all of you with our cell phone numbers so that we can handle any emergency any hour of the day or night."

Lovecchio's eyebrows hit the ceiling. He slumped forward and drooled onto the court calendar.

"Finally, my dear friends, I caution all of you not to be intimidated by my academic achievement and wealth of experience," Graumlich said. "I am merely an attorney. Judge Lovecchio and I may wear robes, but underneath we are simple human beings entrusted with daunting powers. I may not happen to like Judge Lovecchio, but I respect his judicial office. Likewise, I do not ask for your adulation, but will insist upon your absolute respect."

Her speech ended to polite applause. Judge Lovecchio, thoroughly emasculated by the incoming jurist, rose and pounded his gavel.

"Thank you, Judge Graumlich," he said. "According to today's program, this is where the 'old guard' makes a few comments."

Some attorneys snickered, including Lovecchio's lunch buddies. They anticipated a thorough dressing-down of the new judge.

"First, we welcome Judge Graumlich to the Butler County bench. We have enjoyed a long tradition of judicial excellence since 1835. I suppose nothing good lasts forever."

Laughter erupted in the courtroom. Lovecchio blushed.

"No, no. I'm not referring to Judge Graumlich. When I say nothing good lasts forever, I'm talking about my career. I've enjoyed every day as your judge. There can be no higher calling than to work for justice in one's own community. In the past 30 years, thousands of everyday people have passed this bench looking for fairness and an equal shake. Some have gone away disappointed, but many only wanted their day in court. God bless them all.

"Judge Graumlich is correct. It's time for change. She has many ideas. They sound wonderful. I certainly don't want to stand in her way.

"Therefore, it is with great pride and some regret that I announce my immediate retirement as your judge. Thank you all for this wonderful opportunity."

Judge Lovecchio stood to thunderous applause. Courthouse workers, however, sobbed in silence. A new era was indeed coming upon them, something apocalyptic.

Graumlich chased after the senior judge. She found his robe discarded on the floor near his chambers. He was gathering framed photos from his desk when she confronted him.

"What do you think you're doing?" she challenged him.

"Making a hasty retreat."

"You can't do this to me. I can't handle this job all by myself."

"Sure you can, Your Honor." Lovecchio placed a cover over his Olivetti typewriter. "I'll be back tomorrow to collect the rest of my things."

"But Sam, I need you."

"A young lady would need me," he said with a wink. "Judge Graumlich does not."

Chapter Eighteen

The Jackpot

"10-54. Morningside Apartments. Unit 32."

Chief Andy Faxon paid little attention to the radio transmission. Morningside Apartments was a common location for 10-54 calls. In the past year, Zelienople police responded to five dead body reports at the apartment complex – all were young men with cocaine residue in their nostrils. Faxon remained at the station and dispatched two beat officers to the scene; he preferred office work to drug corpses.

When officers called for back-up, Faxon monitored his radio more closely. The victim at Morningside had overdosed, officers at the scene reported. But what they found in plain view startled Faxon. He jumped into his cruiser and sped to the apartment.

He arrived as paramedics were loading the young man onto a stretcher. Investigating officers pulled back a sheet, and Faxon studied the man's face. It was pallid, unmistakably white. A three-day stubble surrounded his chin. His eyes had rolled back. He looked about 20 years old. Faxon nodded to paramedics to take away the dead man.

Faxon climbed up rotted outside stairs to a second floor walkway. He passed several apartments with closed doors and eyes watching behind slightly parted curtains. Apartment 32 was at the far end. A good remote location to end a worthless life, he thought.

"Officer," Faxon called to the lead investigator. "Take me inside and show me what you discovered."

"Sure, Chief. It's the damndest thing. He was using them to cut lines of cocaine. There were just rolls and rolls of them. Here, take a look."

Faxon stepped over three days' worth of Bud Light cans as the officer led him to a bathroom sink. There, stuffed into plastic beer cups, were coiled strips of Pennsylvania Lottery tickets.

"There are hundreds of them, Chief. You can't buy these in rolls, can you?"

No doubt was in Faxon's mind. These tickets were stolen. His only question was whether the tickets could be traced. And, if so, whether the path would lead to Yer-In Yer-Out convenience store on South Main.

"What else did you find?" Faxon asked his investigator.

"His wallet, for one thing. Name is Shawn Hibler. Here's his Ohio driver's license."

Faxon inspected the wallet. Inside was a receipt from Pawndollars in Evans City. Among seven items on the receipt were a ladies ring and a handgun. He put the wallet in an evidence bag and held it close.

"Run a background check, officer. See if he has any priors, especially thefts and any crime involving a gun."

"Sounds like you have a hunch, Chief. What are you thinking?"

"Well, officer, I think we found our Zelienople robber."

The investigator stepped aside as a police photographer memorialized the scene. "We already arrested a suspect, Chief. And he's been arraigned."

Faxon needn't be reminded. His girlfriend's close personal encounter with the Zelienople robber convinced him that the arrested suspect, Matty Moore, was innocent.

Now, Faxon had compelling evidence to prove it – stolen lottery tickets and a pawn shop receipt likely linked to Minka Prybelewski's wedding ring.

It was time to pay a visit to the Butler County district attorney's office.

For the fourth consecutive day, Jimmie Bailey sat alone in his study and called a certain cell phone number. And for the fourth time he heard the same voice mail recording: "Hi. Bill here. Leave your message."

Bailey was not aware of Castle Rock Center's strict prohibition against telephone contacts with its clients. Successful rehabilitation required limitation to communication with substance abuse specialists within the facility. How could addicts break from personal pressures if family members and friends interrupted their treatment with telephone calls?

Bill Pennoyer had surrendered his cell phone, hand-held computer and all other electronic gizmos at the rehab center check-in. He was the center's ward for 45 days. No phone calls in. No phone calls out. The rest of the world had to wait for his re-creation.

But Jimmie Bailey could wait no longer. He spoke at the beep:

"Bill, it's me. Listen, everything has cooled off here. Matty Moore was arrested for the Zelienople murder. Can't go into other details now. People are missing you, so you can come back anytime. Call me."

Bailey wanted to tell his friend so much more. In particular, he wanted Pennoyer to know that the zealous Butler County prosecutor was seeking a speedy trial. He wanted Pennoyer to learn that Matty had been stopped at a police checkpoint and that he met a physical description from an eyewitness. Jimmie wanted his friend to come home as soon as possible;

Pennoyer's absence was becoming suspicious to Ann and others on the governor's staff.

Leigh-Rose Mansion was quiet in early evening. Ann, her mother and baby Hannah were shopping in town. The staff had been excused for the day. Jimmie was alone with his thoughts. And they were not comforting.

The young governor felt a disturbing energy in the room. He always had. When he was a toddler his father, Brock Bailey, found him alone in the room and playing with drawers in his desk. Jimmie remembered loud yelling and a firm paddling from his father, exacting the boy's promise never to touch the desk again. Years later, when his fear subsided, Jimmie returned to the desk and found his father's unloaded handgun. How he wanted to take it to a range and fire it. But his discovery remained a secret – until one Christmas Eve.

Brock had cheated on Jimmie's mother. When he returned to the mansion late on the winter's evening, Jimmie was waiting for him with a loaded gun. Jimmie could not contain his anger and, five bullets later, he called police to an "accidental shooting" at the house. Brock refused to press charges, and the entire matter was sealed in the county's juvenile court files.

The gun was discharged again many years later when Brock faced his son on Kinzua Bridge. Jimmie tried to stop his father on the bridge as a tornado bore down Kinzua Valley. Brock's body was thrown off the bridge by a sweeping vortex of wind. The gun was recovered. Jimmie replaced it in the study desk.

Nothing good came from that gun, Jimmie thought. With a new baby in the house and state police security, he needed it no longer.

Jimmie wiped the gun with a dust cloth and placed it into a plastic bag. Then he walked down the hill toward Leigh-Rose Mansion's back gate. Before him stretched Kinzua State Park and what remained as the southern terminus of

Kinzua Bridge. No park ranger was on duty after dusk. Unnoticed, Jimmie scaled a chain link fence and walked onto the wooden bridge deck.

About a hundred yards in front of him, the bridge deck ended. Its center span, decimated by a July 2003 tornado, was strewn in the valley 300 feet below. Jimmie stepped carefully toward the precipice.

Far below him, Kinzua Creek curled and shone like a baby's hair. Thick vegetation grew along the creek. Dotting the landscape below were thick bushes and tall grasses. Jimmie often stood at this site. He marveled at nature, watching wildlife below and eagles above. He remembered, as a teenager, running across the bridge, timing his sprint as the Knox-Kane railroad train approached. Sometimes, on summer nights, he and his buddies would climb up trestles and hoist themselves onto the bridge deck.

The last time he climbed, Bill Pennoyer was struggling below him. Eventually, both men reached the deck. It was the night Hannah was born.

Jimmie opened his plastic bag and removed the gun. He pointed it into the air and clicked it six times. He then looked for a spot to throw it.

A few seconds later and a few hundred feet below, the Bailey family gun was swallowed up by bramble bushes.

Sylvester Sylvaney was undercover in McKean County. So the private investigator was dressed in a flannel shirt and blue jeans. His get-up would have worked, except that his jeans were uncommonly cleaned and pressed, his fingernails were neatly manicured, and his baseball cap was Husqvarna not John Deere.

Jessie Krone waited on the new customer at the Kane News-Leader business office. She assumed he was trouble, and he was.

"I need to look at your back issues, ma'am," he told her.

"We go back to 1930. Which issue would you like?"

"I'm not sure which day," he replied. "I'd like to do a general search for a particular person whose name may have been printed in your newspaper."

"We don't have a searchable database, but if you give me the name, I might …"

Sylvaney didn't give up a kernel of information. "I'd prefer not to state the individual's name. You know, right of privacy and all of that."

"Sure, Mr. …?"

"I'm sorry. I can't give you my name either," Sylvaney said.

Jessie thought this was about the queerest conversation she ever had with a customer. She motioned for Tom Zachary to join them.

"This is our editor," an exasperated Jessie told the stranger. "He'll take it from here."

Zachary eyed the familiar-looking man. "I know you from somewhere. Let me think."

"No, you don't sir," Sylvaney assured him.

"I never forget a face," Zachary said. "July 2002. Pine Acres Golf Course. The member-guest tournament. You were teamed up with, now wait a second …"

Sylvaney started to blush. This newspaperman had a keener memory than his wife.

"… with the state police commissioner, Josh Gibson," Zachary continued. "That's right, you're the hot shot private eye from Harrisburg."

The jig was up. "Sylvester Sylvaney," Sylvaney confessed.

"No, that's not it," Zachary said. "Let me think."

Sylvaney handed Zachary a card. "Well that sure is a funny name," Zachary said. "I should have remembered that one."

"And you are?"

"Thomas Zachary, owner and publisher and, if I might add, historian of McKean County. If you just let me know what you want…"

"All right," Sylvaney began. "I have been retained by a very important client who is interested in locating a friend. This person apparently has checked himself into a private rehabilitation hospital."

Zachary already had that information. Dennis Padgett had told him that Jimmie Bailey spent $30,000 on the Castle Rock Center for Lifestyle Wellness. But who was the "very important client?" He would be a little coy with the master investigator.

"Is this private rehabilitation hospital somewhere around here?" Zachary asked.

"I-I-I don't know. I was hoping you could help me with that."

"So who's your client?" Zachary inquired.

"I can't divulge my client, sir."

"Well, who's the friend? I can't be of much help, Mr. Sylvaney, if you don't give me more information."

Sylvaney only wanted to look at back issues of the newspaper. But he was losing time and patience with this two-bit newspaper editor.

"If you must know, the friend's name is Bill Pennoyer, Governor Bailey's chief of staff."

Zachary smiled, having obtained an important piece of the puzzle. Things were coming into focus: Jimmie wasn't doing drugs; it was Pennoyer. And Pennoyer had been missing for a while. Rehab was a logical excuse. But why would Jimmie pay for it?

Sylvaney watched Zachary as he computed the new information. "Sir, do you know Bill Pennoyer?"

"Yes, sir," Zachary answered. "Jessie! Please pull the Pennoyer file and share our clippings with this gentleman!"

"I'm very grateful, Mr. Zachary. Do you have anything in your files about his use of alcohol? Any traffic accidents, public drunkenness, abusive conduct?"

"Alcohol abuse is it?" Zachary said. "We probably have something on file about his beer drinking, but, well that depends. Will you share the results of your investigation with us?"

Sylvaney shook his head. "That will not be possible. I'm working solely for my client."

In that case, Zachary thought, Mr. Sylvaney can get lost.

"I suppose an investigator with your pedigree will find this out anyway," Zachary said. "I've been trying to help Bill with his drinking, but he was too far gone. So we talked about getting him some help."

"What did he say to you?"

"Bill told me that he was too well-known to do rehab in Pennsylvania."

"That's what I thought," Sylvaney said.

"So he was going elsewhere, but he made me promise not to give out the name of the facility."

"Where did he go? Just the city, not the name of the hospital."

"All right, Mr. Sylvaney, I can do that. He was going to Toronto."

Good Shepherd Catholic Church was one lousy Sunday collection away from oblivion. Father McWilliams was desperate. He promised the archbishop that he could raise

$50,000 within two weeks. If not, the church doors would be forever closed, the bishop threatened.

McWilliams hastily convened his parish council. The meeting, however, yielded few good ideas. Some council members favored a direct approach, like shaking down drivers at busy intersections or publishing names of parsimonious parishioners in the church bulletin. Others favored an emotional appeal for money, like sending poor children to beg in the streets or advertising for donations: "...for $500, you, too, can buy a pew..."

Pastor McWilliams nixed all of those ideas because, he said, they would demean the church. But he was desperate for fast money, the kind that only gambling can generate.

"We'll call it, 'Casino Night at the Shepherd.' There will be parlor games, Bingo and raffles. Prizes will be donated by local merchants," McWilliams told council members. "Get the word out in the community. Church basement, Saturday from 7 to midnight."

"But Father, are you sure about this?" a council member asked. "There could be trouble in this neighborhood."

"Nonsense," McWilliams replied. "All proceeds will benefit the church. I think everyone will respect that, and act properly."

Council members were skeptical, but mum. If their pastor was able to see goodness in other people, then so should they. But in their minds, Casino Night was an accident waiting to happen.

"I can see fear in your faces," McWilliams told them, "but we have no choice. Do whatever it takes to pull in $50,000 this weekend."

Good Shepherd's blind usher, Mr. Robinson, raised his hand. "I don't play Bingo much, Father, but I'm damn sure it don't make that much money. And dem raffle tickets will git only a couple thousand. How're you gonna do it, Father?"

McWilliams had a plan. He knew a few guys with roulette wheels and decks of playing cards, and he knew other guys with wallets fattened with dirty money. All of those years ministering to imprisoned federal criminals were finally paying off for the pastor.

"Never underestimate the power of prayer," McWilliams told them. "If Saint Stanislaus can raise $10,000 with a bake sale and kiddies carnival, we can do 50 with games of chance. Just get out the word and people will bring their money."

On Wednesday, McWilliams got out the word to Carmen Tavares, Nicky Memisakis and Charlie O'Toole. On Thursday, they spread the word to Tony Oliviero, Porcelli Porgusko and John McGowan. On Friday, the phone tree extended to Sonny Delozier, Ambrose "The Blade" Johnson, Leopold "Little Fatso" Broguglia and the four Cocona brothers currently on probation.

On Saturday morning, Good Shepherd's basement underwent a metamorphosis – from dank storage area to Las Vegas casino. Floors were mopped. Light fixtures were repaired. Walls were decorated with mirrors and glitter. Ladies Guild members strung paper mâché ribbons and festooned Bingo tables with vases of fresh flowers.

McWilliams avoided the main room. Instead, he dragged card tables into two back rooms. He stocked coolers with beer and set out sufficient ash trays for the gentlemen gamers. He placed a stool near a back exit door for six-foot-three-inch and 250-pound ex-professional wrestler Antwon Largo – a recent convert and McWilliams' favorite parishioner and bouncer.

By 7 p.m., the Casino Night crowd began filing into the church basement. The older ladies with clutch bags and Bingo daubers used the Centre Avenue entrance. The younger men with facial scars and gang tattoos used the back basement door. Bingo, pinochle and old maid brought laughter and shouting as dollars flowed in the main room. Meanwhile, blackjack and poker players transferred great wealth in the smoky back rooms.

After a few hours, Father McWilliams retreated upstairs to the darkened church. He checked the front door locks and emptied loose coins from a poor box before entering the main church. Candles for special intentions flickered at the side altar. In the dim light, he noticed the silhouette of a woman kneeling at the railing. She appeared to be unfazed by the raucous party one floor below. McWilliams approached, trying not to disturb her solitude, but a creaking floorboard announced him.

Tanya Harper was no longer alone with her thoughts. She blessed herself and turned to face her pastor. McWilliams saw tears on her face.

"Oh, Father, I am so sorry," she said. "I know the church is closed but…"

"Have you been here all afternoon?" he asked. "I locked up about 3 o'clock. I didn't see you then."

Tanya nodded sheepishly. "I never left after morning Mass. What time is it?"

McWilliams turned his wristwatch to the flickering light. "It's almost 10. You should be going home, Tanya. Get something to eat and some rest. Come back tomorrow."

"It's no use, Father. I can't eat and I can't sleep. Not since they arrested Matty."

"Your son is fine, Tanya. I heard he's free on bond, and that he's staying with his editor in McKean County." McWilliams tried to console her, but his words missed their mark.

"If you don't mind, Father, I'd like to spend the night here. I have a lot of talking to do with my Lord."

McWilliams helped Tanya to her knees and then knelt beside her. He pulled a Rosary from his pocket and started to pray. After a few minutes, Tanya turned to him.

"You know why I'm here, Father. You should be downstairs with your friends. Why are you here praying with me?"

"Unlike yours, my intentions are purely financial," he replied. "Sometimes it's OK to pray for money. Dear God, let this fundraiser be a success."

Tanya and McWilliams returned to their respective intentions. So deep were their thoughts that the laughter and commotion below them seemed to vanish.

Until fists pounded at the church door.

And until they heard the yelling:

"POLICE! RAID!"

Chapter Nineteen
The Audiotape

Tony Alfonzi double-checked the address: 54 West Curtin Street. He pulled his convertible to the curb under shade from a fully mature maple.

The renowned Pittsburgh defense attorney stood in awe of the grand Victorian house. A newspaper editor lives here? Such a home in Alfonzi's Penn Hills neighborhood was rare indeed. Here in Kane, stately brick mansions lined the streets without pretentiousness. The opulence of Tom Zachary's house easily blended into its environment. Lucky guy, Alfonzi thought. There's money in these small towns.

After dragging his trial briefcase up the porch steps, Alfonzi paused to fill his lungs with country air. He smelled fragrance of nearby lilac bushes. Azaleas and mountain laurels, having cast their blossoms months ago, framed a large front porch. Alfonzi noticed two Adirondack chairs beside a matching table. On the table was a pitcher of iced tea with lemons. In the far corner was a slatted wooden swing, complete with seating cushions and fancy pillows. He hadn't seen a place so restful and inviting since a summer vacation with his first wife in Savannah.

Marcy Zachary met him at the door. He accepted her invitation to step inside.

"Please make yourself comfortable, Mr. Alfonzi." She pointed to an antique flowered sofa. "I'll tell Matty you're here."

Alfonzi watched her climb the ornate wooden stairway. She turned at a landing past a stained glass window and disappeared from his sight.

The Zacharys' house was a showplace. One wall of the living room was lined with collector edition books. A well-used brick fireplace separated two column windows dressed in lace. All of the furniture dated from the early 20th Century, he thought. No plywood or particle board in this house, he thought.

Open windows created a pleasant cross-ventilation. Kitchen smells wafted into the living room. Marcy must be baking something, maybe a peach pie, Alfonzi thought. He smiled when he realized that homes this comfortable and peaceful really do exist. People here don't know how good their lives are, he thought.

Matty ambled down the steps with a legal pad and pen in hand. Alfonzi was ready with some important questions.

"Your trial is coming up in a few weeks, Matty. What do you intend to wear?"

"Huh? Is that important?"

Alfonzi shook his head. "For the jury, that's very important. Criminal defendants, especially ones who don't testify, have to look non-threatening. That means a white shirt and conservative necktie. I've never won a case when my client wore a dark shirt to trial."

Matty took notes. "What else?"

"No blue jeans. Wear navy blue or brown slacks with a simple belt. Dark socks, too. And no sneakers, only dress shoes. Got it?"

"Sure, boss. What can I do to help you at trial?" Matty asked.

"Whatever you do, don't laugh or snicker or cry. No matter what the District Attorney says or what his witnesses say, you make no expression. The jury will watch your every move. If they think you are a smart aleck, you'll get punished.

"Also, Matty, don't talk or whisper to me. The court microphones will pick up every little comment you make. You can pass notes to me if you must."

"Sounds like you want me to be a potted plant," Matty said.

"Yes, but don't take it personally," Alfonzi said. "I want to control as much as I can in the courtroom. If my client rolls his eyes, falls back on his chair or spills the water pitcher, I've lost control and I can't help you. Let me be the one to spill the water, OK?"

Matty contemplated his advice, especially the part about not talking.

"So you don't want me to testify? But I'm innocent. I have to tell my story. No one else can testify about what I did that night."

Alfonzi knew that a criminal defendant can insist upon testifying, that there was nothing his attorney could do to prevent that. Still, he leaned on his clients to exercise their right to remain silent throughout the trial. Many cases were lost by rambling defendants who were tricked by the government's cross-examination.

"No, Matty, I don't want you to take the stand. In this case, you could only hurt yourself. Trust me on this one."

"Well, tell me, Mr. Alfonzi, what witnesses will you call to testify on defense?"

The attorney pulled a heavy file from his briefcase and placed it on the coffee table. The file jacket read: "Elliot Chen Forensics, Examination Report, William Herman, Deceased." Matty picked it up loosely, and gruesome photographs slipped onto the floor.

"We paid a lot of money for this, Matty, but sure is worth it," Alfonzi said, stuffing documents back into the folder.

"The great Elliot Chen, he's our witness?"

"Our one and only. He's all we need. After he testifies, there will not only be reasonable doubt, there will be absolute certainly that you were not the killer of Mr. Herman."

Matty looked at Dr. Chen's report. It was filled with charts and graphs. None of it made any sense to the teenager. "What's he gonna tell the jury?"

"Simply that it was impossible for you to have done it. You couldn't be in two places at the same time."

"But I was alone most of the night, Mr. Alfonzi. I have no alibi witnesses."

"That's not true, Matty. Mr. Herman's body is your alibi witness."

Matty gave him a puzzled look. Dead bodies don't testify in court.

"Dr. Chen was the first person to examine the body at Herman's Zelienople home. He performed a number of tests to determine the time of death. One of the tests involved body temperature. By taking Herman's rectal temperature at different intervals and recording the temperature drop over time, Chen determined with medical certainty a range of time when the death occurred."

"Gosh, how did you get Dr. Chen on the scene so fast, Mr. Alonzi?"

"This whole thing is just dumb luck, Matty. Zelienople's police chief called Dr. Chen to the scene when they got the call on Saturday morning. He performed all of these examinations, but the police never paid him. He was never retained by them. So he decided to make his report for us, Matty."

"For a price?"

"Yes, but no price is too high when a man's liberty and life may be at stake."

Matty flipped pages until he reached the report summary. He eyes lit up and a broad smile crossed his face when he read the final sentence: "Based on the foregoing measurements, it is my certain opinion that Mr. Herman was slain between the hour of 1 a.m. and 2 a.m."

Alfonzi watched his client sigh in relief. "Couldn't have been you, Matty."

"No, sir."

"You were …"

"At the police checkpoint on Perry Highway that entire hour."

"Precisely, Matty. There's our alibi."

First day in a new job is the worst day in a new job.

Newly robed Judge Mary Anne Graumlich mulled over her enormous civil and criminal docket. Hundreds of cases awaited her rulings. Dozens of trials were queued up in the fall. She was hassled by attorney conference calls after she stupidly divulged her cell phone number to the Butler County Bar.

Worst of all, one upcoming trial imperiled her annual Jamaican cruise.

Newspapers dubbed it: "Butler County's Trial of the Century" – the case of *Commonwealth v. Matty Moore.* Trial had been set for mid to late October, and the attorneys estimated it would last almost a month.

"Maybe three or four weeks for any other judge, but not for me," Graumlich barked to her law clerk. "We're gonna streamline this thing. You watch me. The case will go to the jury by Friday of the first week."

Efficiency was very important to Graumlich, especially when Jamaica was calling.

Chief Faxon did his best investigative work in the privacy of his bedroom. After a particularly tense but enjoyable tryst with "Saturday Night," he rolled over and grabbed his wallet from a bedside table.

"Don't pay me, Andy," his weekend date cooed. "That would be a crime."

She watched him nervously pull out a driver's license like a teenager hoping to buy a six-pack. Only this driver's license was from Ohio.

"Recognize this guy?" he asked, pointing to the photograph.

"Andy! That's him. That's the robber! Did you apprehend him?"

"In a manner of speaking," Faxon said. "We removed his body this morning after a drug overdose."

"Thank you, Andy," she said. "He was a monster. What about the kid who was arrested? Have you squared things with the district attorney?"

"No, not yet," Faxon replied. "I needed your help first."

He pulled on his cotton sleepwear and shuffled to the bathroom. She called to him through the closed door.

"Andy, I feel really bad about the kid they arrested. Do you want me to talk to the D.A.? You know, I could positively identify this creep as the armed robber who broke into your house."

Faxon spit out mouthwash and popped his head from the bathroom. "That won't be necessary. There's no point in getting you involved in this mess. Besides, we found stolen items in the apartment to implicate him in the burglaries. That should be enough to satisfy the D.A."

"Saturday Night" burrowed under Andy's sheets. She was comforted by the thought that her assailant was dead, but troubled by the thought that her associate in passion kept her hidden.

Maybe if she played it cool, she figured, she could stay in his bed past midnight.

Love was a foreign concept to Bill Pennoyer. But if this wasn't love he was feeling, it was damn close.

Thirty-six straight hours entwined with soft warm skin, brilliant smiles, sparkling eyes and unerring sexual instincts drove him past ecstasy into a new dimension of human emotion. The girl beside him spoke of love in spiritual terms. He answered in language from his heart. It all seemed so natural and so eternal.

Roxanne Randle pretended to sleep, but her mind was buzzing. After years of one-night stands and morning rejections, she was through with testosterone-pumped boys. She wondered whether the average-looking, slightly balding man beside her was finally "the one." He was sweet, tender and, best of all, in no apparent rush to leave her side.

She had never slept with such a man. She hoped Pennoyer would be her last.

In Castle Rock Center terminology, Roxanne was a "recidivist." Despite three stays in rehab, the attractive young lady's addiction appeared to be untreatable. Her promiscuity was attributed by her counselors to a variety of life experiences. One blamed her mother. One blamed her father. One blamed a YMCA camp counselor.

Roxanne only blamed herself. At 19, she quit college and moved to New York. She pursued modeling jobs. Agencies told her that pretty faces were a dime a dozen, but her body was something unique. The more she undressed, the faster money flowed to her. Eventually, she felt cheap and unfulfilled. A year later, she started looking for love.

Having exhausted her circle of friends in New York, Roxanne auditioned for a television modeling job in Los Angeles. Her tryout included both photograph stills and video action. A network producer admired her "lack of inhibition." She was chosen to hold Suitcase No. 17 in a prime-time game show. She was instructed to open her suitcase slowly, bend over it provocatively and hold the pose at least five seconds for the camera. Accordingly, Suitcase No. 17 was a popular choice among male contestants.

Roxanne Randle fan clubs sprouted up throughout the country. Her antics on the show were fodder for YouTube internet videos. Groupies lined up at the stage door, and Roxanne autographed their ticket stubs. Often, she wrote her telephone number for the cutest fan. Her reputation as a "romping sexo" was widespread.

But, while other models slept their way to the top, Roxanne was stuck in the bottom, desperately searching for an "average Joe" she could hold onto forever.

Pennoyer turned onto his side and breathed slightly in her ear. She opened her eyes and faced him. He was an average Joe all right. But average Joes, she thought, are better than at least half of the male population. For Pennoyer, however, there was nothing average about Roxanne. She left him speechless, except for one thought.

"I love you." He snuggled closer to her.

"Do you?" she whispered. "Do you, really?"

"I love you so much, I think I'm gonna explode." Pennoyer brushed a strand of hair from her face. She was beautiful to him in many ways.

"But I really don't know much about you, Bill. Only that you're a senator from Rhode Island and that you have a drinking problem."

"Then you don't really know anything about me," Pennoyer said.

She lifted herself onto one elbow. She felt scorned again. "Just who are you?"

"I'm so sorry, Roxanne. I haven't been honest with you. All this talk about privacy at Castle Rock, well, I guess I took it too seriously."

"I've been honest with you, Bill," she said sternly. "Totally and painfully honest."

Pennoyer felt pain in his heart. How could he be so stupid with her? If this were love, he thought, he'd better be painfully honest as well. He decided to tell her everything.

"I'm in politics, Roxanne, but I'm not a senator," he began. "My name is Bill Pennoyer and I am chief of staff to the Governor of Pennsylvania. I am not an alcoholic. I was sent here by the governor to get away from Pennsylvania."

Roxanne stared in disbelief. "Why did he do that?"

Pennoyer swiveled and put his feet on the floor. "Let's get dressed. I have a great deal to tell you."

She seemed so innocent and trustworthy. Pennoyer was certain she could listen to his story and would understand his perilous situation. The truth was that he had no one else at the moment. And he could hold it in no longer.

They sat inches apart on Roxanne's sofa. She allowed him to take her hand. He began by answering her last question.

"My boss, Governor Jimmie Bailey, sent me here. He paid Castle Rock Center for a 45-day treatment period. The truth is that he wanted me to get lost. And that's exactly how I feel, lost."

"I still don't understand, Bill. Why don't you start at the beginning?" she asked.

"Sure, that makes more sense." Pennoyer took a deep breath. He was about to do what he promised Jimmie he would never do – involve a third person.

"There was a bad man in Pennsylvania. His name was Billy Herman. Billy knew something about Jimmie Bailey, something the governor never wanted anyone to find out…"

"What was it?" she asked.

"His father, Brock Bailey, was unfaithful to his wife. That messed up Jimmie. He fought with his father and, quite accidentally, his father died in a storm. So the governor, panicked. He dumped his father's body into the Ohio River and covered up the whole thing. He didn't want to hurt his chances to be elected governor."

Roxanne tried to understand, but the story was too bizarre for her. "How does any of that affect you, Bill?"

"This man, Herman, figured out what Jimmie did to his father. For the past few years, he extorted money from the governor. A little bit at first and then, later, his demands were in the hundreds of thousands. Everything was hush-hush. Even Jimmie's wife didn't know about the payments.

"Then, earlier this year, Jimmie and Ann had a baby girl. She was everything in the world to Jimmie. Unfortunately, the governor's baby was big news in Pennsylvania, and the extortionist found out. His demands got larger and, when he wasn't paid right away, he threatened to kill the baby."

"Oh, my," Roxanne gasped. "That's awful. What did the governor do then?"

Pennoyer reached into his jacket pocket and pulled out a Dictaphone machine. "Got this from Doctor Bremer's office. Don't worry, Roxanne. There are enough kleptomaniacs around here to keep security officers occupied."

Roxanne watched him load a small audiotape into the machine. He clicked it on and turned up the volume. She could hear rustling and whispers. After a minute, she could hear men's voices.

"Is that you?" she asked him.

"Yes."

"And the other voice?"

"Governor Bailey."

"*Stay here, Bill,*" one voice said. "*I'm going to get closer. That's probably his bedroom there.*"

"*Think that rock's big enough to smash through?*"

"*Yeah, with my 80 mile-per-hour fastball.*"

There was more rustling noise, like someone stepping on dry leaves. Roxanne jumped when she heard a loud crash. *"Run back to the tree line!"* one voice whispered urgently. More rustling before a few minutes of silence. *"OK, Bill, you're up. You have the tape recorder running?"*

There was a thumping sound. Pennoyer showed Roxanne how he patted his pants pocket.

"You had the tape recorder in your pocket?" she asked.

"Yes," he replied. "That was my job. I was to get everything Billy Herman said on tape. We were going to catch him confessing to the murder of our state police commissioner."

"I get it," she said. "That's how you were going to stop the extortion. Get Billy Herman to confess to a crime. That's pretty smart."

"No, Roxanne. That's stupid. Keep listening."

They heard recorded footsteps, first on the sidewalk and then on a porch floor. Next was a creaking front door opening.

"Don't touch that!" Pennoyer's voice was distinctive on tape.

"Who is it? What do you want?"

Pennoyer started to sweat. He knew what was going to happen next. Herman confidently described his murder of Josh Gibson at the foot of Kinzua Bridge. It seemed as though he was proud of his accomplishment, and not worried a bit about the intruder before him. After he admitted the crime, an argument broke out between Herman and Pennoyer.

"Put the damn gun away!" Herman's voice was agitated. *"You'll regret..."*

A gun blast stopped everything. Roxanne heard the thump of Herman's body falling to the floor. She looked at Pennoyer with fear.

"Oh, my God. Oh, my God." Pennoyer's voice was muffled.

"What happened! You were only supposed to scare him. Not kill him!"

"Oh, my God, Jimmie. He pointed a gun at me and I shot first. Look, there it is under his arm."

"Kick it over to his hand, Bill. Make it look like a suicide. Don't touch it. Don't touch anything. Let's get out of here."

Roxanne heard the men running from the house.

"Take your gun, Jimmie. I don't want to touch it anymore."

"Listen, Bill. He had it coming. He was a murderer and an extortionist. It's all over now. The police will find him in a few days. Nobody will know as long as we keep our mouths shut. Promise me…"

Pennoyer shut off the tape. Roxanne slid a few inches away from him.

"You killed a man," she said. "How could you do that?"

"I shot him in self-defense. He was an ex-cop. He would have killed me!"

She cradled his head against her shoulders. "You poor man. You've been holding all of this inside for weeks. What are you going to do now?"

Pennoyer had no plan to return, especially after he broke his promise to Jimmie.

Tom Zachary followed his nose for news, and his nose pointed to Colorado.

His plane touched down at Denver's airport about noon local time. He drained a bourbon and water at the terminal before hailing a cab to Castle Rock.

Zachary's mission was to locate Bill Pennoyer. His objective was to learn why Governor Bailey sent the pseudo-alcoholic to a distant rehab center. It was a long shot, but one Zachary and the Kane News-Leader felt compelled to take. Pulitzer Prizes are not won on the cheap, the editor reasoned.

Castle Rock Center for Lifestyle Wellness was a fortress on the prairie. The perimeter wall seemed to be impenetrable. Metal spikes protruded from it. Security cameras were trained on every square inch of the entrance. With a few guard towers added, the place could easily pass for a federal penitentiary.

Zachary's taxi was met by a guard at the main gate. After he checked Zachary's name against a list of new "patrons," the guard raised a cross-arm. The cab eased through.

A bit intimidated but unflustered, Zachary proceeded with his plan. He checked in at the main conference center and met his substance abuse counselor. He gave his story exactly as he rehearsed it in a measured cadence: he was a small business owner caught in a downward financial spiral; he turned to alcohol for solace and, now, he was hopelessly hooked.

He told his counselor that he needed to join a support group of fellow alcoholics, preferably those from small towns such as his in Pennsylvania. The counselor scheduled him immediately for the morning group session. After completing some paperwork, Zachary was placed in a Tulip cottage. He was strongly advised to avoid contact with other patrons until the morning session.

When night fell, Zachary took leave of his apartment. He walked unnoticed along the macadam path from Tulip to Daffodil to Rose. He looked for any directory of patrons, any listing that may show the name, "Pennoyer." He passed tennis courts and the large recreation center. He walked towards light emitted from the Castle Rock Center community room. He noticed rehab patients returning to their apartments and heading toward him. Some greeted him with a nod or an utterance of indistinguishable language. Others passed him like zombies in a death struggle with their demons.

Zachary stopped a few of them and asked about Pennoyer. One of them was Phillipe Loreaux, Pennoyer's fashion designer.

"*Oui*, he is with the lady, *je présume*," Loreaux told him.

"That is surprising, sir," Zachary said. "Mr. Pennoyer is not one for the ladies."

"*Je ne suis pas d'accord, monsieur.*"

Zachary scratched his head. He was in the communication business, but foreign languages stumped him.

"Sir, *Sprechen Sie* English, please."

"Yes," Loreaux replied. "Mr. Pennoyer is, how do you say, reclining with a young lady. If you understand Latin, I would say he is in *flagrante delicto*."

Could this be the same Bill Pennoyer? Zachary wondered if he had traveled 2,000 miles and spiked his News-Leader expense account only to discover Pennoyer on a play vacation. Oh well, he thought, might as well track down the happy boy anyway.

"I'm staying at the Tulip cottages," he told Loreaux. "Where might I find Mr. Pennoyer?"

"Quite the coincidence," Loreaux replied. "The young lady has been known to entertain at her apartment in the Tulip buildings. But please do not interrupt them. *Monsieur* Pennoyer has been quite eager lately. *Ah, toujours l'amour!*"

Zachary thanked the French man with a hearty, *"gracias,"* and returned to his apartment. He consumed his whey bar and soy milk. Then, weary of the day's travel, he crawled into bed. Tomorrow morning, Zachary vowed, he would confront the promiscuous chief of staff at group therapy.

The coming *tête-á-tête*, Zachary thought, might drive the poor man to drink.

Butler County's District Attorney Gil McFadden rounded up his prosecutors. Trial was fast approaching, and the Commonwealth's case was looking thin. Fresh thinking from fresh minds was needed.

"All right, people. We have our defendant in the area around the time of the murder. We have his fingerprints on a stolen vehicle at the murder scene and we have a positive identification from a witness in a prior armed robbery. Is that enough to convict Matty Moore of capital murder?" McFadden asked. "I don't think so."

One assistant noted that, since Matty's arrest, Zelienople has been free of armed robberies. "I think the jury could take that into consideration as evidence," he said.

"We need more than that," McFadden replied. "We need to establish a motive. We need witnesses."

"How do we do that, Gil?" his first assistant asked.

"Subpoenas, that's how," McFadden said. "We'll smother his family and friends with subpoenas. We'll call them to the witness stand, and the jury will see what kind of trash we're dealing with. Nobody will be able to give this kid an alibi. All of their stories will conflict. They'll stumble over each other to protect Mr. Moore. This is classic stuff, people. The more they talk, the guiltier he'll appear to be."

McFadden's paralegal produced a list of potential witnesses: Matty's parents, his girlfriend Megan and his boss Tom Zachary.

"Serve subpoenas on all of them!" McFadden ordered. "And we'll sequester them so they can't sit in the courtroom and support Moore during the trial."

"That's ingenuous, sir," said a sycophantic assistant. "You're sure to win!"

"Thank you, Kenny. Have I overlooked anything?"

"Yes, sir," the first assistant spoke up. "Police files indicate that Dr. Elliot Chen examined Billy Herman at the scene. We don't have his forensics report."

"Get Dr. Chen on the phone immediately," McFadden directed him. "And add him to our witness list."

Chen was reached at his Pittsburgh office. He gleefully took McFadden's call.

"Yes, my report was completed," he told the DA. "You can't have it."

"Like hell, Chen! It's evidence. I can subpoena your report," McFadden blustered.

"No you can't. My report is privileged. It's attorney work product. No judge would ever command me to give it to the Commonwealth."

McFadden nearly blew a blood vessel. "Work product, my ass! Chief Faxon granted you exclusive access to the body. You worked for the Zelienople police. That's **my** report, Chen!"

Chen relished this "teaching moment" for the old prosecutor. "Look in your file, McFadden. Show me where there's a contract for my services."

Papers rustled, followed by grumping sounds.

"Go ahead, McFadden. Show me any record of payment for my expert services."

More grumping noises.

"I'll save you the time, McFadden. Your boy, Faxon, was too cheap to retain me. So I've gone over to the other side."

"What? You're working for Alfonzi? That sleazy defense lawyer? You can't do this, Chen. I'll have your medical license revoked!"

"A man's gotta eat, McFadden. At least, Alfonzi pays."

Pleased with the havoc he wrought, Chen hung up. He knew a subpoena was heading his way. Alfonzi would protect him. Obviously. Chen was his star witness.

Bill Pennoyer, looking well-rested and oh-so-satisfied, slithered into a front seat. The class of alcoholics filled in behind him. Almost four weeks into the program, Pennoyer was making splendid progress toward sobriety. Of course, when your worst vice is an occasional Rolling Rock Beer, sobriety comes naturally.

His addictions counselor, Catherine, waited for the shuffling feet to be still. She glanced around the seminar room. She noticed a few new patrons in the back row. A couple were repeat customers. She slyly smiled at Pennoyer, her prized student. He would be her little helper.

Catherine warmed up a projector and loaded her PowerPoint presentation into a laptop computer. Her first slide simply said, "Stress Factors."

"Thank you all for coming this morning," she began. "Today, our topic deals with those external factors that lead to our problem behavior. I call them 'stress factors.'

With your help, we will identify those forces in your lives that cause you to break down, and cause you to consume alcohol."

A few hands shot in the air, but she ignored them. Instead, she focused on Pennoyer. Her prized pupil was leaning back in his chair and appeared to be daydreaming.

Catherine pretended to look over her list of names. "Let's see, Bill Pennoyer, would you come forward, please?"

Other group therapy members applauded as Pennoyer ambled to the stage. Catherine greeted him with an arm around his shoulder. She turned him to face the audience.

"You have made excellent progress," Catherine told him. "Your diet has improved. You're exercising more, and you've lost weight. When is the last time you had a drink?"

Truth was Pennoyer had a shot of whiskey each night he helped Roxanne with her sex addiction problem. But now was not the time for truth.

"I've been sober for over a month."

Applause rang out again. Pennoyer smiled at the crowd. Catherine was praising him, but he was distracted by a face in the back row. No, it couldn't be, he thought. That cocked head with a pencil behind the ear. That goofy grin. That familiar blue blazer and brown striped tie.

It was Zachary! Pennoyer froze in place.

"Now, Mr. Pennoyer," Catherine continued, "let's identify some of the factors that led you to be addicted to alcohol. Give me one."

He started to stutter and shake. Catherine tried to calm him. "Just one factor. You can't overcome stress unless you acknowledge it."

"P-p-peop-ple out to get me…"

She typed his response on her slide show. "People out to get you. What do you mean by that? Do you think everyone is out to get you, Mr. Pennoyer?"

"No," he replied, looking directly at Zachary. "Just some people who stick their nose in my business and want to bring me down."

"I see," Catherine said, disturbed by his sudden paranoia. "Are there people in this room who want to bring you down?"

"Yes." Pennoyer started to work on his exit. "I see people who want to hurt me. I feel intense pressure. I must fight it, but I can't."

"Fight it, Mr. Pennoyer," Catherine demanded. "Be strong. Fight it!"

"Can't. Can't fight it. I need a drink. Must have a drink."

Pennoyer shrugged violently to dislodge Catherine's arm from around his shoulder. Two burly security guards intervened and escorted him through a front fire exit. Group members were hushed. Zachary took the rear exit, but soon was lost in a maze of hallways.

"I'm all right," Pennoyer told the guards as held him in a security office. "Just had a minor break-through. I'd like to return to my villa."

After signing a release, Pennoyer scooted up a back stairway to the second floor seminar room. The sex addiction group session was under way. He found an empty chair beside Roxanne.

"What are you doing here?" she whispered. "Have I turned you into a sexo?"

"This is an emergency, Roxanne. I'm being following by the editor of my hometown newspaper. If my cover is blown, I might be arrested."

"This is happening so fast, Bill. What are we supposed to do? Just flee?"

He grabbed her hand and pulled her from the seat. Other women in the room purred in response to his macho aggression. Some men took notes of the event. The counselor clapped his hands to restore order.

Roxanne removed her four-inch high-heels and jogged with him through the conference center. Pennoyer kept looking back to make sure Zachary wasn't following. They reached an elevator and embraced when the doors closed.

"Bill, I'm so worried for you…"

"For us, Roxanne," he said, trying to catch his breath. "We're in this together."

"I have a friend who can get us out of this place," she told him. "It's your personal trainer, Erik. He owes me a huge favor. See, he had some muscle tightness and I, well, no need for those details now."

The elevator doors opened to a basement hallway. Bill and Roxanne sprinted for his villa. She helped him stuff his belongings into his tote bag. She watched him place the incriminating audiotape deep within his pants pocket. They quickly visited her cottage and packed an overnight bag. Then, the couple set off to find Erik.

"Why would your newspaper editor be looking for you?" she asked as they jogged toward the recreation center.

"I dunno. Somebody told him something about me, I guess. Tom Zachary wouldn't chase me all the way to Colorado if he wasn't working on a big story."

"Do you think he knows…?"

"About the killing?" Pennoyer said. "If he does, the cops would be here. No, only one other person knows that I shot Billy Herman, and that's Jimmie Bailey. He won't tell anyone."

Roxanne saw panic in his eyes. She slowed to a fast walk. He likewise eased his pace. When they reached the rec center, she told him to sit on a bench. She wanted to talk to Erik privately, she said. Pennoyer slumped onto the seat and placed his reddened face in his hands.

"Follow me." Erik tapped Pennoyer's shoulder and pointed him toward the rear parking lot. Roxanne already was seated in the personal trainer's Audi. Pennoyer shoved his tote bag in the back seat and followed behind it. Erik's car eased past the front gate, and soon the trio was heading toward freedom.

About an hour into the drive, Roxanne leaned toward the back seat and checked on her paramour. His eyes were closed and, finally, he was breathing easily.

"You two can stay with at my friend's condo in Littleton," Erik told her. "She's vacationing in Steamboat Springs for a few weeks and gave me her key."

"Shhh. I think he's sleeping." Roxanne pointed to the back seat.

Erik lowered his voice. "What's this all about, Roxanne? Patrons aren't allowed to leave rehab until they're checked out. The guards will be looking for you both."

"Bill saw an old acquaintance at the conference center today. The man is a newspaper reporter. We think he's a gate-crasher. Bill thinks the man is a threat. So we had to get out."

Erik was fuming. "Damn press. Always snooping around, trying to get photos of celebrities for their tabloids. We'll catch him. What's his name?"

"Zachary, that's his last name. Bill told me his first name, but I don't remember."

"Should we wake him up and ask him?" Erik whispered.

"No. Just tell the guards that Mr. Zachary is a trespasser. They'll lock him up until the Castle Rock police get there." Roxanne looked at her exhausted lover. "Poor man. He's been through so much. He needs tenderness."

Erik maneuvered his car through the tight downtown streets of Littleton. He pulled to the curb in front of a popular coffee shop. "Here we are. The condo is on the third floor."

Pennoyer awoke when the ignition turned off. Roxanne opened his door and took his tote. Still a bit groggy, Pennoyer stepped to the sidewalk and thanked his driver.

"No problem," Erik said. "I'll cover for you back at the Center. And don't worry, Roxanne, I'll take care of the situation."

As the Audi sped away, Pennoyer looked at his new love. "What situation was he talking about?"

She kissed him gently on the cheek and took his bag. "Oh, nothing worth the worry. How about some lunch?"

Pennoyer pointed to a sandwich shop at the corner. They took a booth by the front window. Everything on the menu looked delicious, especially Coors Beer on draft.

They watched pedestrian traffic for the better part of an hour before Roxanne popped the question. "What do we do now?"

He leaned toward her and spoke softly so the kids in the next booth wouldn't hear. "Well, the beer has loosened up this old drunk and you're still crazy about sex, so let's explore the condo upstairs."

Pennoyer handed the waitress his credit card and waited for his receipt. All the while, Roxanne licked her lips and fussed with her hair.

Why make long-term plans, he thought, when short-term was so much fun?

"Mr. Sylvaney?"

"Yes?"

"Just got a hit."

"Great! It's been five weeks, you know."

"The transaction cleared about thirty minutes ago," the caller said.

Pennsylvania's premier private eye raised his cellphone in delight. Two weeks in Toronto and he hadn't located Pennoyer's rehab center yet. His quarry seemed to have dropped off the face of the planet. Bill Pennoyer finally surfaced.

"What did he buy?" Sylvaney asked his source.

"He paid $32.00 at a restaurant, looks like."

"Give me the address and I'll check him out."

"1930 Aspen Street, Littleton, Colorado," the caller said.

"Effing Colorado! Are you serious?" Sylvaney suspected that Tom Zachary fed him misinformation about Toronto, but now he was certain of it.

"Wait, Mr. Sylvaney! Here comes a second transaction … Mile High Lingerie, $85.76, at Crist Plaza … Littleton again."

Sylvaney started plotting air travel from Ontario to Colorado. Nothing was available until tomorrow.

"Third hit, Mr. Sylvaney," the caller said. "Park Center Drug Store … also in Littleton. Your man is moving fast."

The last thing Sylvester Sylvaney wanted was a fast-moving target. But, at least, Pennoyer was spending money again and leaving a trail to be followed. Once Sylvaney reached Colorado, he could zero in on the free-spender.

He hailed a cab for Toronto's airport. He spent his travel time jotting down Pennoyer's credit purchases: restaurant, lingerie store, drug store. For a guy supposedly recovering from alcohol dependency, Pennoyer was acting more like a born-again bachelor.

The new development required a telephone call to Sylvaney's client. Unfortunately, Ann Bailey could not be reached at the governor's home. So Sylvaney left a message with their mutual friend, the innkeeper at Kane Manor.

When he heard the voice mail beep, Sylvaney recorded the following:

"Greg, please tell our lady that the answer to her question is Colorado. I will be visiting the Denver area tomorrow. There is no treatment center involved, I believe.

"One more thing -- someone is being dishonest with you."

Chapter Twenty–One
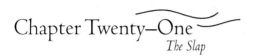
The Slap

By late October, Honorable Mary Anne Graumlich felt confident enough to hear her first capital murder case. So she scheduled a pre-trial conference with the attorneys in *Commonwealth v. Matty Moore* on Monday at 9 a.m., followed by jury selection at 10 a.m.

District Attorney Gil McFadden welcomed the speedy trial. Timing couldn't have been better. Election Day was a week away. A good showing in Butler County Court would erase all those innuendoes about McFadden's incompetence and his gambling habit. And a guilty verdict would smooth the path to his re-election.

Defense attorney Antonio Alfonzi also was happy with the schedule. His opponent had not yet discovered pathologist Elliot Chen's report. Alfonzi would spring that evidence on McFadden at the last minute. Matty would surely be acquitted after Dr. Chen testified about the "impossible timeline," Alfonzi thought.

Judge Graumlich, wearing half-glasses, a white ruffled blouse under her robe and her usual scowl, fixed her eyes on the two combating attorneys.

"Any plea negotiations under way, Mr. McFadden?" she asked through gritted teeth.

"No, Your Honor."

"Mr. Alfonzi? This is your client's last chance to enter a guilty plea."

"We are innocent, Judge Graumlich."

"Yeah, OK. I guess you have a right to trial, but not a long trial. I caution you both..." She wagged her crooked finger at the attorneys. "...I will tolerate no theatrics, no funny business in my courtroom. We will have a verdict in this case by Friday afternoon."

A capital murder trial in five days? Alfonzi was getting nervous. What if McFadden's case dragged on, and Alfonzi had only a few hours left for Dr. Chen?

"Your Honor, our case will be relatively brief," Alfonzi said almost apologetically, "but it may extend into next week..."

"NO, IT WON'T, COUNSELOR!" Judge Graumlich slammed shut her court file. "We're in recess until 10 a.m."

McFadden smiled smugly. "What's wrong, Alfonzi? Afraid you'll run out of time? Won't matter anyway. Your client is toast."

Alfonzi sneered back. "All I need is one hour with Dr. Chen on the stand. He'll rip your case to shreds, Gil. You'll be the laughingstock of Butler County."

"We're not worried about Dr. Chen, Alfonzi. We have a plan for him. The best you can hope for is a jury of idiots." McFadden directed his assistants and his lead police investigator to follow him into the courthouse hallway. There, alone on a bench, sat Zelienople's forlorn police chief Andy Faxon. He tugged at McFadden's sleeve as the prosecution team walked by.

"Give me a minute, Gil," Faxon said. "You need to hear something."

"OK, but I only have a minute." McFadden directed the group to meet him in a witness conference room. The district attorney sat beside Faxon.

"There's been a new development in the case, Gil. You need to ask Judge Graumlich for a continuance."

"Like hell, Faxon! We've got this kid cold and we're picking a jury in a few minutes."

Faxon mustered up some courage. "You've got the wrong guy. I have very strong proof."

"So do I, Faxon. I've got a positive identification from an eyewitness, and we have fingerprint evidence at the murder scene. What have you got?"

"A young man, his name is Shawn Hibler. We recovered pawn tickets for Minka Prybelewski's wedding ring and a handgun. We found stolen lottery tickets from Yer In-Yer Out convenience store. And we have a positive identification from an eyewitness."

"You have this man under arrest, Chief?"

"No, Gil. He died of a cocaine overdose. He's in the County morgue."

"Well, shit, Faxon. I can't try a dead man," McFadden blurted. What he feared most was an aborted trial with a victory by Alfonzi. "What about the gun? Have you recovered it?"

"The gun was sold, Gil. We're trying to track it down …"

"So you haven't linked this man to Billy Herman's murder?"

"Not yet," Faxon replied.

"Good. Then we'll proceed with this trial."

Faxon was incredulous. How could the prosecutor continue in the teeth of so much contrary evidence? The chief protested, "But we have a positive identification by a witness!"

"Who is your witness?" McFadden asked. "Is there someone out there you haven't told me about?"

Yes, there was. Faxon had kept her figuratively and literally under wraps. His "Saturday Night" girlfriend had encountered the raving Shawn Hibler during a home invasion. Faxon could no longer keep his bed companion a secret. So he told the now-aspirating district attorney the whole sordid story.

McFadden processed the facts through his political prism. He had two options. He could expose the Zelienople police chief for his obstruction of justice and his sexual misadventures, or he could ignore the whole situation and proceed to trial against Matty Moore.

He put his arm around Faxon's shoulder and imparted some fatherly advice.

"You're a good man, Andy. You have a bright future. I don't want you to blow it. If the newspapers and radio talk shows learn that the Zelienople police chief failed to report his home invasion because his sex partner was there, you'll be finished."

Faxon knew that, but having an innocent man facing capital punishment seemed much more serious.

McFadden offered some relief. "I'll pretend like you never told me any of this. We'll try the case against this punk and, if he's guilty, the jury will say so. If they return a not guilty verdict, then no harm is done."

"This doesn't seem right to me …" Faxon squirmed from the prosecutor's grasp.

"Sure it is, Andy. Trust the system. Justice will prevail."

Butler County deputy sheriffs herded some newspaper reporters in the hall and directed them to enter the courtroom. Another deputy escorted the defendant, Matty Moore, through the emptied hallway to the courtroom door. For intimidation purposes, McFadden glared at Matty. Minutes later, a courthouse bailiff led a pack of potential jurors through the hallway. One by one, they filtered through the courtroom door. Behind them walked the assistant prosecutors.

"It's time for me to get started, Chief." McFadden rose to his feet and adjusted his necktie.

"What do you want me to do, Gil?" asked a perplexed Faxon.

"Go back to Zelienople," McFadden answered. "Make yourself scarce."

Father Frank McWilliams was summoned to the "Reflection Room," which was located across the hall from Archbishop Ostrow's office. McWilliams had not yet been formally scolded for the Casino Night debacle at Good Shepherd Church. He expected a thorough upbraiding from the archbishop. He could endure anything but a closing of his church.

His worst fear was moments away.

McWilliams was exonerated by Pittsburgh vice detectives after feigning ignorance of the high stakes poker game in his church basement. Sure, he knew the players from his visits to local penitentiaries but, he said, they were "reformed" as far as he could tell. Anyway, he pleaded, "it was all for a good cause."

Pittsburgh's Station 2 commander intervened and absolved McWilliams of all sin. Forgiveness by the archbishop, however, was more problematic. The police raid made page one headlines, embarrassed the neighborhood and placed a target squarely on the struggling parish – a target too attractive for Archbishop Ostrow to ignore.

"Sit." Ostrow commanded the parish priest while firmly closing the Reflection Room doors. "Here's a pen. Sign this check."

The archbishop placed a cashier's check in front of the stunned priest. The draft was payable to Good Shepherd Church in the amount of $500,000.00. McWilliams's face lit up. He smiled as he endorsed the paper.

"Good," Archbishop Ostrow said. "Now keep writing. Make the check payable to the Diocese of Pittsburgh."

"What? Are you serious?" McWilliams asked.

"I don't know what kind of stunt you're pulling, Father Frank, but you're not getting away with it."

McWilliams did as he was told. He handed the cashier's check to his superior.

"Thank you. We received this check from an anonymous donor after the stories hit the newspapers. That was clever, Frank, especially when you were quoted about the church closing if you didn't get enough money."

"But I …" McWilliams really had no "but" to make.

"You had your chance, Frank, and you lost. The damage to your church and our reputation is greater than this check. I've decided to close Good Shepherd once and for all. Start packing because next Sunday will be the last day your doors will be open."

McWilliams sat in stunned silence.

"You'll be reassigned, Frank."

"Yes, Archbishop."

"I think we all learned something from this episode."

"Yes, sir, we have."

Marcy Zachary stood by the telephone. Tom was supposed to call every day at 2 p.m., but apparently he was confused by the time zone difference. "Every day at noon," she had told him. "It's that simple. Mountain Time is two hours behind us."

Zachary finally telephoned her at 6 p.m. Eastern Time.

"Pennoyer was here, Marcy, but he escaped. I think I scared him. I don't understand why; I'm not a threat to him."

"So where are you, Tom?"

"I'm hiding in a golf cart maintenance shed," he said. "Someone reported me as a trespasser and the guards are chasing me. I have to sneak out the front gate without being seen."

"Well, don't rush home," Marcy told him.

"Huh? Why not?"

"The sheriff is trying to serve a subpoena on you. They want you to testify against Matty at his trial this week."

"Gosh, Marcy. I can't do that."

"Everybody is getting a subpoena, Tom. The sheriff served Matty's girlfriend, Megan. They tried to serve old Toolie, but she chased them away with an iron skillet. Jessie hid under her desk at work when the sheriffs came knocking."

"Gee, Marcy, the whole town's getting involved. But none of those people know as much as I do about Matty and Billy Herman. I could connect the dots for the police, maybe even give them a motive. The less I tell them, the better it will be for Matty. Don't accept any subpoena from them, Marcy. Promise me."

"Then keep hiding for a few more days, at least until the trial is over," Marcy replied. "Can you blend in with the other patients there?"

"I don't know, Marcy. Everywhere I look, there are strange people here. It's gonna be real hard to blend in."

"Do your best, Tom."

Ann Bailey felt more like the Ignored Lady than the First Lady. Jimmie seemed as distant as ever. At tonight's dinner table, she tried to engage him in conversation about Matty Moore's upcoming murder trial. Jimmie repeatedly changed the subject and, eventually, told Ann to be quiet.

But she pressed on.

"Jimmie, he's your half-brother. Why don't you take more of an interest in what's happening to him?"

"Stop calling him my brother! He's a punk from the streets of Pittsburgh. I don't know him, and I don't want to know him."

Ann scrunched her napkin and tossed it on her dinner plate. "You can't deny him. He's part of the Bailey family. Instead of pulling away from Matty, we should be supporting him."

"Supporting him? He's a killer! I want nothing to do with him."

"He's a killer, Jimmie? Really? How do you know that?"

"That's what the police say. That's good enough for me..."

"Because, Jimmie, if you have evidence to prove that he's guilty, I'm sure the police would like to see it. From where I'm sitting, he's being railroaded..."

"Stop it, Ann! Just stop it. I have nothing more to say about Matty Moore, his crimes, his trial, nothing..."

Ann pushed her chair from the table. Jimmie's eyes were fixed on the floor.

"Then what should we talk about, Jimmie?"

"Nothing," he mumbled again.

"I know," Ann said, acting perky. "Let's talk about your friend, Bill Pennoyer."

"No, no," Jimmie said, obviously annoyed.

"Yes, we should. I miss Bill. It's been a few months now. How is he doing?"

Jimmie was silent.

"You know, Jimmie, I can't figure this out. I've worked closely with Bill for the past four or five years. I never saw him drink anything stronger than Rolling Rock Beer. How could he have an alcohol addiction and hide it so well? Am I missing something, Jimmie?"

"I've known him since college, Ann. He doesn't drink in public. He's embarrassed about his habit. It reached a point where his health was compromised, that's all. He asked for time off to overcome it. As his boss and his best friend, the least I could do was give him time to work things out. Certainly, you can understand why everything is hush-hush. No reason for the staff or the News-Leader to get wind of this."

"But this is me, Jimmie. You can tell me."

"Well, now you have the story. Just keep it confidential."

"Have you talked to him at all?" Ann persisted. "Is he still in rehab?"

"No, he doesn't take calls. I guess he's still in rehab. Let's change the subject."

"The staff keeps asking me when Bill is coming back. What should I tell them, Jimmie?"

"Tell them to mind their own business."

"Well, can you at least tell me? I'm your wife, remember?"

"Don't be sarcastic, Ann. I've told you everything I know about Pennoyer."

"Have you, Jimmie? You didn't tell me where his rehab center was located."

"That's a private matter, Ann. No one knows."

"You're wrong, Jimmie. I know where Bill is."

He faked a chuckle. "Oh yeah? Tell me."

"Colorado."

"What?!" Jimmie stood so quickly his chair fell backward. "How do you know that? Nobody is supposed to know that."

"Why didn't you tell me, Jimmie? I have a sister who lives in Boulder. We could have visited Bill and stayed with her…"

"How did you find out?" His voice was louder. "Tell me."

Ann walked toward him with a self-assured swagger. "Don't threaten me, Jimmie Bailey. If you had been honest from the start, I would have trusted you. But you sneaked into the house in the middle of night, covered with mud and scratches, scaring my mother half to death. Then you concocted a story about getting into a fight with Pennoyer. The next thing I know is that he's gone, and you're not giving me the full explanation."

"You owe **me** an explanation." He pointed a finger in her face. "Who told you that Pennoyer was in Colorado?"

"I have my sources, Jimmie."

He grabbed her wrist and pulled her violently toward his face. "I'm ordering you one last time to tell me…"

"Let me go!" Ann tried to pull away but his grip was too strong.

"Tell me!"

"I'm entitled to know what's going on with your life, Jimmie. And if you don't tell me, I'm going to find out from other people. Got it?"

He gripped her arm past the point of pain. She grimaced and tried to push back.

"You're hurting me, Jimmie. Stop!"

"Tell me! Tell me now!"

She gritted her teeth as his grip intensified. Through the pain, she uttered: "I hired Sylvester Sylvaney to track him down. I wanted to find out from Pennoyer what happened that night."

Jimmie screamed a profanity. He threw her arms from him and, with an open hand and speed that only anger can create, slapped her face. The blow sent Ann reeling to the right, causing her to fall against a side table.

"Don't talk to me about trust!" Jimmie towered over his fallen wife. After a few seconds, he unclenched his fists, turned and walked away.

When shock abated, Ann began to sob. Real or imagined, she heard a baby's soft cry. She suddenly knew what to do. With all the strength she could muster, Ann pulled herself to her feet and sprinted to the nursery. There, in an otherwise empty room, was baby Hannah – her head raised beyond the side padding of her crib, her eyes sparkling at the sight of her mother.

Ann lifted her daughter, cradling the baby's head against her shoulder. Ann began to shake nervously. The past five years had been erased in one violent second. All that was left was Hannah Maria. She clung to the child like her only life preserver.

Crashing noises came from the study. Jimmie was throwing something around, she thought. Maybe his trophies, his awards or framed mementoes were being tossed. None of it mattered to Ann anymore. If Jimmie wanted to destruct, that was his choice.

Ann stuffed a box of disposable diapers and formula into Hannah's bag. Then she gathered some clothes and items from the master bedroom. She took her keys from a dresser drawer and carried everything down the back stairway. Unnoticed by anyone, Ann stepped outside the back door and to her car. She strapped Hannah in her car seat, slid the bag beside her baby and took a last look at Leigh-Rose Mansion.

The grand mansion had weathered many Bailey family storms – loneliness, unfaithfulness and deadly tragedy. Surely, she thought, the mansion could endure one more. She eased her car along onto the gravel driveway, passing the enormous front lawn where she and Jimmie celebrated their wedding reception. She passed remains of the enormous spruce tree that had been split by lightning during the horrific July 2003 storm. She turned to see the governor's study window. Behind it, she thought, was Jimmie's private Hell.

She repressed any feelings of sorrow for him.

He didn't deserve pity. No abuser deserves pity.

South on Sowers Road and a right turn onto Route 6. Ann was fifteen minutes away from tonight's destination.

Hopefully, Gregory had a spare room at the Kane Manor
Bed & Breakfast. She would call Gloria, her mother, in the
morning. Maybe the proper words to tell her mother would
come to Ann overnight.

The gently bouncing car eased Hannah to sleep. Her little
chest heaved with every long breath. The baby was at peace.
Ann was in turmoil.

Nothing would ever be the same after tonight,
she thought.

Nothing could ever be the same.

Chapter Twenty–Two
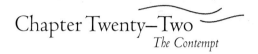

The Contempt

The die was cast at 2:32 p.m. Mountain Daylight Time.

At that moment, Bill Pennoyer swiped his debit card at King Soopers in Littleton, Colorado. Sylvester Sylvaney was waiting in his car only two blocks away.

"Go east on South Park and turn north on Broadway, Sy," said a voice on the investigator's cellphone.

"Gotcha."

"Pennoyer's probably exiting the store. … Wait, he's using his debit card again."

"Where is he now?" Sylvaney asked.

"Looks like a movie rental kiosk," the investigator's friend said. "Movietime, something or other."

"Same address?" Sylvaney asked as he turned left and headed south. King Soopers was a block ahead on the left.

"Yeah," said the voice on his telephone.

"Got a visual!" Sylvaney had Pennoyer in his sights. "I owe you big time, buddy."

"Go get 'em, Sy."

Pennoyer loaded two sacks into the trunk of a waiting car. Sylvaney observed at a safe distance. The face was surely familiar, but Pennoyer's outfit was quite unusual: a bright paisley shirt tapered at the waist, silk bell-bottom slacks and a studded belt. Sylvaney thought Pennoyer looked like a French fashion model, except for his roly-poly waist and thinning hair.

Sylvaney eased his car a bit closer. He watched Pennoyer slip into the passenger seat. Sylvaney tried to observe the driver but their car windows were heavily tinted. He followed them from the supermarket parking lot onto Broadway. He pulled up beside Pennoyer's window at the first traffic light.

A woman was driving – a very attractive woman in Sylvaney's eyes. Pennoyer was smiling and talking with her. Pennoyer had a bunch of grapes in his palm, and he reached over and popped one in the driver's mouth. Sylvaney watched them lock together in a Hollywood movie kiss, a kiss so intense that the lady driver failed to notice a green light.

When car horns began honking, Pennoyer rolled down his window and spit the grape toward Sylvaney's car.

Sylvaney confirmed it was Pennoyer.

And Pennoyer, to his shock, confirmed it was Sylvaney.

"Roxy, quick! Turn right now!" Pennoyer practically grabbed the steering wheel as traffic cleared on East Mineral.

"What the …"

"I'll tell you later. Just keep driving." Pennoyer looked at his side mirror and saw Sylvaney's car making a U-turn to follow them. "Keep going, make your next right turn."

"Who is it, Bill? Who's chasing us?"

"Someone's hired a private investigator from Pennsylvania. Oh shit, he saw us. I'm screwed."

"Jeez, Bill. This is like homecoming week for you. First, your newspaper editor and now a damn private eye. What's going on?"

Pennoyer's breathing was getting faster. "I feel faint, Roxy." He fumbled with his seat controls. "How do you put this thing back?"

She unhooked his seat belt. "Lean forward. Put your head between your knees." She pushed his back forward and

felt his tense shoulders. Roxanne looked up in time to see
Sylvaney's car flying past them on Mineral.

"He's gone, Bill. We lost him."

Pennoyer straightened and heaved a sigh of relief. "I'm
so sorry I scared you," he said. "I feel like I'm running from
the law. Everyone's coming after me."

"Don't be silly, Bill. If the police knew you shot a man,
they wouldn't send a private eye or a newspaperman to arrest
you. There would be helicopters and dogs and S.W.A.T.
teams surrounding us now."

If her words were meant to comfort, they did not.
Pennoyer sunk into his seat and pulled his paisley collar
to cover his neck and chin. "Sylvaney's good, Roxy. He's
the best investigator there is. But I don't understand how he
found me. Only one person knows where I am, and I don't
understand why Jimmie's talking."

"Two people, Bill. Don't forget the editor."

"Not much of a secret anymore, is it?" Pennoyer patted
her knee. Roxanne was his only friend now. He looked at her
with the eyes of a beagle waiting to be petted.

Roxanne shifted into drive and turned the car toward the
highway. "We've got cheese, wine and a movie. Let's go
home and eat, drink and be merry."

"For tomorrow we shall die?" Pennoyer clicked his
seat beat.

"No, Bill. For tonight we shall love."

Judge Graumlich was right on schedule. Her schedule.

The jury in *Commonwealth v. Matthew Moore* was
selected by noon. Juror No. 1, the likely foreman, was retired
plumber Ralph Metzgar. Juror No. 2 was Beatrice Hileman,
a retired nurse. Juror No. 3 was Walt Bienick, a retired
school teacher.

The pattern continued. The rest were mostly retired, old or both. Matty's attorney, Antonio Alfonzi, looked into the jurors' eyes. He imagined each of them with their finger on the electric chair switch. Of course, Alfonzi didn't tell his client about the awful jury. Matty had the innocent and naïve idea that justice would be served.

As bleak as the jury appeared, Alfonzi held onto a glimmer of hope for Matty's acquittal. Hope sat in seat number four of the jury box. His name was Curtis Klepper, and he didn't fit the profile of a Butler County juror. He was young, actively employed and overly polite. He seemed a bit nervous and easily distracted. Most importantly, Mr. Klepper appeared to be too nice to hurt anyone.

Alfonzi hoped that Klepper was strong enough to keep his opinions in the jury deliberation room. Then, perhaps, Matty Moore's trial could end with a hung jury. So the attorney decided to direct his full attention and arguments to Mr. Klepper. All Alfonzi needed was to win the heart and mind of one of the twelve. Klepper was it.

District Attorney Gil McFadden opened to the jury using a selection of morbid photographs. Zelienople's police photographer had captured the murder scene in colorful glory. A pool of blood beside Billy Herman's slumped corpse seemed unusually bright red, as though the shooting had occurred only minutes earlier.

"Objection, Your Honor." Alfonzi interrupted McFadden's opening statement. "These photographs have not been authenticated. We don't know when they were taken, how they were taken and whether they are accurate representations of the scene."

Judge Graumlich let her index finger do the talking. She summoned counsel to the bench.

"Mr. Alfonzi, your objection is overruled. If you don't like the photos, you can cross-examine the police witnesses. I've warned you both about objections. They slow down the trial. They annoy me and the jury. As your punishment, Mr. Alfonzi, your next three objections also are overruled. Do you understand me?"

"But, judge ..."

"Shut up and sit down," Graumlich whispered, while smiling at the jurors who strained to hear. "You may continue, Mr. McFadden."

Happy with three free passes in his pocket, McFadden pressed his case more fiercely.

"Ladies and gentlemen of the jury, the Commonwealth will prove to you that the *criminal* sitting there at defense table, Matthew Moore, pulled the trigger..."

"Objection. My client is not a criminal, Your Honor!" Alfonzi sprang to his feet.

"Overruled. Sit!"

McFadden continued. "As I was saying before the criminal's attorney interrupted ..."

"Objection. I am not the attorney of a criminal!" Alfonzi remained seated.

"Stand when you address the court." Graumlich held her gavel at eye level. She dropped it when Alfonzi stood. "Overruled. Sit!"

McFadden stared at his opposing counsel. Then he turned to face the jury. He rolled his eyes to ridicule Alfonzi's courtroom behavior. McFadden then pointed to the defense table.

"They don't want you to hear the truth, but I'll tell you. In my 20 years as your district attorney, I have never witnessed such a callous, cruel and despicable act in Butler County. With every fiber of my being, I believe that Matthew Moore shot and killed in cold blood..."

"Object..." Alfonzi's rage with the judge exceeded his boiling point.

264 Z<small>ELIENOPLE</small> R<small>OAD</small>

"Overruled." Graumlich interrupted, holding up three fingers to McFadden. His free ride had expired. "How much longer is your opening?"

"I am finished, Your Honor," he said, winking at the jurors.

"Very well," the judge responded. "Mr. Alfonzi, you may begin your brief opening."

The chastened defense counsel stood before the jury. Half of them already made up their minds. So Alfonzi spoke to Juror No. 4.

"Thank you for your service today. And thank you for your promise to keep an open mind about Mr. Moore's guilt or innocence until all the evidence has been presented. What Mr. McFadden said to you is not evidence. Those photographs are not evidence. His opinions are not evidence. The law requires you to pay attention to our evidence as well."

Mr. Metzgar did not make eye contact with Alfonzi. Ms. Hileman was smiling at the district attorney. Old Mrs. Schandelmeier's eyes were closed. But Juror No. 4, Mr. Klepper, listened intently. There was still hope.

"You will hear uncontroverted testimony that my client, Matthew Moore, was elsewhere at the time of the murder. We will fix the time of death through expert medical testimony ..."

"Objection!" McFadden jumped, nearly knocking over his water pitcher. "May we approach, Your Honor?"

Again, attorneys were summoned by the Judge's index finger.

"What now, McFadden?"

"Your Honor," the district attorney replied, "Mr. Alfonzi referred to expert medical testimony. I'd like an offer of proof."

"Gil knows what I'm talking about, Judge. But here it is. We have retained Dr. Elliot Chen for his opinion about the time of death. Dr. Chen will testify that Billy Herman died shortly after midnight. About that time, Mr. Moore was stopped at a police checkpoint on Perry Highway. He couldn't be two places at once. That's our alibi, Your Honor."

"OK. So Mr. Moore wasn't the killer, Mr. McFadden," the judge said. "Let's dismiss this case and we all can go home."

McFadden chuckled. "Not so fast, Alfonzi. You know and I know that Dr. Chen was hired by Zelienople police to investigate. You can't bring him into court to testify against the police. That's a conflict of interest."

"No it's not, McFadden…" Alfonzi started to argue.

"Show some respect, Alfonzi." Judge Graumlich glared at defense counsel. "Don't call him by his last name. It's Mr. McFadden!"

"Sorry, Your Honor," Alfonzi grumbled.

"What's all this about Dr. Chen being hired by Zelienople police?" the judge asked.

"He was never 'hired' because they never paid him, Your Honor. Dr. Chen was the first medical examiner on the scene. He has all of the information. He's a critical witness for the defense."

McFadden edged closer to the bench. "Chen was invited to the scene by Chief Faxon …"

"Be quiet, Mr. McFadden," the judge interrupted. "I'm thinking."

Juror Marion Rouzer's hand was raised. "A smoke break, Judge?"

Graumlich recessed the jury for five minutes. After the last juror closed a side door, the judge returned to her combatants.

"Dr. Chen usually has a lot to say, Mr. Alfonzi," the judge said. "How long do you expect his testimony to last?"

Alfonzi gave a conservative estimate. "Probably about two hours."

McFadden spoke up. "And our cross-examination will take about two days, Your Honor. We will challenge his credentials. We'll go through all the cases where he's testified for criminal defendants, et cetera, et cetera. It will be very thorough, Judge."

A difficult ruling suddenly became easy. Dr. Chen and his rambling days of testimony were not going to delay her Caribbean vacation.

"The objection is sustained. Dr. Chen will not testify." Graumlich banged her gavel as though the bang made her decision providential.

"What?" Alfonzi reeled backward. "This can't be happening."

"Are you questioning my decision?" Graumlich stared daggers.

"Judge, you're sending an innocent man to jail. Dr. Chen's testimony will acquit him."

"Cease your outrageous behavior, counsel," Graumlich scolded. "I have the power to hold you in contempt for such impertinence."

"All defendant seeks is a fair trial," Alfonzi pleaded. "That is not impertinent."

"Bailiff!" Graumlich hollered. "Please confine Antonio Alfonzi to counsel table for the remainder of this trial. He has committed contempt in my presence. When trial is in recess, he is to be held in the Butler County Jail. He is not permitted any visitors, including his client."

"But, Your Honor…" Alfonzi tried to defend himself.

"All is not lost, counsel," the judge interjected. "You may purge yourself of the contempt by agreeing to certain conditions. One, you will not make any more oral objections at trial. If you have an objection, write it on paper and hand it to the bailiff. I will consider your objection during a recess.

Second, you are limited to ten cross-examination questions per witness. Third, the only witness you may call to the stand is your client. That's it. Do you agree to those conditions, counselor?"

Alfonzi looked at Graumlich as though she studied law in North Korea. "I respectfully decline, Your Honor."

"That's unfortunate for you, Mr. Alfonzi." She pointed to her bailiff. "Please place leg irons on both defendant and his counsel while the court is in recess. We will reconvene at 1 p.m.

"Additionally, upon consideration of the Commonwealth's opening statement, the court hereby finds substantial evidence that Mr. Moore is a danger to the community, that his bond should be revoked and that he should be placed in the custody of Butler County Sheriff immediately.

"So ordered!"

Rage reduced to anger. Anger became confusion.

And confusion ended in regret.

Guilt-riddled Jimmie Bailey was alone in Leigh-Rose Mansion. He had committed the very act for which he had condemned his father. Jimmie had abused the only woman who ever loved him. As darkness set in the Kinzua Valley, Jimmie felt profound loneliness.

He wondered if Ann could ever forgive him. Probably not. Even if she did, things could never be the same, he thought.

Little Hannah was gone from his life as well, he realized. Just like that. One stupid act. One moment of irrationality. Would his daughter ever learn what her daddy had done? Would he be part of her life – ever?

All of this thinking was painful. But his hurting thoughts never stopped.

Was he exactly like his cheating father? No, Brock had an affair that destroyed his marriage. Jimmie was not unfaithful to Ann, but his abuse was physical. Was that worse?

Ann had stumbled and fallen when he struck her. Was she injured? She was able to walk out and take their daughter, he thought. How was she now? Where was she now?

Jimmie sat quietly in his study. Through the front window, he watched perimeter security lighting flicker on through stands of pine trees. His telephone, which had rung incessantly all day, was eerily silent as though nobody cared about him anymore.

Why should anyone care? His governorship was ending in a couple years. His career in baseball was over. He had no marketable trade. His family had abandoned him.

Worst of all, he was a punk. Whenever life had thrown a curve at him, he acted upon impulse and emotion. Never had he owned up to his mistakes, taken any blame or said he was sorry. He easily pushed people out of his life. Now, at the ebb of his life, did he have the courage and strength to pull people back to him?

Everything was so complicated now. A man was shot and killed by Jimmie's gun. Jimmie had placed the gun in the hand of his best friend. The killing was in self-defense, of course, but is it self-defense when you've broken into someone's house? Pennoyer would be dead if he hadn't shot first, Jimmie thought. But what judge or jury would be sympathetic to a couple of bungling trespassers, especially when they take along a loaded handgun?

None of this was supposed to happen. The plan was to scare Billy Herman. Throw the rock through his bedroom window. Surprise him at night in his remote farmhouse. Get him to confess to his murder of the state police commissioner. Pennoyer carried a tape recorder to secure Herman's confession. All of that worked out. Once Jimmie had the audio confession, Herman's extortion of him would have ended. That was the plan. It all went awry when Herman reached for his revolver and a panicky Pennoyer unloaded a round into Herman's torso.

But the audiotape. Pennoyer still had it. That would explain everything to the police, Jimmie thought. Herman was a murderer himself, and the governor's extortion payments to him could be verified with wire transfer entries. Jimmie's financial advisor, Dennis Padgett, could provide those records to the police. Given the circumstances, Jimmie thought, Pennoyer's charges could be reduced to manslaughter. Maybe Jimmie could escape with a lesser charge, like accessory after the fact or even a misdemeanor.

Complicating matters was the ongoing trial of his half-brother, Matty Moore. News accounts from the courtroom pointed to a conviction in a few days. Matty's fingerprints were found in a stolen car at Herman's house, and his attorney failed to explain them away. As feelings of guilt bore down on him, Jimmie considered contacting the Butler County district attorney to confess his role in the murder. It was a fleeting thought, however, because the resulting shame to his family would be unbearable. Jimmie decided to contact his best friend instead.

After several attempts to reach Pennoyer on his cell phone at 9 p.m. Eastern Time, Jimmie called the Castle Rock Center directly. An evening receptionist was impenetrable.

"Our policy prohibits direct contact with the public while a patron is undergoing treatment here, Mister …"

"Governor Bailey of Pennsylvania," Jimmie said.

"Mister, governor, king … it doesn't matter who you are. I can't patch you in to Mr. Pennoyer's suite."

"So there is a telephone in his suite?" Jimmie asked.

"Yes, sir. The best I can do is leave a message and, if he wishes, he can return your call."

"Tell him that Jimmie called, and that he must return my call. Also tell him that a private investigator is on his trail ..."

"Just a minute, sir." The receptionist paused. Jimmie could hear some muffled conversation with another woman.

"Hello, Governor Bailey. My name is Catherine. I'm Mr. Pennoyer's life coach here at Castle Rock Center. We have a situation here. Maybe you can help us. Mr. Pennoyer recognized an intruder at a group session the other day. He suffered an episode and escaped from our facility. Do you know his whereabouts?"

Sylvester Sylvaney had indeed tracked down Pennoyer, Jimmie thought.

"This intruder, did you apprehend him?" Jimmie asked.

"No, he remains at large on our property. We will find him," Catherine said.

"Is his name Sylvaney?"

"I don't know. Maybe he signed in using a fake name."

"What name?" Jimmie asked.

"Thomas Zachary."

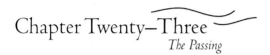

Chapter Twenty–Three
The Passing

District Attorney Gil McFadden directed his final questions to the Commonwealth's star witness, Nata Prybelewski.

"Look around the courtroom. Do you see the man who fired a gun at you on your parents' front porch last August?"

"I do." Nata had identified Matty Moore in a Zelienople Police line-up months ago. Why should she change her story now?

"Could you point to the man so that our jury can see?"

"Yes, sir." Nata stood and leveled her accusatory finger at Matty. Several jurors nodded in approval. Judge Graumlich merely looked at her watch.

"Let the record reflect this witness has identified the defendant, Matty Moore, as the gunman. Thank you Ms. Prybelewski. I have no further questions."

Matty's attorney, Antonio Alfonzi, stood and shuffled a step to the right. His leg irons clanged together as McFadden smiled with sadistic satisfaction. Alfonzi estimated that he could ask four questions on cross-examination before Judge Graumlich would rip off his head. He was wrong by one.

"Ms. Prybelewski, you really didn't have a good look at the robber that night, did you?"

"Objection, Your Honor!" McFadden stood, pointing a menacing finger at Alfonzi. "She testified that she had a good

look, so he's trying to have the witness contradict herself.
He's badgering the witness."

"Objection sustained. Her testimony stands. Don't try to
confuse the witness, Mr. Alfonzi." Judge Graumlich banged
her gavel for extra emphasis.

"Well, then, Ms. Prybelewski, you told police at the
hospital that you weren't sure whether the suspect was white,
black or Hispanic, correct?"

McFadden began to rise, but Judge Graumlich stopped
him with her open palm.

"Whatever objection you were about to make is sustained,"
she told McFadden. "Any statement given by this witness
at the hospital is irrelevant. She positively identified your
client in a police line-up. Confine your questions to that,
counselor."

Alfonzi poured a cup of water from the courtroom pitcher
while he collected his thoughts and curbed his anger. His
next question had better be good, he figured.

"Other than my client, did the police line-up include any
other black men?"

"Your Honor, objection, objection, objection!" McFadden
shouted loud enough to awaken the press corps. "This is
outrageous! Now, he's accusing the brave and courageous
Zelienople police officers of racial bias! Never in my 20
years as a prosecutor have I ..."

Graumlich stopped his speech with a gavel thump. A
second thump halted the swelling murmurs in her courtroom.
She spoke with measured tones, gaining steam like an
eastbound train engine on the Horseshoe Curve.

"Normally, I would call counsel to sidebar so that we
could discuss this matter outside the hearing of our jury.
But Mr. Alfonzi's tactic of injecting race into this trial is
so pathetic and so desperate it mocks the criminal justice
system. I want the jury to hear my response in full.

"Mr. Alfonzi, if you have evidence to support your frail theory of innocence, then come forward with it. Don't insult law enforcement, the prosecutor and the court with flimsy arguments based on racial discrimination. Your client is not here because he is black. He is here because ... well, Mr. McFadden, why is he here?"

"Because he murdered Billy Herman," the district attorney eagerly answered.

"That's the charge, Mr. Alfonzi," Graumlich said. "No one has injected race into this trial until now. And I will not allow you to do so. Do you understand?"

"Yes, but ..."

"That's all, Mr. Alfonzi. I will permit no more questions of this witness. She may step down and is excused. Any more witnesses Mr. McFadden?"

"No, Your Honor," he replied. "The Commonwealth rests."

Graumlich smiled for the first time in a week. The Commonwealth's case had completed several hours earlier than expected. After a 15-minute recess, the defense could begin by 2 p.m. Thursday, the judge calculated. She could frustrate Alfonzi enough to stop his case by day's end as well. A quick jury verdict on Friday and then she could take a weekend flight to the sunny Caribbean.

Alfonzi stood until jurors had filed from the courtroom. He plopped on his chair and turned to his dismayed client.

"You're not testifying," he told Matty. "You can't testify. There's no sensible story you can tell the jury about your fingerprints in the victim's car."

"But I can convince them that I wasn't at Herman's house at the time he died," Matty pleaded. "Just ask me a few questions. You'll see. The jury will like me."

"The jury hates you, Matty. Almost as much as they hate me. The only juror who makes eye contact with us is Mr. Klepper, in seat number 4. He seems to be in our corner. I think he's confused by the evidence."

"Then he wants to hear from me," Matty said.

"No, Matty. We have a chance now for a hung jury. If you testify, McFadden will rip you to pieces. Then we'd have no jurors in our corner."

Matty slumped backward in his chair. He heard a familiar voice talking to him behind the bar. He turned to look past a pair of sheriff deputies.

"Mom, why are you still here?" he asked Tanya as she reached to touch his hand. Two deputies intervened to prevent the contact.

"I'm praying for you, son," she whispered. "That's all we can do."

He noticed a tear in her eye as deputies pushed her from him. "Everything will be all right, Mom. I have a great attorney. You said so yourself."

Alfonzi put his arm around Matty's shoulder. "Thanks for the vote of confidence, kid. I can't guarantee we'll win this, though. Seems like the judge and jury are against us."

Now was probably not the best time, but Matty's attorney had one more issue to raise with his client.

"Since Judge Graumlich found me in contempt and has confined me to the courthouse this week, my law practice is suffering," he told Matty. "I can't return telephone calls. I can't work on other files. I can't send out bills to clients. This is really hitting me in the wallet."

"What are you trying to tell me, Mr. Alfonzi?" Matty asked.

"Simply put, I need another $50,000 to keep my operating running."

Matty shook his head. Now that he was confined to County Jail, he had no access to his trust funds. "How about an I.O.U.? I could sign a paper to promise you twice that much."

"Listen, Matty. I put my neck on the line here for you. I'm in freaking contempt. I have to wear these leg irons in the courtroom. I'm the laughingstock of the defense bar. The least you can do is pay some money to recognize my sacrifice for you."

"I will. I will. I just can't pay you now."

Alfonzi folded his arms and shut his mouth. Matty wondered whether his unpaid attorney would say another word at trial.

Baby Hannah finally settled after a morning of crying and discomfort. Kane Manor's Sunflower Room was large enough to accommodate mother and child, but the Bailey daughter sensed an abrupt change in surroundings. The governor's doting staff members paid no visits. The old bed and breakfast creaked with the steps of passing guests. And, worst of all, Hannah's mother couldn't hide her tearful face.

Greg, the innkeeper, opened his doors and heart to Ann and Hannah. When the First Lady of Pennsylvania appeared at his doorstep last evening, he asked no questions. A veteran of a failed teenage marriage, Greg appreciated the profound heartbreak of a sudden separation. Ann's red eyes told him all that he needed to know.

The Sunflower Room was his largest and most private suite. With two queen beds and a large sitting area near bay windows, Sunflower also was his most sought-after room. Fortunately, the autumn leaf season had ended and demand would drop until cross-country ski season later in November.

But Greg was a man of his word. Ann and Hannah could stay as long as they wanted. He would ensure their privacy while attending to their needs.

After nearly 24 hours in confinement with her infant daughter, Ann needed to venture from the room. When Hannah began to nap, Ann enlisted Greg's housekeeper to watch the baby. She asked Greg for a map of the hiking trail behind Kane Manor. One mile in the fresh air was all she wanted, she told him.

"I've got an hour before I'm needed in the dining room," Greg said to her. "If you don't mind, I'll hike with you."

Ann nodded, and they left through the front door. Greg pointed toward the trail head as he placed a sweatshirt over her shoulders. She mouthed "thank you" and tied the sleeves across her chest.

Meanwhile, the entire episode was witnessed by the governor's financial advisor, Dennis Padgett, from his house across Clay Street. Padgett had noticed Ann's arrival at Kane Manor the previous evening. Innocent? Perhaps. Suspicious? Definitely, he thought. Should he call Jimmie with the information? Not yet. Padgett peered through his binoculars as the couple disappeared into the woods.

"If there's anything you want to talk about, Ann, I'm here to listen," Greg said as they descended toward the valley.

"Thank you, Greg," she answered. "But I really can't. Not right now."

"I understand."

They walked on in silence. He kicked fallen branches to clear her path. The air seemed to cool as they lost elevation. When they reached a clearing about halfway, Ann paused and turned her face to the waning sunlight.

"Do you see it?" she asked him.

"Yes. A bruise on your face."

"Do you understand why I'm not talking?"

"I understand now," he replied.

"Greg, have you ever loved someone so much it hurts?"

No answer was needed. He led her back up the path to Kane Manor. When they reached the front entrance, the foyer telephone was ringing.

Greg excused himself and took the call. "Yes, Mr. Sylvaney. She's right here. Would you like to speak with her?"

He handed the telephone to Ann.

"I found Mr. Pennoyer," Sylvaney told her. "He's no longer in rehab, he's with a girl and ..."

"I don't care anymore," Ann interrupted.

"But I'm so close, Ann. Just another day and I'll get Pennoyer to talk."

"No, Mr. Sylvaney. Just come home. Let Bill live his life in peace."

Marcy stood by the telephone, waiting again for her husband to figure out the time difference between Colorado and Pennsylvania. It took four days' worth of explanation. On Thursday, Zachary finally called at the proper hour, Eastern Time.

"Tom, come home," she told him. "Matty's case has gone to the jury. Your subpoena has expired. You're safe. We expect a verdict tomorrow."

"Great," he said. "I can't wait to get back to Kane. I'm so hungry, cold and tired. Castle Rock Center for Lifestyle Wellness is no place for this country boy. The security guards are still looking for me. Even the prairie dogs are trying to sniff my trail."

"Are you still hiding in the golf cart shed?" Marcy asked.

"No. I couldn't sleep with all those recharging batteries humming," Zachary replied. "Right now I'm in the back of a vending company truck. If I have one more olive sesame cracker, I'll die of savoriness. I think that's a new word."

"Jessie needs you," Marcy said. "She's trying so hard to get the paper out on time, and without Matty there's no local news."

"How's Matty doing?" Zachary asked. "Have you found food that he'll eat? I'll bet he's exhausted when he gets home from the trial."

Marcy told him the sad news. "Matty's bond was revoked by the judge. He's now in the Butler County Jail. I don't know if he'll ever be free again."

"Gosh, Marcy. Don't get all weepy. I'll be back soon and we'll make sure he's free. Matty is innocent. The jury will believe him when he testifies. Has he testified ..."

"Tom, what's that noise?"

"Hey, someone's driving the truck. We're heading past the guardhouse and through the front gate. I'm free!"

Roxanne hand-pressed her lover's paisley shirt and draped it over a kitchen chair. She pulled a hanger from the bedroom closet for Pennoyer's designer slacks. His socks, shoes and underwear were still tousled in the hallway, exactly where they threw them last night.

Their lovemaking had been more intense than ever. It was rough, then tender, then frantic, then romantic, then loud, then playful, then oh so lovey-dovey. Never in her history of conquest did Roxanne have such an enjoyable horizontal experience. Certainly, Pennoyer had appreciated her attention; he thanked her profusely all night.

She smiled at the thought that no other man was attractive to her. Short, stubby, balding Bill Pennoyer, of all the male specimens in the world, was the man who cured Roxanne of her sex addiction. Who could ever imagine that such a man would be as fluent in body language? All of the so-called professional counselors at Castle Rock Center never taught her the lesson she learned from Pennoyer. Sex without love is hollow. "Sex with love is," as Pennoyer mumbled to her between the sheets, "heaven."

Roxanne belted her robe as Pennoyer lay still. They had fallen asleep about 3 a.m. She was awakened about 5 a.m. She sensed that someone was staring at her. She turned to see his grinning face and yearning eyes. He reached to her and pulled her close. Then he ran his fingers through her hair. She felt his warm breath and, in the comfort of the moment, closed her eyes and drifted off. She was secure in a lover's embrace – a feeling that could never be forgotten.

As the Colorado sun filtered through their bedroom shades, she covered him with a comforter. She stood at his bedside for several minutes, just watching his chest fall and rise with every breath. She giggled when he nuzzled his nose deeper into the pillow. She detected his smug look of satisfaction. Perhaps he was dreaming of their night together.

"Sleep while you may, my beautiful man," she whispered. "Tonight will follow today. A night will follow tomorrow. And I will be with you for every night and day."

Roxanne stepped toward the bedroom door. Her foot kicked something that had fallen from Pennoyer's slacks. She bent down to the floor and picked up his audiotape. She recalled the night he played the tape for her. She shuddered when she remembered hearing the desperate shot by Pennoyer, the shot that saved his life but killed a wicked man.

Why was he keeping this tape, she wondered. If police ever listened to it, she thought, her lover would be arrested for murder. "Bill Pennoyer, Convicted Killer," newspaper headlines would scream. And beside the story would be a photograph of the woman "who will love him when he's released in 40 years." The idea horrified her. Pennoyer was the man she wanted to grow old with. She could not face life if he got life. This audiotape was the only piece of evidence that could doom him, she thought. It should be destroyed.

Roxanne placed the audiotape in the pocket of her robe. The bedroom digital clock read 10 a.m. Suddenly, she was hungry. So she decided to attempt breakfast. She entered the small kitchen and rummaged through cabinets for food. The owners, whoever they were, apparently were firm believers in digestive health. All she could find were pouches of instant oatmeal, canisters of prunes and high fiber pancake mix. She looked at the mix – all it required was water. Might as well try it, she thought.

No one ever said Roxanne was good in the kitchen, except for the busboy she once entertained after hours at White Castle. But she remembered how the short order cook there greased skillets and poured batter in circles. A little flip and a flip back and, voila, hotcakes! Seemed easy enough.

Roxanne poked a spout in the pancake box and measured a cup's worth into a bowl. She added water slowly until the mixture became slurry. She beat the bowl with tremendous hip action. After a particularly violent thrust, Pennoyer's audiotape slipped from her pocket.

She placed the tape on a kitchen counter, only inches from a ledge that was two feet above a wastebasket. A simple flick of her wrist, she thought, and the incriminating evidence would be forever lost. If she trashed the tape, would her lover forgive her? Would he understand that she loved him so much that she needed to protect him?

She stared at the tape hoping to move it with her eyes. Its fall into oblivion then would not be from her hand. Maybe if she opened a kitchen window the Chinook winds would blow it off the countertop, she thought.

Roxanne was consumed by the wickedness of the tape. It seemed to pulsate with evil. It needed to be expelled. She began pushing it with her fingers. An inch. Then two inches. The ledge was getting closer.

She poured the batter onto a heated skillet and watched her high fiber pancakes bubble. She flipped them a few times. She dropped her spatula with a clang before returning her attention to the tape.

Bill Pennoyer did not hear his newfound love in the next room. In his dreamlike stupor, he only heard his softening heartbeat and irregular breathing. He imagined that Roxy was beside him, her sweet voice calling to him, her supple skin exciting him again. He allowed a smile to cross his lips. An unexpected warmth crossed his heart.

Peace enveloped him as slowly, ever so slowly, the last lipid lodged in his left ventricle.

When Roxanne pushed his audiotape into the kitchen wastebasket, Pennoyer's heart blockage was complete.

His last breath conveyed only negligible oxygen to his brain – sufficient for him to experience the absolute joy of love discovered.

Perhaps Mr. William Pennoyer didn't know how to live.

But he sure knew how to die.

Chapter Twenty–Four
The Verdict

Antonio Alfonzi won a brief reprieve from Judge Graumlich. She permitted him to address the jury without wearing leg irons. Unfortunately, a wrinkled impression remained on the cuffs of his Hugo Boss trousers.

"You cannot convict my client, Matty Moore, unless the Commonwealth has met its burden of guilt beyond a reasonable doubt," Alfonzi told the jury. "That is the highest level of proof required under law. To convict Mr. Moore, you must be nearly absolutely certain that he fired the gun that killed Billy Herman."

Juror No. 1, Mr. Metzgar, nodded in approval – not approving the burden of proof but approving a guilty verdict. So Alfonzi turned his attention to Juror No. 2.

"Murder in the first degree requires premeditation in Pennsylvania. Mr. McFadden has offered no evidence that my client either knew the victim or that he planned any crime. There is no motive. There is no murder weapon. True, he was in the vicinity a few hours before the body was discovered, but so were about a million other people."

Juror No. 2, Beatrice Hileman, bristled at his insinuation that any member of the Butler County jury could be a suspect in such a horrible crime. Police arrested the best suspect they could find, she reasoned. More important to her, the crime spree stopped after Matty Moore was arrested. That proved Matty's guilt in her mind.

"In our great country," Alfonzi continued, eyeing up Juror No. 3, "a criminal defendant enjoys a presumption of innocence. That is the bulwark of our criminal justice system."

Juror No. 3, Walter Bienick, thought it was bull, all right. Innocence, schminnocence. Why was this kid driving his souped-up Mustang on the back roads of Butler County at 3 a.m.? If he didn't shoot Mr. Herman, Bienick reckoned, Matty Moore was up to no good anyway. He should be punished for whatever he was doing, Bienick thought.

"All of you have taken a sacred oath as jurors to consider only the evidence you heard in this courtroom," Alfonzi argued. "Use your common sense and the law to reach your verdict. Do not use prejudice or rely on anything you heard outside this trial."

Juror No. 5, retired telephone operator Marian Rouzer, sneered. Confine herself to just the testimony at trial? She didn't think so. Rouzer was a talk radio junkie. She followed news from the trial every day on her car radio. And it's a good thing she did. Otherwise, Rouzer would not have learned that Alfonzi flunked the bar exam twice before he squeaked by; Butler County's district attorney had an impressive 97 percent conviction record, and Matty Moore grew up in the crime-infested neighborhood of East Liberty. Only yesterday Rouzer telephoned an afternoon talk show to complain how criminals are coddled in Pennsylvania.

"Now, when you go back into the jury room to deliberate," Alfonzi plowed forward, "remember that Matthew Moore is entitled to all of the rights and privileges of your neighbors, your family and, indeed, every citizen of the United States."

Juror No. 6, the elderly Mrs. Schandelmeier, hissed. That juvenile delinquent deserves rights, she thought – an electrode on his right arm and an electrode on his right leg.

"And so, in closing, my client joins me in thanking you for your service as jurors and we are confident that, when you consider the Commonwealth's weak evidence in this case, you will return a verdict of not guilty."

Alfonzi smiled at his only friend in the courtroom – Juror No. 4. Curtis Klepper seemed to absorb and process each word of Alfonzi's closing. There was still a chance of acquittal, the attorney thought, struggling to find some glint of hope.

Judge Graumlich pronounced her instructions to the jurors before dismissing them to their deliberation room. "We're in recess until they have a verdict," she announced. The crowd stood as the judge exited through her side door.

Before she could unzip her robe, Graumlich encountered her frantic secretary. A young gentleman was waiting in her outer lobby. He had demanded a meeting with Her Honor because his "business was very important." It was something official, he had said.

"I don't want to see anyone," the judge told her. "I've got a headache. So many objections. So many frivolous motions. These attorneys are completely inept. Some days I think this job is a waste of my talents."

But the secretary insisted that she make time. The visitor identified himself as an investigator from Pennsylvania's Judicial Conduct Board. He had papers emblazoned with an official Pennsylvania Supreme Court seal.

Suddenly, the judge's headache was forgotten. "Send him in," she ordered.

Her handshake with the Judicial Conduct staff attorney was perfunctory. "What's this all about, young man?"

"Pursuant to the Judicial Code, I'm required to advise you of a complaint filed by the Pennsylvania Criminal Defense Bar," the investigator said.

"Those weasels! What are they claiming?"

The investigator flipped through a thick document. "In a nutshell, they complain that you acted with reckless disregard of Pennsylvania law when you held one of their members, Mr. Alfonzi, in criminal contempt. They claim you are hostile, biased, incompetent, ignorant of the rules of evidence and, let me quote from page 253: 'a canker on the body of jurisprudence.' It goes on and on."

The judge was filled with rancor when she was called a canker.

"You can tell Judicial Board members that Mr. Alfonzi's conduct was inexcusable. He accused me of being unfair! Imagine that. My trials are absolutely fair. When this jury comes back with a guilty verdict, the criminal defense attorneys will see how fair my sentence will be."

"But the verdict could be not guilty," the investigator said meekly.

"Not according to my bailiff," Graumlich replied. "He's talked to some of the jurors already. One told him that they voted a couple days ago. They're only dragging out the deliberations long enough to get a free lunch today."

"Does the defense attorney know that your bailiff is talking to the jurors?" the investigator asked.

"Hell, no," Graumlich said. "If he did, he'd file another stupid motion for mistrial."

The investigator handed her his business card, slightly bowed and left her chambers. Graumlich shimmied from her robe and collapsed on her leather sofa. No sense in getting upset over weak complaints from lesser attorneys. After all, she was a judge, appointed to her lofty position by the Governor of Pennsylvania.

Accordingly, her thoughts shifted to a certain cabana nestled under the tropical sun thousands of miles to the south. In her briefcase were four nonrefundable airline tickets.

Father Frank McWilliams read each word of the bill of lading. His disbelief was fading. Archbishop Ostrow truly was closing Good Shepherd Church.

"Delivery of all goods and chattel to Diocese of Pittsburgh through its assignee, St. Agnes Church. All such personal property shall be prepared for ordinary over-the-ground transportation by Shipper. Carrier is not liable for any damage or breakage caused in part by Shipper's failure to adequately package such goods for transportation."

For all intents and purposes, the bill of lading was his marching orders.

With help from his stronger parishioners, Father Frank enclosed his largest concrete cast statues in styrofoam and bubble wrap. His marble altar was disassembled and packed in numbered boxes. Smaller religious items were wrapped in towels or green felt and placed in Father Frank's automobile. These he would deliver personally to his sister church.

Everything else was bolted down – the oak pews, kneelers, Stations of the Cross plaques and baptismal font. These would be auctioned off after they were appraised by the Diocese.

McWilliams watched a mover struggling with the church poor box. He helped the worker unscrew it from its pedestal. McWilliams directed him to take whatever coins it held.

Hanging above the poor box pedestal was the only relic he wanted to keep. It was a framed photograph of McWilliams and his law school classmate, the late Governor Brock Bailey. The photograph depicted the elder Bailey's campaign rally at Good Shepherd. McWilliams always viewed the event as more than a political stunt; it was a tribute to the Good Shepherd community and its importance in western

Pennsylvania. McWilliams unhooked the photo and tucked it under his arm. He would keep at least one good memory.

"Father, Father," a mover spoke, trying to shake McWilliams from his daydream. "Could you sign that so we can start driving to St. Agnes now?"

"Yeah, sure." McWilliams scribbled his signature on the bill of lading. He handed it to the mover and averted his eyes from the truck.

"I'm sorry, Father," the older mover said. "You did a good job here. Me and the wife attended Sunday Mass sometimes. Seemed like a real friendly place. I wanted to come to your Casino Night, but the misses said no. Good thing, huh? I coulda ended up in the Allegheny County Jail, heh, heh."

McWilliams tried to smile, but the pain was too great. He watched the movers fold up their ramp and close the truck's rear doors. McWilliams locked the church door and, with head bowed, started his short walk to the rectory. Then one of the movers called to him.

"Father, can you come over here? We need your help."

McWilliams walked behind the parked truck and met him at the driver's window. The mover pointed to the street ahead. "You know him?"

Father Frank looked down and gasped. Good Shepherd's blind head usher lay prostrate on the macadam, inches from the moving van's front tires. "Mr. Robinson, get up!" McWilliams shouted. "You'll get yourself killed down there!"

"I'm not moving, Reverend," the elderly man answered. "And if you were really serious about keeping our church alive, you would be lying next to me!"

McWilliams bent down and whispered, "Robinson, don't make a scene. These movers are working for the bishop…"

Robinson lifted onto one elbow. "I can't hear you, Reverend. Come down closer."

McWilliams crouched like a baseball catcher. "If word gets back to headquarters that we kept these movers from their work, I could be in big trouble ..."

"What you say? Come closer."

Taking baby duck steps, Father Frank waddled closer to Robinson's head. With a violent lunge, the old man grabbed McWilliams by his Roman collar and dragged him to the street.

"Let me go!" Father Frank wrested himself from the man's grasp. He rolled to his left – the moment he heard the "click" from a Pittsburgh newspaper photographer.

The Butler County Courthouse bell rang 2 p.m. Then 3 p.m. Still no verdict.

Gil McFadden paced the lobby. What's taking them so long? The district attorney had expected a guilty verdict immediately after the jurors' empty lunch trays were carted away. At least, that's what the bailiff had predicted.

Matty waited downstairs in a holding cell. His attorney had told him that a long deliberation was a good sign. "Somebody in that room has doubts," Alfonzi said. "And sometimes doubts are contagious and spread to other jurors."

Meanwhile, Judge Graumlich was growing impatient. She promised to treat her family to a buffet at the local Steak and Cake. "Remember, Mom," her 10-year-old told her that morning, "the peanut butter cheesecake is all gone by 6 p.m." If Graumlich was delayed and her child was deprived of cheesecake, there would be hell to pay.

The jury room buzzer rang at 3:45 p.m. Minutes later, Graumlich's bailiff ran breathlessly into her chambers.

"A verdict?" the judge asked.

He shook his head no and handed her a note. It read: "Please send us one replacement juror. If you can't do that, can eleven of us make a verdict? Signed, Ralph Metzgar, foreman."

The bailiff laughed. "Heck, Your Honor, even I know you can't do that."

Graumlich decided he was probably right. There must be some way to force a verdict, she thought.

"Call in the attorneys quickly!" she ordered him.

McFadden was first to arrive. He read the jurors' note and scowled. "Looks like we have a hold-out, Judge."

"How can we get rid of that juror, Gil?" she asked.

"Listen, Judge, before Alfonzi gets here, send back a note telling the juror he must go along with the other eleven. It has to be unanimous."

"I guess that would be fair, Gil, because we really don't know if the juror is holding out for a not guilty verdict or a guilty verdict," Graumlich said.

"Yes, Judge. Put a little fear in him. We don't have all day. Maybe he needs a gentle push in the right direction."

"I never understood why the verdict had to be unanimous," Graumlich groused. "We live in a democracy. Every other vote requires a simple majority. If I could change the law, I would. Then we wouldn't be wasting time waiting for one juror to change his mind."

McFadden decided to take advantage of her ignorance.

"Oh, this is not unusual. Judge Lovecchio had plenty of indecisive juries," he told her.

"What – what did Lovecchio do?"

"He was too busy to write notes to juries, so he usually delegated that task to the prosecuting attorneys," McFadden replied.

"He did, did he?" Graumlich took the bait. "Well, I'm busier that Lovecchio ever was. You write the note, Gil. Get that juror in line!"

McFadden smiled. He was a good note writer. A conviction of Matthew Moore was assured. And next Tuesday, when

Butler County folks voted for district attorney, his success in bringing a murderer to justice would be fresh in their minds.

He handed a pen and scrap paper to the bailiff, and then dictated the following:

Mr. Metzgar, no juror can be replaced. Your verdict must be unanimous. Please advise the misguided juror that he (or she) must change his (or her) vote as soon as possible or appropriate sanctions will be handed down by the court.

The bailiff folded the note in half. He then raced to the jury room, passing Alfonzi in the hallway.

"Do we have a verdict?" Alfonzi called to the flying bailiff.

"No, but we will real soon," the bailiff hollered over his shoulder.

Sure enough, at 4:30 p.m., the jury buzzer sounded. Word spread quickly that a verdict was reached in *Commonwealth v. Matthew Moore.* Judge Graumlich directed the parties to assemble in her courtroom. McFadden stood proudly as jurors filed into the box. Many of them acknowledged McFadden with smiles; Mrs. Schandelmeier actually winked at him.

In the commotion of courtroom observers behind him, McFadden failed to notice a surprise guest taking a seat at his counsel table.

"What the ..., you can't sit here," he scolded. "You're not an attorney."

Zelienople police chief Andy Faxon didn't budge.

"I can't deal with you now, Faxon. Talk to me after the verdict."

"Like hell, McFadden." Chief Faxon's face changed from pink to crimson. "You told me to trust the system, but it looks like you're more interested in your re-election than in justice."

"Go away, Faxon, you don't belong here." McFadden forced a smile to deflect attention from several observant jurors.

"I think I do. I'm going to tell the judge about the evidence you ignored. You know, Gil, the drug addict we found with the stolen lottery tickets and pawn shop receipt for the stolen ring. The positive identification by my girlfriend. Remember?"

McFadden gritted his teeth. His entire legal career, undistinguished as it was, flashed before his eyes. This punk police chief was not going to destroy him, McFadden vowed.

"Here's what I'll do, Faxon. You can sit here, but keep your mouth shut. We'll wait and see what the jury decides. If they have a not guilty verdict, then we're safe. If it's a guilty verdict, then we bring your evidence to the judge's attention. All right?"

"I don't want this kid convicted, McFadden. I can't live with that on my conscience."

"Do we have a deal?" McFadden pressed him.

"Guess there's no choice. Yeah, a deal."

Judge Graumlich took the bench with her usual pomp and flair. The jury foreman passed his verdict form to her. Graumlich donned her reading glasses and scanned the sheet of paper without expression. Her bailiff read the form aloud:

In the case of Commonwealth v. Matthew Moore, we, the jury, find as follows:

As to Count One, murder in the first degree, we find the defendant guilty;

As to Count Two, theft of motor vehicle, we find the defendant guilty;

As to Count Three, armed robbery, we find the defendant guilty;

As to Count Four, aggravated assault, we find the defendant guilty.

Signed by Ralph Metzgar, foreperson.

Faxon tugged at McFadden's sleeve. "Say something to the judge."

"Not yet," he replied. "She's polling the jurors to see if they all agree."

Faxon watched as each juror agreed enthusiastically with the verdict. Only one juror, Curtis Klepper, seemed to hesitate. Alfonzi's objections to the verdict occupied the judge long enough to give Chief Faxon time to plead his case to McFadden.

"You promised, McFadden. This young man is seconds away from being a convicted murderer. You know that's not right. Why are you just sitting there?"

"Shut up, Faxon. I told you I'd bring this up at the appropriate time." McFadden slid his chair away from his tormentor. "Now is not the appropriate time."

"It sure the hell is, McFadden! If you don't tell the judge, I will."

"You can't say anything, Faxon. You're not an attorney. The judge will throw you into jail if you say anything." McFadden pointed to Matty. "Why are you putting your neck on the line for this scum? You're throwing away your career, Faxon."

Graumlich, annoyed by the ongoing banter at counsel table, stared the two men into silence. Confident that all eyes were now upon her, Graumlich announced, "The verdict of guilty is accepted by the Court. Sentencing will be scheduled within 60 days…"

"Your Honor, WAIT!" Chief Faxon bounded to his feet and shouted at the judge.

"Mr. McFadden, who is this impertinent young man at your table?" She seethed at such an interruption of her moment of glory.

"I apologize to the Court," McFadden replied. "This man is a police officer from Zelienople. I promise that such an outburst will not happen again."

Faxon did not back down. "Something terrible has happened here, Your Honor. I really need to speak to you."

"This is highly unusual, young man. You are impeding justice in my courtroom. The trial is over. The verdict has been entered..."

"But if I could have one minute, Your Honor. Just one minute, that's all."

Graumlich looked at the courtroom clock. She could spare one minute. Anything longer and her family would miss the peanut butter cheesecake.

"All right. One minute. But first I have some business to take care of." Graumlich turned to the exhausted jurors. "Thank you for your time. You are now excused from jury duty."

Faxon's jaw dropped as he watched the five men and seven women march from the courtroom.

Exiting with them was any chance he had to upset Matty's verdict.

Chapter Twenty–Five
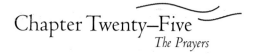
The Prayers

Heavy rain, turning to sleet by mid-day. Possible snowfall of four to five inches overnight.

Winter was moving into Butler County earlier than usual. And the temperature was particularly frigid in Judge Graumlich's courtroom.

"Be seated and be quiet!" was her first order to dozens of excited courtroom observers. "The sooner we get started, the sooner all of us can get home."

No one ever recalled a Saturday session at the courthouse. Graumlich, two days away from her Caribbean vacation, wasn't about to let a Zelienople police chief and a publicity-seeking district attorney delay her. Business had to be completed on Saturday, she told everyone. Matty Moore and his attorney, Antonio Alfonzi, exchanged confused looks. They wondered what Gil McFadden had up his sleeve.

"Place Chief Faxon under oath," Graumlich barked to her courtroom deputy.

McFadden, his conviction secured and his re-election apparent, sprang to his feet. "Objection, Your Honor! The jury verdict is final. You can't take more testimony now."

"Overruled!" The judge was firm.

"But, Your Honor," McFadden pleaded. "This is highly unusual."

Graumlich gestured to the district attorney. He met her at sidebar for a private scolding off the record.

"I had a little talk with Judge Lovecchio last night," she said. "Guess what he told me? He never allowed you to send notes back to the jury. He said something about a 'due process' violation. Is Judge Lovecchio lying or are you lying?"

McFadden reeled. "I-I-I don't recall exactly what Judge Lovecchio did."

"You were dishonest with the court, Mr. McFadden. That's an ethical violation. You could lose your law license over this. Think of the publicity. You would be disgraced right before the election."

"Your Honor, this is all a misunderstanding…"

"See this gavel, Mr. McFadden? Picture it hanging over your head. If you say anything further during this hearing, imagine the gavel breaking your skull."

"Yes, Your Honor," he stammered, returning to counsel table.

Chief Andy Faxon, looking as spooked as a 14-point buck on the first day of deer season, fidgeted in the witness chair. In the audience that Saturday morning was "Saturday Night." If the judge needed his girlfriend to support his story, she was ready to testify.

Graumlich cleared her throat, readying herself for something she had never done: questioning a witness at trial.

"State your name for the record, sir."

"Andrew Faxon. I'm chief of the Zelienople Borough Police."

"Do you have information that could be useful in the case of *Commonwealth v. Matthew Moore*?"

"I do, Your Honor. I have information that proves Matthew Moore's innocence."

McFadden rose to his feet as the audience buzzed. Graumlich raised her gavel. Her dagger eyes forced the district attorney to sit down with a thud.

Faxon waited for silence. When all eyes returned to him, he related the story of Shawn Hibler, how the drug addict was found dead and how police recovered stolen lottery tickets from Yer-In Yer-Out convenience store. Faxon then told Graumlich that videotape from the store's camera clearly showed Hibler as the robber.

Next, Faxon testified that receipts at the apartment proved that Hibler sold Minka Prybelewski's wedding ring to a pawn shop. In fact, the ring was recovered using Hibler's receipt. And, just last night, police obtained a positive identification of Hibler from Nata Prybelewski. She even scribbled a note to Judge Graumlich saying how sorry she was to have fingered the wrong person.

"All right, Chief," the judge said. "Tell us about the murder. Why is Matthew Moore innocent of the murder?"

Faxon was unprepared for such a question. He had no evidence to prove Matty's innocence in the murder of Billy Herman. No fingerprints or physical evidence pointed to Shawn Hibler as the killer. In fact, the bullet recovered from Nata did not match the slug at Billy Herman's farmhouse.

"All I know is what Dr. Elliot Chen said in his report," Faxon said. "The timeline wasn't right. Mr. Moore was stopped at a police checkpoint at the time …"

"Enough, Chief Faxon," Graumlich interrupted the witness. "Dr. Chen's report has been suppressed due to his conflict of interest. Do you have anything else?"

"No, Your Honor."

Attorney Alfonzi raised his hand. "A few questions, Your Honor?"

Graumlich looked at the courtroom clock. She watched freezing rain crack against the courtroom windows. Time was precious.

"A few, Mr. Alfonzi. Just keep it quick."

"Thank you." Alfonzi, free of his shackles, approached the witness. "This new information that you have, Chief Faxon, did you tell anybody about it before today?"

"Yes, sir. I gave a full report to the district attorney before the trial began," Faxon replied.

"And what did the district attorney say to you in response?" Alfonzi asked.

"Objection!" McFadden couldn't help himself. "Hearsay!"

Judge Graumlich aimed her gavel at the prosecutor. "Overruled. I'll deal with you later. The witness is instructed to answer the question."

Faxon looked at McFadden with disgust. "He told me not to worry. He said the jury would figure out whether Mr. Moore was guilty or not. He told me to trust that the criminal justice system would work."

Alfonzi dug deeper. "But what about your evidence? Did he tell you what he planned to do with the information that Mr. Hibler committed the robberies?"

"Mr. McFadden told me to pretend that the evidence didn't exist. He said he wanted a conviction of this punk kid."

Graumlich glared at the prosecutor. "OK, Mr. McFadden, since you made a hearsay objection, you can cure the problem by testifying yourself. Get on the stand!"

"Never in my 20 years…" McFadden repeated his usual argument that his legal experience trumped everyone's in the courtroom.

"Get up here … now!" Graumlich peered over her half-glasses. "I don't care about your 20 years. I care about your last week."

McFadden reluctantly raised his hand for the oath. He grumbled as he sat.

"You may proceed, Mr. Alfonzi," the judge said.

"Is Chief Faxon's testimony accurate, Mr. McFadden?"

"Most of it."

"What isn't accurate, sir?"

"The part about pretending. I don't remember that."

"But Chief Faxon gave you this information before trial, correct?"

"Yes, he did, but we did not independently verify it."

"You would agree that his information shows that Matthew Moore is innocent, at least in the robberies?"

"Yes, but not the murder." McFadden tried to preserve Matty's conviction.

"And you did not share this information with me or with Mr. Moore, did you?"

"No, I didn't. We didn't think it was important enough."

Graumlich interrupted. "I've heard enough. The hour is late. The storm is approaching. I see no need to extend this hearing any further. Go ahead, Mr. Alfonzi, make another one of your frivolous motions."

"Very well, Your Honor," Alfonzi replied dejectedly. "Defendant moves for a mistrial on the grounds that the Commonwealth failed to turn over exculpatory evidence showing the innocence of Matthew Moore."

McFadden was relieved by Graumlich's apparent disdain for Alfonzi's theatrics. "We oppose this silly motion, Your Honor. Mr. Moore is guilty as charged."

Graumlich pounded her gavel one last time.

Ann Bailey was awakened by an unpleasant noise and a pleasant smell.

Freezing rain pelted her bedroom window at Kane Manor. Bacon was cooking in the kitchen below.

As the world outside shivered, Kane Manor offered mother and child refuge from cold November air. The Manor's Sunflower Room, reserved indefinitely for the two famous guests, featured warm afternoon sunshine and aromas from the kitchen below. Today, though, a pleasant autumn had become a wicked winter.

For the past few days, Ann and baby Hannah enjoyed the Manor and its owner's generous hospitality. All of their needs were attended to, except one.

No matter how hard she tried to forget, Ann's thoughts always centered on Jimmie. She wondered if he was suffering as well. Perhaps she would call him later. At least he deserved to know that his baby daughter was safe and cared for.

Innkeeper Gregory Harkins respected his guests' privacy. Ann was invited to breakfast at whatever time she pleased. Her only condition was a private dining room table. After all, Kane was a small town and people talked. So Harkins waited until 10 a.m., when his other guests had checked out, before he knocked on the Sunflower Room door.

"Good morning, Ann," he spoke through her closed door. "Breakfast is ready whenever you are."

Ann snapped Hannah's onesie, put a cloth diaper over her shoulder and picked up her last little friend. "Be right there, Greg."

Harkins ambled down the back stairwell. He grabbed a coffee carafe and two creamers from the kitchen. A plate of scrambled eggs, bacon and buttered English muffin was snatched from the warming oven. Under his arm was something that would make Ann more depressed, the morning's Erie Times newspaper.

"Quite a storm, Greg," Ann said as she angled into her dining chair. "Good day to stay inside, which was what I planned to do anyway."

Harkins served her breakfast and watched her first sip of coffee. He could wait no longer.

"Ann, I am so sorry," he said. "Something terrible has happened, and I don't know how to tell you."

He handed her the Saturday newspaper. The lead headline was a boldfaced dagger to her heart: "Governor's Chief Aide

Found Dead in Colorado." Ann pushed from the table. Her eyes were wide with panic.

"My God, Greg," she said, clutching his hand. "How could such a thing happen? Bill was so young."

"Police say it was an apparent heart attack," Harkins told her.

"Does Jimmie know about this?" Ann asked.

"I assume he's been told. The article says that Governor Bailey had no comment."

Ann grew quiet. She reflected on events of the past week. She had hired Sylvester Sylvaney to locate Pennoyer and talk to him. Sylvaney had tracked Pennoyer to Colorado and confronted him in a Littleton shopping center. Had Sylvaney scared Bill? Enough to cause a heart attack?

"I can't eat any more, Greg. I have to talk to Jimmie."

"I understand, Ann." Harkins helped her to her feet. "If you like, you may use the phone in my office."

"Thank you. I will."

The unexpected winter storm blew icy rain against Good Shepherd's stained glass windows. By late afternoon, when Father McWilliams mounted the church steps one last time, clouds were so thick and black that he imagined Judgment Day. Surely, he thought, Good Shepherd's "Doors to Christ" were about to collapse in the storm anyway.

The gloom did not deter him from one last visit.

His key fit the Diocese's padlock and, as the driving rain bounced upward from the marble portico, McWilliams eased open the heavy wooden door.

He never noticed such an odor before. It was like the smell of an abandoned school house or a vacant grocery store. Good Shepherd smelled like death, as if the Almighty had deserted it and the devil had not yet arrived.

McWilliams pushed through vestibule doors and entered the main church. For the first time in ten years, the tabernacle candle was unlit. The spirit and joy of his parish were nowhere to be found. McWilliams was alone in an empty warehouse, nothing more.

A rare beam of sunlight momentarily illuminated the altar area. But there was nothing to receive the light. The marble altar was gone. Hand-painted statues of the Holy Family and St. Paul had been removed from their pedestals. Not one candle had been spared.

The priest walked slowly down the center aisle. He passed pews that once were filled with parishioners. He had called them his "poor souls."

Winter clouds began to overtake the sunlight. Before darkness had set in, McWilliams observed backlighting of his favorite stained glass window. He had commissioned the work from a Pittsburgh artist. It depicted God dispatching his angels from heaven with the inscription, "All is possible."

McWilliams knelt at the front railing. If all was possible, he thought, his church could be saved. He blessed himself and waited for a miracle.

Noise from the storm did not deter his praying. Neither did the muted sound of approaching footsteps. McWilliams fell deeper into thought, aroused only by the hand upon his shoulder.

He turned sharply. He recognized her face in the growing darkness.

"Mind if I join you?" Tanya Harper knelt beside her pastor and blessed herself.

After a few silent minutes, she turned to him. "Do you believe that? All is possible."

McWilliams could only nod. He had preached that sermon many times, but having encountered Archbishop Ostrow's intransigence McWilliams would admit that much is improbable.

"Why are you here, Tanya? St. Agnes is your parish now. There's no electricity here, no heat, the tabernacle is empty. Good Shepherd is officially closed."

Tanya saw the sorrow in his eyes. "I'm here for the same reason you're here, Father. This is our home. This is where we have a connection upstairs. Actually, I think without all of those candles and statues in the way, our prayers are heard more directly."

McWilliams smiled for the first time that day. "You may be correct, Tanya. Tell me, what are you praying for?"

"Matty was convicted of murder yesterday, Father. He didn't do it. The jury was unanimous, and now he's facing life imprisonment or death. Certainly, God won't let that happen. That's why I'm praying."

McWilliams knew that odds were long that Matty could overcome a guilty verdict but, of course, all is possible.

"I think I know why you are praying, Father," Tanya whispered.

McWilliams nodded in agreement. "That's no secret, Tanya. This church meant everything for me. We started with nothing and we built a place of worship. Few people in our parish had much money to contribute, but they worked hard to make this church a success. Look at it now, though. It's been stripped bare."

Tanya patted his hand. "Let's pray together, for you, Father."

The storm largely passed in about thirty minutes. Skies brightened as they prayed. Soon, early evening sunshine through stained glass windows cast bright colors around them. McWilliams stood and backed from the altar railing.

"It's time to go, Tanya. I've prayed about all I can pray."

McWilliams turned and saw the shadow of a solitary figure in the last pew. He squinted. An older gentleman was on his knees. Good Shepherd was attracting more believers, he thought.

"Father Frank," a familiar voice called out. "I thought I'd find you here."

McWilliams walked closer. Seated in the back pew, resplendent in his purple shirt, was retired bishop John Hogan. McWilliams helped him stand and embraced him like a lost brother.

"Tis a shame what happened here, Father," Hogan said. "It's never easy to lose a church, son."

"My heart is broken, bishop."

"Ostrow must be out of his mind," Hogan said. "Look at this beautiful church. The peace. The beautiful colors. His presence all around…"

"Thank you for your kind words, Bishop Hogan. But I am in the service of the archbishop. I must do whatever he says."

Hogan put his arm around the priest. "Not anymore, Father Frank. You take your orders from me."

"Huh?" was all McWilliams could say.

"Archbishop Ostrow was reassigned yesterday to lead the Baltimore Diocese. I am the interim bishop. Soooo, the moving truck is outside. We have a lot of work to do here. I expect to say Sunday Mass tomorrow."

All is possible, McWilliams believed.

He turned to the lady at the altar railing. Her head was bowed. Her prayer remained unanswered, he thought.

"Just a minute, bishop." McWilliams excused himself and returned to Tanya. He knelt beside her and lowered his head. The priest's joy was temporary. He was moved by his parishioner's deep distress.

Father McWilliams took her hand into his.

"Let's pray together, Tanya. For you."

Judge Graumlich pounded her gavel with a crack. "OBJECTION SUSTAINED!"

McFadden was befuddled. "Your Honor, don't you mean 'overruled?'"

"No, I mean SUSTAINED. I hereby declare a mistrial on all charges. The conviction is dismissed. Mr. Moore, you are free to go."

"What!" McFadden screamed. "You can't be serious. This man is a convicted killer."

"Blame yourself, McFadden." Graumlich wagged her crooked finger at the prosecutor. "You lied to me. You withheld important evidence from the Court. And you're a disgrace to your public office."

"But Your Honor," McFadden pleaded, "don't set this man free. He'll kill again!"

"Oh, thank you for reminding me," Graumlich countered. "Mr. Alfonzi, please make a motion for a judgment notwithstanding the verdict."

"So move, Your Honor," Alfonzi quickly stated.

"Motion is GRANTED!" Graumlich hollered with another bang of her gavel. "This Court finds that the Commonwealth's case is so deficient that a reasonable jury could not find guilt beyond a reasonable doubt."

"What! Judge this is outrageous!" McFadden said, sensing that his re-election chances were depleting like a leaky balloon.

"What's outrageous, McFadden, is the Commonwealth's case. The only thread was a fingerprint found on a car outside Billy Herman's house. A car? That car could have been anywhere before the murder."

Graumlich watched a gaggle of newspaper reporters scribbling her quotes. Might as well destroy his re-election bid, she thought. "Never, in my entire legal career, have I seen a prosecutor as incompetent, unethical and pathetic as you, Mr. McFadden…"

The judge's epithets continued, but all anyone noticed was the unbridled glee of Matty Moore. He hugged his attorney and jumped in the air. The government had tried to convict him and it lost. Matty could return to McKean County and the Kane News-Leader. He could finally pursue the story that plunged him into trouble – solving the murder of Josh Gibson.

Matty ran from the courtroom and into the arms of his girlfriend, Megan.

"I knew you could beat this, Matty," she said above the din. "Let's go out and celebrate."

Matty kissed her forehead. He hugged her tightly.

"First, I have to find my mother," he said. "I knew she was praying for me."

Chapter Twenty–Six
The Mourner

William Pennoyer's flag-draped casket was carried through the doors of Kane Memorial Chapel and into a swirling snowstorm. Hundreds of public officials, friends of the governor and local residents watched in stone silence as state police troopers folded the Commonwealth's blue flag and handed it to Governor Bailey.

Tom Zachary studied Jimmie closely. Like his daddy Brock, the young governor had a knack for drama. Zachary had seen that act before. The show of grief seemed genuine, but Zachary knew it was phony. How could Jimmie seem so in control, yet so cold, upon the death of his best friend?

Something else was strange. Ann Bailey had not interacted with her husband during the 90-minute memorial ceremony. Ann was seated with her daughter and her mother on the opposite side of the chapel. Perhaps, she wanted to keep her baby away from public glare, Zachary thought. But why did Ann continue to avoid Jimmie after the ceremony?

"Tom," a voice called behind him. "It is 'Tom,' right?"

Sylvester Sylvaney, his trench coat layered with fresh snow, saddled up to the newspaper editor. "Funny, isn't it? Just the other day we were talking about Pennoyer, and now he's dead."

"Yeah, funny." Zachary continued to watch the estranged Baileys.

"You know what else is funny, Tom? Pennoyer wasn't at a rehab in Toronto like you told me. He was in Colorado."

"No kidding, Sy! But a great investigator like you probably checked it out before you traveled to Canada."

Sylvaney disregarded the jab. "What else do you know about Pennoyer that you're not telling me?"

Zachary shook his head. "I don't give away information for free, Sy. Read the newspaper."

The two men watched pallbearers load Pennoyer's casket into a waiting hearse. The governor's limousine, engine running and lights on, was second in line. A trooper was brushing accumulating snow from its windshield. Meanwhile, Ann, her baby and her mother had stepped through slush and ice en route to the chapel's parking lot. There they were ushered into the waiting car of Kane Manor innkeeper Greg Harkins.

"What's with that, Sy?" Zachary pointed to Ann's hasty exit.

"Things are complicated right now, Tom. Don't get involved."

"What do you mean, 'complicated'? Are they separated? What do you know, Sy?"

"I can't say. Everything is confidential."

Zachary turned to face him. "So that's it. Ann was your client. She wanted to know where Pennoyer was."

"It's confidential," Sylvaney repeated.

"Ann found out that Jimmie spent $30,000 on Pennoyer's rehab, didn't she?"

"She never told me that," Sylvaney replied.

"So what did she tell you, Sy?"

Sylvaney pulled Zachary backward into the warmth of the chapel's lobby. "I'm only telling you this, Tom, because it may help us understand what happened here. After midnight, early on August 15, Governor Bailey returned home from a government trip. He was covered with mud, his clothes were torn and he had scratches all over his legs. He told Ann that he was in a fight with Pennoyer."

"With Pennoyer? That's crazy," Zachary said.

"So, all of a sudden, Pennoyer is missing. Ann is worried. She wants me to track him down and find out the real story."

"And you tracked him down?" Zachary asked.

"Eventually. First I found his Jeep parked at the Pittsburgh Airport. It was covered with mud and there was a kayak tied to the roof."

"Both of them got into mud, I suppose," Zachary said. "But this is the end of the story, Sy. Pennoyer's dead. Your client doesn't seem to be interested anymore…"

"I'm interested, Tom." Sylvaney's eyes sparkled. "You see, I'm an old school investigator. Even when the client quits, I keep going."

"You'd be a great newspaper reporter, Sy."

Sylvaney laughed. "I can dig, but I can't write."

"I can write," Zachary countered, "but my digging skills need help."

Sylvaney escorted him outside. They observed Jimmie's limousine and a convoy of state vehicles pull onto Chestnut Street as the hearse headed toward Pennoyer's final resting place. The crowd slowly dispersed.

Zachary watched Sylvaney's eyes scanning the mourners. Zachary grew impatient. He began to walk down the chapel steps, but the investigator pulled him back.

"Don't go! Not yet," Sylvaney said.

"What do you see?" Zachary asked.

"Over there, by the tree. The woman in black with the shapely legs. Watch her."

Zachary noticed the shapely legs immediately. "Why? Who is she?"

Sylvaney flashed a mischievous smile. "She, my friend, is the key to your story."

Zachary tried to recognize her face through swirling snowflakes. There was nothing familiar about her. Obviously, grief had overtaken her. Her eye shadow was streaked by tears.

"Her name is Roxanne Randle," Sylvaney told him. "She's a game show model from Los Angeles. She and Bill met at the Castle Rock rehab center. They had frequent sex, or so I hear."

The woman dabbed a tear as Pennoyer's hearse rolled from sight. She carefully placed one high heel after another as she struggled to reach the chapel parking lot. Zachary tried to imagine Bill canoodling with such a beautiful woman. Life is stranger than fiction, he thought.

"What are you going to do, Sy? She's walking away. There goes our story."

"I can't stop her, Tom. She and Bill saw me in Colorado. I was chasing them. I'm sure Roxanne remembers me. If she sees me now, she'll run again."

Zachary took his cue and followed her to the parking lot. He caught up with her as she was hand-brushing snow off her car handle.

"Here, young lady," he called. "Let me help you."

"You're so kind." Roxanne sniffed into a tissue. "It's only a rental car, so you don't have to make it perfect."

"A rental?" Zachary reached through the driver's door and popped the trunk lid. "Here's a scraper. This will do a better job."

She watched him clean her car to perfection. She slid into the driver's seat and touched up her makeup. He reached past her, turned on the ignition and started her defroster. "You'll be ready to go in a minute or two."

"That's OK," she said to him sweetly. "I'm in no hurry."

After a few seconds of awkward silence, Zachary began his sneaky interview.

"That was a beautiful ceremony today," he said. "Bill Pennoyer was a lucky man to have so many friends. Even the governor paid his respects."

"Don't talk to me about the governor." Her cheery attitude was gone. "If you knew what I know about the governor, you'd want him to stay away from your funeral."

Zachary was stumped. What did she know? What made her so hostile?

"Well, Governor Bailey and Bill were best friends," he said. "Did you know that?"

"This is what I know, mister," she said with a scowl. "Friends don't do what the governor did."

"What did he do?" Zachary tried a direct approach.

"What did he do? He killed the only love of my life. I'm convinced of it. Bill didn't deserve this. He was chased by people because of Jimmie Bailey. He was scared and threatened. The stress killed him."

Maybe Zachary was one of those "people" Roxanne was talking about. But he didn't chase Pennoyer when he found him at the rehab center; Zachary just wanted to ask him a few questions.

Her windshield was warm enough to melt away the snow and ice. She thanked him again for his kind deeds.

"May I speak with you later, ma'am?" Zachary tried to keep the interview going.

"I'm afraid not," she replied. "I'm going home to California. I need some time alone."

"If you change your mind, give me a call." Zachary handed her his business card, then stepped back as she closed her car door.

"Thomas Zachary, editor of the Kane News-Leader." She read the card with increasing anger. "You're the newspaper writer who scared Bill at the rehab center! I'll never talk to you again!"

Roxanne sped away, leaving Zachary in a cloud of snow and ice. He turned toward Sylvaney. The investigator held his head in his hands.

Zachary hollered to him: "I told you I wasn't good at digging!"

Gil McFadden always viewed himself as a survivor. But even the five-term district attorney understood when an election was lost.

After his colossal failure in *Commonwealth v. Matthew Moore* and public flogging by Judge Graumlich, McFadden's hopes for another four years as Butler County's top prosecutor were dashed. His campaign workers abandoned him. Telephones stopped ringing. Even the radio talk show callers ridiculed him for botching the only case he tried in ten years.

Facing certain defeat and growing more despondent by the hour, McFadden called together his assistants and staff. He thanked them for their help over the years. As a reward, he said, all of them could take a vacation day with pay.

When the last secretary exited the office, McFadden sat behind his computer. Finally, he was alone with the Internet. He typed the only Web address that gave him comfort, "bookiedelight.com."

A poker hand popped on the screen.

His hand contained three queens, one ten and one ace. He clicked the window that said "Place a Bet." He entered his credit card number. "Verified," the screen said. "Open with a Bet -- $100 or $250 or $1,000?" He clicked on $1,000. Immediately, three other poker hands vanished. He was playing only against the house.

McFadden discarded the ten and ace. Two cards were dealt – a seven and the fourth queen. His eyes lit up. Best hand he ever played on this website, he thought. The "Make

a Bet" window was flashing again. He typed in $50,000.00.
"Please retype to verify," the website asked. McFadden again
typed "$50,000.00."

He watched the house's hand revealed, card by card. Ten,
seven, six, nine, eight – all were spades.

In horror, McFadden saw his four queens vanish beneath
the words, "House wins, straight flush. Another game?"

No one was around, so he kept playing.

And he kept losing.

Matty Moore returned to Kane News-Leader offices
with the fanfare of a knight returning from the Crusades.
Helium balloons were strung from every computer terminal.
Streamers were suspended from the ceiling. Dozens of
fair maidens, including office manager Jessie Krone, were
waiting with arms open.

After accepting dozens of hugs and kisses, Matty called
to Jessie. "Where's Mr. Z? I need to tell him about my
Josh Gibson story."

"He's back in the shop," Jessie told him. "Someone has
to work on tomorrow's paper."

Matty found him editing page proofs. The editor was
rearranging photographs from today's memorial service. Bill
Pennoyer's sudden death was front page news.

"Oh, Matty, welcome back." Zachary barely looked up
from his task. Matty understood that putting the newspaper
to bed each week was task number one. But he expected a
more joyful reaction from his boss.

"We need to discuss some matters," Zachary said to his
intern. "Let's talk in my office."

This was serious, Matty thought. His editor rarely
allowed anyone to enter his office, other than the Texas Hot
Dog delivery boy.

"Sit down, son." Zachary closed his door and muffled sounds of the office celebration. "There's no easy way to say this. Matty, you know I have a world of respect for you, but ..."

"But what, Mr. Z?"

"We have to let you go, Matty." Zachary couldn't maintain eye contact and started to fumble with a paper clip. "Let's just say your summer internship is over and it's time for you to start college."

"Mr. Z, I love it here. The News-Leader is my new home."

"Matty, I've spoken to the admissions director at the Bradford campus. She will enroll you in a few freshman classes and, if you go full-time next summer, you can be on track for a degree in four years."

"Bradford is pretty close, Mr. Z. Are you saying I can work with you on the weekends?"

Zachary twisted the paper clip until it snapped. "I'm afraid that won't be best for us. If it were up to me, you could work here all the time. But it's not up to me."

Jessie tapped on the door and opened it a crack. "C'mon you guys, we're about the cut the cake. Don't be party poopers!"

"In a minute," Zachary replied, motioning her to close the door.

Matty was confused. "Who is it up to, Mr. Z? You own the newspaper. It's your decision who you hire and fire."

"Newspapers are different, Matty. We're not like other businesses. Readers feel close to their hometown newspaper, as though we're part of their lives. Advertisers identify with their local paper, too. They want to feel comfortable paying us to promote their merchandise. We work hard to become part of everyone's family."

Matty sighed. "And I'm not part of the family, am I?"

"Don't take this the wrong way, Matty. Those people partying in the office love you. Marcy and I love you. We opened our house to you, for Pete's sake. But after you were arrested, well, the readers and advertisers said things to me."

"Let me guess, Mr. Z. They asked you why a killer was working for the News-Leader, right? But I was acquitted. The judge said there wasn't enough evidence to convict me. Don't people understand that?"

"No, they don't, Matty. All they understand is that Butler County's prosecutor did a lousy job. A killer is still free, and most everybody thinks it's you. That's why I'm helping you get back to school. You can keep a low profile, be a good student and maybe, in a few years, you can return to the News-Leader."

"You're afraid that, if I stay here, you'll lose readers and advertisers?" Matty asked.

"I'm sure we will," Zachary said. "I'm trying to save you and the newspaper."

Matty thought of an alternative. "Mr. Z, what if we track down the real killer of Billy Herman? That would clear my name. With your contacts and my energy, we can pick up where the Zelienople detectives left off. What do you say?"

Zachary shook his head. His rejection of Matty's idea was interrupted by an internal telephone call. "Jessie," he hollered into the receiver, "I told you we'd be there in a minute."

"Tom, I think you better come to the front desk. You have a visitor. She says it's important." Jessie then whispered into the telephone: "I recognize her. She's one of the models who hold a suitcase on that TV show."

Zachary's face flushed with excitement. Roxanne Randle? She wants to talk?

"Escort her back to my office, Jessie," Zachary said. "And try to keep the noise down, OK?"

Zachary directed Matty to stay. He wanted his best reporter to hear the conversation.

Roxanne had removed her coat in the outer lobby. When she strode into Zachary's office, she carried both an air of sophistication and a white business envelope.

"I apologize for my earlier rudeness, Mr. Zachary." She slid into the chair next to Matty. Her legs barely folded into the cramped area. "My conscience told me to visit you before I return home."

"Your conscience? Why is that?" Zachary asked.

"After my lover died, I returned to Castle Rock Center to claim his things. One was his cellphone. As you might expect, Bill Pennoyer had a large number of voice mail messages while he was in treatment. Most of them were strictly business, but I retrieved one that surprised me. It was a call from your governor."

"What was the message?" Zachary asked.

"The message was short, something about Matty Moore being arrested for the Zelienople murder and that Bill should relax." Roxanne turned to the teenager beside her. "You're Matty Moore, right?"

"Yes, ma'am.

"Your attorney said you probably were here," Roxanne said. "I was so relieved to hear that your case was thrown out. I know you didn't commit the murder."

"How?" Matty and Zachary asked in unison.

Roxanne slid the white envelope across Zachary's desk. He ripped it open and pulled out an audiotape.

"Bill wanted to keep this," she said. "It was the only evidence he had to prove he fired the gun in self-defense. It's all on the tape, Mr. Zachary. Their voices, the sound of a rock thrown through the window, a gunshot. You can hear everything Bill and Jimmie Bailey are saying – the whole scheme to get Billy Herman to confess to his murder of the police commissioner."

"You kept this tape? Why, Ms. Randle?" Zachary asked.

"No, actually I threw it out. I thought the police could use it to convict my sweet Bill. But when I heard Jimmie Bailey's voice mail, I realized an innocent man had been arrested. So I dug through the trash and found it. I'm giving it to you because I believe only a newspaper would have the guts to report the whole story."

"Would you stay while we listen to the tape, Ms. Randle?" Zachary asked.

"I've listened to it too many times," she said. "One more thing before I go, Bill told me that Jimmie Bailey wanted the dead man's confession on tape. He said that would stop the dead man from extorting money from the governor."

Zachary suddenly remembered the unexplained wire transfers from Bailey's money market account. After Roxanne exited his office, Zachary telephoned the governor's financial manager to confirm his suspicion.

"A few months ago, we spoke in confidence about some of Jimmie Bailey's wire transfers," Zachary reminded Dennis Padgett of their interview. "I had one more question. You told me about the Castle Rock Center wire transfer, but you said there were others. Those other transfers, the ones that totaled about one hundred thousand dollars, whose account did they go to?"

"Are we still off the record?" Padgett asked nervously.

"Sure."

"Let me look ... Central Bank & Trust, Butler, Pennsylvania. The account holder's name was Mr. William G. Herman."

Editor and reporter stared at each other in silence. Between them was the audiotape that would bring down a governor.

Zachary loaded the tape into a player.

"Take notes, young man. We have a story to write."

Chapter Twenty–Seven

The Footsteps

Ice and drifted snow crunched under his feet. Sowers Road, the scene of many joys and horrors, was still and silent. Tom Zachary paused to witness its silvery beauty.

"I should have taken this walk many winters ago," he told himself. "And I should have arranged this talk with the governor long ago as well."

Having abandoned his car in a snow drift, Zachary approached the governor's mansion on foot. Each step brought the editor closer to his prey.

Jimmie Bailey's free ride was about to end. The editor's reserve of sympathy had run dry. No pity remained for the young man. His parents' tragic deaths had long passed. His struggle to run an unwieldy state while raising a young family seemed irrelevant now. Being McKean County's native son was not enough for Jimmie to escape scrutiny by his local newspaper.

This time, Bailey's callousness and deception were unforgiveable. Zachary's gifted young reporter barely escaped a murder conviction. Matty Moore's reputation was scarred because Bailey had arranged for the real killer's getaway. And Bailey stood by silently while Matty faced a death penalty.

Zachary had listened to the audiotape in disbelief. How could Jimmie be so cowardly? The governor had handed his best friend a loaded gun and told him to confront Billy

Herman. Someone was bound to be shot, Zachary thought. No matter who died in the Zelienople house, Jimmie would be free of Herman's extortion. The governor's plan had worked brilliantly, for a while.

As in Jimmie's other misdeeds, truth eventually surfaced. Jimmie never dreamed that Pennoyer would entrust a television model with that damning audiotape. Pennoyer had been Jimmie's most loyal soldier, but love intervened.

Zachary and Matty had worked all night. Their story of the governor's role in Billy Herman's murder was complete, except for one thing. They needed reaction from Jimmie Bailey. So Zachary telephoned the governor thirty minutes ago, told him the News-Leader was about to print a story implicating him in Herman's death. He asked for the governor's response. After a long pause, Jimmie simply told him to "come over."

Leigh-Rose Mansion stood at the end of Sowers Road. Zachary trudged the last 100 feet through sun-sparkled snow flurries. He observed two state troopers guarding the front gate. They waved him through. They said the governor had authorized his visit.

Zachary approached the mansion with trepidation. He knew that Jimmie acted impulsively and that he owned a gun. He also knew that desperate men backed into a corner do desperate things. How Jimmie would react to his accusations was a coin flip, Zachary thought. Jimmie could either admit his guilt or kill the messenger. But Zachary understood his job. He took a deep breath and trudged on.

About a foot of fresh snow blanketed the driveway and front yard. No one had entered or exited overnight, except for a trail of footprints that led from the mansion's porch northward toward Kinzua State Park. Zachary mounted the front porch steps and rang Bailey's doorbell.

No answer.

Zachary began to worry. The footsteps. They were fresh. Jimmie appeared to have abandoned the mansion after Zachary's telephone call. Jimmie probably knew the editor would follow his steps and find his story.

Sensing the historical significance of the moment, Zachary took photographs of Jimmie's footsteps leading from Leigh-Rose. The editor then flipped up his collar and braced for a chilly and difficult walk toward Kinzua Bridge.

Zachary stepped down a steep bank near the property's northern gate. He saw footprints gathered in close proximity where the gate had swung open. Zachary followed a trail past the gate and into Kinzua State Park.

The footsteps veered onto the park's entrance road. Pine trees, their branches thick with heavy snow, flanked Zachary's path. The thick forest obscured his view of the viaduct bridge now about 200 yards ahead. Zachary peered into the distance, hoping to see Jimmie at the end of his trail. But snow-laden pines and the sun's glare impeded him.

Footsteps diverted from the road onto railroad tracks. Zachary followed. He could finally see what remained of the Kinzua Bridge deck. It was empty. He saw no Jimmie Bailey.

A few hundred yards farther, the footsteps turned from the tracks and onto a park trail. Zachary sighed in relief. He saw only fresh snow on Kinzua Bridge. Whoever made these tracks, he thought, changed his mind. The bridge evidently had lost its attraction.

Zachary turned to follow the new path when, suddenly, a white blur flew inches from his head. He heard a splatter on the tree behind him. Zachary ducked as his heart nearly shot through his chest.

"I'm getting rusty, Tom." Jimmie hollered at the editor from a picnic pavilion about 100 feet away. "I would have nailed you in my prime."

Zachary stood up, grateful that Jimmie's weapon was only a snowball, but surprised by his child-like playfulness.

"Had you going there? Didn't I, Tom?" Jimmie yelled.

"Yeah, I thought maybe you ended it all on the bridge."

Jimmie threw another snowball into the valley. "Maybe you don't know me that well after all."

Zachary disagreed. "I know you very well, Jimmie. That's why I'm here."

Bailey fired a snowball and it splattered against the park dumpster. "I can't stop your story. Write what you have to write. But every story has another side, Tom. Isn't that true?"

"I suppose," Zachary conceded. "But not this one. You killed a man, and you let your brother be condemned for it. I'm having trouble finding another side of that story."

Jimmie shook snow from his gloves and sat on the picnic table. "Come, join me here, Tom. Let's talk."

Zachary stepped through the last 50 feet of snow and ice. He stomped slush from his boots and sat beside Jimmie. Zachary pulled a steno pad from his coat. These quotes had to be perfectly recorded, he thought.

"You know, Tom, when I was a child, my mother and I would sneak off to this spot. She'd pack a picnic lunch and we would watch the steam engine cross the bridge. That's one of my earliest memories. I miss her, Tom."

"She was a great lady, Jimmie. But that doesn't excuse what you did …"

"We buried here over there, Tom, at the overlook cemetery. She was a young woman. What happened to her was terrible. I can't get that kidnapping out of my mind."

"It was tragic. But that was nearly 25 years ago, Jimmie. We've all moved on."

The governor shook his head. "Not me. I never moved on. Sure, I married a great lady and we have a wonderful daughter, but I didn't move on. There was always an emptiness that nobody could fill. She didn't deserve to die."

Zachary felt a touch of pity, but resisted the emotion. "Nobody deserves to die. Not Sallie Bailey. Not Pennoyer. Not even your enemy, Billy Herman."

Jimmie was expressionless. "Maybe so, Tom. But there's one person who deserved to die, my father. He was a monster. He abused my mother. He cheated on her. He was despicable and only cared about himself. When the tornado threw him off this bridge, my world was a better place."

Zachary was not a grief counselor nor would he draw comparisons between Jimmie and his father. He reminded himself that he was a journalist. All he wanted was a story.

"Tell me, Jimmie. Why didn't you simply tell the police that your father was killed by the tornado? Instead you took his body and threw it into the Ohio River. You tried to cover it up, but Billy Herman discovered what you did. He extorted money from you and …"

"It was stupid, yeah. But let me tell you something you can quote for your story. When my father was killed in the tornado, I felt cheated again. Not because I lost my last parent, no. I lost my opportunity to kill him myself for what he did to our family."

"But, Jimmie, he was already dead. You couldn't kill him again."

"No, you're wrong." Jimmie looked him squarely in the eye. "I killed him. When I drove his body to Pittsburgh and onto the West End Bridge, that's the night I killed Brock Bailey. I pulled his wretched body from the trunk and, with the strength Mom gave me at the moment, I heaved him into the Ohio River. I felt good about what I did, Tom. And I still feel good. Nobody was going to deprive me of that satisfaction – not you, not the state police commissioner and not Billy Herman."

"So you threw the rock through Billy Herman's bedroom window?"

"That was me," Jimmie said.

"Like you threw the rock at the bear when we were here last spring?"

"Yeah, I forgot about that."

"You told me that you threw the rock just to scare away the bear, remember?"

"I never wanted to kill the bear, just to scare it. That's right, Tom."

"And you threw the rock to scare Billy Herman?"

"That's all we ever wanted to do, Tom. Just scare him. We had to end his extortion of me. I couldn't keep paying him forever."

Zachary jotted the last quote, then continued, "But why Pennoyer? Why would you send him into the house with a loaded gun?"

"Herman was a former cop. We knew he'd be able to defend himself. I couldn't have Pennoyer walk in to that house unarmed. And it's a good thing; otherwise, Herman would have shot him."

"What's the difference now, Jimmie? Pennoyer's dead anyway."

"Yeah, I know. That's exactly what Ann said to me this morning."

Zachary was surprised. "You told Ann about all of this?"

"Had to. Ann's all that I have left now. Her voice was about the only thing that kept me from jumping off that bridge this morning. She gave me hope. There's a chance, a slim chance that she'll forgive me."

Jimmie hopped down from the picnic table. "Can I tell you something off the record?"

Zachary tucked his steno pad into his coat pocket. He nodded yes.

"Ann made me promise to do something," Jimmie said. "I had to make another call."

Zachary heard sounds of approaching footsteps. He turned to see three state troopers approaching the picnic pavilion. "She made you call the police?"

"She said that was my first step."

Jimmie stood and put his wrists behind his back. One trooper bound him with handcuffs. Another asked if he was finished with his interview. They led the governor back toward the park road. Zachary followed close behind.

Before Jimmie was placed into a waiting police cruiser, he turned to Zachary.

"This is probably my last executive order, Tom."

"Tell me, governor."

"Write it Tom. The whole damn story."

Epilogue

Father Frank was a regular. About twice a month, he presented his clergy card and a guard escorted him through the steel doors. McWilliams enjoyed visiting the imprisoned. It was a corporal act of mercy.

Pittsburgh State Correctional Institution was temporary home for many of his parishioners and permanent home for others. When Father Frank passed through the cellblocks, he recognized many of the faces. He brought greetings from family members. He offered humor and spirit. He gave them hope for another day.

McWilliams traveled through a concrete block passageway into D Block, the prison's minimum security facility. It housed a notorious prisoner he had never visited – a criminal convicted of voluntary manslaughter.

Jimmie Bailey didn't fight the charge. He was guilty. He entered a plea and asked the Court for compassion. His wife and infant daughter stood beside him as his sentence was pronounced. Five years in prison. Public opinion was split; about half wanted probation and the other half, a life term. Jimmie would have accepted either if Ann forgave him.

Minimum security rules permitted face-to-face contact with visitors. McWilliams settled into a small interview room while a guard rounded up the ex-governor.

People may have wondered how it all came to this, but Father Frank understood. He had heard the confession of Jimmie's father, Brock, and he witnessed the sin's toll on Jimmie. McWilliams saw generations of Baileys corrupted by money, fame and power. He stood by helplessly as their marriages failed and as they withdrew in self-pity. He watched as Brock and Jimmie inevitably realized that nothing outside a marriage is as important as what is inside.

But, as Frank's father always told him, life is a journey. Each man takes his own steps and, if he's lucky, he'll end up at the right destination.

Jimmie Bailey had many steps ahead, the priest thought. All of them upward.

McWilliams paced the interview room. He didn't know why Jimmie had asked him to visit today. He never ministered to the ex-governor before. He probably was not a Catholic. He never set foot in Good Shepherd Church. As far as Father Frank knew, the young man was either agnostic or non-denominational. But clearly he was a lost sheep, and McWilliams was comfortable in the role of shepherd.

The guard led Jimmie from an outdoor exercise yard through a common dining area. McWilliams was struck by the sight of Pennsylvania's former governor in a bright orange jumpsuit. The other obvious change was his full, nicely-trimmed beard.

"Father, forgive me for I have sinned." Jimmie shook his hand.

"We're all sinners, Governor."

"Yes, Father Frank, but I was caught."

Jimmie looked fit and rested. Gone were the worried face and the stress of public office. His major activity was counting days. About 300 to go.

"How are they treating you, Jimmie?" McWilliams asked.

"They put me in a good pod. Most of the guys here are white collar. Some of them embezzled or cooked the books. Some are tax cheats. I'm the only violent person here."

McWilliams accepted the comment. He had read excerpts of Tom Zachary's series from the Kane News-Leader. McWilliams knew about Jimmie's juvenile record and his now infamous slap of Ann Bailey.

"Have you changed?" Father Frank asked.

Jimmie laughed. "After a year in this place, a man changes. Everybody changes. They go from petty criminal to pious Christian. I've never seen so many Bibles or heard so many prayers."

"How about you, Jimmie?"

"I've changed in many ways, but Jesus hasn't visited my cell yet."

"Well, I'm a poor substitute for Jesus," McWilliams said. "Why did you invite me?"

"I need a friend on the outside, Father. Somebody who can smooth things over for me."

"Why? What's happening with Ann and your daughter?"

Stress returned to Jimmie's face. "They moved back into Leigh-Rose. That's a good sign. Her mother visits them from time to time. But Ann has visited me only three times. I feel like I'm losing her."

"These things take time, Jimmie."

"It hurts so much, Father. I never thought it would come to this. I've prayed and I've paid a lot of money so none of this would happen."

"Paid money? What are you talking about?" McWilliams asked.

"A donation. Didn't you get it, Father?"

Yes, he remembered. The anonymous donor finally was revealed. When Good Shepherd was deep in the throes of ruin, the Diocese received a cashier's check for $500,000.

"That was you?!" McWilliams had suspected Matty Moore. "Why?"

"Everything was going downhill for me, Father. I decided to do something to change my luck. So I had Padgett strike a check and hand it to the archbishop."

"That's a lot of money, Jimmie."

"Didn't work, Father. Look where I am now."

"I'll say it again. These things take time," McWilliams told him. "Would you mind if I give you some cheap psychology?"

Jimmie nodded. After paying half a million, how cheap could it be?

"You may not believe this, but your father loved your mother very much. I heard his confession shortly before his death. I can't tell you what he said. Trust me. He loved her."

"Do you think all of my problems were caused by my parents?"

"Some maybe. Most were caused by you, Jimmie. You have to take responsibility for your actions. You've hurt the people you love most, just like your father did. It's time to move on. There are a woman and a baby waiting for you to change."

Cheap psychology, but right on the money, Jimmie thought.

"I'll be your friend on the outside," McWilliams said. "You just have to change on the inside."

"Thanks."

Dennis Padgett slid the paper across to Matty. "One last signature."

Matty scribbled his name and held the pen high.

"Congratulations," Padgett said. "You are the proud owner of the Kane News-Leader."

"Pride of the Alleghenies!" Matty yelled.

Applause erupted at the corner table of Golden Wheel Restaurant. A new era was starting in McKean County. Everyone felt the energy.

"Speech! Speech!" the diners shouted.

Matty took a deep breath. He recalled every detail of an unforgettable summer – the thrill of seeing his byline on a front page story, the excitement of chasing a killer and the absolute terror of a criminal trial. He had grown through all of it. And now, nearing graduation from Pitt-Bradford with a business degree, he made his first investment decision.

"I have a few announcements to make. First, Toolie has agreed to write a weekly advice column. Why should she give out advice for free?

"Second, I've hired Dennis to be our business manager as well as my personal financial planner. His family will be well taken care of.

"Third, Jessie Krone will be the newspaper's editor-in-chief. Of course, I'll be doubling her present salary."

"Finally," he pulled Megan close, "we're engaged to be married next summer."

Another cheer rang through the restaurant.

"But what about Mr. Zachary?" Jessie asked.

Matty saved his best announcement for last. "He agreed to be my publisher, on one condition – he asked for a two-year vacation. Finally, he's writing his book."

Tom Zachary stared at his stuffed bookshelves. He tapped a pencil on his knee. He adjusted his swivel chair up and down, up and down.

The Zacharys' grandfather clock rang 11 chimes. He was now three hours sitting behind his computer. He had produced only one sentence: *There was a bridge in Pennsylvania.*

"Marcy, come look."

Being Tom Zachary's wife had its good points. He was funny, loyal and considerate. But when he was writing, he was serious, moody and mean.

Marcy leaned over his shoulder and read the sentence. She wanted to be encouraging, but her reaction had to be brutally honest. If he wanted to spend the next two years, at home, in her way, sacrificing her time, messing up her schedule, then his book had better be successful.

"Tom, it's a lovely sentence," she said. "So well constructed. I see a subject and verb. You even added a prepositional phrase."

"Yes, yes," he said excitedly. "What do you think, Marcy? You know, the first sentence is very important. People won't buy the book unless the first sentence hooks them in."

"It's OK, Tom. But, I was expecting something more. A little more action."

"So you think 'was' is not a strong enough verb?"

"You're so smart, Tom. You saw that right away. You're such a gifted writer." Marcy rubbed his shoulders as he deleted the sentence.

A few minutes passed. Zachary tapped the space bar with his thumb. The cursor flew across the monitor. No ideas were coming. Marcy sensed his frustration.

"Wasn't that tornado awful?" She rubbed his temples as if to massage her thought into his brain. "It blew apart Kinzua Bridge. Nobody expected it. That seems to be a key part of your story."

"Marcy!" Zachary nearly fell off his seat. "That's it! I have a great idea. I'll start the book just as the tornado strikes Kinzua Valley. And I'll write the whole scene from the perspective of Glen Weaver. You remember. He was the park ranger."

She kissed his forehead and instinctively left him in the company of his creativity.

His fingers pounded the keyboard.

Flying debris battered Glen Weaver's cabin with such fury and noise that he barely heard the two gunshots. Hunkered beneath an old oak desk, the Kinzua Park ranger covered his face with a forearm. The fierce storm had uprooted a decaying pine tree and sent it crashing through the eastern wall. He had scrambled into the tiny cabin for protection, dropping his radio into a swelling pool of rainwater at the front steps.

Weaver tried to warn the men on the railroad bridge of the tornado watch, but now his safety was more important than chasing trespassers from the closed park.

The time was 3 p.m. A funnel cloud was bearing down the valley. Weaver struggled to his feet and grabbed his Nikon. He focused his camera through the cabin's western window and snapped the shutter. It would be the last photograph of Kinzua Bridge.

The End

AUTHOR'S NOTES AND COMMENTS ON THE RIVERS OF PITTSBURGH MYSTERY TRILOGY

I congratulate all readers who have completed the trilogy – *Tonight in the Rivers of Pittsburgh, Woods on Fire* and *Zelienople Road*. Before I move on to my next project, I'd like to revisit the scenes and characters of the trilogy one last time.

Many readers have suggested that I explain some details in what one reviewer called "an intricately plotted novel." And, indeed, there are many details. But each has some importance, if not immediately in the chapter then later in development of the plot.

I undertake this task at some risk. As author of these stories, I understand the weaknesses in some of these situations, particularly logistical problems that arise when characters move from scene to scene. If these notes do not completely explain all details, or if I omit some peculiarity that should be further explained, the reader can email me at brianweakland@aol.com

Before we begin this footnote exercise, I repeat that all characters are fictional. Many readers have asked whether certain characters are based on specific people in their communities. These similarities are purely coincidental. The characters are based on a blend of personalities and characteristics of people I've met over the course of my career. To the extent that these characters seem real,

I'm flattered because I have tried to accurately reflect personalities of Pennsylvanians.

Additionally, some readers have commented on my lack of running narrative and the constant shifting of perspective between characters. Most readers, however, enjoy the breeziness and humor of my prose and my use of changing points of view. There is an explanation for this. The novels are adapted from a screenplay that I initially wrote. Each chapter represents two or three "scenes" of a movie. Each scene adds a fresh idea to the plot through the actions and dialogue of different characters. While other authors prefer to tell a story viewed only through eyes of a central character, I believe a storyline is much more dynamic when many characters are engaged.

Again, I thank my wife Louann for her help and editing prowess. I thank my very supportive publisher, Tom Costello. And, as always, I appreciate the diligence and creativity of my illustrator, Taylor Callery.

TONIGHT IN THE RIVERS OF PITTSBURGH

The series begins with an unexpected but horrific tornado that destroyed the center span of the Kinzua Viaduct Bridge in McKean County on July 21, 2003. The Prologue describes this disaster from a park ranger's perspective. While our fictitious Ranger Glen Weaver escaped unscathed when a tree crashed through his cabin roof, in reality one park worker present during the storm was injured when a roof fell on him. It was the only injury caused by the tornado.

p.10 – Tanya Duncan's scene with a "teenage boy" was the last section written for the book. Upon my review of early drafts, I concluded that more forewarning was needed about the governor's illegitimate son. My primary duty to the reader is honesty. The existence of Matty Moore could not be sprung on the reader in Chapter 22. That's why the novel is scattered with clues, including this reference to a teenager in the Prologue. (See also Chapter 13.)

Incidentally, my working title for the novel was "The Governor's Son." Imagine the misdirection that such a title would cause. The "Son" would be viewed as Jimmie throughout until Matty appeared in a late chapter.

pp.16-17 – Family history is very important in Pennsylvania. The fictional Leigh family's story is fairly typical of settlers in central and western Pennsylvania in the 1700s. In fact, I am a descendent of indentured servants in the service of Lord Baltimore as well. The difference with the Leigh family, of course, is the discovery of oil riches by patriarch Austin Peter Leigh and the inheritance of his wealth by his daughter, Marie.

pp. 18-20 – The description of Leigh-Rose Mansion was necessary because it plays such an important role throughout the trilogy. It was the home to Brock Bailey, the site of his wife's kidnapping, the location of Jimmie Bailey's wedding to Ann Negley, and scene of the governor's final fall. The Mansion's location is critical due to its proximity to Kinzua Bridge, its railroad tracks, Kinzua Valley and overlook cemetery – all important locations in the trilogy.

p.31 – Good Shepherd Catholic Church, placed strategically in Pittsburgh's Hill District, is intended to show the great disparity between the haves and have-nots in Pennsylvania. Governor Brock Bailey, wealthy and powerful, chose the poor and lowly church as the scene for his re-election campaign start-up.

p.32 – The distance between Pittsburgh International Airport and downtown Pittsburgh is ridiculously far. Governor Bailey shares my frustration when I make this trip as well. Reference to many potholes on the trip foreshadows the accident to occur later on Fort Pitt Bridge.

p.33 – Yes, the Grant Building beacon flashes "Pittsburgh" in Morse Code.

p.34 – The Pope was indeed in Toronto on March 5, 2003, the date of Bailey's fictional trip to Pittsburgh.

p.36 – Introduction of "the tall old man" a/k/a Louis Rose added tension to the scene at Good Shepherd Church. Louis first appeared as Brock's older brother in Chapter 1, but readers likely glossed him over because he had joined the Army and moved to Germany (p.21). He would return to the story with a vengeance – placing a bomb in governor's limousine, conspiring for a contract killing, disposing of Brock's body and sharing his brother's loot.

p.37 – The choir's song, "Wade in the Water," portends trouble that will happen soon when Governor Bailey's limousine crashes and falls into Monongahela River.

p.39 – St. Luke's gospel passage was carefully chosen. Its reference to giving "your shirt" to your enemy foreshadows the act of Jimmie giving his father a white shirt in Chapter 21.

p.39 – Brock Bailey standing beside a pregnant black girl reflects his relationship with Tanya, his mistress, and their illegitimate son.

p.41 – The first appearance of Tom Zachary, Kane News-Leader editor, illustrates his special interest in the Bailey family, which continues through the trilogy.

p.42 – The Ladies Choir sings "Swing Low Sweet Chariot," a traditional spiritual sung at funerals, again foreshadowing approaching death.

p.44 – Anyone familiar with the design of Fort Pitt Bridge would be stumped by the details of this accident. The governor's limousine would be traveling west on the lower level of the bridge, where the sides are protected with thick steel beams. It is doubtful whether even a speeding, fully loaded tractor-trailer could crash through these beams, let alone a limousine. I ask the reader for a willing suspension of disbelief.

p.46 – The young personal injury attorney is Antonio Alfonzi, who appears as Matty Moore's attorney in *Zelienople Road*. Alfonzi's office is located on Fort Pitt Boulevard.

p.47 – Bailey removed the telephone cord from a wall jack. A reader commented that, in Chapter 5, Father McWilliams's telephone rings. This conflict is easily explained because the operating telephone rang his kitchen, and Bailey disabled a telephone in the priest's study.

p.51 – New character, Tanya Duncan, is introduced with references to her boyfriend. The boyfriend's identity is revealed to the reader when a helicopter is located at her house. Brock Bailey's helicopter was a curse and a blessing for the plot to work. He could travel at whim to Harrisburg, to Virginia and to his home in northwest Pennsylvania. But when he perished in the Kinzua tornado, his helicopter had to vanish. Thank goodness that Louis Rose, with his Army training, could fly it away from Leigh-Rose Mansion and, thereby, confound the Brock Bailey investigators.

p.53 – Chocolate chip waffles are my specialty as well.

p.57 – Brock was working on the fictitious Labor Protection Act, which allowed police officers to honor picket lines of private company unions. This law would later cause Pittsburgh police to suspend its search and rescue operation for Brock because private Mon Valley union divers went on strike.

p.60 – Since publication of *Tonight in the Rivers of Pittsburgh*, various state governors have behaved badly. I truly hope my novel did not inspire such conduct. New York's governor was caught cheating on his wife. New Jersey's governor didn't wear a seat belt and was seriously injured in an automobile accident. South Carolina's governor, like Governor Brock Bailey on this page, dallied with his mistress in Argentina.

p.63 – The places described in Tampa are real. Given the timing of Brock Bailey's announcement in March 2003, the New York Yankees would be training at "Legends Field" in Tampa. After the publication of this novel, the Yankees renamed their spring training stadium to "George M. Steinbrenner Field." Legends Field is the correct name for 2003, but all of you Yankee fans who object may pencil in "Steinbrenner Field" on pages 63 and 70.

p.71 – After the novel was renamed, I added this section about a network news reporter at Monongahela River's edge. His opening words, "Tonight in the Rivers of Pittsburgh," appear at the top of page 72 quite coincidentally.

p.74 – Brock Bailey confessed to the priest for two reasons. First, he needed to explain himself to someone who had a car. Second, whatever he said to Father McWilliams was privileged under Pennsylvania law. That's why he kept open the confession as he drove away.

p.79 – The "dome light" story is taken from a real kidnapping that occurred in Centre County in the late 1970s. The father of a kidnap victim was instructed to take ransom money and drive to a certain location. He was to keep his dome light on so that kidnappers could locate his car. The victim was released unharmed. FBI agents arrested the kidnappers when they used the same public telephone on Penn State's campus to make two ransom demand calls. Agents staked out the public phone area. Memo to kidnappers: never use the same telephone twice.

p.83 – Brock tells Father McWilliams of his bouts with depression, particularly after his wife was declared dead. Brock says he contemplated jumping from Kinzua Bridge, but instead thought of his lover, Tanya, and returned home. Throughout the trilogy, numerous characters are poised to jump from the bridge, but no one ever does.

p.95 – Tanya made "another call." Who she called was never revealed. Some may speculate that she called Louis

Rose, her conspirator friend. But Chapter 11 reveals that Tanya only communicated with him by email and regular mail. A better guess would be that she called her mother in East Liberty.

p.98 – Frank "Josh" Gibson, state police commissioner, is introduced. Although he bumbles through the Brock Bailey investigation, he eventually succeeds in solving the case. Only at the end does he trade his integrity to keep his job with the new governor. This dereliction of duty prompted one reader to complain that police are not portrayed with respect in my novels. My answer is two-fold: first, no one in authority is portrayed with respect in my novels and, second, Zelienople Police Chief Andy Faxon is a hero in *Zelienople Road*. P.S. to reader: Josh Gibson was OK until he messed with the Indian curse.

p.99 – The legislation giving physicians sole discretion to order autopsies in suspicious deaths, opposed by medical malpractice attorneys, comes into play in Chapter 14 when a nurse's mistake is covered up by hospital doctors.

p.110 – The fuzzy-faced officer Billy Herman is introduced. His investigation of Brock Bailey's disappearance would lead to discovery of a silver treasure in Kinzua Valley and a deadly confrontation with Commissioner Gibson. Billy is one of several characters who appear in all three books, although his appearance in *Zelienople Road* is, well, pretty stiff.

p.112 – Jimmie Bailey's agent and confidante, Bill Pennoyer, appears whenever Bailey needs advice or a partner in crime. And, yes, he is named after the founder of Pennsylvania, William Penn.

p.122 – I never swam in the Monongahela and never met anyone who did. Several years ago, however, we had three goldfish that outgrew their tank and ended up swimming there.

p.131 – The story about ironworkers falling to their deaths was entirely made up.

p.134 – Although Pennsylvania is a fierce battle ground between political parties, the combatants in the novel (Jimmie Bailey and Lindy Todd) are not defined by party labels. In fact, the words "Democratic" and "Republican" are nowhere printed in the book. At p.184, Jimmie identifies with no political party.

p.174 – The kidnapper's obituary appears in his local newspaper. Reference is made to Hector Quattone's second wife, Jane. Could Jane actually be Sallie Bailey, the kidnapped wife of the governor? The answer appears in Chapter 17.

p.178 – A deer appears, the first of several deer appearances foreboding danger.

pp.186-90 – Brock's post-seizure hallucinations contain several allusions to his illegitimate son (a black child seen through the mansion's window), to the death he would suffer from the bridge and to the later-discovered murder of Sallie.

p.192 – The true identity of "Loranger" is revealed as Brock's older brother "Louis." Loranger is a blend of Louis and Army "Ranger." Louis's training in the Army comes in handy when his character is called upon to rig explosives, physically move heavy boxes, fly helicopters and drag his brother's corpse.

p.196 – This IV-bag mix-up with fentanyl is based on an actual hospital death. However, in that case, the nurse intended to doom the patient.

p.204 – Tanya Duncan's decision to donate her $2 million to the church poor box, eventually led to a ten-fold return on her investment. Her son, Matty, ended up with more than $20 million in the resolution of Brock's estate. Tanya was the only character to actually change for the better. In many ways, her act here represents a climax in the story.

p.218 – People may differ, but I believe the Allegheny Mountains extend as far east as Mansfield. No matter what they're called, the mountains and hills of Mansfield are about as beautiful as any in the eastern United States.

p.219 – The elderly woman exclaims that she is voting for "the governor's son." The working title of the novel was "The Governor's Son."

p.227 – "Two shadows, pale and naked" also was considered as a title, but wiser heads prevailed.

p.236 – One of my favorite chapters is "The Discovery." In it, the reader discovers the tragic death of kidnap victim, Sallie Bailey. First, though, the reader is misdirected by a description of Jane Quattone, the mysterious second wife of the kidnapper. When Jane gains access of Hector's off-site storage area, she discovers her husband's long-held secret. The former machine operator at the Cellowrap Products company put the product to good use by wrapping Sallie Bailey's body in cellophane. My apologies to those readers who held out a candle that Sallie Bailey would return to the story and save her family. Sallie's demise was necessary to force Brock to return to Kinzua Bridge and visit her grave.

pp.252-53 – Jimmie should not have shredded his father's trust document. Not only did he have a duty to preserve his father's legal papers for the probate proceedings, his destruction of the trust actually cost him about $20 million. Here's how: Brock's Last Will poured all of his property into the Thomas J. Bailey Revocable Trust. The trust, by its terms, gave ten percent of his money to Tanya Duncan, with the remainder to Sallie Bailey's "heirs at law." If Jimmie had followed the trust terms, $5 million would be paid to Tanya and $45 million to Jimmie (who was the only surviving heir of Sallie). But Jimmie shredded the trust document because he wanted nothing to go to Tanya. Therefore, without the trust, Pennsylvania law split Brock's estate between his heirs at law – Jimmie and Brock's illegimate son Matty. Each received about $25 million. It's always a good idea to think before you shred.

p.254 – A seemingly innocent tale of the News-Leader editor's new business cards takes on great significance later when Zachary hands a card to Jimmie on the funeral train. Jimmie puts the card in his shirt pocket, at p.273. When Brock's bloody black shirt is taken off and replaced with Jimmie's white shirt, shortly before Brock's corpse is tossed over the West End Bridge in Pittsburgh, the business card is still in the shirt pocket, at p.301. After Brock's body was recovered from the Ohio River, state police commissioner Josh Gibson discovered the business card in Brock's shirt pocket, at p.344. Gibson learned that the business cards were printed by the News-Leader in July, so Brock's body could not have been floating in the Pittsburgh rivers since the traffic accident in March.

p.348 – The "tapping at his chamber door," of course, is my tribute to Richmond's favorite macabre poet, Edgar Allen Poe.

p.375 – The Kinzua Bridge has not been repaired since the July 2003 tornado damage. The Pennsylvania General Assembly, however, has allocated sufficient funds to construct a viewing platform at the edge of the bridge's southern section. Completion of the viewing platform is expected in 2010.

p.380 – The novel literally ends with a cliff-hanger. Commissioner Gibson is left standing on the Kinzua Bridge and contemplating his immediate future or lack thereof. Whether Gibson jumped or not is left for the second book of the trilogy, *Woods on Fire*. The last sentence, "It would take about six seconds," was crafted to keep the reader guessing.

WOODS ON FIRE

A brilliant red sky, reflected in the Allegheny River, graces the cover of *Woods on Fire*. To most readers, a forest fire was suggested by the cover. But the true meaning of "Woods on Fire" is not revealed until page 102, when the Peacemaker tells Megan Broward that Woods on Fire was an early 19th Century Seneca Indian leader. But anyone who could understand the Iroquois language knew that fact on page 12, when Brother John recited an incantation from "TI-OOH-QUOT-TA-KAU-NA," which is the Iroquois equivalent of "Woods on Fire."

p.26 – A seemingly insignificant episode was the major clue in Jimmie's involvement in the later killing of Billy Herman. Jimmie hurled a rock at the Kinzua Park bear, only to scare him and not to kill him. In chapter 27, someone threw a rock through Billy Herman's bedroom window only to scare him. Who else but Jimmie would be throwing a rock?

p.29 – The 90-year-old Toolie is introduced. She is a character that all of us have interacted with at some point during our lives, but probably didn't give her much thought. Most established restaurants have a "Toolie" on their staffs, and wise diners seek her out.

p.54 – Jimmie Bailey and Bill Pennoyer together "trespass" into Billy Herman's hospital room. Often throughout the book, these two characters work in tandem. Here, Jimmie threatens the life of Herman. This is another clue in the mysterious killing of Herman.

p.60 – Tom Zachary ridicules a job prospect of Matty Moore. "What could be more boring than writing reviews of Pittsburgh books?" This represents my personal view of the sorry support Pennsylvania newspapers give to local authors and publishers. Please pardon my one-sentence editorial.

p.62 – All of Toolie's idiomatic expressions are part of the American lexicon, even "Lookie, Lookie, Archway Cookies!" My favorite is "Cripes Hanna," an expression usually uttered in my childhood after my behavior deviated from the norm.

p.71 – Blackbeard's Rum is an illusion to the English captain who, legend says, raised a sunken Spanish galleon off the cost of the Carolinas in the early 1800s. He retrieved millions of dollars in silver, which he tried to return to England during the War of 1812. He supposedly transported the silver over land as far as Gardeau, in southeastern McKean County. There, legend says, he buried the silver in the hope that he would recover it after the war.

Also, rum was seen as the demon for Pennsylvania's Indians. William Penn had hoped to keep rum away from the Delaware Indians so that they would act less savage-like. Brother John's consumption of rum in the Prologue was, therefore, a drink in protest of the white man's domination of Pennsylvania Indians.

p.104 – Mr. George, the Peacemaker, describes the Indian curse. Harm will befall any white man who disturbs the ground where silver was buried under Kinzua Bridge. The curse actually worked fairly well. Commissioner Gibson and Billy Herman were murdered. Professor Dulaney was killed in a bear attack. Bill Pennoyer died at an early age. Only Jimmie Bailey survived, but other harm came to him. Matty Moore poked around the ground under the bridge, but the curse did not apply to him – he was not a white man.

p.128 – Tom Zachary tells Matty Moore of his desire to write a book. He finally sits down to write the book of his career in the last scene of *Zelienople Road.*

p.134 – Some McKean County residents believe that "Kinzua" was a word attributed to the Valley by

Delaware Indians and that "Fish on Spear" may not be the literal translation.

p.244 – The nightmare forewarns the reader of an approaching death. In Jimmie's dream, a black vehicle driven by Billy Herman threatens his family. Jimmie's best friend, Bill Pennoyer tries to stop the car. The driver, though, shoots and kills Pennoyer. In the last scene of the book, "one body slumped to the floor" and "one heart stopped beating." If readers followed the clues and understood that Pennoyer was the intruder, then either Pennoyer or Herman was killed in the final scene.

p.264 – I wrote this section upon my return from the dentist. Like Ernest Hemingway, I believe an author needs to experience pain before he writes about it.

p.292 – Pennoyer is troubled by a threat he heard from Billy Herman – that he would kill the Bailey's newborn daughter. He remembers that Jimmie has a gun. He realizes that Jimmie would "take matters into his own hands" if he knew of Herman's threat. Assuming that Pennoyer told Jimmie about the threat, then Jimmie would be a likely suspect in Herman's death.

p.313 – Some readers reported their joy in learning that Toolie found romance and security with Mr. George. Every pot has its lid, I'm told. Because she is such a delightful character, Toolie did not perish in the novels and will live in perpetuity.

ZELIENOPLE ROAD

The Prologue highlights the "Great Delegation" of judicial decision-making, otherwise known as the American Jury System. We entrust 12 members of the public-at-large, none of whom likely has any experience in criminal or civil law, to make the most complicated analyses and difficult decisions in our society – decisions that have horrific economic repercussions and even life-and-death consequences for others. And we justify this system by saying, "It's the best that's ever been invented." Similar to my treatment of other great institutions that played roles in the *Rivers of Pittsburgh Mystery Trilogy,* the jury system can be easily skewered for comic relief. As the coming chapters illustrate, this jury is probably the worst of all time. Jurors' minds were made up before the trial began, and they delayed their verdict long enough to get a free lunch.

Chapter 1 – Initial police descriptions based on shaky eyewitness testimony can be misleading and may detour the investigation. Here, Chief Faxon describes the suspect as a "black male" rather than as a male wearing a black hoodie. As a result, Matty Moore was detained at a police road block and, perhaps, the white criminal eluded police.

Chapter 2 – There is no old farmhouse on Zelienople Road that is along Connoquenessing Creek. The house and its design are fictional. The New Castle Street Bridge over the Connoquenessing is real.

Chapter 4 – Common Pleas courts in Pennsylvania are lower trial courts. Pennsylvania voters elect their county judges. The Governor appoints judges to fill vacancies. Some watchdog groups complain that legislatures and bar groups are more qualified to select judges than are voters. I don't think it makes a lick of difference. It's just politics.

Chapter 5 -- I am indebted to Cyril Wecht, M.D., for his expertise in forensic pathology, as demonstrated by his exceptional book, *Mortal Evidence: The Forensics behind Nine Shocking Cases* (Prometheus Books, 2007). Dr. Wecht, however, is not the template for our fictitious Dr. Elliot Chen. Dr. Wecht's forensic skills are much more admirable and his professionalism is topnotch.

Dr. Chen's removal of eye fluid is a technique for determining time of death. A reading of potassium levels can be taken from eye fluid (vitreous humor) inserted at the back of the eye. If too many hours have passed, however, the reading is considered scientifically unreliable. Wecht, *Mortal Evidence*, p.103.

Chapter 6 – The Padgett family dinner was inspired by a childhood friend, whose parents and brother passed much too soon. He requested that all of his family be gathered for a dinner on one page of *Zelienople Road*. My best to you, Dennis.

Chapter 7 – Pennoyer was housed in the "D Sector" at the Castle Rock Center. His accomplice in crime, Jimmie Bailey, was housed in the "D Sector" of the state correctional center later in the Epilogue.

Chapter 11 – These newspaper typographical errors were a couple doozies I discovered as a newly hired proofreader at The Centre Daily Times in 1975.

Chapter 12 – Another reference to Bill Pennoyer's heart. Roxy warned him in Chapter 9 about staying in the sauna too long, and its bad effect on his heart. There are later references to the toll of excessive exercise on his heart. (He had a pain in his heart in Chapter 19.) Add that to his poor diet and romantic flings and his demise is only beats away.

Chapter 13 – Prosecutors have an ethical duty to the court not to bring criminal charges against a questionable suspect. Here, McFadden wanted a conviction at any cost, for nothing more than his political gain. Later, he ignores exculpatory evidence, which not only results in a mistrial but could possibly subject him to disbarment under the Pennsylvania rules of ethics.

Chapter 14 – Sylvester Sylvaney was the investigator hired by gubernatorial candidate Lindy Todd to investigate Jimmie Bailey during their campaign, in *Tonight in the Rivers of Pittsburgh*.

The Zelienople Police line-up, containing only one black man, was impermissibly suggestive and probably unconstitutional – especially when the police earlier identified the robber as a black male.

Chapter 19 – The best advice a criminal defense attorney can give his client is: wear a white shirt and don't say a word. The best advice Matty could give his attorney was this: don't rely on one witness to win your case. While Dr. Chen's potential testimony on the time of death would be devastating to the Commonwealth's case, things happen in court, like your expert witness being disqualified. Also, if Matty insisted on testifying, his attorney could not stop it.

Chapter 20 – Chen probably would have been disqualified as Matty's expert witness in real life. The forensic pathologist was asked by Chief Faxon to examine the body at the murder scene. Whether he was paid by Faxon is not critical. The question is whether a professional consulting relationship had already developed with the authorities at the time Chen offered himself to the defense. Alfonzi should have subpoenaed Chen's report and then hired another pathologist as his expert.

Chapter 21 – Matty Moore is Jimmie Bailey's half-brother because they are related through one parent only. A stepbrother is the son of one's stepparent by a former marriage, according to Webster's New Dictionary. And, yes, I don't understand the difference either.

p.s. to readers: Sorry about the slap. It was a critical dramatic event, which allowed the author to isolate Jimmie Bailey from other supporting characters. Rest assured that Jimmie and Ann are working things out, but he'll be doing housework for eternity.

Chapter 22 – I've never visited King Soopers in Littleton, Colorado. It looks like a gigantic store on Google Earth, though.

Chapter 23 – Bill Pennoyer had to die if the spotlight was to center on Jimmie at the end of the novel. I concocted a number of scenarios for his death, including a traffic accident on Zelienople Road or maybe something self-inflicted. But Pennoyer was too lovable a character to exit with trauma. So I chose the happiest death imaginable.

Chapter 24 – "The judge was filled with rancor when she was called a canker." This is my one-sentence ode to poet-humorist Ogden Nash. ("The Lord in His wisdom made the fly, and then forgot to tell us why.")

Chapter 25 – If the judge only declared a mistrial, then the Commonwealth could refile charges against Matty Moore and retry the case. However, the second order on Alfonzi's motion for judgment of acquittal ended it all – the double jeopardy clause of the Constitution would prevent Matty from being twice put in jeopardy for the crime of which the judge acquitted him. Some commentators describe the role of a judge in a criminal jury trial as the "13th juror." Rarely will a judge upset a jury verdict, but here, obviously, it was the right call.

Chapter 27 – Zachary and Bailey meet in a picnic pavilion near Kinzua Bridge. Some of the proceeds from *Rivers of Pittsburgh Mystery Trilogy* have been donated to the Kinzua Bridge Foundation to defray costs of its construction of such a picnic pavilion. The Foundation is active in preserving the bridge as a national treasure, as well as supporting the Kinzua State Park. I encourage readers not only to visit the bridge and learn about this fascinating piece of American history, but to support the Foundation as well. Contributions can be made to: Kinzua Bridge Foundation, Inc., 17137 Route 6, Smethport, PA 16749. All contributions are tax deductible.

Epilogue – The story ends where it all began.

About the Author

Brian Lee Weakland is a native of Altoona, Pennsylvania, and an honors graduate of Penn State's School of Journalism. He won the Associated Press Community News Reporter Award and Keystone Press Award for investigative reporting as a staff writer and news editor for The Centre Daily Times in State College, Pennsylvania. His work has been published in Pittsburgh Magazine as well as numerous national journals. A graduate of the University of Pittsburgh School of Law, Brian has written extensively on the dynamics of judicial decision-making and politics. He has taught university-level writing courses at Penn State and Pitt. Brian lives in Richmond, Virginia, with his wife and two daughters.

Brian loves to hear from his readers. You can reach him at brianweakland@aol.com

WA